CRY BABY

CRY BABY

WHAT'S THE LIFE OF YOUR CHILD WORTH?

DAVID JACKSON

ISBN-13: 9781499235104

This one's for Eden,
who keeps me smiling.

Also by David Jackson

Pariah

The Helper

Marked

TUESDAY, JANUARY 4
10.21 PM

She awakens because the voice in her head commands her to.

'*Wake up, Erin. Come on, now. Time to get up.*'

Her eyes flicker open, blink a few times. It's like trying to see through gauze.

Light. It's light in here. Daytime? No – it's an insipid, artificial light.

She realizes she's staring at the ceiling, even though it appears to be miles away. Her room feels stretched up into space. Is this her room? She turns her head slightly, but it takes an effort. As though her spine has fossilized and rotating her neck could snap it. She sees items of furniture – a dresser, a closet, a nightstand. Their edges are blurred and they seem to quiver, but they look familiar to her.

Why do they move like that? What happened to me?

'*Erin? Are you awake?*'

That voice. Where is it coming from? Am I not really awake? Am I stuck in a dream?

And then it's as if she gets sucked into a black hole. Something opens up in the pit of her stomach and she feels as though the rest of her body is being pulled into it. The room swirls. A pounding starts in her skull. She wants to vomit and scream at the same time.

Because she remembers.

It hits her like a shell blast. Sends a shock wave through her body that seems to lift her into the air and drop her onto the bed again.

1

Adrenaline floods her system, wrenching her out of her stupor. She turns her head to explore the other side of the room. She knows what she wants to see, but dreads that it will not be so.

Georgia. My precious little Georgia.

The crib has wooden slats down the side, but the light in here is too dim, damn it, and she can't see beyond them with this diluted sight of hers. There's no sound either, but Georgia could be asleep, please let her be sleeping. Erin throws her feet over the side of the bed and places them on the floor. She is surprised at first to see that she's wearing shoes, has all her clothes on in fact, but the terrible memories tell her why, and they tell her to expect the worst, and now she is starting to cry even before she has seen, because she knows, she knows what she will find. She pushes herself off the bed with arms that feel as though they're made of cotton, and when she gets to her feet the floor seems to lurch, to the left and then to the right, like she's on a ship being tossed in a storm. But she has to make it over to the crib, has to check that her darling is all right, and as she stumbles across the room she blinks furiously, tries to bat away the tears and the mist that keeps obscuring her vision, and she finally makes it to the crib, steadying herself on its rail as she stares down and reaches in and touches…

… nothingness.

The covers are undisturbed. Heart-wrenchingly crisp and crease-free.

'GEORGIA!'

She screams the name, as if expecting her baby to come running, or at least call back, even though she is only six months old. But there is no logic in Erin's mind now. The fogginess is dissipating only to be replaced by blind panic.

'Erin! Listen to me!'

Still the voice. She cannot work out where it's coming from, but right now she doesn't care. She cares about only one thing, one person. Nothing else matters. Nothing in the universe is more important.

Whimpering, she turns on the spot, scanning the room, struggling to concoct explanations. Trying to make herself believe that her daughter somehow escaped from the crib and is hiding somewhere nearby, even though Erin knows it's impossible, even though she knows what happened to her baby but doesn't want to acknowledge it.

Because that's the thing, isn't it? I know what happened to her. I know it, I know it, I know it. But please don't let it be true. Please!

And so she throws open the door and bursts into the living room, her eyes desperately searching, and she sees the stroller over by the apartment door and she weaves her way over to it, her legs turning to jelly and the tears running down her face, because again she knows what she will find. And as she spins the stroller around to face her and peers into its hollowness, a yelp of pain escapes her lips.

'Erin! Stop this. Listen to me!'

She screams angrily to drown out the voice, then runs into the kitchen. It's a tiny area, and she can see immediately that it's empty. She tries the bathroom next. Yanks aside the shower curtain just to be sure, because you never know. With what has gone on, you just never know.

Back into the living room. One more room to try. The second bedroom. Where she keeps all the baby stuff because there is no space in her own bedroom. Here is where there are cuddly toys and diapers and a diaper disposer and a changing mat and clothes, lots of clothes, and all kinds of lotions and potions and powders and medicines…

… but no Georgia.

She is not here. She is not in this apartment. Which Erin has suspected all along. This is no dream. This is real. Her world has been taken from her, and she doesn't know what to do about it. How do you find a baby? Where the fuck do you start to look for your baby?

Her legs give way and she falls to the floor. In the second bedroom, surrounded by all the baby things, she drops to the carpet and lets out her grief and anger in long drawn-out wails.

'Erin! Can you hear me?'

This damned voice. Why am I still hearing it? What are you doing to me?

Erin claps her hands to her ears.

And then she feels it.

The earpiece. In her right ear. If she had not been panicking, if she had not been recovering from her drug-induced state, she would have realized it was there all along.

She unplugs it. Stares at it. Tries to understand. Who put it there? And why?

The man who took my baby?

Images flash in her head. Of coming home from the drugstore at about seven o'clock this evening. She'd bought some diaper rash cream for Georgia, plus a new bib. She'd paused at the apartment door, dug around in her purse for her keys. She eventually found them, unlocked the door, pushed it wide open. Started to wheel the stroller into the apartment.

She heard nothing. Her attacker came at her from behind. Was on her in an instant. He must have been hiding in the shadows of the hallway, just waiting for her. Yes, she remembers now. The smell. The chemical smell of the cloth that was clamped tightly over her mouth and nose. So tightly she thought she would asphyxiate. She had to breathe, couldn't stop herself. Had to take a deep breath, suck in some oxygen. And with it those chemicals. She felt them burning in her throat, and she remembers her consciousness dissolving, the long fall into blackness.

That was, what, more than two hours ago? Two hours in which the attacker could have taken anything. Money, the television, whatever.

But he chose my baby. Why did he have to take my baby?

She stares at the earpiece. Knows that she has to replace it. It might be Georgia's only chance.

She brings it slowly, tentatively, back to her ear. Hears a tinny voice as it approaches. When she inserts it fully the voice gains volume and bass, and she catches the end of a sentence:

'... *in the apartment.*'

She opens her mouth, wanting to speak, but realizes how ridiculous that would be.

Talk to me again, she thinks. Please, tell me something about Georgia.

'*Erin, did you hear what I just said?*'

Her lips part again. Why is he asking me a question? How am I supposed to communicate with him?

'*It's all right, Erin. You can speak. I'll be able to hear you.*'

'Wh-what?' she says. 'Hello?'

'*Hello, Erin.*'

Her eyes dart. How can he hear me?

'Where are you?'

'It doesn't matter where I am, Erin. You just need to calm down and listen to me.'

'You've… you've bugged my apartment.'

'No. Only you, Erin.'

She doesn't understand. He's not making sense. Why is he messing with my mind like this?

'What do you mean?'

'Stand up, Erin. Go back into the living room and sit down. You need to relax. You need to get your head together again.'

Stand up? Go into the living room? How does he know I'm not standing up? How does he know what room I'm in right now?

'You can see me? You're watching me?'

'Just do as I say, Erin. Into the living room. Take a seat on that comfy leather sofa of yours.'

Her face creases up. She wants to cry again. He knows so much. She feels so invaded, so defiled. What else does he want from her?

'My baby. Do you have my baby?'

'All in good time, Erin. All in good time. Just do what I tell you, and everything will be fine.'

She scrambles to her feet. Her head is still muzzy and she feels nauseous, but she does what he asked of her. She heads back into the living room, pauses in front of the sofa.

'Sit on it, Erin. Go ahead. It's not a trap. I just want to explain things to you.'

Jesus. He can see me in here too.

She turns a full three-sixty, examining the walls for cameras. Where are they?

'Erin, will you just sit down? Please.'

She lowers herself onto the sofa.

'Okay, I'm sitting.'

'Yes, I know.'

'How do you know? How can you hear and see me?'

'I can hear you, but I can't see you. I see only what you see.'

'What? I don't understand.'

'Look down, Erin. At your coat.'

She obeys his instruction. Looks down. She's wearing her short woolen coat, above a long black skirt and brown boots. The coat is buttoned up, just as it was when she arrived home.

But something is different. She sees it instantly.

A large brooch. Intricate gold-colored metalwork holding a blue gemstone at its center. She twists it toward her to take a better look.

'Hello, Erin.'

The greeting puzzles her. 'What are you—'

'That's a sad face. Your makeup is running down your cheeks.'

It hits her then. She understands.

'No. No...'

'Yes, Erin. The brooch. It contains a miniaturized camera and microphone. That's how I hear you. That's how I see what you see. Open up your coat.'

For a moment she cannot move. Is it true? Are such things possible?

'Go ahead. Unbutton your coat.'

Slowly, she unfastens each button. She pulls the coat open. She sees the wire that comes from the back of the brooch, through the material of her coat and into the inside pocket.

'What do you see, Erin?'

'A... a wire.'

'Look in your pocket. See where the wire goes.'

She reaches into the pocket. Her fingers touch something hard. She takes hold of it and pulls it out. It's a black plastic box, attached to the other end of the wire.

'The box. What is it?'

'A radio transmitter, plus a battery pack. Now put it back in your pocket, Erin.'

She stares at the box of tricks. What is going on here? Why would anyone go to such lengths?

'Erin, did you hear what I said?'

'Yes. I mean... No. I don't want this. I don't want you spying on me. Why should I—'

'You want your baby back, don't you?'

Georgia. He's admitting it. He has my Georgia.

'You took her.'

Yes. I took her. She's cute. Little dimples when she smiles. Just like her mom.'

Erin's face contorts again. Don't cry. Stay in control. Find out what he wants.

'Why? Why did you steal her from me? She's only six months old. She needs me.'

'She's fine. I've got formula. I've got diapers. Everything she needs. Besides, I don't plan to keep her very long.'

A surge of dread pulses through Erin. 'What do you mean? What are you going to do with her?'

'Relax. I'm going to give her back to you. That's what you want, isn't it? You want Georgia back with you, don't you?'

'Yes. Yes. Please. Just bring her back to me. I'll give you anything you want.'

'Anything?'

'Yes, anything. If I've got it, you can have it. Just name it.'

She hears a low chuckle. It's carries the echo of evil thoughts. But she doesn't regret what she said. She will truly offer him anything. Her own body if that's what it takes.

'I don't want anything you own, Erin. I just want you to do something for me.'

It will be something sordid. Something degrading. But she doesn't care.

'I'll do it. If you promise me I can have my baby back. You can watch me on your camera. I'll do it for you.'

'You haven't heard what it is yet.'

'Then tell me. I'll do whatever you want. Tell me what it is you'd like me to do.'

There's a pause. It's probably only a couple of seconds, but it presages what is to come with ominous force.

'I want you to kill someone.'

10.23 PM

Lord and master of all he surveys. That's how Marcus Wilson sees it. Small though it is, this is his dominion. He is in charge.

His solid wooden desk is expansive and elevated above the rest of this room. The sides of the desk are completely enclosed in wood paneling. He could easily imagine that he is the captain on the bridge of an old sailing ship, scanning the horizon as his men toil to push this vessel through the choppy waters.

And those seas can get real rough, all right. They can seethe and foam and rage. But Wilson isn't fazed. He's in control. He knows exactly how to see this ship through any storm. He is its captain.

Well, actually he's a sergeant. But that's enough. These stripes on his arm and this position behind the huge desk mean that he is in charge of this part of the Eighth Precinct station house, yes sir. And it's an important job, too. A vital job. He acts as the first point of contact with people who come in off the street, and so the way he handles those people can affect their dealings with the police for good or for bad. Sometimes that means being compassionate. Sometimes it means being unyielding. Sometimes it means kicking ass. Every situation is different, and in a city like this you never know what's going to come through those doors next. Each time he says to himself that he's seen it all, a new and surprising scenario develops right in front of his desk. It's one of the things Marcus Wilson loves about this job.

Take tonight, for example. Just an hour ago, a homeless guy came in to ask if he could curl up and sleep right next to the desk, because it was the only place he felt safe. After that, in came a woman who asked for a permanent police patrol of her building because every night someone would attach some kind of vacuum device to the wall of her apartment and start sucking all the air out of it. And then, only five minutes ago, there was the woman who wanted to know if the cops could arrest her cat for breaking the curfew she had imposed on it.

Wilson dealt with them all. Calmly, professionally, he responded to their requests in ways that left them with the lasting impression that yes, the boys and girls in blue really do care. We don't all adhere to stereotype, thinks Wilson. We don't all eat donuts and drink coffee and hit people with sticks and shoot unarmed civilians and take bribes and chew gum. Some of us believe in those three words written on the sides of the patrol cars. Courtesy, professionalism, respect. That's what it's all about.

And that's precisely what he'll apply when dealing with this latest arrival at the station house.

The man is short. From Wilson's lofty vantage point, everyone else in this room looks small, but this guy looks to be on the more unfortunate side of the five foot six mark. Wilson would put the man's age at about thirty-five, give or take. He's pale and blinks a lot – as though he's averse to bright light. He wears a gray hooded sweatshirt, zipped right up to the neck, and unbleached denim jeans. Curiously, the laces on his green sneakers don't go through the holes; instead, they have been wrapped around the shoes, passing under the soles several times before being knotted tightly on top. As he approaches the desk, his hand keeps shooting up and scratching behind his ear in an exaggerated manner, the way a rabbit or a cat might scratch with its back foot.

Here we go, thinks Wilson. Another strange one. The characters I get through here, I could write a book.

The man comes right up to the desk, but he keeps his gaze low. Only once or twice does he allow it to flicker upward to take in the view of Wilson.

'Aw, Jeez,' says the man, and then he veers away again. Keeps walking right over to the other side of the room, then down the length of the far wall, muttering to himself and scratching behind his ear.

That's okay, thinks Wilson. I'm an imposing sight. I can be frightening to some people.

Wilson is a big man, with a wide head. He thinks he looks like an oversized Yaphet Kotto. When his face is set, he can look pretty mean. But he also knows that when he affixes the right smile, he can look like a big soft teddy-bear. Kids love him when he does that smile. Maybe it's time to do one now.

The man comes back again, still muttering. Eyes fixed on the floor.

'Aw, Jeez. Jesus-Cheeses. This is bad, this is bad, this is bad. I can't do this.'

The man turns away again. Starts to shuffle off.

Wilson sighs. 'Sir? Excuse me. SIR!'

The man stops in his tracks, his back still to Wilson.

'I'm in trouble now. Big trouble. Yessiree. Big, big trouble with the big, big sergeant. Oh my.'

Wilson notices that a couple of uniforms have appeared, and are now leaning back against a noticeboard, watching the fun.

Okay, he thinks. Stay calm. Show them how this is done.

'Sir,' says Wilson in his most appeasing tone. 'Could you turn around, please?'

The man does nothing for several seconds. Wilson opens his mouth to repeat his request, but then he notices a subtle movement: the man turning one of his feet slightly to his right. Then the man follows it with the other foot. Then the first foot again. Gradually and painstakingly, the man continues to move in this way until he has turned all the way around.

This could take some time, thinks Wilson. Be nice to the guy. Show him how friendly we all are here. Just one big happy family. Welcome, brother, to our happy station house. The cherry pie is almost done, and in the meantime we can offer you a choice of delicious beverages. Now sit yourself down, brother, and tell us of your troubles.

'Good,' he says. 'You don't need to worry, okay? Sir? Could you look at me, please?'

The man lifts his head a fraction of an inch, but his eyes stay locked on the floor.

'That's it,' says Wilson. 'Bring your head up... A little more... Good. Now look up at me.'

The man's eyelids blink furiously, as though he is having to make a supreme effort. After much apparent turmoil, he eventually manages to align his gaze with Wilson's face.

Now, thinks Wilson. Do it. Do the smile.

He does it. The biggest, daftest grin imaginable. The one that would cause his kids to break out into fits of helpless laughter.

'Waaah!' the man yells, his face registering extreme terror. He turns and scurries away, back to the security of the wall.

Wilson drops his smile. Darn it. This is getting ridiculous. Hearing snorts of laughter, he turns to his right, where the two uniforms are having a whale of a time. He turns his mean face on them, and instantly they become paragons of sobriety. One of them takes it as his cue to make himself useful, and starts to saunter over to the man.

'Hey, buddy. You okay there? Come on, let's get over here and sort this out.'

The man's response is to shuffle closer to the wall and press his forehead against it. He continues to mutter.

'Hey,' says the uni, more aggressively now. 'You hear what I'm saying to you?' He reaches out a hand and places it on the man's shoulder.

Big mistake.

The man screams and then whirls away from the wall. He clutches his shoulder where the cop just touched it. Acts as though he's just been shot there.

Startled, the cop jumps backward and reaches for his sidearm. His partner starts to race over, his hand also on the butt of his gun.

'He hit me,' yells the man. 'He hit me. 10-34. Assault in progress. 10-34.'

He continues yelling and screaming while the two officers circle him warily. Wilson shows the palm of his hand to the patrolmen, warning them to stay calm. Then he makes a pushing motion, telling them to back off. Slowly, the cops retreat.

'Hey,' says Wilson. 'Hey, mister. Come over here. I ain't gonna hurt you. Do you want me to send those two cops away?'

The man glances at Wilson, then back at the unis. 'Yeah,' he says, his hand still pressed to his imagined wound. 'Away. In the slammer. Put 'em in the slammer. 10-34.'

Wilson jerks his head, telling the cops to disappear. They look at him questioningly, but Wilson maintains his glare until they obey his command and move into the records office.

'There,' says Wilson. 'See what I did for you?'

'Yeah.'

'I got rid of them, didn't I?'

'Yeah.'

'Just you and me now, all right?'

'Yeah. You and me. Me and you. Me and the big sergeant.'

Wilson can see that the man is growing calmer by the second, and he beckons him over.

'Come a little closer, man. Come talk to me. Tell me what's on your mind.'

The man sidles gradually toward the desk, allowing his eyes to jump up much more frequently than before. Wilson decides not to attempt the smile again, but he's got another trick up his sleeve.

'You want some candy? I got candy here.'

He picks up a plastic bowl that he keeps on his desk for whenever there are young children in the station house, although its contents are constantly being depleted by passing officers when he's not looking. He tips it to show the man what it holds.

'Go ahead. Take some.'

The man cranes his neck and peers into the bowl. He seems mildly interested, but then he pulls his head back in and shakes it.

'Five blues, seven reds, thirteen yellows. All prime. Primes are good, but you're a stranger. Don't take candy from strangers. Look before you leap. Never look a gift horse in the mouth. All that glitters is not gold.'

Wilson looks with puzzlement into his bowl, then replaces it on his desk. Never had a reaction like that before.

'So it's because I'm a stranger? Okay, then, let's fix that. My name is Sergeant Marcus Wilson. How's that? We friends now?'

The man scratches again. Then he brings a hand up and starts touching the thumb to each finger in turn, over and over.

'One-three-seven-one,' he says.

'What?'

'One-three-seven-one.'

Wilson nods. 'Yeah. That's my shield number. What about it?'

'Thirteen-seven-one. Thirteen is prime. Seventy-one is prime. Seven is also prime. Thirteen times seven is ninety-one. Put the one on the end gives nine-one-one. The emergency number is nine-one-one. The World Trade Center disaster was on nine-eleven. Nine hundred and eleven is also prime.'

Wilson can't remember what a prime number is, but he bobs his head more appreciatively now. 'That's pretty good. You like numbers, huh?'

'I like numbers.'

'Is that why you came here? Something to do with numbers?'

'No. I don't know.'

He's rocking now. Still touching his thumb to his fingers, but rocking back and forth on his heels.

'Okay, so not numbers. You know what this place is, don't you? You know where you're at?'

'Yeah. Police station. Nine-one-one. Emergency, which service do you require?'

'That's right. This is a police station. Do you have an emergency? Some kind of crime you need to report?'

The rocking increases in tempo. Wilson believes the guy is getting more agitated. On the verge of losing it again.

'Hey,' he says. 'It's okay. We're here to help you. Tell me what the problem is, and we'll see if we can fix it for you, all right?'

'Yeah. Aw, Jeez. Aw Jeez. It's bad, it's bad.'

He's getting more anxious. Another few seconds and he'll be tearing off toward his wall again.

'Did somebody hurt you? Is that it? Or maybe you saw something? Somebody do a bad thing, and you saw it happen?'

The man starts scratching again. Both hands this time, flapping frantically behind his ears.

Wilson isn't sure what to do now. Say something or keep quiet? Which is the least likely to detonate this guy?

But then the man stops beating his ears. Panting heavily, he brings a hand to the zipper of his hooded sweatshirt. Takes it away again, brings it back again.

Wilson watches, a little concerned now. Years of training and experience have taught him to be wary of people who suddenly decide to reach under their clothing. Especially those who appear to be in a disturbed state of mind.

'Aw Jeez,' the man says again. He takes a deep breath, as if he has just made a momentous decision. Then he grabs the zipper, pulls it all the way down, and opens up his sweatshirt.

Wilson's eyes widen at what he sees. This changes things. Wilson had started to believe this situation would come to nothing. Another amusing but innocuous episode to add to tonight's list. But this – this is different. This situation has just shown him a serious edge he can't ignore.

The man's shirt is soaked in blood.

'Sir,' says Wilson. 'Are you hurt?'

'N-n-no. Oh boy.'

'Then whose blood is that?'

The man's jaw works up and down and his eyelids flutter as he tries to force out the words.

'It's my… It's my m-m-mom's.'

'Your mom's? It's your mother's blood?'

'Yeah. My mom's blood. She's dead. I killed my mom.'

10.36 PM

'What? What did you say?'

'I want you to kill someone, Erin.'

She'd heard him correctly the first time, but saying it again doesn't make it any more believable.

'What are you talking about? That's crazy.'

The voice remains calm. *'I don't think it's crazy. I think it's a good deal. If you want to see your baby alive again, then that's what you need to do.'*

She shakes her head. This has got to be a joke. A test. He's pushing me. Trying to find out just how far I'd be prepared to go. He's not really expecting me to agree to this.

She pushes out a mirthless laugh. Lets him know she appreciates the morbid humor.

'All right, can we get serious now, please? I want my Georgia back.'

'Yes, I know you do. And that's why I'm giving you this opportunity. I'm perfectly serious about it.'

No. No. This is insane. He can't mean this. Nobody in their right mind would suggest something like this.

'You want me to kill someone? You're seriously suggesting that I kill another human being?'

'Only if you want Georgia as much as you say you do. If you love her, then prove it. Her life for somebody else's. Is that such a hard bargain for an adoring mother to agree to?'

'Yes. Yes it is. It would be hard for anyone to agree to. It would be hard if you had stolen ten children of mine. You're asking me to take someone else's life. Do you understand how repellent that idea is to me? Do you have any concept of how alien it is to me?'

'Really? You surprise me. That's not the impression I have of you.'

This stops her. Impression? What impression? All he's got is a few minutes of listening to me over a microphone.

'That's because you don't know me. You know nothing about me.'

'Actually, I know a lot more about you than you think. I didn't just pick you out of a hat, Erin. You were chosen. Carefully selected.'

A chill races through her body. The situation she's in is devastating enough without the added suggestion that it could possibly go much deeper.

'What do you mean, selected? I don't understand. How was I selected?'

'I can't go into all the details. Suffice to say that you were chosen on the basis of your potential.'

Wait. What? He's talking as though I'm the subject of some kind of experiment here. Like I've been under a microscope all my life and didn't even know it.

'Chosen by whom? By you? Why? And how? You mean you've been watching me?'

So many questions. Her mind is a whirlwind of questions. Nothing makes sense. Nothing is believable. This just doesn't happen to people.

'Like I say, Erin, I can't go into details. But you're definitely right for this. I know you have it in you.'

'No. You've got me all wrong. I don't know what you've heard about me. I don't know what research you've done on me. But you picked the wrong person. Doesn't matter what threats you make, to me or my baby. I can't do what you ask. I'm sorry.'

She hears a low laugh through her earpiece.

'Oh, Erin. You're priceless. You're perfect for this. It's precisely because you think you can't do it that makes you so suitable. This will be good for you, believe me. It will bring out an inner strength in you that you don't even know you possess. You will discover so many new things about yourself.'

He's insane. Has to be. He sounds calm and rational, but he's got to be out of his skull. This is too twisted for words. Why is he doing this? What possible motive could he have if he's not crazy?

'I don't want to discover new things. I'm happy as I am. I just want to get on with my life. Just me and my baby. Please, if you really have

Georgia, you should give her back to me. I won't say anything about this to anyone. Just hand her back, and we'll forget all about it. Okay?'

'*Erin, Erin, Erin.*' The voice is so patronizing now. Making her feel like she's a naughty child who needs to learn her lesson. '*Stop all this. You can't make it go away. It is what it is. Whining and pleading won't change things. Besides, it's beneath you. Start showing some of that fortitude I talked about.*'

A wave of fury suddenly engulfs Erin. 'NO!' she yells. She leaps to her feet. Grabs her lapel and brings the brooch right up to her mouth. 'NOOOO! You give me my baby now, you fucking piece of shit! You hear me, you son of a bitch? Give me back my baby, or so help me God I will track you down and I will kill you. Do you hear what I'm saying, you cocksucker?'

She stands there panting after her tirade, burning tears of anger running down her face.

'*My, my. What a potty mouth you have when you get riled. But you know what? I believe what you said. I believe you could kill me right now, if it meant getting your baby back. You see? You can do it. You can kill for your baby. You've already taken that first vital step.*'

'Fuck you,' she says. 'I've had enough of listening to your crap. I'm calling the cops. You can watch if you like. If you get so aroused by watching what I do, then observe this, you prick.'

She walks over to the phone. Picks it up from its cradle. Holds it in front of the brooch.

'You see this? Watch what I do.'

'*Erin, put the phone down.*' The voice has a hardened edge to it. A hard, sharp edge that threatens harm.

'Watch. See? I'm pressing nine. See how I press the nine key?'

'*You're being silly, Erin. Don't be so childish.*'

'Now a one. Are you getting all this? Can you see what I'm doing here? Your game is over, mister. Give up now, or you are in so much trouble.'

'*Erin. I am not going to warn you again. This is your last chance.*'

'Oh, yeah? Last chance for what? What are you going to do about it? Scared now, aren't you? Shoe's on the other foot now. Are you watching? One more digit. Ready for this, you cowardly bastard?'

'*Erin, if you make that call, you will regret it for the rest of your life.*'

Erin stabs at the key. Does it with great emphasis to let him know she's not afraid of him. She's in control now.

'Now all I have to do is press this call button. See? This one here?'

She hovers her index finger over the button – the one with the little icon of a green phone above it.

And then the man says something that makes her think again.

He says, *'Do you want me to hurt your baby? Is that really what you want?'*

'What?'

'Because I will hurt her. If you complete that call, I will damage your baby.'

She stares at the phone. Her finger is still aimed at the call button, but now it's quivering. And over the camera, the man will see that he has put doubt in her mind.

'You're bluffing. You wouldn't hurt a baby. Nobody would hurt a little baby.'

'Ah, see, that's where you're wrong. This child might mean everything to you, but it means nothing to me. It's a means to an end, that's all. I don't care if it lives happily or suffers a very painful death.'

Erin wavers. What do I do? If I stop this call now, he's won. He will know how weak I am. I can't let him believe he's stronger than me.

'You know what? I think you're lying. I'm not even sure you've got my baby. She could be dead already, for all I know. And even if you do have her, you won't hurt her. You know why? Because if you harm just a hair on her head, this conversation is over. I will take out the earpiece and I will smash the brooch and your little game will be over. The only reason I'm still talking to you now is because I'm giving you a chance to put things right. You've got three seconds. After that I'm calling the cops. What's it going to be?'

She hears a brief burst of what sounds like handclapping. *'Bravo. Nice try. You've got guts, Erin. It's why I chose you.'*

'Three,' she says.

'Won't work, though. Not against me. There's no point in trying to fight this.'

'Two.'

'*But maybe it's for the best. We need to get off on the right foot. Establish the ground rules. Maybe this is a lesson you need to learn the hard way, just so we work together better in the future.*'

'One.'

'*Okay, Erin. If that's what you want. I'll let you choose. What's it to be? Georgia's fingers? Her tiny button toes? Maybe those shiny blue eyes of hers? What do you think? Which bits of her are you going to sacrifice?*'

Tears are streaming down her face now. Her finger is shaking uncontrollably over the phone. I can't do this, she thinks. I can't endanger Georgia. But I have to do it. It's the only way to save her. I have to do it. Please, please, please, let this be the right decision.

She presses the call button. Brings the phone to her ear.

'*Oh, Erin.*'

His voice in one ear, speaking with quiet finality. The ringtone in the other. Please answer. Answer the damn phone.

And then she hears it.

The scream.

The high pitched shriek of her child.

She's heard Georgia cry a thousand times, and she knows it's her – knows that without doubt. But this cry pierces her. It shoots through her ear and into her brain and on down through her heart and her gut, ripping her insides to pieces as it fires through her body. And all she can think is, No, no, no, what have I done? And she drops the phone and yells something. Calls for him to stop as she fumbles for the phone. Pleads with him not to hurt her baby. Look, I'm ending the call, see? Can you see? Please tell me you can see this. Please stop hurting Georgia. She's just a baby. Please stop. Please. Please.

And then she's on the floor and she's screaming and crying and wishing the world beneath her would open up and swallow her and end her life because of what she has done to her poor sweet baby.

11.05 PM

Detective Second Grade Callum Doyle would go home now if he could. But he can't. He has almost two hours of his shift left. He started work at four this afternoon, and isn't due to finish until one in the morning.

The unsociable hours are one of the downsides of being a New York City detective. Doyle thinks it's a pity that the criminals in this fair city haven't yet adopted the more reasonable nine-to-five working day to which anyone with common sense adheres. Maybe they should form a union. Take strike action. The criminal fraternity is certainly being short-changed in this regard.

That said, tonight it would seem that the felons have finally seen sense. Either that or they've all taken themselves off to a conference somewhere. It has been a deathly quiet shift in a deathly quiet day. The Christmas and New Year festivities are well and truly over. Not so much drunken carousing. Not so many suicides. The two ends of the happiness spectrum have been replaced by a middle ground of people returning to the mundanity of everyday life. This is a lull, though. The brief respite provided by the holidays will soon be forgotten, and people will resume where they left off. They will return to their feuds, their hatreds, their greed, their pettiness. Conflict will be re-ignited. All will be as it was. As though the message of Christmas was written in disappearing ink.

Doyle can't wait.

Which is not to say that Doyle has less love for his fellow humans than the rest of us. In an ideal world he would be the first to vote for scrapping the police force. He would be the first to sign up to no more murders, rapes, robberies, assaults and other forms of nastiness. But it's not an ideal world, is it? These things happen, and if they're going to happen then they may as well happen on Doyle's shift, because right now he is bored stiff. He is bored of paperwork, and he is bored of taking phone calls from mentally disturbed people who want to report aliens under their beds, and he is bored of trying to keep himself interested in things that don't interest him.

He is not alone in this. When he looks around the squadroom, he sees his colleagues yawning, stretching and scratching. It's not as if they can even do much in the way of chasing up leads on active cases. When it gets this late, people don't like to receive calls from cops, asking them what they saw or heard or did. They want to go to bed. Requests for interviews at this time of the night just make people irritable and uncooperative.

Rachel, his wife, might also be a tad annoyed if he called her again. He spoke to her less than an hour ago. And an hour before that. And an hour before that too. She saw right through it. Said, 'You don't build up credit, you know. Making all these calls tonight when you've got nothing else to do doesn't mean you don't have to call on other nights. You're not allowed to average things out like that. It's in the rulebook.'

He smiled at that, but although he didn't protest, he actually did have reasons for calling other than boredom. That's the thing with working these late shifts. He misses out on precious family time. The evening meal together. Putting Amy to bed. Earlier, his daughter told him on the phone about a flower she had made with the new craft set she received for Christmas. To anyone else it would be insignificant news, but to Doyle it was fascinating. He listened intently to her squeaky little voice and told her how clever she was and about how he was dying to see it, and then she told him she would leave it by his bed for him to see, and he wished he could be there right then, sitting with her on her bed and looking at this beautiful flower his child had created.

And sometimes, when he gets all melancholy like that, he thinks about how he has let his family down. He thinks about all the terrible things he has done. Things that include killing and maiming. Things he cannot tell anyone about. Things he finds difficult to admit even to himself. He knows he has been changed by these things, and sometimes it worries him that he will lose himself and he will lose his family. And then he gets scared.

Shit!

Too much time to think, that's the problem. Snap out of it, man.

He clears his throat. Gets up from his desk. Rotates his shoulders and shakes the tension out of his arms. He's spent the last hour typing up DD5 reports – a task which he hates – and his posture feels all out of whack. He reckons he's not built for desk duties. He's built for being active. For doing stuff. In his younger days he boxed. He was good, but not brilliant. Not top-notch enough to make it his career. But he's never stopped doing the exercises. He still jogs, he still does the sit-ups and the press-ups, and he still pounds the punch-bag. And he doesn't do all that just so he is better prepared for the demands of typing.

Doyle picks up the mug from his desk. Given to him by Rachel, it has a picture of Popeye on it. 'Popeye,' she explained at the time. 'Because you're Doyle. Popeye Doyle? The French Connection?' To which he replied. 'Thank you, Olive. Where's me spinach?'

He strolls over to where Tommy LeBlanc is pouring himself a thick, strong dose of coffee. Sets down his mug next to LeBlanc's.

'Fill her up,' he says.

LeBlanc smiles. 'Regular or premium?'

'Gimme the highest octane you got.'

LeBlanc brings the jug across and pauses. 'You really need this? With all the excitement we got going on here?'

Doyle shrugs. 'What can I say? I like living on the edge.'

Not so long ago, most of Doyle's conversations with LeBlanc were not as amicable and relaxed as this. LeBlanc is the youngest and least experienced member of the Eighth Precinct detective squad. That in itself does not make him a bad or ineffectual cop, and in fact Doyle now thinks of him as having the makings of an excellent detective. A few months ago, though, his view of LeBlanc was as a snot-nosed fashion-obsessed newbie who probably didn't know shit. Which, Doyle now accepts, was completely unreasonable of him. What prompted that way of thinking was that LeBlanc's usual partner on the squad was, and still is, a man called Schneider, who hates Doyle's guts. It was guilt by association – a specious syllogism that went something like: Schneider hates Doyle; Schneider's partner is LeBlanc; therefore LeBlanc hates Doyle too. And without any evidence that this had some basis in fact,

Doyle went on the defensive and mentally slotted LeBlanc into the category of 'opposition'.

Things came to a head last October, when Doyle and LeBlanc were paired up for the first time on a case. From the get-go it was not a harmonious partnership. Doyle did his best not to involve LeBlanc. He didn't even let him into his thought processes. It didn't help matters that this particular case, involving the torture and murder of a teenage girl, really fucked up Doyle's mind, and that the man he believed to be the killer was adept at fucking up Doyle's life. A partner he could have trusted and relied upon would, he now acknowledges, have been a tremendous asset.

Doyle knows all this. He got it wrong. He made a mistake. He acted like an asshole.

But good things can arise from bad situations. And arising from this one was what he learned about LeBlanc, which is that underneath the trendy suit and the skinny tie and the snazzy glasses and the waxed blond hair there is a stand-up guy who has balls. A guy with a moral compass that points in the right direction despite the spiteful magnetic pull emanating from people like Schneider.

In short, Doyle has taken a shine to LeBlanc. He would welcome the opportunity to partner up with him again, and this time on much more conducive terms.

Says Doyle, 'You get any good toys for Christmas?'

LeBlanc's smile shows that he doesn't mind the jibe. His youthful, fresh-faced appearance belies the fact that he is actually only a few years younger than Doyle.

'Yeah. I got a nice train set. You want, I'll let you come over and use it some time. It's got little action figures and everything.'

'Cool. Is it as nice as our subway? Does it come with a pickpocket and a homeless guy and a drunk and a flasher?'

'Sure does. Even has this one little guy, throws himself onto the track at random intervals. It's very realistic.'

Doyle issues an exaggerated sigh. 'Ah, don't you just love the romance of those traditional toys? Much nicer than the modern crap.'

He takes a sip of his coffee. Tries to peer through the grime-caked windows of the station house.

'What's wrong with people tonight? Don't they know there are things worth stealing out there? People worth assaulting? This rate, we'll be out of a job.'

LeBlanc starts back to his desk. 'It won't last. Make the most of it. Something big goes down now, you'll be here all night. Just type up your fives and punch out. Tomorrow you'll be praying the shift could be as peaceful as this.'

Doyle nods. Wise words from such a young head. Make hay while the sun shines. Except that the sun isn't shining because it's a miserable, depressing January night, and making hay is the last pursuit he's likely to undertake in a squadroom full of tired, bored cops.

He sighs again, this time for real, and drags himself back to his desk. He sets the coffee mug down on a Guinness coaster, then flicks the head of the bobble-headed leprechaun that was bought for him by the squad as a welcoming present. Something to do with him being Irish, ho, ho.

He sometimes wonders what would have happened to him if he'd stayed Irish. If he hadn't been whisked across to New York when he was only eight years old. Would he still have become a cop? A member of the *gardai*? Was he always destined to become an enforcer of law?

And sometimes he wonders whether that's still what he is. Whether the line between right and wrong is still as clear as it seemed to him when he was a hopeful young man in the Police Academy. That line seems so much fuzzier now. Some of the things he's done...

His phone rings. He snatches at the receiver and stabs the flashing call button before some other bastard can steal his action.

'Cal? It's Marcus, downstairs.'

Marcus Wilson. The desk sergeant. Doyle likes Wilson. He likes LeBlanc too. Hell, it seems to Doyle as though he likes everyone at the moment except the criminals, who are just not living up to expectations tonight.

'Hey, Marcus. How's it going?'

'Oh, the usual. You know how it is. Busy, busy, busy. Right?'

Doyle frowns. How is it that Marcus has so much to do, while we're sitting here with our thumbs up our asses? Where's the fairness in that?

'Yeah,' he says. 'Up to our eyes here. Whaddya got?'

'A live one. You interested?'

Am I interested? All the activity we got going on, not a moment to ourselves, and he asks if I'm interested?

'Shoot,' says Doyle.

11.11 PM

'**E**rin, you need to stop this now. You need to calm down.'

She is on the bathroom floor, having just spent the last fifteen minutes with her head in the toilet bowl. There is nothing but bile left in her stomach. She can still taste the foul acidic fluid in her mouth, steadily dissolving her teeth. She wishes it would continue on through her jaw and her skull, liquefying them as it goes. Wishes her whole body could dissolve into a rancid puddle on the floor.

'*Erin, are you listening to me?*'

She's not sure she can be bothered to answer him. Everything seems too much effort now. She is responsible for injuring her own baby. No mother can be forgiven for that.

'*ERIN!*'

'WHAT?' she yells back. Then, softer: 'What? What do you want from me? What did you do to Georgia? Is she… Is she… ?'

'*She's alive, if that's what you're asking. You can still get her back alive. But what you need to understand is that I'm not fucking around here. I am serious. When I say I am going to do something, I will do it. Do you believe me, Erin?*'

'Yes,' she whispers.

'*Do you?*'

'YES! But…'

'*But what, Erin?*'

'I need to know. What you did. Is she hurt? Badly, I mean?'

'*She'll live. That's all you need to know. I could've hurt her a lot worse, and next time I will. But there won't be a next time, will there? You know now that you have to do what I say. Isn't that right?*'

'Yes. But…'

'The buts again, Erin? More buts? Are you sure you want to keep questioning me like this?'

There is a razor-edged tone to his voice. A tone that will cut. A tone that will slice her baby into tiny pieces. Ever since she heard Georgia's cry of pain, all kinds of images have been jumping into her head of what might have been inflicted. Images of wounding and dismemberment that no mother should conceive of happening to her child. She will have nightmares about those images when this is over. She will have them even if she can get her Georgia back safely.

But there can be no ifs about it. Protecting Georgia is paramount. She *will* get Georgia back. Even if that means…

A life. Another human life. He wants her to take a life in exchange for the life of her baby.

She knows this already. This is nothing new. But she has to keep repeating it to herself. Has to try to make it real in her head. Because still it seems so absurd that anyone could demand such a thing.

She says, 'It's just that… I don't know if…' Her lower lip begins to quiver as she wrestles with the thought of what she is being asked to do. 'Physically, I mean. I don't know if I am physically capable of killing someone. I could say yes to you now, and then… later, when I'm actually there, with another person, the person you want me to kill, I'm not sure I could do it. Do you understand what I'm saying? It's not that I'm saying no to you now, okay? But, but… even if I agree now, that doesn't mean I would have the strength to… you know… when it comes to it.'

'Erin. Remember what I said to you before. You've been chosen for this. I picked you because I know – I know, all right? – that you're perfectly capable of this. You're stronger than you think. You can do this.'

She shakes her head in confusion. What does he know? What does he know about me that I don't even know myself? Where does he get the idea that I'm capable of murder?

Because that's what this is. Murder. It can't be dressed up as anything else. There will be no pretending that I didn't mean to do it. It's all being planned in advance right now. It will be deliberate, cold-blooded murder. And just because I'm being pressurized into it, will that make me any less guilty? Will an argument of that kind wash with a judge and jury? *I was only following orders.* Yeah, right. Heard that one before. You really want to be associated with the type of people who tried to use that as an excuse?

She says, 'What if they catch me? If I do this and I get caught, I'll go to prison. They'll take my baby from me. Even if I do what you say, I could lose Georgia.'

'Don't worry about that. I know how clever and resourceful you are. You won't get caught. I'll be with you all the way. I'll tell you what to do.'

He makes it sound so easy. Like cooking a meal, or learning to drive a car. You get up, you go out, you kill someone, you come home. What kind of day did you have today, dear? Oh, you know, the usual. Managed to squeeze in a murder in my lunch hour. Nothing special.

She's still not sure she can do this, but what choice does she have? Doesn't she at least have to try? Doesn't she at least have to get some more details? Try to familiarize herself with the situation? Maybe, once she gets a lot more information, maybe then it won't seem so daunting. Maybe he's already got something in place for his victim, and all he needs is some-body else to push a button or something like that. Couldn't that be it? Is she jumping ahead of herself, making something out of what could be nothing?

'Tell me what you want me to do.'

'That's my girl. First thing is to get up off that floor. Go over to the mirror.'

She gets to her feet. Walks unsteadily over to the washbasin and stares at herself in the mirror above it. What a mess. Her dark hair looks like it's just been subject to a small explosion, and a section of it is covered in puke. Her tears have carried dark rivulets of mascara down her face, her lipstick is skewed across one cheek, and a glistening mucus trail runs from her nostrils down to her chin. Right now she'd make a terrific evil clown.

'Nice.'

She nods in agreement. 'I've had better days. When I've showered, when I've slept properly, I'll look better. In the morning I'll look okay again. And then we can talk more about what you want me to do.'

'Uhm, no, Erin.'

She looks in the mirror at the brooch pinned to her lapel. Tries to picture a man's face behind it. A face that will match this voice of pure evil.

'What? What do you mean, no?'

'I mean not tomorrow. This can't wait. This happens now.'

She feels her pulse start to race again. How much more of this stress can her body take?

'Now? No. I can't. I'm not ready.'

'Erin, you can't sleep. Not without your baby. You're just trying to put off the inevitable. And the longer you put it off, the longer you go without Georgia. It happens now, or not at all. And if it never happens, then Georgia never comes back to you. Do I make myself clear?'

She nods into the mirror. She was fooling herself. She could have guessed it would have to be now, while he has her in the palm of his hand. She just didn't want to face up to it.

'I... I need to get cleaned up.'

'You can do that. You can wash, fix your makeup. Then we go, Erin. Okay?'

'All right. But... but I don't know anything. You haven't given me any details. I don't even know who you want me to kill. Who is it? Somebody important? An enemy of yours? Who?'

There's a lengthy pause then. It lasts so long she thinks the connection has been broken. She looks quizzically at the brooch.

And then it starts. A low rumble of amusement that steadily increases in volume and pitch until it becomes a roar of laughter in her ear.

'Who?' he gasps through his laughter. *'You want to know who I want killed? That's great, Erin. That's wonderful.'*

And then he continues to laugh.

And she doesn't understand why.

11.23 PM

'So,' says Doyle. 'Shall we start with some names here? I think that'd be good, don't you?'

It's not clear to Doyle that the man seated on the other side of his desk has heard the question. He seems distracted, his eyes snap-glancing at different points in the squadroom. Doyle knows this isn't going to be easy. The eye-rolls that the uniforms gave him when they brought the guy up told him he had his work cut out with this one.

So be it, thinks Doyle. Kills some time, if nothing else.

'What do you think?' he prompts. 'Some intros?'

The man's gaze flickers across Doyle's face, but moves on again.

'My name's Doyle. Callum Doyle. I'm a detective here. You know what a detective is?'

'Yeah,' says the man, and it's the first word Doyle has heard him utter. 'Like a cop.'

'Well,' says Doyle. 'Not just *like* a cop. I *am* a cop. I investigate crimes.'

'Crimes, yeah. I did a crime. Aw, Jeez. Jesus-Cheeses. It's bad. Are you gonna kill me?'

Doyle flinches in surprise. 'What? Kill you? No. Why would I... No. Nobody's gonna kill you, okay?'

'Have you got a chair up here?'

'A chair? Yeah, we got chairs. You're sitting on one.'

The reaction is unexpected. The man leaps off his seat, then spins to look down at the chair he has just vacated. His hands grasp the hair on both sides of his head as he stares in horror. Doyle jumps to his feet too, ready to tackle this guy if he his actions become more extreme.

'*Is that it?*' yells the man. '*Is that the chair?*'

'What chair?' says Doyle. 'What do you mean?'

'The chair. The electric chair. Bzzzz. Are you gonna fry me? Like bacon? Like sausages?'

'No. Look, it's just a chair. Like mine.' Doyle gestures to both chairs, then picks up his visitor's and shows him the underneath, feeling a little ridiculous at the need to do this. 'No wires. See? It's not electric. Now, could you sit down again for me, please?'

Another brief glance. 'Not electric?'

'No.'

'No sizzling?'

'Nothing like that.'

Slowly, the man edges toward the chair. He starts to sit down, then changes his mind and stands again. He performs another visual inspection to satisfy himself, then lowers himself cautiously.

Doyle looks behind him. Sees that he's attracted an audience, including LeBlanc, who now has a huge smirk on his face. Doyle realizes he's just become one half of a double act.

He turns back to the man. 'Let's start over, all right? I just wanna ask you some questions. Nobody here is gonna hurt you.'

'No sizzling.'

'No.'

'What about lethal injection? Or gas? Or firing squad? Or—'

'No! None of that. Just questions. Simple questions. That's my job. I find things out. I help people.'

'You said you're a cop.'

'Yes, I am.'

'So do you help criminals?'

'Well...'

'I'm a criminal. You won't help me. You'll probably shoot me. I see it all the time on the TV. Cops shoot criminals. Or they lock them up. That's what you'll do to me.'

Jesus, thinks Doyle. This is going nowhere.

'One step at a time, all right? I don't even know if you *are* a criminal yet. All I know is what you told the sergeant downstairs. You remember talking to him? To Sergeant Wilson?'

'One-three-seven-one.'

'What?'

'Sergeant Marcus Wilson. Nine-one-one. Lots of primes. He has candy. Prime candy.'

'Uh, yeah,' says Doyle, feeling lost.

The man flicks a hand toward Doyle. 'You don't have a number.'

'A number? I'm not sure what you—'

'You got a bent nose, though.'

Doyle starts to lift a hand to his face. It's true, he does have a slight kink in his nose, a legacy of his boxing days. Not many people have the effrontery to point the fact out to him, though.

'Okay, so you know about my nose, you know my name, you know what I do for a living. How about we even things up a little? Let's start with your name.'

The man resumes his random search of the squadroom. His leg begins to shake, and he starts tapping the fingertips of his hands together.

Doyle tries to head off another flare-up: 'You don't want to tell me your name? Why's that? We're friends, aren't we? Friends tell each other their names.'

Nothing doing. The man doesn't so much as turn his head toward Doyle.

'Why won't you give me your name?'

Doyle decides to wait it out. He sits and watches, but the man says nothing.

'Look,' says Doyle, a little too firmly because he can feel his irritation building, 'if you want me to help you—'

'You'll put me in jail,' the man blurts out. 'If I tell you who I am or where I live, then you'll know, and you'll see what I did, and you'll lock me up.'

'But isn't that why you came here? To tell us what you did? Why did you do that if you don't want to give me more details?'

'My mom.'

'Your mom. What about your mom?'

'She said I should always say when I've done something bad. She made me promise. I always keep my promises.'

Doyle sits back in his chair and watches the man eyeing up the squad-room like a pigeon scanning for crumbs.

Great, he thinks. A guy fesses up to murder, but he won't tell me who he is or where he lives.

Just great.

11.48 PM

He wouldn't allow her to shower.

It would have meant removing the brooch and surveillance equipment, and he wouldn't permit that. Instead, she had to wash in the hand-basin, doing what she could to clean the vomit from her hair, and then re-apply her makeup.

'Very nice, Erin. Very pretty.'

His voice sickens her. She doesn't want to be told how she looks. Not by this monster. She doesn't feel attractive. She thinks she still looks like shit.

'What now?' she asks.

'Now? Now we go out.'

'Out where? I still don't know where you want me to go. Is it somebody's home?'

A chuckle again. *'Could be.'*

'I don't understand. How am I supposed to know where to go if you don't tell me?'

'You mean you haven't figured it out yet?'

Figured what out? What's there to figure out? He wants me to kill someone, and he won't tell me who. What am I supposed to deduce from that?

'No. Tell me.'

'It's perfectly simple, Erin. I'm leaving it up to you.'

'Leaving what up to me?'

He laughs. *'The choice, stupid. The choice of victim.'*

She stands there in shock, staring at her own open-mouthed reflection. How many times is this man going to surprise her?

'W-what?'

'You heard me, Erin. You can decide. Should be easier that way.'

Easier? How is it easier? If he tells me who to kill, then I go and do it. But this? Deciding who should die at my hands?

'No. Please. Don't ask me to do that. I can't pick someone to die. Killing someone is going to be hard enough, but I can't decide who that will be. You have to do that.'

'What's the problem? This way you can choose someone you hate. Someone you always wanted out of your life. A boss who made your life hell, maybe. A boyfriend who cheated on you. A school bully. There must be lots of people you wouldn't mind getting a little revenge on.'

'NO! We're not talking about putting a laxative in someone's drink, for God's sake. This is about killing them. I don't want anyone to die. Nobody has hurt me badly enough for me to want them dead.'

'Well, then, you'll have to pick someone at random. Frankly, Erin, I don't give a fuck. Pick who you like. As long as you kill them, that's all that matters.'

'Why? What do you get from me reducing the human race by one? Because that's what it amounts to. I could understand if you wanted me to kill your worst enemy, or you were trying to make some kind of statement by taking out a politician or a religious leader, but it's not even that considered. So why? For kicks? Is it just to experience the power of controlling another human being so completely? Is that all this is to you?'

When it comes, the response gives her no answers: *'You're wasting time, Erin. We need to get moving. Your baby needs you.'*

Georgia again. Always he is there with the reminders about Georgia, and with them, the underlying threat to her existence. Not that she needs reminding. Georgia is her everything – always at the epicenter of her thoughts. He knows this, and he will continue to use it against her.

But now she's having second thoughts again. How in Christ's name can I select a victim? What gives me the right to do this? Who would I choose? Where would I find them at this time of night?

'Erin. Get your ass into gear. Let's go.'

The voice startles her into action. She leaves the bathroom. Back into the living room. She doesn't know what she's going to do or how she's going to do it. The only thing she does know is that she cannot defy this man any longer. She will have to wing it. Go along with his plans for as long as she can, hoping that something will crop up, something will go her way for once, because God knows everything's been against her so far. Talk about victims – well, yeah, here's one, the biggest victim of them all, and when are you are gonna give me a fucking helping hand here? Please, somebody, help me.

She moves toward the apartment door. Goes to open it.

'Uhm, Erin. You planning to use your hands?'

She pauses, perplexed. How else would she open the damned door?

'Duh! To kill, Erin? Are you going to strangle them to death, or do you think maybe you should take a weapon of some kind?'

A weapon. It hadn't crossed her mind. Generally, the idea of using weapons never crosses her mind. Why would it? Her life now consists of looking after her baby. What connection could that possibly have to implements of pain and death?

Unless, of course, your baby is snatched violently from you and hurt. Hurt so bad it screams for you to intervene.

Oh, yes, she thinks. Put me in a room with that guy, and give me a weapon. In fact, no weapon needed. I will tear him apart with my bare hands. I will gouge out his eyes and bite off his ears and stamp my heels into his—

'ERIN! Get with the program. Are you signed up for this or not?'

'Yes. Yes. A weapon. Uhm…' She looks helplessly around her.

'The kitchen,' he says in despair. 'Something sharp maybe?'

She goes where she is told. Slides a huge carving knife out of the wood block on the counter.

'That's a bad-ass knife, all right. But a little impractical, don't you think? What are you going to do, walk around the city looking like you're Norman Bates's mother?'

She returns the knife to the block. Takes out a smaller one. Black plastic handle, five inch blade, sharp serrated edge.

'That's fine. Don't worry, it's more than capable of doing the job. Now put it in your pocket and let's get out of here.'

Again she's slow to respond. She stares down at the knife. The last time she held it, she was cutting into tomatoes. It's hard to imagine herself thrusting it into the flesh of a human being. And is thrusting best, or do you slash? Or chop? How much force is required for such an act? Do you have to be strong? Or does it part flesh easily, like slicing through a soft peach? Do you hold the knife in the usual way, with its blade upward, or do you hold it the other way round, ready to plunge it downward into your victim, again *à la* Norman Bates's mother?

'ERIN!'

She jumps. 'All right, all right.' She's nowhere near ready for this. She doesn't know how to kill, has no inclination to kill.

She hurries to the door. Hurries because she senses she has pushed her baby's kidnapper to his limit, and not because she is eager to carry out his bidding.

She slips the knife into her pocket. Pulls open the door to her apartment.

She lets out a small cry when she sees the man standing in the hallway, staring right at her.

WEDNESDAY, JANUARY 5

12.05 AM

Says Doyle, 'You eaten recently? You want something to eat? A drink, maybe? You want a soda?'

'Do you have Seven-Up?' says the man.

'Uhm, I'm not sure. I could go take a look if you like.'

'I like Seven-Up. Especially from the Seven-Eleven. Seven is prime. Eleven is also prime.'

'They are, huh?' says Doyle, trying to hold the attention of this man by feigning interest on a topic he knows nothing about.

'Yeah. Seven is also a lucky number. Thirteen is unlucky, but it's also prime. Thirteen is made up from four plus nine, both unlucky in Japan. In Japanese, the word for four sounds like the word for death, and the word for nine sounds like the word for pain. Very unlucky. Very bad numbers.'

'And let me guess,' says Doyle with mock enthusiasm. 'Four and nine are both prime, right?'

Doyle thinks he's hit on something when the man actually lets his eyes alight on Doyle's face for more than one second. At last, he thinks, I've made a connection.

But then the man turns his head aside, as if turning to an invisible companion next to him. He jerks a thumb in Doyle's direction and says to his imaginary friend, 'You hear that? He thinks four and nine are primes. You believe that? Ha!'

Doyle feels instantly ridiculed. Jesus, how am I letting a guy like this make me feel two inches tall?

He says, 'So … they're not primes?'

'Ha! Not primes. Of course not. They're squares. No number can be both a square and a prime, but it can be a square of a prime. Four and nine are squares of primes.'

Doyle's head is whirling now, and he's starting to feel like this is going really off-topic. That in addition to making him feel like the class dunce.

'Tell you what,' he says. 'I'll make you a deal. You tell me your name, and I'll go fetch you that Seven-Up. Whaddya say?'

What he says is nothing, and Doyle's frustration level climbs ever higher.

'I gotta call you something,' he says. 'If you won't give me your real name, I'll have to give you a nickname of some kind. Is that okay with you?'

The man's not interested. Doesn't appear to be listening. Doesn't appear to be in this room, mentally.

'How about Rainman?'

This from Schneider, languishing at his desk across the squadroom. He is a large, square-framed man with an equally square head topped by close-cropped steel-gray hair. Schneider looks like the type of cop who would crush a suspect first and ask questions later. He takes no prisoners with Doyle either, and makes no secret of the fact. The animosity has been present ever since Doyle joined the Eighth squad, and Doyle long ago abandoned any hope of extinguishing it.

Schneider presses on: 'You should take him to Atlantic City. Get him counting cards in the casinos. What with his proficiency with numbers and your luck in getting away with things, you'd clean 'em out.'

This is nothing new to Doyle, Schneider not being one to waste an opportunity to cast a shadow on his past. It is Doyle's hope that, even if Schneider never tires of it, others will, and someone will eventually tell him to shut the fuck up. All Doyle needs to do in the meantime is to keep his nose clean – something that, unfortunately, doesn't always come naturally to him.

He does now what he has found works best with Schneider, which is to ignore his jibes. Doyle's suspect, on the other hand, has already formed an opinion and is less reticent in keeping it under wraps. He leans conspiratorially toward Doyle.

'I don't like him. He's mean. And he looks like Spongebob Squarepants.'

Doyle can't prevent himself from laughing out loud, and as he does so he looks over at Schneider, who seems to sense that he is the butt of a joke and is muttering angrily to himself.

Doyle returns his attention to the stranger on the other side of his desk. He is starting to warm to this guy.

Which is probably not the best attitude to have toward someone who may have just disemboweled his own mother.

12.06 AM

She wasn't expecting to meet anyone in the hallway at this time of night. She certainly wasn't expecting someone to be right in front of her apartment door. As if he'd been about to knock.

Or as if he'd been listening.

She wonders how long he's been standing there. How much he's heard.

'Who the hell is that?'

The voice sounds so loud in her ear that it makes her wonder if her visitor can hear it too. She reaches a hand to her hair to make sure that it's hiding the earpiece.

'Mr Wiseman!' she exclaims in surprise, but also answering the question.

Mr Wiseman is in his sixties. Short, slim and slightly stooped over. As if in apology for the absence of hair on his head, his eyebrows have bloomed to form a shelf of thick, lustrous gray. He lives in the adjoining apartment, apparently with his son Leonard, although she has never seen or heard the latter. According to the elder Mr Wiseman – and here she's a little fuzzy on the detail because she never listens to his stories properly – his son was hit by a car about twenty years ago and broke his spine. Wheelchair-bound ever since, he refuses to leave the apartment, relying on his father to do everything for him.

When Erin moved here just a month or so ago, Mr Wiseman was the first to knock on her door and say hello. Since then she has chatted to him several times in the hallway. Mostly mundane stuff, but in spite of his own family burdens he has always seemed peculiarly concerned for her welfare.

'I'm sorry,' he says. 'I didn't mean to alarm you. It's just that… I heard noises.'

His voice is gentle and filled with concern, which does not go unnoticed as it carries over the microphone.

'Great. A do-gooder. Tell the Jew bastard to fuck off.'

She feels the urge to snap. She wants to bring the brooch to her face and yell into it. What stops her is the realization of how crazy she'd look.

'Noises?' she says, because she has no better answer at the ready. She racks her brain for even the feeblest of explanations.

Wiseman cranes his neck to look past her and into her apartment. She tries to act casual in the way she steps toward him and pulls the door almost closed behind her.

'Yes,' says Wiseman. 'Noises. Crying. And yelling.'

'Tell him to keep his huge prying schnozz out of your business.'

'Maybe it was the TV? I did have it on a little loud tonight. I'm sorry if—'

'No. Not the TV. It was your voice, Erin. You were shouting, and you were really upset. I just wanted to check if everything was all right.'

'Sure, Samuel. Everything's fine. No problems.'

'Samuel? You're on first name terms with this Hebe? Christ. Like I said, Erin, you need to tell the kike to take a hike.'

The venom of this racist sickens her. She hates him even more than she did before, if that's possible. She guesses he's probably homophobic too. Guesses he's probably anti-everything. She doubts that a more detestable creature has ever walked this earth.

Wiseman continues to look at her for answers. 'So… the yelling?'

She struggles for an answer. The voice in her ear makes it even more difficult to concentrate.

'I just thought of something, Erin. Yeah! This guy! He could be your victim.'

'What?'

The shock of the suggestion forces the word from her mouth. Wiseman blinks at her, obviously wondering how it's possible that she didn't hear his question. Then he narrows his eyes, which almost disappear as his bushy eyebrows collapse in on themselves.

'Are you all right, Erin? Is there someone…' He nods at the door behind her, then lowers his voice. 'Are you in some kind of trouble?'

Trouble? Am I in trouble? Other than my baby being snatched and me about to commit murder, what kind of difficulties could I possibly be in?

'He's on to us, Erin. Waste him. You don't even need to step out of the building. You could get this over with right here and now.'

She tries to laugh. Tries to make light of the scenarios being thrown at her from all directions. But what comes out of her mouth is a humorless bark.

'No,' she says. 'Nothing like that. Look, if you must know, I was having an argument with my ex. Over the phone. Things got a little… heated.'

Wiseman stares, and his stare is filled with suspicion.

'He doesn't believe you, Erin. What are you waiting for? Kill the Jew bastard.'

'Heated?' says Wiseman. 'More like a raging inferno, I'd say.'

She gives a little shrug and an attempt at a smile. 'What can I say? I picked the wrong guy.'

Wiseman nods sagely. 'It happens. I was fortunate. My Esther was with me for forty years before she died. Is there anything I can do to help?'

'Yeah. Get ready to join your dead bitch in hell, Samuel.'

Shut up, she thinks. Shut the fuck up, you loathsome piece of crap.

'No. Thank you, but I just need some space, you know?'

Wiseman nods, but she can tell he's not wholly convinced. He continues to stand there, awaiting her next move. And she's not sure what that should be.

He says, 'Going out somewhere?'

'Out?' she says, but how can she deny it? She's coming out of her apartment with her coat on, for Christ's sake. 'Uhm, yeah. For a short while.'

'He's too fucking nosy, Erin. Whack him now.'

'At this time of night?' says Wiseman. He tries to look over her shoulder again. 'Are you sure…'

She reaches behind and grabs the door handle. Pulls the door firmly shut behind her. Wiseman stares at her again, eyes saying, *Tell me the truth now, Erin. If you're in trouble, I can help you.*

But you can't help me, Samuel. Nobody can help me. I have no choice in what I'm about to do.

She puts her hands into her pockets. Recoils slightly as the fingers of her right hand encounter the knife.

'Yes,' she says. 'I'm meeting up with some friends. They just got into the city.'

'Erin, do you know what time it is? It's after midnight.'

Another shrug. Saying, *What's the big deal? Why shouldn't a woman go out after midnight?*

'I was supposed to meet them earlier. For a meal. But then ... well, that's when it all blew up with my ex. So... so I'm catching up with them at a club.'

'A club,' he repeats, but in a much flatter tone. He looks her up and down, and she knows he's thinking that she's hardly dressed for partying.

'I didn't have much time to get ready,' she explains. 'And if I don't go now, I won't see them again for a long time. So if you'll excuse me...'

She starts to move past Wiseman, heading for the staircase.

'Erin,' says Wiseman. 'Aren't you forgetting something?'

She halts. Why do people keep asking me if I've forgotten something? What the hell can it be this time?

She turns to Wiseman. Questions him with her eyes.

'Your baby?' he says. There is an earnestness to his voice now.

'Uh-oh. I told you, Erin. This Hebe won't give up. Do yourself a favor. Do Georgia a favor. Why make it any harder than it already is?'

She tries not to listen, but she finds her fingers closing around the handle of the knife.

'What?' she says. 'Oh!' She laughs. 'No, it's okay. She's with a babysitter.'

Wiseman takes a step closer. Her grip on the knife tightens. Would it be so hard? Couldn't I just whip this knife out now and stick it in him? All these questions of his, all this suspicion. I could end it with one swift move. I could get my Georgia back.

Wiseman points at her door. 'A sitter? In your apartment?'

She tries to think. Every time she comes up with an answer, Wiseman finds something else to query. The lies are growing. He's going to catch me out. I'll say something inconsistent with what I said before, and he'll latch onto it. Please don't do that, Samuel. Please don't make me kill you.

'Do it, do it, do it!'

It's like he knows what I'm thinking. As well as seeing and hearing what I see and hear, he can read my mind. He knows I'm crumbling.

'Uhm, no,' she says. 'Another friend. She's looking after Georgia at her place.'

'She's staying with her? Overnight?'

She hears his incredulity. And why wouldn't he be surprised? Georgia is six months old. Who the hell lets their six-month old baby do a sleepover? What kind of fucking stupid tale are you weaving here, Erin?

'I know,' she says. 'Sounds crazy, huh? But Lois is a real close friend, with young kids of her own. Georgia will be fine. I wouldn't do this normally, but like I say, this is my only chance to see my friends.' Another thought occurs to her – a way of allowing her to bring some of the threads together: 'Of course, my ex doesn't see it that way. That's what the argument was all about. He seems to think I should spend twenty-four/seven with Georgia, even though he's out of her life for good, the prick.'

She's pleased with that. She's especially proud of the way she has included a subtext that warns, *Only a complete asshole would accuse me of being a bad mother.*

But Wiseman seems to have other thoughts on his mind. He moves even closer to Erin. Dangerously close. Less than an arm's length away. A dagger thrust away.

'Who's Lois? You've never mentioned her. In fact, I thought you said you had no real friends in New York.'

Please, Samuel. Don't do this. Don't push me like this. Don't give me an excuse.

She can feel her arm muscles tensing. Ready to bring out the knife. Ready to drive it home. One brief jab. That's all it will take to bring Georgia back again.

'Do it!'

'I, uhm … did I say that? Oh, yes. I meant Manhattan. Lois lives on Staten Island. That's what I meant.'

Everything seems to freeze then. Wiseman and Erin staring at each other, not moving, hardly even breathing.

He knows, she thinks. He can sense there's something badly wrong here. He's going to do something about it. He's planning to go back to his apartment and call the cops. I can't let him do that. I can't let him jeopardize Georgia's life.

Her right arm starts to move, seemingly of its own accord. She can't prevent it. It's bending at the elbow. Her hand is coming out of the pocket, still clutching the knife. The knife with the five inch blade and the serrated edge. The knife that means the difference between having Georgia and not having her. It's coming, it's coming…

'Now, Erin! Now!'

And then it stops coming. It stops because Wiseman has reached out and grabbed her forearm. Not in any attempt to defend himself – he has no idea what imminent danger he's in – but in a warm, benevolent way. It's a touch of friendship.

'You know,' he says, 'that I'm always here, don't you? If ever you want me to look after Georgia for a couple hours. I'm pretty good with kids.'

'Ha! I'll bet he is, the old pervert.'

Erin drops her gaze to the floor. She cannot look Wiseman in the face any longer. Oh my good God, she thinks. What am I doing? Was I really about to take the life of this innocent selfless man?

She wants to answer. She wants to tell Wiseman everything. She wants to cry and to let him know of the trouble she's in and to plead for his help.

And the only way she can prevent herself from doing all that is to get the hell out of here.

'I gotta go,' she mutters, still looking at the floor.

She turns and pulls away. Scurries to the stairs and descends as quickly as she can, never looking back. She doesn't want to see the expression on Wiseman's face. Cannot bring herself to look again into the eyes of the charitable neighbor who so nearly became her sacrificial lamb.

If I could do that to Samuel, she thinks, if I could contemplate hurting a gentle soul like him…

… then what could I do to a complete stranger?

12.12 AM

They observe from a distance.

Doyle is at LeBlanc's desk. Hunched over, talking to LeBlanc in a low voice. They both have their eyes on the man who has confessed to murder and nothing else. The nameless suspect is sitting at the water cooler, looking sidelong into a paper cup and muttering.

'So what do you think?' LeBlanc asks.

Doyle digs deep into his knowledge and experience of human behavior and comes up with, 'I think he's a little… special.'

LeBlanc nods. 'Good special or bad special? You make him for a killer?'

'Who knows?' says Doyle as he observes the man dip his index finger into his cup of water and swirl it around. 'Like this, no. But I haven't pushed him real hard. Every time he goes near the edge, I feel I have to back off. I don't know what he's capable of if I really lean on his whacko button, and I'm not sure I want to find out.'

'You got an ID on him yet?'

'Nope. Guy won't give me nothing except he offed his mother. I got no victim, no crime scene, no witnesses. He won't even tell me how or why it happened. What the hell am I supposed to do with that?'

'You could try a mind meld.'

Doyle shifts his gaze to LeBlanc. 'A what?'

'You know. Like Spock. Where you put your fingers to his noggin and listen in to his thoughts.'

'Thanks, Tommy. You're a great help. I can see now how you made detective. Besides, I'm not sure I want to start moseying around inside this guy's brain. I might never find the exit door.'

LeBlanc glances at his watch. 'We're getting near end of shift. What's your plan?'

Over at the cooler, the man is now on his knees, trying to peer up the spout of the water dispenser. Doyle can't help but smile. He feels there's a million miles between them, but that, given time, he could build a bridge across that gulf. He could make a connection. There was another guy once: he didn't have the same mental problems as this one, but he was a challenge in his own idiosyncratic way. A guy called Gonzo…

Doyle shakes his head. 'He's gonna have to become somebody else's problem. Someone who knows how to talk to people like this.'

'Who? Psych Services? You won't get them out at this time of night.'

'I know it,' says Doyle.

A sense of failure runs through him as he leaves LeBlanc's desk and heads over to the cooler, where the confessed murderer is tinkering with the spigot. To Doyle he looks so harmless, so childlike. It's hard to imagine him viciously spilling the blood of another human being. But Doyle knows only too well that appearances can be deceptive.

'Hey!' he says. 'Whatcha doing?'

The man gets up from the floor and holds out his paper cup. 'You drink this stuff? It tastes funny.'

'Come on,' says Doyle. He nods toward the hallway, then starts walking in that direction.

The man puts down his cup and starts to follow. 'Where are we going?'

'Downstairs. I have to put you somewhere while we find someone to talk to you.'

'Why can't I talk to you?'

'We've been talking. You won't tell me anything. I still don't even know your name.'

They start down the stairs, side by side. Doyle can see the worry on the man's face. He sees the twitching start up, the fingers tapping together. Doyle feels sorry for him, but what choice does he have?

They get to the bottom of the stairs. The man hesitates on the final step.

'Come on,' says Doyle. 'Not far now.'

'Albert,' says the man.

'What?'

'Albert. You can call me Albert.'

Doyle brightens. Is this it? Is this the breakthrough?

'Your name is Albert?'

'No.'

Shit.

'So… why did you pick that name?'

'Einstein. I like Albert Einstein. He was good with numbers.'

Doyle sighs. Not the breakthrough he was hoping for. A name, yes, but not this guy's name. It's not enough.

'Let's go, Albert.'

He leads him around to the front desk. Since we're now into the midnight tour for the uniforms, Marcus Wilson has gone home, and has been replaced by a portly, round-faced sergeant called Costello. In many ways he resembles his namesake, the comedian Lou Costello, but unfortunately that doesn't extend to his sense of humor. This Costello is about as entertaining as hemorrhoids.

'Whaddya got, Doyle?'

'Guy says he killed his mother.'

Costello looks Albert up and down, then returns his attention to Doyle. 'And did he?'

'I don't know. I can't get anything else out of him.'

Costello stares down at Doyle in a way that suggests he's less than impressed with his powers of interrogation.

'So you wanna book him or not?'

Doyle shakes his head. 'Not yet. I need help on this. Someone who can get through to him. What I'll do, I'll write it up, put in a request to get an expert out here first thing. Meantime, we'll have to put him on ice. You mind doing that for me, Sarge?'

There's a sneer on Costello's face. Like he thinks this is a huge imposition.

The man who has called himself Albert leans toward Doyle and whispers. 'He ruined the candy.'

'What?' says Doyle.

'The candy. He ate some. One blue, one red, one yellow. No more primes.'

'What's that?' says Costello.

'Nothing, Sarge,' says Doyle.

Costello stares his contempt. Several seconds elapse before he deigns to turn his head and call over his shoulder.

'Presley. Get in here!'

Albert speaks to Doyle again: 'Elvis Presley. Jailhouse Rock.'

Doyle starts to smile, but Costello snaps another glare at him. Doyle shines back a look of wide-eyed innocence, but feels a little like a mischievous schoolkid.

One of the uniforms appears from a back office, a crumb of food on his chin.

'Another guest for the night,' says Costello. 'Put him in our presidential suite. And don't forget to turn down his sheet and put a chocolate on his pillow.'

Presley beckons toward Albert. 'Okay. Come on, bud.'

Albert stays where he is. 'Aw, Jeez,' he says.

Says Presley, 'What are you waiting for? Let's move it.'

'Aw, Jeez,' Albert says again.

Doyle looks at the man next to him. He can see the agitation building up in him again. This won't go well.

Obviously not the patient type, Presley abandons his warm invitation and starts to close the gap between him and Albert. Albert starts to fold in on himself, making himself as small a target as possible.

'Nine-one-one. One for the money. I'm all shook up. Whole lot of shaking going on. This is bad, this is bad.'

Before Presley can turn this into the riot it doesn't need to be, Doyle shows his palm, halting the cop's advance.

'It's okay. I'll bring him down. All right?'

Presley looks to his sergeant for advice, who in turn shrugs his indifference. Presley steps aside and sweeps his arm in front of him in a be-my-guest gesture.

'Come on, Albert,' says Doyle. 'Everything's cool. There's nothing to worry about here. I'll come with you, okay?'

Albert taps his fingers together again. His eyes dart around the room, like he's a frightened animal desperately seeking an escape route.

'It's all right,' says Doyle. 'Come on. Walk with me.'

He puts a hand to Albert's elbow. Slowly guides him toward a staircase that leads down into the bowels of the building. Albert shuffles along uncertainly, and Doyle senses that Presley is becoming irritated at the snail-like pace. But he's not going to allow Albert to be bullied into losing his tenuous hold on things.

They start to move down the stone steps. The stress emanating from Albert is palpable.

'Green mile,' he says. 'Dead man walking.'

'No,' says Doyle. 'Nothing like that. We're just gonna put you somewhere for the night. Somewhere you'll be safe. Tomorrow we'll bring you out again and get somebody to talk to you.'

They get to the bottom of the steps. A corridor stretches ahead of them, painted in a drab gray. The lighting is fluorescent, and one of the strips in the ceiling keeps flickering. On each side of the corridor are the grim bars of the holding cells. Although Doyle's night has been quiet, down here it's a veritable social club. Somebody is singing Danny Boy; another is telling him to shut the fuck up; another is belching; a drunk is explaining to anyone who can hear how he once met the Queen of England in Times Square.

There are smells here, too. Of vomit, of alcohol, of piss. And underlying all that, the odors of decay and dankness and human misery. This is not a pleasant place. It's old, and it has witnessed too much. Another wash-down with detergent – even another coat of battleship gray – will do nothing to lift spirits in here.

Albert wants to move no farther, and Doyle can't blame him. Presley, though, seems to feel no such compassion.

'C'mon, fella. I ain't got all night.'

Albert is trembling visibly. He looks down the corridor and his mouth opens and closes and he shakes his head and his eyes are wide with fright.

Doyle tries telling himself it's for the best. This is a goddamn suspect. He says he killed his own mother. You wanna feel sorry for someone like that? You wanna treat him as a special case, just because his brain is wired a little differently? Lots of killers have loose connections. What makes this guy such a charitable cause? Lock him up, Doyle. Lock him up, type your report, and let the morning shift worry about him.

Presley's thoughts seem to be running along exactly the same lines. Only he's more willing to put those thoughts into action. He grabs hold of Albert's arm.

And that's the flashpoint.

That's what causes him to turn into a whirling dervish, screaming and slapping at Presley. Driving the cop backward with his frenzied attack. Causing him to fall to the floor and then landing on top of him, still screaming and hitting.

Doyle pounces on Albert. Grabs him around the ribcage and yanks him away from Presley. Doyle loses his footing and hits the floor himself, dragging Albert down with him. A few feet away, Presley gets up, a murderous expression on his face.

'You fucking piece of shit,' he says. He advances on Albert. Gives him a good kick to the stomach. Reaches for something on his belt. Pepper spray.

'No!' Doyle cries. He releases Albert and jumps to his feet, then barrels into Presley, forcing him backward until he slams into the wall.

'What the fuck, Doyle? He's a lunatic. Look at that crazy fuck.'

Doyle follows Presley's gaze. But he doesn't see what Presley sees. He doesn't see a raging maniac, filled with hatred and violence and a desire to destroy.

He sees a cowering, frightened man, curled into a ball, his arms tightly wound around his head while he sobs and shakes and rocks and mutters to himself.

Doyle goes over to him. Kneels down. Rests his hand gently on Albert's shoulder.

'It's all right,' he says. 'It's okay. We're not gonna put you in a cell, okay?'

He continues to talk. Calm, soothing words that he hopes will find their way through to this man who is doing his best to close himself off from the world. A man who struggles to come to terms with this confusing world at the best of times.

Now what? thinks Doyle.

Now what do I do with him?

12.40 AM

She doesn't feel safe.

She came here from Brookville, Pennsylvania, where she worked as a payroll manager for a lumber company. That's where she met Clark Vogel, who worked in the company's export division. She fell in love with him instantly. Tried to play hard to get, because that's the way she'd been brought up, but her desire got the better of her. She surrendered to it, and within six months they were married.

The child was not so quick.

They tried for two and a half years. They told themselves it was fun trying, and at first that was true. At first they believed it was normal to have to wait patiently for the miracle of conception. But time stretched and their belief didn't. Their enjoyment began to be pushed out by the fears and the doubts and the stress. Making love became a chore, at least for Erin. It became a means to an end – an essential but almost tedious procedure to be endured for the sake of what she really wanted. Clark felt this, of course. As much as she did her utmost to issue all the right noises and actions, it was obvious to her that he sensed her detachment and discomfort. Slowly but surely she felt him being turned off, like a dimmer switch gradually being lowered until all that remains is a cold wintry twilight.

She could not have this. Her want of a baby became a need and then a mission. She had to use every trick in the book – some of which would have been unthinkable to her once – to keep him aroused and at her service. She knows now how selfish she was, but at the time she was beyond reasoning with. The child was everything, and the fact that it seemed increasingly beyond reach only made it more of a cherished goal.

Her attitude was nearly self-defeating. Clark was not immune to the pain of being relegated to secondary status. When they weren't having sex they argued furiously, or spoke not at all. He turned to the bottle, and to be honest she was glad of it, because it made him more susceptible to being taken advantage of in the bedroom. But the cracks in the marriage were widening, its foundations crumbling. She knew that the end of its short life was on the horizon, and the sadness of that knowledge was immeasurable.

And then it happened.

The baby. Georgia.

She timed her appearance in the womb to perfection. No better cliffhanger was ever written. Her tiny barely-formed hands took hold of that relationship and drew it back from the precipice.

Erin metamorphosed. Her fear and her irascibility dropped away. She apologized to Clark. Explained to him that her irrational behavior had been out of her control. She pleaded for a new start, and tried her best to become the loving wife she once was. All was fine again.

For a while.

When Georgia arrived, Erin found a new focal point for her love. She was the best mother ever. Clark, on the other hand, was forgotten about again. He became a hovering presence in the background. When she casts her mind back to those times, she realizes how badly she treated him. And when the marriage finally succumbed to the rot that had seeped insidiously into its structure, and collapsed around them, she was not surprised. Not even particularly saddened. She had her baby, and that was enough.

Coming to New York was meant to be a fresh start. She knew little about it other than it presented a profound contrast to her existing lifestyle, and that's what she needed. Something different. Something new. An escape.

But now she's afraid, and not just because of what's happened to Georgia. She has heard countless times that New York is one of the safest cities in the country now. That even this part of the East Village – once one of the most violent, drug-infested neighborhoods in the city – has been tamed.

But...

That's what they add. A big fat but.

But watch what you do and where you go and at what time, they say. Don't act like an easy target, they advise. Be aware of your surroundings, they warn.

Doesn't make a girl feel safe.

She passes a group of three Hispanic men coming out of a bar on Avenue C – a street they would probably refer to as Losaida Avenue, the name being a Latino corruption of 'Lower East Side'. The men leer at her and beckon to her and make lewd suggestions to her. But she keeps her gaze fixed on the tall buildings looming ahead, her chin uptilted, acting proud and streetwise and unafraid.

When their drunken voices fade into the distance, she releases a sigh of relief. And then she laughs.

She laughs because she has just realized where the danger lies on these streets. It is here, in her. She is the one carrying the weapon. She is the one seeking a victim. She is the one carrying the promise of death to anyone who appears in her sights. And it is only as she acknowledges this that she senses it is time to leave this wide, sprawling avenue with its lights and cars and people. It's time to become unseen, a shadow amongst shadows.

She turns left at the corner of the next block, onto one of the side streets just a couple of blocks short of the Stuyvesant projects. There are no bars here. No nightclubs. No reason for most people to venture this way. It is much darker here, and that absence of light makes it seem colder. The bitter frosts have not yet arrived in this city, but looking into that tunnel of blackness ahead of her makes her shiver.

But she walks. She takes a deep breath of the cold air and starts walking.

Perhaps, she thinks, someone will try to attack me. He will come at me out of a doorway or from behind a dumpster. He will leap at me and try to put his hands on me and he will give me an excuse. He will give me a reason to kill him – something that I can use to tell myself that it was a justifiable action on my part. He attacked me and I killed him in self-defense, and that's an end of it. I will be able to live with myself if that happens. I will not feel guilt every time I look into the eyes of my baby.

'Good choice, Erin,' says the voice in her ear. *'Dark up here. Deserted. Nobody will see what you do. You've got all the makings of a great killer.'*

She doesn't want to hear this. Doesn't want to be told what an emotionless hunter she's becoming. I'm doing this because I have to, she thinks, not because I want to. There's a difference. A world of difference.

And then she becomes aware of a presence. Across the street. A clatter of something metallic, followed by some tuneless male singing. She halts and tries to make her eyes see through the gloom.

From out of the shadow of a tree he appears. A homeless guy, looking big and burly in the many layers of old clothing he wears. He's pushing a shopping cart ahead of him, piled with all kinds of crap.

Erin glances up and down the street, checking for onlookers. Nobody is here to see. She steps off the curb. Starts to walk toward him. He continues to shuffle along, one leg moving more stiffly than the other. As she gets closer, she realizes he is singing lines from 'Camptown Races':

'I bet my money on a bob-tailed nag, someone bet on the gray.'

It is only when she steps onto the sidewalk that he notices her. He stops moving, stops singing. Just stares wide-eyed at this figure homing in on him from out of the darkness.

When she gets within a few feet of the man, she is able to get a better look at him. He is black, somewhere in his sixties. His round face is cracked and grainy, like old leather. There is a tuft of white hair on his chin, and he wears a baseball cap. His bulky coat is tied up with TV cable, its frayed ends showing the metal core.

'Oh, yes,' says the voice. *'Now you're talking. Perfect, Erin. Absolutely perfect.'*

She continues to stand and watch the man, and he stares back.

'What could be better? Nobody will miss him. Plus, you get to rid the streets of another vagrant. That's so great, Erin. I admire your thinking.'

She says nothing. She wants to say no, this isn't the one, and then to move on. But she can't. She can't because part of her is thinking yes. If I have to kill someone, if I really have no choice in that matter, then shouldn't it be someone who has no attachments? Someone who makes no contribution to society? Someone who is, in fact, a nuisance and a blight on this city? I could keep on going. I could walk all night long and not find a more suitable candidate. Isn't this a no-brainer?

The man opens his mouth. 'I bet my money on a bob-tailed nag,' he sings to her, but in a more subdued voice now. 'Somebody bet on the gray.'

'Camptown Races,' she says.

He narrows his eyes. 'Some know it as Camptown Ladies.'

'Yeah?'

He nods. 'Because of the way it goes. The Camptown Ladies sing this song.'

'Doo-dah. Doo-dah.'

He nods again. 'You know it?'

'I know it.'

She thinks, Why am I doing this? Why am I even speaking to this guy?

But she knows why. She knows what beginning she is creating here, and what ending it will surely give rise to.

'Who are you?' asks the man.

'Just a passing stranger,' she answers.

''Cept you're not passing. You're here, on my doorstep.'

'Your doorstep?'

He gestures at the space around himself. 'It's the only home I got.'

She reaches up and pushes an imaginary doorbell. 'Ding-dong.'

He pulls his head back in surprise, then gradually lets his neck muscles unwind again.

'What you doing out here, girl?'

She shrugs. 'Walking. Thinking. Dreaming.'

'Dreaming 'bout what?'

'Getting my family back.'

She knows it's a surprise answer, and she watches him chew on it for a while.

'That's a good ambition. Family's important. Prob'ly the most important thing on this earth.'

'You got family?'

He pauses again, then looks up to the sky. When he lowers his eyes again, she can swear they are glistening.

'Once. Long time ago.'

'What happened?'

Erin, what the hell are you doing? Waste the stinking hobo, and let's get you the fuck out of there.

'I forget,' says the homeless guy, but it's obvious that he hasn't forgotten. He reverts swiftly to his questioning: 'Girl, what are you doing?'

'I… I needed someone,' she answers. 'And then you came along.'

'Me? I can't help you. I can't help nobody. You should go now. Leave me be.'

'What if I think you can? What if I say you could be the only person on this earth who is able to help me?'

The man looks at her, long and hard.

'Girl, I don't know what troubles you. All I know is that I am what I am because I'm no good. I was no good to my family, and I can't do no good for you either. Now go home, before you make me angry.'

He moves off, wheeling his collection of items that are of meaning to him alone.

You're losing him, Erin. There goes your chance of seeing Georgia again. Maybe your only chance tonight.

'Wait!' she calls. She jogs after the man, then puts a hand on his shopping cart to stop him. He halts, but turns worried eyes on her hand. She pulls it away.

'I want to show you something,' she says. She is almost breathless, and not because of the jogging. It's because she has decided.

'Show me what?'

'Show you how you can help me.'

'I told you. I can't help nobody.'

'Yes. Yes, you can. Two minutes of your time, that's all I'm asking.'

He studies her, and while he does so it seems to Erin that a bubble has enclosed them. It is just the two of them in the world now, debating moves that will lead to life or death.

'You're a strange one,' he says.

'How so?'

'Asking me for help. Normally it's the other way round. Me asking folks for stuff. Money, food, a drink. Something I can sell.'

'Must be hard.'

'It's all I know. What I don't know is people be asking me for things. Makes me feel…'

'What?'

'Special.'

No, she thinks. Don't say that. Don't turn this into something it's not. Don't make me feel guilty about this.

'Then maybe you should help me. Maybe it's an opportunity you shouldn't waste.'

'Excellent, Erin. Nice move.'

The man pulls on the wisp of white chin-hair.

'Two minutes?' he says. 'I guess I can find two minutes in my hectic schedule. What's on your mind, girl?'

'Not here,' she says. 'Over there.'

She nods at the building to her right. It's a huge apartment building in brown brick. It's only about ten stories high, but it has a massive footprint. The ground floor level is set back, the upper stories being supported at the building's perimeter by thick brick columns. The passageways running behind those columns are shrouded in darkness.

The man turns his head slowly, following her gaze. 'You want me to go over there with you? Why?'

'That's where it is. What I want to show you.'

'Yes, Erin. Brilliant.'

She finds the voice intrusive. She doesn't need his fatuous remarks. She just wants to get this over with.

She wonders if the homeless guy will refuse her. If he does, she's not sure what her next step will be. Desolate though the street is at the moment, she feels far too exposed out here on the sidewalk to do what she needs to do.

But he relents. 'Show me,' he says simply. And as he starts pushing his cart toward the building, she almost wants to tell him he's making the worst decision of his life. Almost wants to call him an idiot for being so trusting of her. Yes, she looks like a harmless young woman, but doesn't he know that appearances can be deceptive? All these years on the streets, and he hasn't learned how to avoid risking his life?

But maybe that's it. Maybe he doesn't care anymore. Maybe he's had all the shit that life can throw at him, and what's another pile of crap to add to his load? Maybe he just doesn't give a damn whether he lives or dies.

That's what she tells herself. That's her rationale. That's what will make this easier.

She walks with him. Leads him into the murkiness behind one of the brick columns. There is a faint smell of urine here. Somewhere in the distance a dog barks, and the sound of an argument escapes from one of the open windows above them.

'Dark here,' says the man.

'Yes,' she says. 'And cold too.'

'I don't feel the cold no more. Got used to it. One night it's gonna take me in my sleep, and I won't even feel it.'

'Is that your hope, or your fear?'

'It's my expectation. People like me don't live long in a situation like this.'

'You want an end to it?'

'Sometimes.'

She can feel her tears starting to build. He's giving her all the right answers. All the wrong answers. Unwittingly, he's taking down the barriers. Almost giving her an invitation.

'Then why do you carry on? What makes you keep going?'

He thinks on this for a while. 'Cowardice,' he says. 'I keep going because I'm too scared to stop. Too scared to deal with things. I move on. I've always moved on. It's what I do. What I am.'

'Do you want it to stop?'

She sees the whites of his eyes. Sees a glimmer of understanding in those tired eyes.

'What about you?' he asks. 'What is it *you* want?'

She steps toward him. Even this close she can't make him out too well. She can hear his heavy, animal-like breathing.

'I want my baby. Will you help me get my baby back?'

'I... I don't know. Can I do that? Do I have that power?'

'Yes,' she says. 'You do.'

And now her tears are flowing. The end is in touching distance.

She says, 'Can I… Can I hold you?'

The man works his jaw. She hears him swallow, and then a small murmur deep in his throat. She suspects she has touched him. A deeper touch than he's had in a long, long time. She thinks he might be crying too. But she doesn't want to know.

She moves into him. Presses herself against this big bear of a man. Lays her head against his chest and hears a pulsing of pure emotion. A song of sorrow and of regret and of ungrasped opportunities.

And in her own head she hears the voice. Screaming at her to do this. Almost apoplectic in its demands for her to make the final move.

She ignores the words. This is not for him. Not to satisfy the thirst of his deranged mind. This is for Georgia. Solely for Georgia.

May God forgive me.

The motion is swift and simple and brutal. She almost doesn't realize she's doing it. It's as if something mechanical takes over, completing without feeling what she began. A single forceful thrust.

She hears a grunt, and she takes a small step back, her fingers still wrapped around the handle of the knife. The man stares into her eyes, then down at the knife buried deep in her gut, then back up again. He does not show rage or fear or surprise, and when he speaks his voice is low and calm.

'You killing me, girl? Is that what this is? You killing me?'

'I'm sorry,' she says. 'It's for my baby. You're saving my baby.'

'I am?' His mouth twists into a semblance of a smile. Perhaps the first time he has felt cause to smile in a decade. 'Then that's good. That's a good thing.'

He lifts his arms from his sides. Wraps his big bear-paw hands around hers. They tighten, and for a moment she is afraid he will crush all her fingers. He pushes her hand away, and he grunts again as the knife slides out of his belly. He holds her like that for a while, and now she's not sure what to do. Try to run? Try to stab him again? And while her mind races, the voice keeps yelling at her, issuing its commands, its threats, its promises. For that brief time, nothing seems real. She is in a fantasy world, where she fights a bear while unseen demons shriek and wail.

'Tell me the name,' says the man.

'Who?'

'The baby. The baby's name.'

'Georgia. Her name's Georgia.'

And now his face cracks into a real smile, an unmistakable smile reflecting fond memories.

'I knew a Georgia. Long time ago. She needed me too. I let her down. I won't let your baby down.'

And with that, he forces her hand upward. Brings it to him again, the tip of the knife pressing into his chest, just to the left of the sternum.

'Here, girl. Here.'

She is crying. She cannot see. She can only feel. She is deaf to the voice, blind to what she is doing. She wants it to stop now.

When it happens, she is not sure how much of it comes from her, and how much from the man. She knows only that the blade seeks its target, takes its prize.

Another grunt. Movement. The man sliding slowly down the brick column behind him as his legs give way. His grip on her is still strong, and he pulls her down with him, causing her to sink to her knees. She moves her head closer to his, hears his breathing become ragged.

'Sing to me, girl,' he says. 'Sing that song you always used to sing.'

And she does. How can she not? She sings to him about the Camptown ladies and about the race track that is five miles long and about how she bet her money on a bob-tailed nag and about…

He's gone.

She feels him go, and he lets her go too. Sets her free as he releases his grip. Sets her free as he once sought to break free himself.

She hopes that, in his last moments, he found some kind of peace.

'Thank you,' she whispers to him. 'Thank you for giving Georgia back to me.'

And then she cries some more. Sits there amidst the smell of piss and blood and death, and cries.

Sounds start to break through. The slamming of a door, and then footsteps running into the distance. Far-away sirens. Night-time city noises. Her world becomes painfully real and frightening again.

'Erin! Get up! We need to get you out of there.'

He's right. She knows he's right. To go through all this and then still end up without Georgia would be a travesty. She has to listen to that voice now, even though it is the focal point of her hatred. Her fury at what she has just done is all turned on that voice.

She gets to her feet. Stares down at the big bundle of rags that used to be a human being. You saved us, she thinks. You gave up your life for us.

'Erin, are you listening to me?'

She forces herself to listen, even though she has an almost irresistible impulse to take out the earpiece and stomp on it.

'What?' she says. 'What do you want from me?'

'We have to go, but there's something else you need to do first.'

She's confused. Hasn't she done enough? What more can she possibly do here?

'What do you mean?' she asks.

So the voice tells her. It whispers its words of horror to her. Gives her a task to do that is beyond her comprehension.

Truly, these must be the words of the devil himself.

1.18 AM

Doyle slams the receiver down.

'How is it,' he says, 'that we're the only people willing to do any work at nights? What are we, idiots?'

LeBlanc replaces his own telephone receiver. 'We're the boys in blue. Without us, they wouldn't be able to sleep peacefully in their beds. But yes, we're idiots too.'

'You know what gets to me most? When people say they'll call back, and then they don't call back. What's that all about? Why promise something if you have no intention of doing it? Why not just be honest about it? Why not just say, I'm real busy for the next two weeks, try somebody else?'

'You'd prefer that?'

'Sure I'd prefer it. At least then I'd know where I stood. This way, I have no idea if these people are ever gonna call.'

Doyle is frustrated, but what frustrates him most is that much of this is his own doing. He should have followed procedure. He should have handed Albert over to the unis downstairs and then just walked away. Let them deal with it. Let them lock him up and keep watch over him. He wants to scream and rant, let him scream and rant. I should be on my way home now, like all the sensible detectives on the squad, instead of wasting my time making stupid phone calls that nobody wants to return.

'So now what?' LeBlanc asks.

Doyle blows air out of the side of his mouth. He has tried every number he can think of for help on this, including social services, hospitals and mental health charities. Most of the calls weren't answered, it being an ungodly hour of the day to be telephoning for anything. When he could, Doyle left a message. Of the ones who answered, some said they couldn't do anything right now, but they could try to get someone to him in the morning. The word Doyle didn't like there was 'try'; it suggested to him there were no guarantees. And then there were the respondents who put the ball firmly back in Doyle's court by suggesting he should put the guy into a cell for the night. Which annoyed Doyle even more because he was already fully aware that that's exactly what he should have done.

'I'm out of ideas,' he says.

He looks around the squadroom for inspiration. He doesn't get much of that from Albert, who is sitting at the water cooler again, trying to figure out the mechanics of the plastic tumbler dispenser. The only other person here is LeBlanc, who has stayed to help out Doyle with the phone calls. Everyone else has gone home to their warm apartments to sleep in their warm beds next to their warm partners. At eight o'clock in the morning the new shift will arrive and they will pick up the 60 sheet and decide what merits being turned into a case requiring their investigative talents. Until that time – barring a major incident such as a homicide – the members of the Eighth Precinct Detective Squad are not required here. They certainly shouldn't be spending their precious slumber time acting as nursemaids.

Says Doyle, 'You should go home, Tommy.'

LeBlanc shrugs. 'What, and miss all the action? How could I sleep knowing you're having so much fun here?'

It occurs to Doyle that he knows very little about LeBlanc's home life.

'You got nobody waiting for you? Someone pining for your presence in her boudoir?'

'Me? No.'

'Seriously? I pegged you as having a little blonde piece squirreled away somewhere. A farmhand from Iowa or wherever it is you came here from. Thigh-high boots and a Stetson.'

'Hold up, Cal. Is that really what you think of my personal life, or is this some kind of wild fantasy of your own?'

'I'm a married man, Tommy. I don't think of any women other than my darling wife, you know that.'

LeBlanc smiles. 'Then if anyone should be going home, it's you. You need to make a decision about Albert here.'

Doyle looks at Albert again. He's now yanking the tumblers out, one by one, and stacking them on the windowsill.

'Yeah, I know,' says Doyle.

'There's always that offer from the hospital.'

Doyle shakes his head. He has already considered and rejected that option. The offer was to put Albert in a secure unit for the mentally ill for the night. Doyle has seen those places, and knows that Albert wouldn't last five minutes. He's not insane. He just has… issues.

See, there you go again, Doyle. Feeling sorry for the guy. If walking into a station house covered in your own mother's blood after you've just sliced and diced her doesn't count as insane, then I don't know what the hell does.

'I'll find something,' he says. 'Hey, if your place is so empty, maybe you could—'

LeBlanc jumps off his chair like a spring has just come up through the seat. 'Well, it's been nice knowing you, Cal. Time I hit the sack, I think.'

LeBlanc grabs his coat and comes around his desk, grinning at Doyle. He starts to walk out, but pauses when he gets level with Albert. He points at the stack of tumblers.

'Prime number?'

'Seventeen,' says Albert. 'Prime.'

LeBlanc turns back to Doyle. 'See, Cal. It's all a question of knowing how to communicate. Now if you—'

The phone on Doyle's desk rings.

Says LeBlanc, 'Maybe sometimes they do call back.'

Doyle snatches up the receiver. He listens. Grabs a notepad and pen and scribbles down some notes. Ends the call.

He looks up at LeBlanc.

'You still going home?'

He watches as LeBlanc tries to read his face.

'Yeah. I think. Shouldn't I be? Why are you asking?'

'I just caught a homicide. Interested?'

Doyle doesn't have to wait long for an answer. They're both tired, but they've both had one of the most boring days they can remember. Things just got a lot more appealing.

'Count me in,' says LeBlanc. 'Only…'

'What?'

LeBlanc jerks his head toward Albert.

'What about him?'

They turn their gazes on Albert. He doesn't look up, but seems to sense he's being watched.

'Where we going, fellas? Can we put the flashing lights on? Not the sirens, though. Too noisy. Too noisy. And not too fast. I get nosebleeds.'

1.22 AM

At the apartment she breaks down.

As soon as she closes the door against the world, she leans back against a wall and lets her emotion pour forth. She slides down that wall, sobbing her heart out.

It's all over, in so many ways. Over for her, over for Georgia, over for that poor homeless guy, whose name she doesn't even know.

What she has just done is a crime. A crime in legal terms, but also a crime against everything she believes in. No, not just a crime. An abomination. What she has done is monstrous. She is not sure she will ever be able to forgive herself. She certainly will never forget what occurred on this god-forsaken night in January. Her only hope is that Georgia will make it all right for her. Georgia will lessen the enormity of her pain and guilt. Erin will look into her baby's eyes and say, *It was for you. I did it for you. You are alive only because I gave up everything I am for you.* And there will come a time when she can stop repeating it. The memories will begin to fade like the scars they are. Always present, still causing the occasional twinge, but a part of the dim and distant past. Memories of events so incredible and grotesque she might one day be able to convince herself that they were contained in something she read or dreamed.

That is her hope.

'Oh my God, Erin. That was fucking awesome. You did it. I said you could do it, and you did. I picked you, Erin. I believed in you, and I was right all along.'

'Good for you,' she murmurs, her voice dripping with sarcasm. 'Give yourself a round of applause. Now tell me where I can find Georgia.'

'Come on, Erin. Don't be like that. You did good. You found the strength. You didn't think you could kill someone, and you conquered those doubts. I helped you do it. You should be congratulating me.'

'You're a gem, you really are. A shining diamond. I'll be eternally grateful. Now where is my baby?'

'Of course, as victims go, he wasn't exactly a prize catch. I mean an old nobody like that. You didn't set your sights too high there, Erin.'

'He was a man, goddamnit! A human being. He walked and he talked and he felt things. And most of all he had blood in his veins until I spilled it all over the ground.'

As she hears her own words, something occurs to her. She raises her hands and stares at them. Sees the dark blood caked on them.

'Oh God,' she says.

She gets to her feet. Races into the bathroom. She turns on the faucet over the sink, squirts huge gobbets of liquid soap onto her palms and then rubs them together frantically under the hot stream. She watches the pink-tinged water disappear, and keeps on rubbing and washing until every trace of the blood has gone from her hands and the water runs crystal clear.

When she is done, she stands with her hands on the edge of the basin, staring at herself in the mirror. She is exhausted and ashamed and sick to her stomach, and she thinks her face reflects all that. She thinks she looks like a junkie or a whore or a pathetic drunk. Maybe even someone who would willingly resort to murder.

She needs her antidote.

She looks directly at the reflection of the brooch. Turns her sternest gaze on the man who is looking back at her through that tiny lens.

'Where. Is. Georgia?'

'See, Erin, a wino is one thing. But would you have been able to handle a normal person? I mean, someone who had more to live for? What do you think? I mean, if the right guy had come along tonight. Or a woman, even. Doesn't have to be male, right?'

She slaps her hands on the basin. 'Fuck you! Stop these games. I've had enough. It ends now. I gave you what you wanted, and now it's your turn. Give me my baby!'

'The main thing is, though, you survived your baptism of fire. You popped your cherry with that...'

'Are you hearing me, asshole? I said...'

'... homeless dude. It should be a walk in the park next time.'

'... give me my— What? What did you say?'

'I said it should be a—'

'No.'

'What's the matter, Erin? Surely it's no big deal now? You can't start playing the virgin queen after what you did. It's just a question of—'

'No. This is a joke, right? You're playing with me.'

He goes silent. She thinks, He's going to burst out laughing in a moment. He's going to say, Of course I'm fucking with you, Erin. Had you going, though, didn't I?

But the silence continues, and her fear intensifies. No, he cannot mean this. Surely he cannot expect any more of me?

'We had a deal,' she says. 'A life in return for my baby. That's what we agreed.'

'Did we, Erin? One life? Is that what I said? Did I really ever say only one death would be enough?'

She observes herself in the mirror. She looks so unsure of herself, so subservient. How can she hope to defeat this man acting as she does?

She makes herself stand up straight. Shoulders back, jaw set, eyes glaring. She doesn't feel strong, but she can at least try to appear strong.

'Uh-uh. Forget it. You said I had to kill someone. Singular. That's what you said.'

'I didn't say that would be the end of it, though, did I? In any case, I'm not going to quibble with you about this, Erin. You're hardly in a position to argue. You want your baby back, then you do as I say.'

'No. Absolutely not. I have given you all I have to give. I won't do it. I can't do it.'

'You have no choice in the matter. It's decided. You have to accept it.'

'No. Fuck you. Give me Georgia. Now!'

A pause. She wonders what he's thinking. She prays he will see sense. She prays he will be able to see that he can squeeze no more out of her, that she is physically and mentally incapable of giving him what he desires.

'*Oh, Erin, you should see her now. Georgia, I mean. Cute as a button. That soft little face. Those tiny bunched fingers. You should see— Oh, but I'm forgetting. You can't see her, can you? Pity. You'll just have to use your imagination. It's not quite the same, I know. Not the same as holding her and smelling her and hearing her and talking to her. It must be real hard not being able—*'

'STOP IT!' she yells. She lowers her voice. 'Please. Don't do this to me. Don't hurt me like this. I'm begging you.'

And then she catches sight of herself in the mirror again. Sees that she is slumped again, that her eyes are pleading, her lip quivering, her fingers stretched out like those of a starving street urchin. Look at you, she thinks. This is what you really are. Without strength, without willpower, and therefore without hope. There is no escape. He has won. As long as he has your baby he will always win.

'*I don't want to hurt you, Erin. I want to help you. I want to give this baby back to you, I really do. But first you have to prove yourself. Believe me, you'll feel so much better about yourself when we're done.*'

'When? When will we be done? You could do this to me forever. How many more deaths? One? Five? Twenty? How long do you intend to make me kill for you?'

'*That depends. How many lives do you think your baby is worth?*'

She will not answer that question. She would kill a hundred for her child. A thousand. She would go on killing until she died herself. That's how much she loves her baby. It is infinite. But she cannot tell him that.

'Enough of the games,' she says. 'I need to know when this will be over. No estimates. No holding information back for later. Tell me exactly what you want from me.'

There's a longer pause now. Surely he can't be making this up as he goes along? He must have a goal for me in mind. He must have already decided this. And that means he's merely trying to make me suffer.

'*Midnight,*' he says finally. '*It'll be over by midnight.*'

She tosses his words over in her mind, examining them for holes.

'Which midnight? Tonight?'

'*Yes, Erin. Midnight tonight.*'

That's still almost twenty-four hours away. A full, agonizing day without my baby.

'We had a deal,' she says, but her delivery is meek. Thrown out almost petulantly.

'*This is the deal. Midnight tonight. That's assuming you do what needs to be done.*'

'Which is what?'

He makes her wait yet again. Then: '*Five more lives. You have until midnight to kill five more.*'

She shakes her head, trying to agitate some other meaning out of what she has just been told.

Five?

FIVE?

She was expecting maybe one or two, and even then she wasn't sure she was capable of doing that. But five? In a day? She's sure that not even the most prolific serial killers took victims at that rate. This is more like – what do they call them? – spree killers, that's it. The kid who wanders into his high school with a gun. The guy with a machete in the shopping mall. The people who lose it mentally, and then usually end up losing their lives too, either at their own hands or those of the cops.

'That's ridiculous,' she says. 'You want me to kill a total of six people? In a day? No. No way.'

'*What's the problem, Erin? Like I say, you've done it once already. One down, five to go. Kill another one, and you'll already be one third of the way there.*'

'Don't give me the salesman act. A dollar a day is still a lot to pay over a year. We're talking about people here. I don't have the strength to kill that many.'

'*Yes you do, Erin. That's what I'm trying to prove to you.*'

'I don't want you to prove it. I don't want to be any different. I just want my baby back. Please. Give her back to me.'

'*I will. At midnight. When you've completed your mission. I promise. No catches. No strings attached. Five more deaths by midnight tonight and you get Georgia. Alive and with no further harm.*'

She analyzes his words again. They seem so clear, so unambiguous. She cannot find any get-out clause.

But that doesn't make her task any easier.

'I'll get caught. How can I kill six people in a day and get away with it?'

His voice is reassuring. *'I'll help you. There will be no connection between your victims. No links with you, either. And at midnight it will stop as suddenly as it began. You'll get your life back. You'll get your baby back. You can carry on as normal.'*

'Normal? How could I be normal after something like that? I'm losing it already, after killing that homeless man. What will I be like after the next one, and the one after that?'

'That's the deal, Erin. Take it or leave it. Of course, you know what will happen if you leave it.'

She continues to stare into the mirror. She shifts her gaze away from the brooch and locks it onto her own eyes. Tries to see through those eyes and into her own head.

Earlier she told herself she would kill any number of people for the sake of her baby.

Now she is searching her soul to find out how true that was.

Now she is trying to see if she has what it takes to continue her trail of death.

1.43 AM

Word gets around fast when there's a homicide. People abandon their sleep, abandon their lovemaking, abandon their cars – all for the possibility of a glimpse of a corpse. Roll up, roll up, folks – come and marvel at the fascinating spectacle of the man with no heartbeat and no breath. No living person on this earth can replicate what this man is doing. Prepare to be amazed.

The large woman in the belted overcoat and slippers isn't helping the situation. Marching up and down alongside the yellow cordon tape, she seems to be doing her best to whip the growing throng into a frenzy, despite the attempts of a female police officer to silence her.

'We found him,' says the woman to the onlookers. 'My son and me. He dead. That guy over there, he dead. Blood everywhere. And the way he was looking at me? Oh, Lord, I ain't never seen nobody stare at me like that before. The devil has been here. This is Satan's work.'

Doyle and LeBlanc approach the female uniform.

'What've we got?'

The officer points to where the crime scene technicians are working around the body. 'DOA's a homeless guy. People around here know him as Vern, but I don't know if that's his real name. Looks like he picked the wrong spot to sleep it off tonight.'

Doyle's grunt is non-committal. He chin-points toward the lady who is still relating her experiences to anyone who will listen. 'Who's she?'

The cop curls her lip in disdain. 'She lives in the building. Her son came home shortly after one, and woke her up. Told her there was a dead guy outside. She came out for a look-see, and now she seems to think it's her duty to tell the whole fucking world about it.'

Doyle finds the officer's attitude irritating, and so when he nods, it is more in dismissal than gratitude. He moves toward the woman in the fluffy slippers, then holds up his gold shield in front of her face.

'Ma'am, we're detectives from the Eighth Precinct. You mind if we have a word?'

'A word? I got lots of words. There's a dead guy over there. Outside my building. Where I live. I saw him, with my own eyes. The blood. All that blood. It's the devil's work.'

'Okay. I hear your son found the body. Is that right?'

'Thass right. But he's only a kid. Only seventeen. I'm trying to bring him up nice. Trying to give him a chance. How am I s'posed to do that when there's people being mutilated on our doorstep? What kind of world are we living in? Don't get me wrong, I love my country. But this kind of thing, it ain't right. The government should do something.'

Doyle wonders why her precious seventeen year old is wandering the streets at one o'clock in the morning, but doesn't say.

'Where's your son now?'

'Upstairs, in our apartment. I tole him to stay up there. Ain't no need for him to see something like this more than once.'

'We'll need to talk to him later, if that's okay. What did he tell you when he came into the apartment?'

'He said there's a dead guy outside. What else is he gonna say? He said it was the homeless guy, and he was cut bad.'

'So you came outside to check?'

'Damn straight. My boy don't lie to me. If he says something is so, then it's so. I grabbed my flashlight and I came straight down here. Now I'm wishing I hadn't seen what I seen. Wishing my boy hadn't seen it neither. The way he was staring at me. All that blood. Lord, I will have nightmares about that for the rest of my days.'

'All right. That's very helpful. You mind giving your details to the officer here? We'll get back to you.'

Doyle motions the female uniform over, and notices how she rolls her eyes to display her lack of enthusiasm.

Doyle drops his voice when he speaks to the officer, but gives it an edge. 'From now on, you're her friend. Get her apartment number, and listen to what she's got to say. Above all, lose the attitude. She's loud because she's scared. She's trying to help, and we should be grateful for it.'

The officer straightens up in respect, and nods. And because he gets that from her, Doyle repays her with a smile.

He ducks under the cordon tape and heads toward the hubbub around the body. LeBlanc walks at his side.

'Could be a tricky one,' says LeBlanc.

'How do you mean?'

'Finding the perp. Guy like this is an easy target. Probably no real motive. A couple of crack-heads, maybe. Some gangbangers out to earn a stripe. They come across an old wino, and that's it.'

Doyle says nothing. He knows LeBlanc is probably right. This city, there are all kinds of drunks, junkies and crazies wandering the streets at night. They get into arguments that would make no sense to the sober or the sane. They pick fights they don't even know they're starting. Sometimes they're just unlucky. They say the wrong thing or look the wrong way at someone, and suddenly a blade or a broken bottle appears. And then it's game over. And because the victim is what he is, not that many people give a damn.

The sad thing is, the Police Department probably won't give much of a damn either. This man will be of no interest to the politicians; he will have no city hall muscle pushing for his case to be solved. There probably won't even be a family or friends wanting to pursue this. Nobody will miss him. Nobody will care if the killer is caught or not. The PD will make all the right noises to begin with, and with any luck they might get a break. If not, well, sorry Vern: you've just become a statistic.

The CSU guys have set up lights in the area surrounding the body. It's as clear as day here now. You could do shadow puppets. You could wait for the fat lady to come on and sing.

You could stare at a dead guy.

Roll up, roll up…

Doyle and LeBlanc step into the brightness and take stock of their work for the night. There's not much to see – certainly nothing to suggest this was the work of anything unearthly, as the loud woman was claiming. A figure curled into a fetal position at the base of a brick column. A tattered gray coat, brown corduroy pants, scuffed leather boots. A length of some kind of electrical cord used as a belt. The front of the coat carries large dark stains – presumably the victim's blood. Doyle can clearly see the holes that have been punched through the coat and into the flesh beneath. The man's face is hidden behind a peaked cap that has either slipped or has been pulled down. Doyle wants to see this man's face. He wants to know—

Wait a minute.

Doyle moves away from the scene. Starts retracing his steps.

'Where you going, Cal?' says LeBlanc.

Doyle doesn't answer. He sees the female police officer. She has her notebook out and is talking to the large woman Doyle spoke to earlier.

'Excuse me,' he says. 'Ma'am?'

The large woman turns fearful eyes on him.

'I'm sorry,' he says. 'I just wanna check on something you said earlier. The man back there, the homeless guy – you said he was staring at you. Isn't that what you said?'

'Uh-huh. Lord, I'll never forget those eyes. All that blood.'

Suddenly Doyle's neck-hairs are bristling.

'So was it you who pulled his cap down over his face?'

'Yessir, it was. I couldn't close his eyes. Couldn't bear to go near them. The hat was the next best thing. People should not have to look at—'

But Doyle has stopped listening. He's jogging back to the where the body lies. LeBlanc looks at him quizzically.

'Cal?'

Doyle offers no explanation, because he doesn't know what this is yet. That woman saw something nobody else gathered here has seen. The devil's work, she called it. Something that got her real scared.

He turns to the CSU gang. 'You done here? You mind giving us a look at the guy?'

One of the techs moves closer to the body, reaches out a gloved hand. Takes hold of the very edge of the cap's peak. Gingerly lifts it away from Vern's face.

'Jeez,' says LeBlanc.

They are all looking, all staring. A crime scene photographer moves in for some close-up shots.

What they see, carved deep into the man's forehead, is this:

Doyle is certain he has the same thing on his mind as everybody else: *Shit, our killer thinks he's Zorro.*

2.25 AM

He has given her until two-thirty.

She told him she needed to rest, to recuperate. To gather her strength for what's to come.

Since then she has just been lying here on the bed, staring up at the ceiling. Wondering what the hell she can do to extricate herself from this living hell.

Questions have been bouncing endlessly around her skull. Why me? Why choose me, of all people? Lots of people have babies. He could have picked any one of them. Did it even have to be a baby? Why not an older child, a wife, a husband? Hell, some people would kill just to get material things back. Others would do it for money. Some would probably do it for the sheer adrenalin rush.

So why me?

And why six people? Six victims. Not five or seven, but six. Is there a significance to that number? That might make some kind of sense if he were selecting the targets – the six people in his life who most pissed him off, say – but he's not. He's leaving it up to her. He's not guiding her to those people in any way.

And then there's the biggest question of all: Just who is this guy?

Every time she hears his voice she tries to put a face to it. She has spent much of the last hour putting people she knows or has met in front of a microphone, speaking those words. None of them seems right.

Has she met him, in the flesh? How does he know so much about her? Where does he get his information?

More questions.

She wonders about the technology she has been made to wear. Just how far can equipment like this transmit sound and images? It can't be miles, surely? Is he just outside her apartment? Perhaps parked up in a van on her street? Could he be that close?

The thought makes her shiver. Shiver with the fear that this monster could be so near, but also with the realization that perhaps, just perhaps, this could be the first glimmer of hope. If he is there, outside… If she can catch a glimpse of him, maybe even seize an opportunity to—

'It's time, Erin.'

She looks across at the clock. Two-thirty in the morning. It has come so quickly.

She feels her heart rate step up again. She sits up, swings her legs over the side of the bed. She stands up, and the sudden elevation causes her to feel nauseous.

'I don't suppose…' she begins.

'What?'

'That you'd reconsider? That you'd see how unnecessary this is?'

'It's necessary, Erin. Later, you'll understand.'

Understand what? What is this supposed to teach me, other than how to become a murderer?

She puts her hands in her pockets. Finds the knife. She pulls it out, and sees that it is still stained with the old man's blood.

'Wait,' she says.

She goes into the bathroom again. Washes the knife in the sink, then dries it on a towel. As she does so, her eyes alight on all the baby things here. The bath bubbles, the rubber ducks, the talc, the musical plastic boat. Her eyes sting. She would give anything to be able to bathe her little girl again. To hear her giggle. To watch her kick and splash in the foamy water.

And then her eyes move back to the knife.

The contrast hits her hard. The early stages of precious life versus the build-up to early death. The thought of what she is about to do seems even more ugly, more inexcusable.

Then I'll go to hell, she thinks. If that's what it takes to save Georgia, I'll pay that price. I'll accept the eternal damnation. Maybe the cops will track me down. Maybe they'll stick me in prison for the rest of my life.

Whatever this guy in my ear tells me about keeping me safe, he can't give me any guarantees. Something could go wrong. Once the police realize what they're facing, they'll concentrate all their efforts on stopping me. How could I possibly hope to retain my freedom when every cop in the city will be looking for me? When all the technical resources they possess are devoted to finding me?

But if they do, then that's okay. As long as it happens after Georgia is out of harm's reach. After that, I don't care. They can do what they like to me then.

But maybe it won't come to that. I have to cling on to the hope that he'll make a mistake. He'll show himself, or unintentionally disclose something about himself.

I'll be waiting for that moment. Listening intently. Watching everyone around me. You'll make a mistake, you sonofabitch.

And then you're mine.

'I think it's dry now, Erin. You want to get a move on? You've got people to kill.'

She drops the knife back into her pocket, then walks out of the bathroom. At the door to the apartment she takes a deep breath, then leaves.

As soon as she enters the hallway she thinks she catches a small sound. Like a latch gently clicking into place. She looks over at Mr Wiseman's door, and sees a line of light below it.

She waits. Listens. No more sounds except the pulsing of her own blood. The building is deathly quiet.

Solemnly, she descends the stairs in search of a victim.

3. 10 AM

Nobody saw anything, nobody knows anything, nobody has anything useful to say. It's not an unusual story. This time, however, it's probably true. The killer or killers are probably miles away by now.

Doyle and LeBlanc are working the door-to-door in the apartment building. Right now, it's the only thing they've got to go on. They don't even know who the victim is. Other precinct detectives have been dragged out of their beds to assist with the canvass, but they know it could take hours to talk to everyone in a building this size, especially since half of the residents seem reluctant to open their doors. Because we all open our doors when they're being pounded on at three in the morning, right? Yeah, right – with a shotgun in our hands we might consider it.

The hope is that somebody in this building might have heard something happening outside. Or might have come home late and seen something unusual. Or might have some more information about Vern. Or might have seen suspicious characters hanging around the building. Or…

Yeah, lots of mights. So while we're at it, why not the biggest 'might' of all – that the killer himself might open one of these doors? There he'll stand, blood all over him and a maniacal glint in his eye. He might even confess on the spot. 'Remarkable work, detectives,' he will say. 'I am astounded at how swiftly you have traced me to my humble abode. Given your undeniably prodigious powers, it would be a mistake on my part to do anything other than surrender myself to your custody forthwith.'

Or that might not happen.

A more likely scenario is that they will obtain nothing of value in this building. They will then widen the search to encompass other nearby buildings. They will contact local soup kitchens, charity workers, homeless hangouts. The media will be asked to invite concerned citizens to contact the police with any information they might have.

And it will all come to naught.

It will come to naught because, not to be too cynical about this, few will shed tears over the demise of another drain on the city's resources, especially with the economic climate being how it is. Nobody will give this story prominence, and nobody chancing across the story will give it the attention it deserves.

That's what will probably happen.

But…

There's a chance the cops could get lucky. This time they have got something going in their favor, because whoever killed Vern wasn't satisfied with merely killing Vern. The perp could have just stabbed the victim a couple of times and then disappeared into the night – a lightning strike, with no hanging around even to determine if the wounds were fatal. He – or *she*, because let's face it, Doyle, these are modern times, with equal opportunities for all – could have absconded to distant shores after leaving nary a trace.

But not this killer. This killer chose to make a statement. He chose to leave a mark.

To somebody, somewhere, that mark means something. Maybe our killer really does believe he's Zorro. Maybe it's a gang symbol of some kind. Maybe it's a tag used by a graffiti artist. Whatever, it wasn't chosen at random. It has significance. And Doyle's hope is that its significance is known not only to the killer but to those near to him. And that's the one thing that makes Doyle's target bigger and easier to hit.

Clinging to that hope, Doyle continues knocking on doors.

3.27 AM

'**Y**ou're not trying, Erin.'

She's heading uptown on First Avenue. About the fifth time she's traversed this particular block.

'I *am* trying.'

'*Then try harder, for Chrissake. You want this baby back or not?*'

'What do you want me to do? Take off my clothes to attract someone? What am I supposed to do?'

'*At least that would be showing some initiative. You've already passed up several opportunities.*'

'They… they weren't right.'

'*You don't have the luxury of being choosy, Erin. Time's ticking away. Tick-tock, tick-tock.*'

'Shut up. Just shut up, okay? I can't concentrate.'

She feels stupid, speaking to thin air like this. She also feels like a hooker, parading up and down the streets as if she's touting for business. Earlier on she did encounter a woman she thought might have been a hooker. Despite the cold, the girl was wearing a skirt that barely covered her ass, and her dead eyes appraised Erin as she passed her on the street corner. Erin got the impression that the girl was checking her out as possible competition – someone who might be prepared to snatch away the money she needed for her crack habit. But as the distance between them closed, the girl just sneered, as if passing judgment that Erin presented no threat to her livelihood.

Erin thought about killing her.

She didn't do it because she didn't hate her enough. After her experience with the homeless man, she has decided that the next one can't be like that. Not someone who has done her no harm – someone towards whom she harbors no ill feelings. A sneer doesn't count. That's not worth a life.

The same went for the other possible victims she encountered on her current travels. Another wino, sleeping it off on a bench, covered in flattened cardboard boxes. He would have been so easy. No need to wake him up. Walk over to him, put the knife in, walk away. Job done. Another box ticked.

But no. She couldn't bring herself even to pause in her walk when she saw him. It would have been history repeating itself in all its profound sadness.

And then there was the drunk guy who meandered towards her along the sidewalk. She desperately wanted him to make her hate him. She stopped as he came level with her. She willed him to make crude suggestions to her, to make a grab for her. An excuse, she thought. Just give me a fucking excuse. Please.

But no, again. The young man beamed idiotically at her and said, 'I'm in love. The world is a beautiful place. You're beautiful too.' And then he continued on his way.

What was she supposed to do with that? How did that merit a blade in his love-filled heart?

She has the uneasy suspicion that this could go on some time. Maybe he's right. Maybe I'm not trying hard enough. Maybe I can't do this again. Where are all the dangerous people when you want them? Where are the vultures, the parasites, the leeches? Why are the shadows so empty of demons tonight?

'Miss?'

She jumps, startled at the voice suddenly at her side. She turns. Sees the car that has pulled up alongside her. Sees the face looking out at her from the open passenger window.

Cops.

She has dreaded this, but felt it had to come. A lone woman, wandering the streets at three in the morning. No purse, no friends, and seemingly no purpose. Why wouldn't they stop and ask questions?

'Oh. Hi, officer.'

She flashes them a big smile. Like this is so ordinary. Why shouldn't I be doing this? What's the big deal?

But inside she's shaking. Her hands are buried in her pockets and one of them is grasping the knife and she's scared witless. She's scared they will become suspicious and they will want to frisk her and they will find the knife and it will all be over. Goodbye, Georgia.

'Oh, shit. Don't fuck this up, Erin. Stay cool. Nice and easy.'

For the first time, she can sense fear in his voice. It surprises her, but also comforts her. He's not as in control as he wants her to believe. He is not so supreme.

'You all right?' the cop asks.

She notices how he looks her up and down as he puts his question. Checking her out.

'Fine,' she says, still breezy. 'Getting cold though, huh?' She brings her shoulders up to her ears, emphasizing this fact. Also letting the cop know that this is the reason her hands are in her pockets. Nothing to do with a weapon. No, siree.

'On your way somewhere?'

'Careful, Erin. Watch what you say. I've got the baby here, don't you forget that.'

He's trying to scare her, but it's not working, because for once she has the upper hand. He's crapping himself, and they both know it.

'Just a stroll. I do it most nights. I'm an insomniac.' She sees the blank look and hastily adds, 'I don't sleep so good. Sometimes a good walk helps me to chill out.' She speaks clearly and with confidence. Letting him know she's not drunk, not doped up.

'You want my advice,' says the cop, 'you should stick to walking around your apartment. I don't wanna scare you or nothing, but being on the streets at this time of night, that ain't such a good idea.'

Yeah, she thinks. I could be attacked. I could get stabbed by someone with a knife in her pocket.

'Thank you, officer. I'm sure you're right. I'm on my way home now anyway.'

He studies her some more, then says, 'Okay. Be safe now.'

She nods. Starts to walk away. She hears the radio car's engine rev up and then she glances at the vehicle as it glides past her. The cop isn't even looking her way.

'You did good, Erin. I knew you could do it. That's what will keep you and Georgia safe. That's what will make sure you come out on the other side of all this.'

The patronizing bastard. He's trying to cover up. Trying to make it sound as though he knew what he was doing back there. But she knows. She felt his fear. And that gives her hope.

She turns right at the end of the block. Onto East Tenth Street. Across the street is a large mural painted onto the wall. After that, a couple of shuttered storefronts. Then mostly apartment buildings and dark empty sidewalks.

'Where the fuck are you going, Erin? There's nothing down here. Haven't you figured it out yet? You need people.'

'I need you to shut the fuck up, is what I need. I'm doing my best, okay? If those cops see me again, they'll get suspicious. Is that what you want? Do you really want me to—'

She stops because she hears something. A car approaching from behind, slowing to a crawl. She doesn't turn, but slows her own pace. Please don't let this be the cops again.

'Erin, you need to step up your game. You need to—'

'Shut up.'

'What? What did you—'

'Shut up. There's somebody coming.'

The car draws level with her. She risks a glance to her left. It's a large dark sedan, but she doesn't know anything about makes. She can't see inside. She looks straight ahead again and keeps on walking.

The car drifts past. A few yards ahead it pulls into the curb. The passenger side window yawns open.

'Ah. Now that's more like it. Go check it out, Erin.'

Yeah, sure. Because we all go and check out suspicious cars in the middle of the night, right?

She keeps walking, but now her heart is pounding furiously – at least a dozen beats to every heel-click. Who's in that car? Someone with a gun? A gang of youths, ready to burst out of there and drag her to the ground and rape her? What good will her pathetic little knife be then? Of what use to her Georgia will she be if she ends up in a hospital, or even the morgue?

She wants to turn and run. All her instincts tell her to get back into the light of the Avenue. To flag down a taxi or any damn car and plead for them to take her away from there.

But she doesn't, because of her baby.

She gets to the car. Acts as though she's not aware its occupants are waiting for her.

'Hey! You want a ride somewhere?'

She bends at the knee. Peers inside. Just the one guy, it seems. Pale shirt, open at the collar. A gold necklace. He has a widow's peak. Hard to tell from here, but his skin looks badly pock-marked. His mouth is a weird shape too – like he once had a hare lip and it was fixed by a back street surgeon for twenty bucks.

'He's a looker, Erin. Don't let your heart rule your head on this beefcake.'

She hears a laugh in her ear. Go ahead, she thinks. Laugh while you can. Laugh until I get a chance to gut you like a fish.

'Maybe,' she says to the driver. 'You going my way?'

'Baby, whatever way that is, I'm going there. Hop in.'

She hesitates. Her fingers close more tightly around the handle of the knife.

'Invitation's all there, Erin. What are you waiting for?'

She looks up and down the street. She doesn't want to get in this man's car, where he may try to do God knows what to her. She wants to go home. She wants to see her baby. She shouldn't be out here on this cold night, contemplating death and mutilation.

She opens the car door. Climbs in. There's a smell of alcohol here, mixed with stale smoke. The man smiles at her, showing her nicotine-stained teeth.

'Where to?'

She's not about to tell him where she lives, and has no idea where to tell him to drive. She just points straight ahead and says, 'That way.'

He seems to like that. He nods and drives off.

'What you doing out here, anyhow?'

'Just killing time,' she says. 'I don't sleep much.'

'Uh-huh. So what do you do to kill time?'

'Tell him you murder people, Erin.'

'I walk. Sometimes I find people to talk to.'

'Yeah? Is that it? Just talk?'

'Sure. What else?'

'Well, maybe nothing. Talking's okay. How much action did your mouth get tonight?'

'Not so much. It's been quiet. You're the first.'

'The first, huh?' He looks across at her. 'You know, you don't look like a typical...'

'Talker?'

'Yeah. Yeah, that.'

'Well, maybe I'm not typical. Maybe I'm not like others you might have met before. Maybe I just really enjoy a good... conversation.'

'That would be different. Real unusual, in fact. You do know that a good speaker can earn a lot of money, don't you?'

She shakes her head. 'I'm not interested in money. I'm interested in sparkling wit and repartee.'

'Repar-what?'

'Repartee. From the French.'

'Oh, so you do French too, huh?'

'I do a lot of things. I'm very versatile.'

'You certainly are, Erin. Good job. You've got him hooked.'

The driver laughs. A dirty, lascivious laugh. She knows what he's thinking, and she knows that she's encouraging him. But it's still his call, she tells herself. He can still walk away from this if he so chooses.

The man reaches into his pocket. Pulls out a small bottle of scotch.

'You want some? Wet your whistle? Help you loosen up a little?'

'I'm plenty loose already,' she says. 'And my whistle couldn't be any wetter.'

Jesus, Erin, she thinks. Where is this coming from? Where did you learn to act this way?

She watches him take both hands off the wheel as he unscrews the cap from the bottle and takes a swig of the amber liquid. He smacks his misshapen rubbery lips and says, 'Ah, that's good. Sure you won't join me?'

She shakes her head, and wonders what to say next. But then she realizes that he's pulling the car over. Her nervousness returns. She starts to think maybe she should have swallowed some of that scotch after all. Downed the whole bottle, in fact, just to take away her jitters. This is it, she thinks. This is the moment where he decides whether to live or die.

'Why are we stopping?'

It's a stupid question, but she has to ask it. Has to give him an opportunity to redeem himself.

He chugs some more scotch, then screws the cap back on and slips the bottle into his pocket.

'Makes it easier to talk. You said you like talking, didn't you?'

Her mouth is drying up. It's hard to say anything right now. 'Yes, that's what I said. What do you want to talk about?'

'You. What's your name?'

'Erin.'

'Hey, Erin. My name's Ed. I like you, Erin.'

'You do?'

'Yeah. A lot. I'd like to show you how much I like you. Is that okay with you, Erin? If I show you, I mean? You'd like to see that, wouldn't you?'

She doesn't answer. She feels like she's on a scary carnival ride and she wants to get off. But it's too late. It's already in motion. They've crested the rise and have started the almost vertical descent. She can see the emptiness below her and she knows they're about to plunge into it. There's no going back now. He's decided he wants to go there, and he's dragging her down with him.

'Look, Erin. Are you ready?'

He's unzipping his fly now. Digging around inside and pulling himself out. Showing her how excited he is.

'Ha! Well, will you look at that!'

God no, she thinks, and her stomach lurches, and the rollercoaster is gathering speed, thundering down the track now.

'I think...' she says. 'I think maybe I should go now.' And she takes her hand out of her pocket, the pocket that has the knife in it, and searches for the door handle on this unfamiliar car, the type of which she has never been in before and has no idea how to open. She runs her hand over the door's surface, searching for the right latch or button to get her the hell out of here, while all the time trying not to take her eyes off this man for fear of what he might do next. And when she decides that she has no option but to tear her gaze away so that she can escape, she realizes what a dreadful mistake she's made. Because what she hears then is a fierce 'No!' from the man, who then grabs her by the hair, grabs it with both hands and yanks her head down toward his lap, toward his pathetic excuse for manhood, yelling at her to talk to him, to use her mouth and fucking talk to me, you bitch, you fucking whore. And her hand searches again, not for the door handle this time but for her pocket, which no longer seems to be there, where the hell is it, where is my damn pocket, where is my knife? And she feels his heat and his wetness and his stench on her face while her fingers search frantically. And finally, yes finally, God be praised, it's there, she finds the pocket, her fingers plunging into its warmth, touching its offering, its secret contents. She takes it, grasps it with relief, she's never felt such relief, and she brings it out, and she has no hesitation now, she begins to stab, to poke to thrust, to damage. And she hears his grunts of pleasure turn to shrieks of pain, and even after he releases his grasp on her hair she continues to stab, working her way up his body, up his abdomen and his chest and to his throat, yes his throat, where she opens him up from ear to ear and feels not his semen now but his hot blood pumping onto her face, and she sees the surprise in his eyes, the shock of it all as he loses his life force and dies right in front of her, right there in his own car with his tongue hanging out and his dick hanging out, and the voice of her persecutor baying for blood in her ear. And gradually her train ride slows and stops and it's all over. It's all over.

'Fuck!' she screams into the dead driver's face, spittle flying at him. 'Fuck you!'

'*Nice job, Erin. Messy, but nice.*'

'Fuck you too.'

She can feel something running down her face, and she's not sure if it's tears or blood. She could be crying, yes, because she feels so enraged and so distraught and so fucking emotional right now. Every single emotion she has seems to be bursting out of her simultaneously, including love. Love for her baby, because that's what this is all about, isn't it? That's why I'm doing this. That's why this piece of shit had to die, and actually, you know what, I don't feel much regret over this one. This is a world apart from the poor homeless guy. This one is scum. This one asked for it.

She takes a moment. Tries to talk herself down. Tries to give her rational mind a look-in. She needs to get out of here.

She opens up the glove compartment. It's full of junk. Sunglasses, pens, business cards, candy wrappers. But also a small packet of tissues. She rips it open. Does what she can to wipe the blood from her face and hands.

'Don't get too clean, Erin. Not just yet.'

She knows what that means. Her work here isn't quite done.

She looks again at the driver. His eyes are wide and fixed straight ahead, as if staring in terror at an oncoming truck about to plow into his car and crush him to a pulp. Blood is still oozing out of that huge gash across his neck. His face is ghostly white.

She picks up the knife again, examines its deadly edge and sharp point. She knows what's coming next, and strangely she is not so repulsed this time. She thinks it is partly because she has done this before, but mainly because of what this man represents. He is a predator. He seeks out vulnerable women and tries to subject them to his evil will.

Didn't I give him a chance? Didn't I tell him I wanted to get out of the car? He could have been nice to me. He could have dropped me off somewhere and driven away. Why did he have to be so disgusting and violent? Why did he have to choose that path?

Well, you did. And actually I'm grateful, because you don't deserve to live and my daughter does. It's a good trade, because her life is worth infinitely more than yours.

'I'm ready,' she says.

When he gives her the instruction she hardly hesitates. A few swift strokes, and she's done. She even thinks she carries it out with a little more gusto this time. Her cuts perhaps a little deeper – scraping against his skull, in fact.

She cleans herself up again with the remaining tissues. Wipes the knife and returns it to her pocket. She looks out onto the street. Deserted, quiet, dark. As though nothing has happened. Everyone asleep in their beds, unaware of the sexual assault, the violence, the slaying, the mutilation that has taken place just yards away from their cozy bolt-holes.

She gets out of the car and scans her surroundings, double-checking that she remains unseen. She realizes she's still on East Tenth Street, just a couple of blocks away from her home. Which is useful seeing as how she needs to cover the distance while dripping in a man's blood.

She puts her head down and starts to walk. Hopes that nobody notices her, nobody sees the mess she's in.

She gets only a few yards from the car when the noise blares behind her, startling the shit out of her.

The car horn.

For the briefest of moments she imagines the driver sitting there, pushing in desperation on the horn, doing whatever he can to summon help, someone to get him to a hospital. He's sitting there and he's moaning and gasping for breath and he's leaning on the horn button, making it send its plaintive cry into the night for him.

And then she shakes her head. He's dead. I know he's dead. He must have fallen forward, that's all. That's all it is.

But still she runs for home, not once looking back.

4.07 AM

'So tell me again why you ain't got a girlfriend.'

This from Doyle. He's sitting in the police sedan next to LeBlanc, taking a break from trying to find anyone who knows anything about the demise of Vern. Teasing LeBlanc is a lot more entertaining.

'I didn't tell you the first time.'

'Well now's your golden opportunity. You got… you know… problems?'

LeBlanc stares at him, and Doyle finds it hard to keep his face straight.

'No, I haven't got *problems*. What do you mean, problems? What kind of problems?'

'I don't know. Any kind of problems. Problems of an intimate nature.'

LeBlanc continues to stare. 'No, I don't have intimate problems. And if I did, you'd be the last person I'd be confiding in.'

'Well, so, what is it then? What's holding you back?'

'Nothing's holding me back. You think a guy's always got to have a girlfriend? Didn't you ever have a time when you were without a girl? Or can't you remember that far back?'

Doyle smiles. He's not much older than LeBlanc, but he's not going to let the discussion be deflected onto him.

'I remember, and actually no, I was never without a girlfriend. Sometimes I even had several at the same time. You, on the other hand, seem disturbingly uninterested in women.'

'Disturbing? What's disturbing about it? Why does that bother you so much?'

LeBlanc's voice is becoming comically high-pitched, and now Doyle really is struggling to contain his amusement.

'Doesn't bother me at all,' says Doyle.

'Well, good.'

'Can't speak for other people, though. All those rumors…'

'Rumors? What are you talking about, rumors?'

'The rumors. You know how other cops can be, right? The way they talk? Somebody says something, somebody else believes it, and suddenly it spreads like wildfire. Everyone ends up believing something that has absolutely no basis in fact. It always amazes me how that kind of thing happens.'

LeBlanc sits bolt upright, all ears now. 'Wait. Who's been saying this? What rumors?'

Doyle's confession that he's just made all this up is sitting on the tip of tongue. He's about to let it out when something else demands his attention. It's the car radio, which has been blathering in the background all the time they've been sitting here. Experienced cops develop an innate radar, capable of filtering out the noise while remaining subconsciously alert to items of interest. And now Doyle's radar is definitely pinging.

'Eight Adam to Central, K.'

'Go ahead, Eight Adam.'

'Central, confirm the report of a DOA in that car on East Tenth Street.'

'Ten-four, Adam. Stay with it, we'll put the calls out.'

Doyle looks across at LeBlanc. 'That's just a coupla blocks from here.' He grabs up the radio and requests more details. And what he hears sends a tingle up his spine.

'Central,' he says, 'show us as responding, K.'

As he fires up the engine, LeBlanc says to him, 'You don't think…' and leaves it hanging in the air like that, because that's exactly what they both think.

They get to the scene in minutes. The first thing they hear when they get out of the car is the steady mournful drone of a car horn. There is a small gathering of people – not nearly so many as there was for Vern – but only because word has not gotten around yet that this is a homicide scene. Anyone else who has woken up probably thinks it's just a faulty car alarm.

A uniform approaches the detectives, greets them, then leads them over to the Ford sedan.

'The horn going off when you got here?' Doyle asks. He has to raise his voice to be heard above the noise.

'Yeah,' says the uniform. 'That's why the vic was found.' He jerks his thumb toward a stout balding man standing on the sidewalk. 'Guy over there is the superintendent of that apartment building. He lives on the ground floor at the front. The noise woke him up. When it wouldn't stop, he came out to tell the driver to shut the fuck up. That's when he found the body.'

Doyle and LeBlanc try to peer into the black interior of the vehicle.

'Here,' says the uniform, handing Doyle a flashlight.

Doyle shines the light through the window. He can see a figure slumped onto the steering wheel, plus a lot of blood, but that's about it.

'Anyone move the body?'

'No. The super says he opened the car door, but closed it again as soon as he saw what was inside. When we got here I checked the vic for vitals, but that's all.'

'Okay. Let's wait for crime scene. Let them take some pictures and check it out before we move him.'

He hands the flashlight back to the officer, then he and LeBlanc head over to the man who reported this.

The building superintendent is wearing a thick trench coat over pajama pants and sneakers. He rubs his jowls nervously as the detectives approach.

'Mister…?' says Doyle.

'Stavropoulos.'

'Mister Stavropoulos, we're detectives from the Eighth Precinct. Can you tell us what happened here tonight?'

'The noise. Can't you stop the noise? I have sensitive ears. Noises like this make me crazy, you know?'

'We will, just as soon as we can. I understand you were the first one to find the victim. Is that correct?'

'Yes, it's correct. It was the noise, you understand? I can't sleep through noise like that. This is a noisy city, I'm used to noise. But this, right outside my window? Nobody could sleep through this. You think you could sleep through this?'

'No,' says Doyle. 'I'm sure I couldn't. And that's why you came out here, right?'

'Yes. I looked out of my window. I put my light on so that he could see I was looking out of my window, but he wouldn't stop. I didn't understand why he was doing it. So I came out here. I'm not afraid. I can handle punks. But still he didn't stop with the horn.'

'So you went over to the car.'

'Yes. Even though the noise was killing my ears I went over there. I knocked on the car window, but the man didn't even look at me. I thought, this man's drunk. He's drunk or he's on drugs, or he's had a heart attack or something. I never thought… well, I never thought it would be this. All the blood and everything. Horrible. I never saw anything like that before.'

It's LeBlanc who puts the next question: 'Mr Stavropoulos. What time was this, when you first woke up?'

Stavropoulos looks at LeBlanc with a slightly surprised expression, as though he's just realized he's there.

'Are you a detective too?'

'Yes, sir, I am,' says LeBlanc.

'You look too young to be a detective. They let you work on big cases like this?'

'Yes, they do. So what time did you get woken up?'

Stavropoulos thinks for a moment. 'About a quarter to four. Unheard of, right? Nobody should be woken up at a time like that. But the noise, you know?'

'I understand. And then you looked out of your window, right? Did you see anyone on the street?'

'Not a soul.'

'What about when you went outside? See anybody then?'

Stavropoulos shakes his head. 'Not a soul. Whoever did this, they just vanished. Like a ghost.'

Sure, thinks Doyle. A ghost. Only this guy wasn't frightened to death. Someone very solid went to work on him.

They thank Stavropoulos, then question a few of the other bystanders while the Crime Scene Unit detectives arrive and do their stuff. Eventually, they get the all-clear to take a closer look at the body.

'So are we taking bets?' says LeBlanc as they approach the car again. 'On this being our Zorro guy?'

'I got a bad feeling about this, Tommy,' says Doyle. 'Something tells me we're in for a long night.'

At the car, a squat Chinese man straightens up from his examination of the interior, then turns his bespectacled eyes on the detectives.

'Hey, Norm,' says Doyle. 'How's tricks?'

Norman Chin, one of the city's leading Medical Examiners, gestures helplessly to his left ear.

'What?'

Doyle raises his voice. 'What've we got?'

'What's that?' says Chin. 'Speak up.'

Doyle frowns, then steps up his volume even further. 'You okay to move the body? Cut off this noise?'

Chin looks at the corpse, then back at Doyle. 'You know what, I think I should pull the body back and kill the noise.'

Doyle nods. 'That's a great idea, Norm.'

'What?'

'I said I think that's— Are you yanking my chain?'

A mischievous grin appears on the medic's face. 'Who, me?'

Chin holds up a wait-a-second finger. Leaning into the car again, he gently pulls the driver back into his seat. The horn stops, and from behind Doyle comes the sound of Stavropoulos thanking God for an end to his torment.

Doyle's eyes remain fixed on the victim. He holds his breath as it is raised into view. Someone angles a light straight into the driver's bloodied face.

'Jesus,' says LeBlanc.

Doyle takes a step closer, not quite sure he's seeing correctly. But he's not mistaken. The cuts are there, all right. Slap bang in the middle of the man's forehead. But it's not what Doyle expected. It's much, much worse:

'You see what I see?' says Doyle.

'Yeah,' LeBlanc breathes. 'Yeah, I do.'

'We were wrong. About the homeless guy. It wasn't a Z. It was a 2.'

The two detectives take their eyes off the victim and look at each other.

'So,' says LeBlanc. 'If Vern was number two, and this guy's number three...'

Doyle finishes the sentence: 'Then where the fuck is number one?'

4.25 AM

Numb.

That's how she feels. Detached, somehow. As though she's not really here. Just looking out through somebody else's eyes, the way that man looks out at the world through the brooch pinned to her coat.

She has been sitting here on a chair since she got home. A wooden chair rather than the sofa, because she's still covered in blood and doesn't want to ruin her furniture. Doesn't want to soil it with the blood she has just spilled.

And she spilled a lot of it. She can still feel it gushing out of the man's neck. Hitting her in the face, hot and wet and somehow alive.

She knows she should wash it off, but it almost seems a futile gesture. Like wandering through the remains of a house that's been smashed into pieces by a hurricane, and then picking up an overturned chair, as if that somehow restores order.

She's not sure she can ever remove this blood. Not completely. Even if she could wash a hundred times, she will still feel as though it is there. As if it has seeped into her skin and become as permanent as a tattoo – an eternal reminder of what she has done.

And yet she is not as upset as she was after the homeless guy. This man was garbage. Scum. He deserved to die.

Did he? Did he deserve it? Does anyone *deserve* to die?

Oh, Jesus, Erin. Let's not get philosophical about this. You don't know what that piece of shit would have done. You don't know what he's done to other women either. Maybe he would have raped you and then murdered you. You did what you had to do to protect yourself and get out of there.

Yes, but I got into his car in the first place. Doesn't that make me at least a little bit guilty?

Why should it? Are you saying girls shouldn't wear short skirts or smile at strangers? Next you'll be saying they shouldn't be revealing their ankles either. How far do you want to take an argument like that, Erin? No means no, end of.

Yes, but…

Oh, fuck.

Listen to me. Setting up a debating society in my own head. As if it's not already crowded enough in there with Mister Voiceover.

'Are you all right, Erin?'

Right on cue. Right on fucking cue. Come on in, join the party, why don't you? Put your two cents in. Not that you need an invitation. Since when has that stopped you? When did you ever stop and consider that the interior of a woman's head is the very last place you should be intruding.

No fucking manners, some people.

'Erin? Did you hear me?'

'I heard you, all right? Have I got a choice not to hear you? I can't just walk away from you, in case you haven't realized. Maybe your wife did, and your mother, and all your other friends and family. Maybe that's why you're doing this, because it's the only way you can get someone to listen to your stupid boring voice. And maybe it's why you don't show yourself either, because you're ugly and weak and afraid and everybody hates you. Is that it, asswipe? Because you're a nobody, a nothing, and this is the only way you can give yourself some feeling of control? I bet it is. I bet if you walked through my door now, even I could kick your ass. That's how pathetic you are.'

'My, my, Erin. Are you annoyed at me?'

'Me? Nooo. Why would I be angry at you? You only drugged me, stole my baby and made me kill people. What's there not to like?'

'I told you. It's for a reason. It's all for your benefit.'

'That's right. I forgot. You're showing me the light. Hallelujah, brother. Praise the Lord and pass the ammunition so I can blow another fucker off this planet. Thanks for that. I feel so righteous now.'

'You shouldn't feel guilty about killing that last guy. He had it coming.'

'FYI, I've just had this discussion in my head. Your contribution isn't needed, thank you very much.'

'*Did he hurt you?*'

'Oh, don't even go there, all right? Like you're concerned for my welfare. Like you're somehow looking after me. Don't stick that label on yourself along with all the other ones that add to your delusions, okay?'

'*But I am looking after you, Erin. You'll see. After this day is done, you'll understand.*'

'Yeah, right.'

She decides this conversation is over, and gets up from the chair.

'*Where are you going?*'

'To get cleaned up. You want to come with me? Feel free to say no to that.'

She goes into the bathroom and puts the light on, then looks at herself in the mirror over the basin.

Christ. It's worse than she thought. Those tissues barely made a difference. She's covered in it. It's on her face, in her hair, soaked into her coat. She looks like Carrie in the movie of the same name.

She starts to unbutton her coat.

'*Whoa, Erin. What the hell do you think you're doing?*'

She ignores him. Continues unbuttoning. Starts to shuck off the coat.

'*Hold it right there. Don't be stupid. You know what will happen.*'

She pauses, the coat off her shoulders but her arms still in the sleeves. 'I need to get clean.'

'*Uh-uh. Forget it. I told you. You need to wear the surveillance equipment at all times. You don't take it off, not even for a minute.*'

She pulls the coat back on, but doesn't fasten it. 'Are you crazy? Look at me. You think I can go out again looking like this? I am covered in that man's blood. If the cops stop me again I'm done for. Even if I didn't have any blood on me I'd have to change, because those cops from before will be looking for me as soon as that body in the car is found. Send me out like this and you might as well call the cops yourself. I won't get five yards without being arrested.'

There's a long pause while he contemplates her argument. Ha! Didn't think this one through, did you, mastermind? You're not so infallible.

'All right, Erin. What do you suggest?'

'I suggest I take a shower, is what I suggest.'

'How do I know that's all you'll do?'

'You don't. Obviously I can't get in the shower with all this equipment, so you'll just have to trust me.'

'No dice, Erin. I don't do trust. That's not how it works.'

Big surprise, she thinks. He doesn't trust me.

'All right, then you come up with an idea. I have to get cleaned up. You tell me how I'm supposed to do that while sticking to your rules.'

Another long pause. Then: 'Go get a hanger from the closet in your bedroom. Hang the coat on the bathroom door, the brooch facing out. You can take the earpiece out when you're about to get into the shower.'

She falters then, her fighting spirit suddenly dissipating again. 'I... You'll see me. If I do it like that, you'll see me getting undressed.'

'Take it or leave it, Erin. I'm giving a little here. You need to do the same.'

Giving a little. Yeah, right. Giving yourself a little erection while you watch a strip show, is more the truth of it.

Fuck.

But she knows she has to do what he asks. She can't bear to stay covered in this sticky dark blood from another human being any longer.

She fetches the hanger, drapes the coat over it, then hangs it in position on the bathroom door. Stepping back, she stares at the brooch. It feels strange not to have it attached to her and looking out. Now it's at a distance, with its beady little eye on her. Like having a stranger right there in her bathroom – a peeping tom about to watch her get naked.

She turns her back to her watcher as she starts to undress. While she disrobes she listens intently for any sounds over the earpiece – any sign that he's getting a little too interested in this spectacle. That dirty bastard. He's probably—

And then a thought hits her.

Maybe she can use this. She didn't think she possessed anything she could use in a fight against this man, but maybe she does. Her body. Her sexuality. Maybe the sight of someone being murdered isn't the only thing that turns him on. If he's at all interested in women...

Yes. Could that be it? Could I do it?

A tremor runs through her.

I can't be obvious about it. Nothing too quick, too artificial. I have to take my time. Build up to it. Start with a little teasing. Get him interested. Get him thinking about me in a different way. Not as a pawn for executing his death warrants, but as an object of desire. Someone he might fantasize over. Someone he thinks about so much he will be unable to control himself. He will need to see properly, up close and personal. Not through a crappy little lens. He will need to smell and hold and caress. And to do that, he will need to get closer. So much closer. Close enough to kill.

Yes!

Her original intention had been to protect her modesty as much as possible. Keep his pervy little eyes off of her. She planned to get behind the shower curtain before removing the last of her clothes, keeping a robe within arm's reach for when she got out. That way he would see nothing.

But now she has a different plan.

She is down to her underwear. Blue bra, white panties, thick winter pantyhose. Not the sexiest attire, but hey, seducing the abductor of her child wasn't originally in her diary for today.

She peels off the pantyhose. Then she takes a deep breath. Pulls in her stomach and sticks out her chest. Childbirth took its toll, but in the months following she put a lot of work into getting her shape back. The one thing she appreciated about motherhood, however, was a much bigger rack: she went up two whole cup sizes while pregnant, and her boobs don't show any sign of shrinking just yet, despite the fact she abandoned breastfeeding as a lost cause.

She sneaks a sidelong look into the mirror. Not bad. Well, except for that blood on your face. That kinda ruins the effect you're aiming at, Erin. Not exactly subtle in the makeup department.

Still, beggars can't be choosers. If this works, maybe he won't be lifting his gaze that high.

She turns.

Tries to make it seem casual. An 'I need to go over here now' kind of move, rather than a 'feast your eyes on these bad boys' one.

She doesn't know what she's hoping for – maybe not a cry of 'hubba hubba', but at least a lewd comment or even a mild gasp of arousal – but she gets nothing.

Press on, she thinks. He might even have turned his own microphone off so as to cut off his groans while he jerks off.

Maybe you'd like to come over here and do the five finger shuffle, you pervert. I can promise you that your groans won't be the only things that get cut off.

She reaches in behind the shower curtain, then bends forward while she turns on the water, affording him an even better view of her cleavage. As she twists the control, one of the bra straps falls off her shoulder. She leaves it there.

Come on, fella. Say something. Anything. Show me you're interested. Show me that watching people being sliced open isn't the only way you can get your rocks off.

She straightens up, then moves closer to the coat on the door. Looks straight into the brooch. He's got a perfect view of me now, she thinks. Close up and semi-nude. A bra that's possibly on the verge of revealing more than it should. A few smears of blood that might even add to the attraction as far as this crazy fuck is concerned. You don't want to say anything? All right, how about I make you talk?

'Is it okay if I take out my earpiece now?'

He pauses before answering: *'Yes, Erin. Put it on the shelf above the basin, where I can see it.'*

His response couldn't be more disappointing. He seems more interested in the damn earpiece than he does in her. His voice is dull, flat. Like he finds this tedious. Distasteful, even.

Yeah, well, the feeling's mutual, mister. You think I'm stripping off in front of you because I like you? Think again.

Actually, no. Don't think again. Don't think at all. Let your hormones do what they're supposed to do. Let them pump up your organs and get you racing over here, stud. Come and prove to me what a hot-blooded caveman you are. And when you do, I'll show you just how hot your blood really is. I'll let you see it and touch it for yourself.

This isn't going to work.

He's not into me. Hasn't got the faintest interest.

Don't give up, Erin. Don't abandon the only plan you've got so easily.

She walks back to the basin, pulling out the earpiece as she goes. With her back to the camera again, she reaches behind and unhooks her bra, then lets it fall to the floor. She tries telling herself that he's mere inches away from his monitor now, desperately trying to catch a glimpse of her tits. She forces herself to imagine that his breathing is heavy, panting almost. Maybe it's not true. Maybe the sight of a naked woman is abhorrent to him. But if there's a chance, just a slim hope...

She slips off the panties, careful not to bend forward too much. This isn't one of those ludicrous sex-romp movies. She's not auditioning to be a porn star here. Just a little titillation. Get his cogs rotating. Get him hungry for more.

If you want more, mister, then you'll have to ask for it. For now, this is all you get.

She side-steps into the shower. A slight turn to reveal the curve of a breast, and then she's out of his sight.

The water is warm on her back, and yet she notices that her hands are trembling, her breath fluttering. What are you doing, Erin? Are you insane? You really think it's a good idea to entice this lunatic into your home? Do you really want him lusting after your body?

She turns and pushes her head into the stream of water, anxious to drown the doubts. I've got nothing else, she thinks. No other source of hope. I need to be at least trying to do something.

And then she's crying again. Sobbing silently, her shoulders heaving. At first she can't understand what's prompted this, but then she realizes it's the freedom. It's the sudden comprehension that, for these few brief minutes, she is out of his grasp. She does not have to listen to him, doesn't have to put up with his satanic commands and his spiteful remarks. She has been untethered from that mystical third eye she has been forced to wear. No longer is he able to look where she looks, see what she sees. He has been cast out from her body. Exorcized.

And Christ does it feel good.

She wants to stay here forever. While she washes herself again and again with shower gel and shampoo, until her eyes sting and her ears are plugged with soapy foam, she wishes she never had to go back to her nightmare. She wants to scrub and scrub until there is nothing of herself left. She will be rinsed down the drainage hole and away from this place of disembodied voices and eyes. She does not want to hand over her body to the demons again, to give them the power they demand from her. Without her they are nothing. They need her physical form to give them life, the ability to move and be heard. She would like nothing better than to withhold all that from them for eternity.

But she knows she cannot.

Georgia is in there. The demons are holding her hostage. And the only one who can save her is her mother. Good has to vanquish evil – all the stories say so. Erin knows she has to find the courage to cross back into the underworld.

Where are you now, God? I could do with a little help here.

She turns the shower off. She can delay no longer. She needs to connect again, because that's the only way to her baby. That's her umbilical cord.

She reaches for a towel from the radiator. Dries herself off as best as she can while she remains standing in the tub. Then she grabs her bathrobe and puts it on. No more sex play. No more acting the temptress. It was okay while she was filthy and disgusting and caked in drying blood. The soiled appearance paired well with whoredom. But now she is clean. Bright as a new pin. She doesn't want to contemplate sordid, unholy things.

She steps out of the tub. Grabs another towel and wraps her hair up in it. She inhales deeply, and likes how the air smells. The perfume of summer and flowers and freshness. Nice things. Pure things.

Then her eye catches sight of her coat on its hanger over the door, and her mental pictures begin to decay and become infused with gore and violence. She sees the unfocused image of a man bent over a screen, staring at her. Waiting for her to return to his domain, as she knows she must.

She retrieves the earpiece from the shelf and looks at it for a while. She is painfully aware that putting it back into place will transport her into his hands once again, but she also knows that it is a path she cannot refuse to tread.

She puts the tiny speaker back into her ear. Her world lurches.

'Hello again, Erin. Feel better for that? Have to say, you look pretty refreshed.'

She doesn't say anything. Just glares coldly at the brooch.

'Come and get the equipment, Erin. Pin the brooch to your robe, and put the battery pack into your pocket.'

Remaining silent, she follows his instructions. She grimaces at the blood on her coat as she removes the brooch, anxious for it not to get on her fingers again. Finally she pins it into place on her lapel and drops the black plastic box into her pocket.

'Okay, Erin. I think you should get ready again, don't you? Dry your hair, put some more makeup on, do whatever it is you girlies do.'

'Not yet.'

'What do you mean, not yet? You've done a lot already, sure, but there's still plenty of work to do. Four more, remember?'

'Yes,' she snaps. 'I know. I know exactly. You don't have to keep telling me.'

'Hey, Erin. Don't be like that. I'm just trying to—'

'How's Georgia?'

'What?'

'Georgia. How is she? I want to know how my baby is.'

'She's asleep. Like a log. Is she always this good at night?'

'Sometimes. Not always. Is she… does she look happy?'

'Happy? Yeah, I'd say so. Sweet dreams, I'd say.'

Erin nods, even though he cannot see her. 'Good. I need her to be happy. I need to know that… that…'

'Erin, she's fine. And she'll stay fine. Just a few more hours, okay. A few more… people.'

'Right. Right. But later, okay. I need to rest. I'm so tired.'

'I don't think that's such a good—'

'Please. Just a couple hours.'

Silence for a while. Then: 'It's your call, Erin. You know what needs to be done, and you know how long you've got to do it. You make the call.'

She makes it. She leaves the bathroom and goes through to her bedroom. She turns the bedside lamp on, and the main light off. Then she lies down on the bed.

'Just leave me in peace for a while, okay? Let me sleep.'

'All right, Erin. But leave the lamp on, okay?'

She stops responding again, and waits for the buzz of thoughts in her head to die down so that sleep can steal in and claim her.

5.16 AM

Everything has changed.

Two murders carried out within hours of each other by the same killer is serious enough. But the possibility of a third victim? One they haven't even located, let alone identified? Well, that's just set all the alarm bells ringing. Ringing even louder because there is every chance that this is just the beginning. Where there's a one, two and three, there may be a four, five and six on the way. They can't let that happen.

And so it's with a certain sense of urgency that Doyle returns to the squadroom with LeBlanc in tow. There is much work to be done.

The last thing he needs right now is to deal with Albert.

He's trailing behind a female uniformed officer called Sheridan. She looks pissed.

'Wait there,' she commands Albert, finger in the air. When her charge obeys, Doyle half expects her to pat his head and give him a biscuit. His amusement fades when she turns back to Doyle and he sees that her expression has darkened to a thunderous level.

To her credit, she keeps her voice low: 'Where the hell have you been, Cal? I've been stuck with this fruitcake for hours.'

Doyle tries to look pained. He approached her to look after Albert while he was out on the first call. Turned on his boyish Irish charm and told her how he'd be eternally grateful for her assistance.

'Sorry, Frankie. I caught a second homicide straight after the first. This could turn into something big.'

'Yeah, I heard about that, and that don't exactly make it better, Cal. I should be out there too, trying to catch the perp, 'stead of running a crèche here for your adopted orphan. I am so gonna get my ass kicked at the end of my tour if I've got nothing to show for it.'

Doyle puts his hands out to placate her. 'All right. Lemme talk to your sarge. I'll square it with him, okay?'

He's not relishing the prospect of trying to square anything with Costello, but he knows this is his own fault.

He chin-points at Albert. 'You get anything out of him?'

'Oh sure,' says Sheridan. 'It was riveting. I was almost tempted to take the matchsticks out from my eyelids. Now I know everything about Einstein and some theory he had about his relatives.'

Doyle is tempted to smile, but doesn't want to get into further hot water with Sheridan.

'What about his mother?'

'Nothing about his mother specifically. Just about his relatives in general.'

'No. Albert's mother. The one he says he offed.'

Sheridan shrugs, unfazed by her faux pas. 'To be honest, I gave up trying to go there. Every time I steered the conversation that way, he went all weirdy on me. Scratching his head and mumbling to himself. Asking me if I was planning to shoot him, like that.'

Doyle looks over Sheridan's shoulder at Albert, who is counting something on his fingers. He sighs. 'All right. Thanks, Frankie. I owe you one.'

'You owe me big time. If I asked you to sleep with me, you wouldn't be able to refuse, is how much you owe me.'

'Are you gonna ask me that?'

'I might, if I ever get desperate enough. See you around.'

'Yeah,' says Doyle as he watches her leave. He looks across to LeBlanc and holds up his fingers to let him know he'll be just five minutes, then heads over to Albert.

'How's it hanging, Albert?'

Albert looks down at his pants, as if he should be able to see something hanging there.

'I mean,' says Doyle, 'are you okay? Everything all right?'

Albert offers him a quick glance. 'You've been gone a long time. Hours.'

'Yeah, well, I had work to do. You're not my only worry tonight, believe it or not. Officer Sheridan was okay though, wasn't she?'

'Yeah, but...'

'But what?'

'She's a... a girl.'

'What, that makes you feel uncomfortable, Albert?'

Albert suddenly makes one of his frantic scratching motions behind his ear. Doyle is tempted to step back in case something should come flying out at him. But he wonders if he's on to something.

'You feel awkward with her? Is that it?'

'Yeah. Awkward, yeah. Not comfortable. Like my mattress. That's not comfortable either. It's all lumpy. She's lumpy too.'

Doyle wonders how Sheridan would react to being called lumpy. He also wonders whether Albert is suggesting that he'd like to lie on her to compare her with his mattress.

'Did that bother you, Albert? Do women make you want to do bad things?'

Albert starts up his eye-dancing then, but Doyle presses on: 'Does Officer Sheridan remind you of your mother?'

Albert's gaze suddenly locks on Doyle, and he girds himself. Tenses for a sudden and possibly violent reaction.

But he doesn't get one.

''Course not. My mother is smart. She knows stuff. She knows about prime numbers. Officer Sheridan thinks Isaac Newton is a singer. When I told her he was the guy with the apple, she asked if I was talking about iTunes.'

Doyle lets out a snort of laughter, partly because of what Albert has just said about Sheridan, but also through sheer relief. He didn't really want to delve further into any warped relationship that Albert might have had with his mother. Sigmund Freud he ain't. In fact, he finds that whole area of walking around in people's minds just a little disturbing.

Doyle gestures to the chair next to the water cooler. 'Sit down, Albert.'

Albert slides onto the chair. Crosses his legs and interlaces his fingers. Starts rocking slightly while looking straight ahead at nothing in particular.

'Listen to me,' says Doyle. 'This has suddenly become a really busy night. Everyone in the station house is busy. We can't afford to assign officers to look after you every single minute. You came here for our help, right? Well, then, let us help you. Give me some information. Anything.'

'I, uhm…'

'Yeah?'

'I, uhm… I got some Edifix building blocks. For my birthday. I made a robot out of them. Then a house. Then a helicopter. Then another robot. Then a—'

'No, Albert. Something useful, okay? Something about why you came here tonight. You told us you killed your mother. Was that the truth?'

'Yes. The truth. I always tell the truth. The truth, the whole truth and nothing but the truth. Tell me no secrets, tell me no lies.'

His rocking is more vigorous now. Faster, like he's on a racehorse.

'How?'

'How what?'

'How did you kill her? With a knife? A gun? A rock? How did you do it?'

'Aw, Jeez. Aw, Jeez. This is bad. Very bad.'

'Come on, Albert. If you killed her, then you should be able to tell me how you did it. So what did you do? Stab her in the heart? Cut her neck open? What?'

'Aw, Jeez. Can't say, can't say. It's too bad. You'll hang me. You'll fry me in the chair.'

Doyle lifts his face to the ceiling. This is such a waste of time, and right now time is a precious commodity.

'You know what, Albert? I don't think you killed your mother at all. I think this is all a big lie to get attention.'

'No. I told you. I don't lie. Bad things happen to people who lie. My mom told me that.'

'She tell you that bad things happen to people who hold back too? People who know something wrong has happened and won't tell the police about it? That's a crime too, you know.'

Albert's rocking is frantic now. He starts tugging on his hair. Grasping at it just above his ears and twisting it so hard it looks like he could tear it out.

'I *did* tell you about it. I told sergeant one-three-seven-one, and I told you. I always tell. Even when it's really bad I tell. That's why I told my Mom about Louie.'

Uh-oh, thinks Doyle. Uh-fucking-oh.

'Louie?'

'Yeah. Louie. I killed him too.'

Icy finger running down the spine time. Another killing? Really? You wanna just casually throw it into the conversation like this?

'You killed Louie?'

'Yeah. I didn't want to tell my Mom, but I had to. She woulda found out anyhow.'

'Found out what, Albert? What happened to Louie?'

'I was s'posed to look after him. When I left him he was warm, and when I came back he was cold. I didn't look after him properly. I was bad.'

'Albert, who was Louie? Was he a member of your family?'

'Yeah. Family. Yeah. I was s'posed to take care of him, but I didn't. We had to get rid of him.'

'Get rid of the body? How, Albert? How did you do that?'

'We… we flushed him down the toilet.'

Doyle suddenly wants to collapse on the floor in a heap of despair.

'Albert. Was Louie… was Louie a fish?'

'Yeah. I had him for a whole year. Then I forgot to plug in his water heater. I needed to charge my Nintendo and I forgot to plug his heater back in. He got cold and died. It was my fault. I killed him.'

Doyle closes his eyes and bows his head for a few seconds. Tiredness pours into his skull. Somebody please drape a blanket over me and leave me here until this is over. I want to wake up and find out that Albert has gone away and the number killer has been caught.

He looks again at Albert. Looks at this fragile human being who is constantly on the edge of being shattered into a million tiny pieces. He watches him sway and fidget and pull at his hair in frustration at not knowing how to deal with this hostile incomprehensible world.

'All right, Albert,' he says in his most soothing voice. 'All right.'

As he tries to restore Albert to what must count to him as some kind of normality, Doyle wonders what the penalty is in this state for killing a fish by neglect.

5.57 AM

If she slept, she's not aware of it. Perhaps a couple of minutes – nothing more. It feels like there's just too much adrenalin in her system. As though there's a drainage point that's blocked somewhere so that there's nowhere for the hormone to go. It just stays in her bloodstream, circulating. Prodding and poking fatigued organs into staying alert, just when they're on the point of drifting off. Her brain especially. All those thoughts flashing through with reckless abandon. Giving off sparks as they collide and combine and turn into surreal images and suggestions and fears. There's an ache in her chest, and she puts that down to the adrenalin too. The anxiety has tightened all her muscles until her ribs feel they could snap under the pressure. She dreads to think about the strain her heart is under. That's a muscle too, right? Why should that remain unaffected? Could it be at breaking point? Is it on the verge of exploding in her chest, just as that man's blood seemed to explode outwards, firing from his throat like some alien creature's biological weapon?

Here we go again. Back to that episode in the car. Back to the slow-mo replay of her repeatedly plunging a stainless steel blade into flesh. Feeling each puncture as it travels through her hand and up her arm. Hearing his screams trying to compete with cries of bloodlust coming over her earpiece, but not really hearing either. It's all just noise, just high-volume static as she does what needs to be done. And then the look in his eyes – that expression of incomprehension and terror as her gaze finally meets his. That profound questioning and pleading as she shows him the sharpness in her fingers, just before she flashes it across his neck and opens up his fountain, sets it free in a glorious spray of Technicolor – everyone go 'ooh' and 'aah', folks, because you don't see displays like this too often.

Did I really do that?

She did. She knows she did. But it could have been a dream. It could have been another existence. It could have been something she was only told about. She could believe that. If she were on a psychologist's couch and the shrink told her it was all a figment of her fervent imagination, she could accept that. She could never do such things in reality. She's not that kind of girl. What, me get into a car with a complete stranger? Heaven forfend! Flirt with him? Get him aroused? And then – what's that you say? – stab him to death with a kitchen knife? Oh, no, no, no. You've got the wrong person entirely. That's not the way I was brought up. You need to look elsewhere if it's murdering prick-teasing scumbags you want.

While we're on the topic of prick-teasing...

That wasn't me either. I don't do that. I don't take off all my clothes in front of a camera. I didn't even do that for my husband, let alone a baby-snatching insane person. I don't put on shows like that, because if I tried I would feel self-conscious and embarrassed and I would just come across as an awkward, fumbling amateur who doesn't even have the body to make up for it.

She cringes. Yes, all right, it was me. I did it. I tried to make that man all hot under the collar, even though all I probably did was to make him piss his pants laughing. Excuse me, Mr Nobby Bigcock, while I just bend at the waist in the most unnatural pose ever to retrieve that pair of lace panties I just took off for no reason whatsoever and dropped in a way that suggests I have lost all motor coordination of my fingers. That's what it must have looked like to him. Absurdly comical rather than alluring.

Okay, so I'm exaggerating. It wasn't that bad, surely? Was I really that obvious?

Maybe not. But did he betray a glimmer of interest? No. Not a word, not a murmur. Not even an ejaculation, if you'll pardon the pun.

But just suppose...

Suppose it worked. What now? If my semi-naked form is now permanently etched in his mind, what's my next step? How do I capitalize on that and move it forward?

She has no idea. She's not even certain it's possible to work up a definite plan at this stage. She may just have to play it by ear. Try to sound him out. Throw in a remark here and there. 'I hope you didn't make a recording of me in that bathroom.' Or, 'I hope you don't plan on seeing any more of me.' That kind of thing. And then he'll say something like, 'What if I told you I'm very interested in doing just that?' And then she'll know. She'll know he's taken the bait, and all she'll have to do is reel him in. Sure, that's how it will go.

After that internal pep-talk, she suddenly feels more confident about her strategy. I just need to go easy, she thinks. Keep up the sexual pressure. A glimpse of flesh here, an innuendo there. Nothing too overt. Not like, say, pulling my robe open and saying 'Come and get it.'

Not that he'd see that, of course. The camera's back in place. He can see only what I see, and right now all that I can see is a ceiling with a big crack in it. Because, Mata Hari though I'm aspiring to be, I haven't yet gotten around to installing a mirror on my ceiling. So you'll have to make do with that, fella. That's the only crack you'll see tonight, my friend. You'll just have to—

And then it hits her.

He can't see me!

Of course he can't. He looks out from me. Right now he's probably not even doing that. He's probably taking a nap himself, or reading a magazine or something. Why would he want to devote a couple of hours to staring at a ceiling?

So what if—

Oh, Jesus!

What if…

She catches her breath, suddenly afraid of moving an inch or making the slightest sound – anything that might betray the fact she's wide awake.

She wonders how much time she's got. At some point it will enter his head to give her a wake-up call, reminding her that she's got corpses to amass. But maybe not yet. He left the ball in her court. She told him she was desperate for sleep and would get back to the killing when she was good and ready. Since then he's been silent. He hasn't tried to interrupt her rest, and maybe he won't for at least another hour.

So…

God, can I do this? Should I risk it?

But her hand is already moving. Sneaking up on her dead-still body as if it isn't connected to it. Her fingers touch the warm fuzziness of her robe, then slide up to the pocket. They feel the stretched outline of the fabric against the hard box contained there. They continue their way up to the mouth of the pocket, then dip smoothly inside. They plunge slowly downwards – God, this pocket seems so deep – until they touch the hard foreign object there. She takes hold of the box – tight hold for fear of dropping it – then slowly begins to withdraw it. Up, up it comes. It should be such an easy thing to do, and yet it seems the most difficult thing in the world. She keeps her eyes focused on the ceiling, willing herself not to make any sudden movement, fearful of revealing the fact that she is awake. She draws the box along her robe, unsure as to whether it has cleared the top of the pocket but needing to make sure. She brings it up as far as her hip, and only then does she move it sideways and down onto the bed.

It's done. Phase one is complete.

She feels the need to suck in huge lungfuls of air, but prevents herself. Her heart is hammering against her chest, trying to push what little oxygen she allows in around her system. She feels dizzy and her stomach seems clenched like a fist.

And now for the difficult bit.

Fingers moving again. Back onto the robe. Up, up, up. Keeping them low so there is no danger of them being seen. They touch the swell of her left breast, then the snake of wire. They follow the lead. Careful now, careful.

She can't risk leaving this to blind groping. She raises her head from the pillow slightly. Just a couple of inches. Enough to look down and see what she's doing. Her hand is almost there. Just a little more…

She touches the brooch. Gently at first. Then she slides finger and thumb around its outer edge and grips it tightly. Holds it as firmly as she can. There must be no sudden movement.

The pin of the brooch goes right through the lapel of the robe, but she chose not to fasten it behind because she knew it would be there only temporarily. She thanks God now that she made that decision earlier.

Slowly, painstakingly, she starts to pull the brooch upward, toward her face. She slides it along the cloth to keep it steady. At least a minute passes for every millimeter of travel. It's almost imperceptible to her, so surely it must be the same on his screen?

She loses all sense of time. In fact, she doesn't want to know how long this is taking. She can't rush it. It has to be done this slowly.

But Christ it seems to be taking a fucking age to get this pin out!

Maybe it's already out, but she can't see. Another fraction of an inch, just to be sure.

Slide it along. There you go. Fingers starting to ache now, neck muscles starting to spasm.

But now it's out. It's got to be. It must be clear now.

She lets her head sink back into the pillow. Rest for a minute. We're almost done.

But he'll speak soon. He'll try to wake me up. If we're going to do this, we have to do it now.

She lifts her head again. Keeps her eyes fixed on the brooch as she slowly lifts it into the air. Not by much – just enough to keep it clear of her body.

There. That'll do.

With her free right hand she grips the edge of the bed. Starts to pull herself across the covers. Sliding while she holds the brooch in place, her left elbow braced against the bed to keep it steady. She hopes this looks as steady to her enemy as it does to her. Hopes he's not watching an image that's bouncing about all over the place, making him wonder what the fuck she's doing. If the ceiling were completely featureless he might not even notice, but there's that damn crack up there.

She keeps moving, inch by painful inch. Again it takes a lifetime, but finally she gets her body clear. No screaming in her ear yet.

She licks her lips. Her mouth is so dry. Her neck, still elevated, is screaming at her to abandon this unnatural pose.

But she can't take her eyes off the brooch now. Not now she's come this far. She knows as soon as she does, her hand will take its opportunity to do its own thing, like a naughty schoolboy out of sight of its teacher. She has to keep a stern watch on that hand. Keep it in line.

Okay, next step…

She begins to lower her hand. Gently, gently does it. Keep the brooch upright and level. Keep its beady little eye fixed on that crack in the ceiling. Down, down, ever so slowly down.

And it's there, on the bed. Oh my God, it's there.

She tries to release her grip, but her fingers have locked in position. Please don't make a cracking noise, she thinks. Not that close to the microphone. It'll sound like a gunshot to him.

But she gets them open, and pulls her arm away.

Free! I've actually managed to free myself. I did it!

Her heart is pounding furiously now. Practically bouncing off her ribcage. She feels like she's just run a marathon instead of moving a few inches on a bed.

She's right on the edge of the bed. She shifts a little more. It's easier now that both hands are free. She twists her body, drops one leg into space, feels touchdown on the soft carpet. Then the other leg. Then her body. Sinking below the level of the bed like a predatory river creature lowering itself into position to grab the next passer-by. Finally she pulls down her head, her eyes still wide and unblinking, until she is lying on the floor.

She is still wearing the earpiece. She presses on it with her finger, forcing into her ear canal. No voice. No noises at all. He hasn't seen.

He hasn't seen!

She takes a deep breath. She can smell carpet and dust. It makes her want to cough, and she has to bring a hand to her mouth to stifle it. She doesn't know how sensitive the brooch microphone is, but she's taking no chances. One tiny noise might be all it takes to ruin this.

She looks over at the bedroom door. It's open – probably enough to squeeze through without opening it further. Things are going her way for once. If she had closed the door, she doubts this would be possible.

She thinks about squirming across the carpet on her belly, like a soldier trying to stay below enemy fire, but is worried that it will make too much noise. Instead, she gets into a kneeling position, her front half supported by her forearms. She can move much more quietly this way, but…

Will he see?

She lifts her head above the parapet that is her mattress. The brooch sits there, staring, watching, waiting. She has no idea what its field of view is, but surely it can't detect anything this low down?

The ceiling, yes. It will see the ceiling. Maybe even some of the walls. But down here, no. Hell, she thinks, I could probably stand up and walk out of here and he wouldn't know.

But she's not going to do that. She's not going to jeopardize her scheme now after all this effort.

So she stays on her knees. Moves slowly and surely and, above all, silently. A strange, ungainly hunter with its eyes locked on its prey. The door. If she can just get to the door.

A thousand things could go wrong. A million. An unexpected noise, perhaps. Sirens from outside, or the gurgling of a radiator – the heating in this old building makes odd noises sometimes. She could press on the one floorboard that squeaks – she has never noticed the floor do that before, but this could be the one and only time it does. Or maybe her robe will come undone and the belt will catch on a shoe under the bed and nudge it against the bedpost. Or maybe—

Stop it, Erin! Your belt's fine. The floor is fine. Nothing will go wrong. Believe it.

But he could just decide enough time has passed. He will have become hungry for more killing – ravenous even. The demon will need feeding. It will have to summon its servant to bring its fast to an end in the only way it knows.

What will I do then? If he speaks to me now, what will I do?

He's not going to, Erin. You've got plenty of time. And even if he does, you say nothing. Pretend you're fast asleep. He can't question it. He knows how exhausted you were. Now get a fucking move on!

She gets to the door. This is going to be tricky. It's going to be tight. Just a nudge and the door will move. And unlike the floorboard, this probably *will* squeak, because doors always squeak. And even if it doesn't, the light will change. There are lights on in the living room – stronger than the lamp in here. If the door moves, shadows will shift in the room. They will pan across the ceiling and he will know.

She pulls her elbows as close together as she can manage while still allowing her to move. She edges her shoulders through the gap. So far so good. But now there are my hips. My fucking huge hips that I have always hated and that are now going to take out their revenge in retaliation for my neglect of them.

I promise. Get me through here and I will diet, I will exercise. I will turn you into the most shapely hips known to man. Please, just do me this one little favor.

She moves, the pain of expectation written on her face. She waits for the door hinges to betray her presence, squealing treacherously away. She waits for the boom of his voice in her ear – the school principal's roar, demanding to know what the hell she thinks she's playing at.

But then she's through. She looks back to make sure. The door hasn't moved. He has no idea she has left the bedroom.

You did it, Erin! You fucking did it, you crazy bitch!

She rolls to one side, away from the door, and leans against the wall – let him try to see through a fucking wall! Only now does she allow herself to breathe just a little more deeply.

Don't get cocksure now. Don't get blasé. Don't ruin this.

But she breathes. At least she can do that. She can suck up the oxygen of freedom, just as she imagines a prisoner of war might have done on emerging from an escape tunnel.

You can't linger, though, Erin. Time isn't limitless. You have to act, and you have to do it now.

And then she almost wants to burst into laughter. Mad, humorless laughter.

Act? I have to act? Okay, so tell me what the fuck I'm supposed to do.

Ha! Jesus Christ! You didn't think this through, did you, Erin? You were so obsessed with casting off those technological shackles, you gave absolutely no thought as to what you might do with your newly gained liberty.

There had been a vague intention somewhere at the back of her mind to get to the phone and call the cops, telling them her story in hushed but frantic tones. But now that she gets that idea out into the yellow lamplight, its flaws and cracks are all too obvious. Call the cops? Really? You want them to know what you've been up to for the past few hours? *Yes, Ma'am, this child abduction story is all very interesting, but you mind if we get back to these murders you mentioned?*

So if not the cops, then who? Tick tock, Erin. He's gonna come calling soon. Was this all for nothing? Are you just going to slink back onto the bed without doing a damn thing?

She gets to her feet. Panic is starting to creep up on her. She needs help, and she doesn't know a soul in this damn city. Here almost a month and she doesn't really know anyone.

Kind of your own fault, though, don't you think? You haven't exactly gone out of your way to make friends here, have you? You and Georgia – that's all you've thought about. Happy to exist in your own little bubble. Well now the bubble's burst, Erin. Somebody's poked a big fat finger into it, and left you exposed and alone.

Think, Erin, think!

And then her feet start moving. Carrying her across to the apartment door. She's got to talk to someone and she needs to do it fast. And the only person she can think of who is near enough and sympathetic enough to approach is good old Mr Wiseman. She doesn't know what he can do, doesn't know if he'll even understand what she's telling him, but what choice does she have? She's out of time, goddamnit, and she can no longer think straight, but she has to talk to someone, has to let somebody know what she's going through. She can't do this alone anymore. Somebody has to help. Please, Mr Wiseman, please understand, please believe, please know what I should do.

She opens the apartment door as quietly as she can, telling her fingers not to fumble with the locks, not to permit the escape of any metallic snaps or rattles. She pulls open the door – not too wide, because she still maintains the belief that all doors have a perverse tendency to squeak when you least want them to – and slips out into the hallway.

It's cold out here, made colder by the single naked light bulb casting a deathly glow. Pulling her robe tightly around her, she pads over to Wiseman's door. She takes a deep breath and thumbs the doorbell. Hears the urgent jangling inside the apartment.

Come on, come on. Wake up. Open the door. I haven't got long.

She wants to pound on the door. Yell at Wiseman to get his lazy ass out of bed and open this fucking door, doesn't he know there's a girl here in trouble, doesn't he realize he's the only one in the world who can help her?

But there's no sign of him. Not the slightest noise from inside. So she raises her hand again. Puts her thumb out in readiness for leaning on that doorbell. Prepares herself for the sounds inside the apartment, the insistent alarm that is her only voice right now. Her cry…

Her cry.

Georgia's cry.

That's what she hears. Over her earpiece. Georgia crying. Georgia screaming.

It comes as a terrifying jolt that threatens to blast her apart. And in the split-second it takes for all her wily plans to drop into the infinite blackness that has just opened up beneath her feet, the horrifying, petrifying implications strike into her heart.

He has seen something or he has heard something.

He knows.

He knows!

6.32 AM

So now he's interested, thinks Doyle.

His lieutenant. Cesario.

Marching into the squadroom with this sudden sense of urgency in his step. Where was that when Vern was at the center of interest? Who was hitting the panic button back then?

He knows how Cesario would answer. He'd say the same thing that all the white shirts above him would say: *It's not about who the victims were, or what they did. In our eyes they get equal treatment. It's about numbers. The fact that we've now got two connected homicides, maybe more.*

Yeah, right. All equal in the eyes of the law. Homeless black wino and respectable looking white businessman who owns a car and wears a suit. Both the same. Right. It's purely the numbers that've made Cesario leap out of bed and hightail it over here.

Still had time to dress, though. No throwing on the nearest things to hand for Cesario, oh no. He's as immaculate as ever and smelling of roses. Not a crease or a stray hair to be seen. No chance of him being mistaken for one of the disheveled, unshaven bums under his command, some of whom haven't seen a bed in what feels like a week.

But maybe I'm being too hard on him, thinks Doyle. Maybe I should give him the benefit of the doubt. I should stow the cynicism, at least until he does something more to deserve it.

Cesario barely breaks step as he barks an order. 'Everyone. My office. Now.'

Which is nice. Which is a great way of thanking his loyal detectives for the hard hours they've put into this so far.

Cynicism, you can come back in now.

6.34 AM

So what she does now is to drop everything. Her thoughts of escape, of seeking help, of talking to Wiseman – all gone, all abandoned in a bat of an eyelid. All she can think about now is saving her baby, her Georgia, God what have I done, what danger have I put her in?

And then she's running. Back into her apartment and flinging the door closed behind her. Dashing across the living room, into the bedroom. Flying onto the bed and grabbing hold of the brooch. Bringing it to her face. Showing him that she's here, she's right here where she's supposed to be, and she's not causing any trouble, not calling the cops or doing anything that would endanger her baby, because that would be stupid, wouldn't it, and why would I do such a thing?

'Stop it!' she yells. 'Don't hurt her. Please. Don't hurt her. I'm right here. I didn't mean anything. I didn't talk to anyone. Please. I just needed to… I just needed a little freedom, okay? Just a little time to myself. Please.'

'Erin? What—'

'Is she okay? Please tell me she's okay.'

'Erin. You broke the rules, Erin. You know what happens when you break the rules.'

She can still hear Georgia's wailing in the background. It's breaking her heart. She doesn't know what he's doing to her baby, but the sound is killing her.

'No! Please don't. I won't do it again. I promise. Stop hurting her. Stop it!'

'Where did you go to, Erin? Did you make a phone call, is that it?'

'No. I swear. I thought about it, but I didn't. I couldn't bring the police into this. They'd find out about the people I killed. I didn't call them or talk to anyone.'

'I don't believe you, Erin.'

Again she doesn't know what he does next, but Georgia's screaming suddenly intensifies. How can he be doing this?

'NOOO! I'm begging you. Stop! In God's name, stop. She's just a baby. I swear I didn't do anything. I took off the brooch, that's all. That's all I did.'

And then she loses it. Despite all the crying she has done in the past few hours, she manages to step it up now. She sobs so hard it feels her chest could burst. It's like a huge fist is gripping her heart and squeezing every last bit of emotion out of it.

'Erin,' says the voice. *'Listen to me. I'm not hurting her. I'm not doing anything to Georgia. I should, because of how you've behaved, but I'm not. She's hungry, is all. That, and I think her diaper needs changing, judging by the stench in here.'*

It takes a while, but the words eventually percolate through to Erin's consciousness.

'What? You're not... She's not hurt?'

'No, she's not. No thanks to you, Erin. You put her in danger. Maybe I should do something about that.'

'No. Please don't. I'll be good.'

'You'll be good? You won't try anything like that again?'

'No. I swear. She's all right? She's really okay?'

'She will be when I feed and change her. What were you thinking, Erin?'

What was I thinking? I don't know. I didn't think, did I? Not properly. I had no idea what I was doing. More importantly, he doesn't know either. He has no idea. Georgia crying – it was just coincidence. She's all right. He hasn't hurt her. Oh, thank Christ for that.

She almost wants to laugh with the relief. From the most profound sorrow to the most maniacal laughter in a heartbeat. That's the control he has over her. That's his power. She knows that now. There's no escape.

'I don't know. It was stupid. I just wanted to run away from all this.'

'If you run away, then you run away from Georgia. You do understand that, don't you?'

'I... Yes. Yes, I understand. I'm sorry.'

She means it. She's not saying this just to mollify him. She feels sincerely apologetic and grateful and all the things she hoped and promised herself she would never feel toward this man.

'All right, Erin. Just this once, I won't punish you. But you have to—'

He is interrupted by the sound of a buzzer. In Erin's apartment.

'What's that?'

Oh, God, no. Not Mr Wiseman. Please don't ruin this after I've just mended it.

'It's… there's somebody at the door.'

'Who? Who's at the fucking door, Erin?'

She can hear his anger building, his distrust of her returning. That can't happen. For Georgia's sake she has to forestall it.

'It'll be Mr Wiseman. My neighbor.'

'Why? Why's he here?'

'I…'

'Erin.' Stern now. Threatening. A simple utterance of her name that drips with the promise of harm to her daughter.

'I called at his apartment, okay? While I was out of the bedroom.'

'You did what?'

'I… It's okay. He didn't answer. I changed my mind. I came straight back.'

'Oh, Erin. You weren't going to tell me that, were you? What else haven't you told me? Because I swear, Erin. If you—'

'Nothing. There's nothing else. I didn't mention Mr Wiseman because I didn't think it was important. He didn't answer his door when I called. That's the truth.'

The buzzer sounds again. More insistent, it seems.

'All right. Answer the door. Get rid of the old Jew. But before you do that, pin the brooch back on. No more games, Erin. No more slack.'

Erin puts the box of tricks back in her pocket and re-attaches the brooch. Wiping the tearstains from her face with her sleeves, she gets off the bed and walks through to the apartment door.

The buzzing starts up again. Cuts out when she noisily puts the chain in place. She doesn't want him barging in here. If he seriously believes she's in trouble, he might push his way in and search the place. He would find the bloodstained clothing, and wouldn't that give her some explaining to do?

She opens the door the few inches the chain allows. It's Wiseman, all right, and he's wearing the edgy expression of someone who's on the verge of calling in all the emergency service personnel in the city.

She smiles at him. The most reassuring smile she can muster in the circumstances.

'Samuel! Hi. It's so early. Is everything okay?'

This throws him. He was probably planning to ask her the exact same thing.

'Okay? Yeah, I'm okay. What about you? I thought I heard...'

'What?'

'I... Someone just called at my door. That wasn't you?'

'Me? Call at your apartment? No. Why would I be trying to see you at this time in the morning?'

Look at me, she thinks. Ignore the red-rawness in my eyes and see instead how they emanate pure innocence. How could someone like this be guilty of lying?

He appears flummoxed. He tries to see past her into the apartment, but he's got only a few inches of space to push his gaze into, and she's blocking most of it.

'Somebody did,' he says. 'And then a door slammed. Sounded like your door. And then there was your voice. Like you were crying again – no, not just crying. Like you were begging. Was that you, Erin?'

Was that you, Erin? He says it with such softness in his voice, such charity. *Can I help you? Do you need me?* Her lip wants to quiver and her chest wants to heave and she wants to let it all out. Pour out all the hurt and the sorrow inside her. Let him see what a devastated human being this is in front of him.

But she doesn't. She holds her false smile in front of her and says, 'You know what? I heard a bang too. In the hallway. It woke me up and I yelled something. That must have been what you heard. Sometimes I don't know what the hell's going on in this building. You think it was Grace again?'

'Grace?'

'Miss Frodely. From downstairs. You know what she's like with her Alzheimer's. Always wandering around the building at night, knocking on doors and stuff.'

Wiseman sighs and shakes his head. 'No, I don't think it was Miss Frodely. And it didn't sound to me like you were yelling at someone to keep quiet. It sounded like you were upset. Maybe even a little... afraid.'

Oh, God, you are such a wise man, Mr Wiseman. A little too perspicacious, if that's the word I'm looking for here. Why can't you just be like everybody else – insular and not at all interested in the affairs of your neighbors? Why do you have to be so nice to me? So nice that you make me want to cry?

'Afraid? Really? Is that how it sounded to you? No, not at all. It's just that... Well, to tell you the truth, I'm having a tough time of it lately. Clark – he's my ex-husband, the one I was telling you about? – he's been saying things to me. Hurtful things. About how he thinks I'm a bad mother, and that maybe it would be better if he had custody of Georgia.'

'Oh,' says Wiseman. 'That must be tough on you. I'm sorry to hear that.'

'Yeah, it's tough. It's driving me crazy, if you must know. My emotions are all over the place, I'm not sleeping right... The slightest thing makes me cry and go nuts.'

Wiseman nods like the sage old owl he is. 'You want my advice, you should see a doctor. They can give you pills for things like that. These days, they have a pill for every problem under the sun.'

Except for this one, Mr W. Oh, if only there was a pill for my problem here. One little pill to wipe away these horrors. What a miracle cure that would be.

'I'll do that,' she says. 'Thank you. Talking to you has made me feel a lot better.'

'Any time,' he says, but continues to study her.

She knows what he's thinking. He's thinking that this woman isn't just mildly distressed; she's off her rocker. She's lost it. Her behavior puts Miss Frodely in the shade. Here she is, running up and down the hallway, pressing buzzers, waking people up, slamming doors, yelling and crying, going out at weird times of the night. Two tablets with a glass of water won't help her. This sorry sight should be in a mental institution.

Well, let him think that. Better that than he should suspect the truth. A few minutes ago, yes, she would have told him everything. But not now. That bridge has been well and truly burned down. He can't help me now. Nobody can.

She says, 'I think... I think I'll go make myself some tea. Can't see myself getting back to sleep now.' She dredges up another weak smile – see, everything's hunky-dory.

It should be a conversation closer if ever there was one, but Wiseman is still on a scent. 'What about your friends? Do they know about what's going on in your life?'

'Uhm, well, I don't really have any—' She stops dead, suddenly aware that she's landed herself in a trap of her own making. 'Oh, you mean, the people I went out to meet in the night?' She emits a laugh that even she thinks is thin and unconvincing. 'Oh no, I couldn't drop my petty little problems on them. Besides, they're all so successful and happy. I wouldn't want them to know my own life is so crappy compared with theirs, you know what I mean?'

She's not sure if that was a save or not, but suddenly it doesn't seem to matter, because Wiseman doesn't appear to be listening. His gaze has dropped from her face to her chest area. For a brief and embarrassing moment she wonders whether her robe has come open and flashed the old guy. But then she realizes it's worse than that.

The brooch. He can see the brooch. Who the hell pins a brooch to a bathrobe? Moreover, what kind of brooch has a thin black wire trailing from it – a wire which then disappears into a pocket?

Shit.

She moves back behind the door. He won't know what it is, she tells herself. He's old. He'll think it's some new kind of music player or something.

'Listen,' she says. 'I should go. Thanks again for your concern. It's really good of you.'

She doesn't wait for him to complain or ask another question. She just shuts the door, then leans against it and breathes a sigh of relief.

'I told you before. You should whack the old guy. He's nothing but trouble.'

Sure, she thinks. Kill Samuel. Then she'd have to kill his son too before he raised the alarm over his missing father. And then why not kill Miss Frodely too? Throw in the building super and she'd have her six-pack. Just an hour or so's work and she'd have her baby in her arms again.

Right. Because the cops would never figure that one out, would they? Wouldn't dream of questioning her if everybody else in her building got wasted.

She figures that keeping out of the way of the cops is going to be hard enough as it is, without bringing them right to her door.

She wonders what trail of clues they're following right at this minute.

6.49 AM

'Does anybody know what the hell is going on here?' says Cesario.

A small group of detectives is gathered in Cesario's office. Despite the Lieutenant's sartorial splendor, he seems unduly ruffled. Doyle suspects he's already had his ear chewed by the Chief of Detectives about curtailing this purported killing spree before it goes any further.

Eyes fall on Doyle. Which is only right seeing as how he caught the case, but still it's pretty intense pressure.

'We've got two possibly related DOAs, that we know of. There may be more.'

'Wait,' says Cesario. 'Wait a minute. *Possibly* related? They've both got numbers carved in their foreheads, and you say *possibly* related?'

Okay, thinks Doyle, so we're off to a great start here. I get two sentences out and already he's picking holes.

'What I mean is that they're possibly the work of the same killer. We don't know that yet.'

'Anything to suggest it's not the same perp?'

No, thinks Doyle. Nothing concrete. But that's not how it works, and you know that as well as anyone in this room. We don't go making unfounded assumptions. We work with what we have. Otherwise we'd close off paths that should remain open.

'On the surface, there are similarities. The numbers on the heads – that's the most obvious one. The vics were both killed with a knife. They were within a few blocks of each other...'

'But?'

Doyle takes his time searching for the right choice of words, in an attempt to preempt another attack on his views. 'It's the method that's bugging me. The attack on the homeless guy was short and sweet. Two stab wounds, to the gut and the chest – that's it. This second vic, though – this was frenzied. A dozen knife wounds at least. One of them opened up his neck from ear to ear. It was a helluva lot messier than the first one.'

'And that tells you what?'

'I don't know what it tells me. It brings up questions, though. Why not a fast kill like the last one? Why pick someone in a car instead of a guy who's just walking the streets? And why the sexual element this time?'

Cesario furrows his brow. This is news to him. 'The sexual element?'

'Yeah. The driver had his pecker out when we found him.'

Cesario's face registers his surprise. 'You think this could have been a woman did this? A hooker, maybe?'

Doyle shrugs. 'We can't rule it out. I still don't get the difference, though. Why wait for things to get that far? Why not just waste him as soon as he opens his window or the car door?'

From the back of the room, Schneider – the detective who usually partners LeBlanc and who has nothing but contempt for Doyle – pipes up: 'Maybe he always drives around with his dick hanging out. I know I do.'

Jay Holden, a shaven-headed black detective with a vicious looking round scar above one ear, chips in: 'Yeah, but you get away with it 'cause nobody ever notices.'

'Hey,' says Schneider, pointing to his crotch. 'This thing is so visible I can make turning signals with it. And who are you to talk? Even the sparrows ain't interested in your puny little worm.'

'All right,' says Cesario. 'Can we quit this juvenile locker room showdown, please?' He turns to Doyle again. 'Anything from Forensics or the ME?'

'Not yet. Plenty of prints in the car, but too early to say who they might belong to.'

Cesario looks around at the tired, grim-faced detectives. 'What do we know about the victims?'

It's LeBlanc who answers. 'Not much on the homeless guy. He gets called Vern, but that's about it. No full name, no address, and so far, nobody who really knew him. He was a loner. We're hitting the shelters, the churches, all the usual places. The other guy's name is Edwin Steppler. He worked as a kitchen salesman. He's divorced, lives alone near Washington Square Park. We talked to his ex-wife. She didn't seem too grief-stricken over his demise. Says she wouldn't be surprised to learn he spent his nights cruising the streets for fun either.'

'Anything else to connect the two DOAs?'

LeBlanc shakes his head. 'Nothing. These two are chalk and cheese.'

Cesario blows air. 'Okay, so now the big question. These vics are numbers two and three. So where's number one?'

Silence in the squadroom. Nobody wants to answer that one. Doyle feels it's left to him again.

'Most likely scenario is that we just haven't found the body yet. It could turn up in the next five minutes or it might not show up for weeks. Just because they're killed in order doesn't mean we have to find them in order. The alternative is that we've already found the first victim.'

All eyes on Doyle again, most of them puzzled. Cesario gives the question a voice. 'What do you mean by that?'

'A number one is just a vertical slash. It could easily be mistaken for any head wound, especially if there are other cuts on the body. What I'm saying is that maybe we've already had a DOA fitting that description and we just didn't assume it was numbered.'

Cesario nods slowly. It's a good thought, and Cesario knows it. See, thinks Doyle, I'm not just a pretty face. Which, by the way, I've proved to you before, Lieutenant.

'All right. Check the files, especially the autopsy reports. See if any precinct caught a DOA with a head wound that could be interpreted as a number one.'

He pauses for a moment. 'Now the even bigger question. How do we stop this whacko before there's a number four?'

Doyle goes to answer, but LeBlanc lets him off the hook. 'We put out an APB on this. Everyone is looking for this perp. Stop and frisk is the order of the day. Short of alerting the public to be more vigilant, there's not much else we can do.'

Cesario shakes his head. 'The last thing we want is to cause panic out there. But if this continues we're gonna have to release it to the press.' He points a warning finger at his detectives. 'What I don't want to leak out is this numbering thing. The media already know about the marks left on the homeless guy, but I want to keep it at that. Don't go spreading stories about some kind of body counting system. There's a difference between alerting people and scaring them out of their wits. Shit, it gives me the creeps just thinking about it.' He raises his hand as if to run it through his hair, then seems to think better of mussing it up. 'All right, get out there and catch this maniac, before someone feels it necessary to wake up the mayor.'

As he leaves, Doyle ponders the task of finding the killer. He's got the uneasy feeling that all the detective work in the world might not be of much help here. If they get anywhere with this case, it'll probably be through sheer chance or coincidence rather than brilliant sleuthing.

But unless Lady Luck gets off her lazy ass and helps them out soon, somebody else is going to die.

7.45 AM

'*'m not asking you to get ready for a freaking catwalk, Erin. Just choose a damn coat!*'

She's in the bedroom, taking out clothes from her closet, examining them, and putting them back again.

'It's not easy,' she snaps. 'It's not like guys' clothes. Most of my coats don't have inside pockets.' She takes down a blue padded jacket. Unzips it and looks inside. Bingo.

'This'll have to do,' she says.

'*Finally! Okay, now go over to the mirror and swap the brooch over. You'll have to make a hole in the jacket to thread the wire through, and that means—*'

'You want me to make a hole in my jacket?'

'*Yes, Erin. A hole. It's not the worst thing you've made a hole in recently, so quit bitching. Attach the brooch in exactly the same way as it was on your other coat. You'll have to unplug the wire from the box again to thread it through, and that means I'll lose the picture and sound, so I'm giving you exactly five seconds to reconnect. You understand, Erin? Five seconds. One second over and you're gonna hear little Georgia scream till her lungs explode.*'

'Yes. I understand.'

She goes to the bedroom mirror. She is dressed in a tight gray sweater and black pants, the brooch pinned over her left breast and the transmitter box bulging in her pocket. Getting dressed was an experience. He insisted on having her in full view the whole time. She had to prop the brooch up against a table lamp. She kept the bathrobe on while she dressed her lower half, then kept her back to the camera while she slipped off the robe and put on her brassiere and sweater. Throughout, she made no attempt to be sexy about it. She was far too shaken by what had occurred during her earlier scheme to be making devious plans for the future.

She opens a drawer in her dresser and takes out a pair of nail scissors. She puts their sharp point to the shiny cloth of her coat and begins to twist it as she drives it through to the other side. Wouldn't it be great, she thinks, if this was his throat? Turning and pushing sharp scissors into his jugular. Wouldn't that be so satisfying, so much fun? Or, even better, his eyeballs. Yes. His eyeballs. I could do that. I could happily blind him. It would be such a fitting penalty for all the staring at me he's been doing. And then on to his other soft fleshy areas. Oh, yes.

'All right, Erin. Now the wire. Five seconds, remember?'

Yeah, I remember, jerk-off. I remember everything you said and did. It'll stay in my brain long after I've killed you.

She unplugs the wire from its box, pushes it quickly through the hole in her coat, whispers 'I am so going to enjoy watching you die' to the disconnected brooch, then reattaches the cable.

'Good girl. Now get the coat on, and we're ready to roll.'

She drops the box into the inside pocket and pins the brooch in place. Then she slips the coat on and stares at herself in the mirror.

Back to normal again. Clean, tidy, dressed. Not caked in clotting blood. Who would guess what horrors she committed during the night? Who would guess that she's about to do it all again?

'The knife, Erin. Go get the knife.'

Reluctantly, she tears herself away from her mirror-image, then goes through to the bathroom. The knife is on the edge of the basin. She picks it up by her fingertips. She's not convinced it's completely clean. Look there – isn't that a spot of crimson?

'Erin? What's the problem?'

She looks up. Sees herself again, in the bathroom mirror this time. Only now she has a knife in her hands. It takes away the normality she had achieved. From Jekyll to Hyde in the time it takes to pick up a knife.

'I can't,' she says. 'I can't go through that again.'

'Erin, we went over this. I told you—'

'No. It's not just the killing. It's the blood. It got everywhere last time. I was covered in it. I was lucky nobody saw me. But now it's busy out there. I can't walk around with blood all over me. I won't get five yards.'

'Then don't make such a mess of it next time. Hell, you practically sawed that guy's head off. Do it like you did with the wino. A simple stab through the heart – that's all it takes.'

'There'll still be blood.'

'Yes, in all probability, there will still be some blood loss. For fuck's sake, Erin, what do you want me to say? Unless you can perfect the art of knife throwing in the next five minutes, you're out of options.'

She continues to stare at herself. Her image keeps getting replaced by an earlier one. When she was drenched in blood. When it was clinging to her, clawing at her.

'I… I need another weapon.'

'What? What kind of weapon? Oh, yeah, I forgot. There's that rocket launcher you keep in your underwear drawer. Get real, Erin.'

'Stop making fun of me. I'm serious. I need a different way of doing this.'

A pause. A sigh. Then: *'Okay. What about your hammer?'*

She thinks about this. Wonders why he said *'your* hammer.' Not *a* hammer. Not go out and buy a hammer. How does he know she has a hammer? She doesn't have many tools, but a hammer she does possess. Mr Wiseman lent it to her when she told him she needed to fix a loose floorboard.

A hammer? Yes, maybe. Maybe that would be okay. Surely there would be a lot less blood that way.

'All right,' she says. She walks through to the kitchen area. Opens the cabinet beneath the sink. There it is, sitting innocently on top of a box of soap powder. Just waiting to be called on to do something useful. Like knocking in nails. Or caving in skulls.

She puts down the knife on the counter, then bends to pick up the hammer. She hefts it in her hand. It's heavy. Those two vicious-looking claws sweeping back from the solid head as if it has been streamlined for maximum momentum. In the wrong hands – and her hands couldn't be more wrong – it could do some serious damage.

'*Happy now? Sure you don't need to go to Central Park to pick up a few boulders?*'

'It… It won't fit in my pocket.'

'*Then take a fucking purse! Jeez, do I have to do all your thinking for you? Put it in your purse along with your tissues and your lipstick and all the other crap you women carry everywhere you go.*'

She closes the cabinet. Turns to head back to the bedroom.

'*Oh, and Erin… Take the knife along too. You're still gonna need it. For what comes later, you know?*'

8.31 AM

'**D**OYLE!'

Crap, thinks Doyle. What have I done now? He looks up to see Cesario summoning him into his office. Whatever happened to courteous invitations? A cheery note would be nice: 'Lieutenant Cesario would appreciate your company at a little get-together at his place; bring cakes' – that type of thing.

Doyle gets up from his desk and heads toward his boss's lair. Cesario hasn't been in the job all that long, and Doyle feels he hasn't really figured the man out yet. Sometimes he seems okay; other times he acts like a complete asshole. In the past he has given Doyle breaks when things haven't been going well, but he has also landed on him like one of those cartoon ton weights when he's decided that Doyle has pushed things too far. Which, Doyle admits, he is somewhat prone to do.

So let's be positive. Maybe this is one of the give-the-guy-a-break moments.

'I just had a very interesting conversation with a guy at the water cooler,' says Cesario.

Then again, maybe it's not.

'Uh-huh,' says Doyle. Because a little chat with Albert could be about any one of a billion things, selected at random.

'About numbers mostly. But also about why Oreos are the wrong shape. You wanna tell me about him?'

'Uhm, yeah. He's a suspect.'

'For what?'

'A homicide.'

'A homicide.'

'Yeah.'

'And who do we think he might have killed?'

'His mother.'

'His mother. Okay. And did he?'

'That's the thing. We don't know. He says he did it, but that's all he'll say. He won't give us his address. He won't even tell us his name. I call him Albert because he's a fan of Albert Einstein. You know, the scientist?'

'Yes, Doyle. I have heard of Einstein. Believe it or not, some of the bosses in the NYPD actually went to school. So how did he come to be a collar?'

'He just walked into the house. Gave himself up. There was blood all over his shirt.'

'So what's his status now?'

'Pending, I guess. I'm trying to get somebody from Psych Services to come in and talk to him. I'm also trying to find out where he lives, but, well... he ain't exactly top priority right now.'

Cesario nods. Leans back in his chair. Here it comes, thinks Doyle.

'Okay,' says Cesario. 'So far so good. Now here's the thing that's bothering me. What the hell is he doing by the water cooler?'

Doyle shrugs. 'It fascinates him. And he likes playing with the cups.'

'He's a homicide suspect, Doyle. You just told me that. Since when do we leave homicide suspects sitting by the water cooler?'

'It's not like he's gonna poison it, Lou. I got nowhere else to put him.'

Cesario pulls a face like he thinks Doyle is the village idiot. 'How long have you been a detective, Detective? This guy may have just wasted his own mother, and you think he should be left to roam around a police station house? Hell, he's not even cuffed. What were you thinking? You know the rules. Get enough on him to charge him, then get his ass down to Central Booking. Until then, lock him up, just like we do with all the suspects. With everything that's going on right now, we haven't got time to be chasing after people who decide they want to play games. Now get him outta here. I don't want him hanging around my squadroom anymore. Got it?'

Doyle nods. 'Got it.' He turns, then halts in the doorway. 'By the way, what's wrong with the shape of Oreos?'

He sees Cesario raise a warning finger, then decides not to wait for an answer.

He goes and finds Albert, who has seemingly tired of examining plastic cups and is now bent right over and staring down at his shoes – the sneakers with the laces wrapped all the way around them.

'Albert?'

Albert doesn't look up. His head twitches as he flicks his gaze from one foot to the other and back again.

'Whatcha looking for, Albert?'

'I'm checking.'

'Checking? Checking for what?'

'Balance.'

'Balance?'

'Yeah. They have to be the same, or my balance goes kooky.'

'Well, I wouldn't want for your balance to get all kooky. Is that why you tie your laces all the way around your sneakers like that? To help your balance?'

'No, that'd be ridiculous. It just holds them on better.' He ventures a glance across at Doyle's shoes. 'You should try it. Yours don't look very secure at all. How do you run after criminals with loose shoes like that? Plus, they're dirty.'

Doyle checks out his shoes. 'You got me there, Albert. I should definitely do something about my slack footwear here. Listen, you mind coming with me?'

'Yeah.'

'What, yes you mind, or you don't mind?'

'No.'

Unsure as to what answer he's been given, Doyle makes it less complicated: 'Come on, Albert. Walk this way with me.'

'Walk this way,' Albert sings. 'That's by Run DMC. Of course, they didn't tie laces in their sneakers at all. Not at all. That's crazy. They could get hurt.'

'Foolhardy,' Doyle agrees. 'What kind of role models are they, huh? Come on, Albert.'

He leads him down the hall, and then into one of the interview rooms. The one containing what the detectives call the cage – actually an area on the far side of the room, penned off from the rest by steel mesh. In the center of the room is a table and chairs, and along one wall is a large, two-way mirror.

'Take a seat for a minute, will ya?' says Doyle.

Albert lowers himself warily onto one of the plastic chairs, but keeps twisting his head toward the cage.

'Okay, Albert, here's the deal. You can tell me where you live and exactly what happened, and then we can clear up this whole mess. Or – listen to me here, Albert – I have to lock you up. Now what's it to be?'

'The water cooler. I like it by the water cooler. It makes funny noises.'

'No, Albert. The water cooler is not an option anymore. Are you gonna tell me where you live, so we can see what happened to your mother?'

Albert looks at his feet again. 'I think I need to re-tie my laces. I feel a bit kooky.'

Doyle sighs. 'All right, Albert. Get on your feet.'

'Aw, Jeez. Don't wanna go, don't wanna go.'

'Albert, it's okay. Chill. I'm not gonna take you downstairs again. Not to the cells. I know how you hate it down there, and I wouldn't do that to you. But here's the thing. My boss says I gotta put you somewhere safe, and that means putting you into this little room here. You see it?'

Doyle points toward the cage, and Albert ventures another glance at it.

'In there? That's for people? It's not for dogs, or rabbits?'

'No, it's not for animals, although I'm not so sure about some of its previous occupants. What do you think? It ain't exactly the Waldorf Astoria, but would you mind sitting in there for me? I'll keep checking on you. Later I'll bring you something to eat, maybe a soda. How's that sound?'

'Seven-Up. I like Seven-Up.'

'Seven-Up it is. You cool with this?'

'No dogs?'

'No dogs.'

'A rabbit would be okay, though. I like rabbits.'

'I'll see what I can do. Go ahead, Albert. Try it out.'

Albert gets off his chair. He shuffles into the cage and looks around at his new surroundings.

Gently, so as not to alarm his prisoner, Doyle closes and locks the door. 'All right in there, Albert? I'll be right back. Make yourself comfortable on the bench there.'

Albert sits himself down on the extreme end of the wooden bench that is bolted to the floor.

'Monkeys,' he says. 'This place would be good for monkeys.'

10.15 AM

This is proving more difficult than she thought.

It was never going to be easy anyway, but the streets are busier now. Much busier. It was even worse during the rush hour, but it's still bad enough.

She has been wandering the street for over two hours now. Trying to figure out how she's going to do this.

For one thing, it's got to be someone she dislikes. Hates with a passion, preferably. That creep in the car was so much easier to deal with than Vern. It was almost a pleasure to dispatch him. Well, no, not a pleasure. Let's not get carried away here. It could hardly be called a pleasure to open up any human being like that. But let's just say it wasn't such a hardship – not after what he tried to do to her. He was sick. A stain on humanity. Who did he think he was, treating me like that? Where did he get the idea that—

Okay, Erin. Calm down. He's the past, and now we have to think about the future. Move on.

So, back to the point. Which is that she's still massively upset about Vern, and she's not nearly so saddened by the demise of Mr Creepy. Conclusion – she should stick to people she wouldn't be inclined to piss on if they were on fire.

Problem is, where do you find people like that? If you're new to a city, and you don't really know anyone well enough to like or dislike them, where the hell do you start? Night-time was different – that's when all the disease-ridden cockroaches come out to play. But now? It's just a sea of people. Normal people. People who are going shopping or dining or to get their hair done or to place a bet or to meet friends. People who don't even notice me and who have no opinion about me. People who, in particular, harbor no thought of copping a feel or trying to make me gag on their genitalia.

She has tried to come up with a mental list of suitable candidates. In her head she scribbled a title: 'People I Could Willingly Kill.' Then her imaginary pen moved down the page and…

… and that's as far as she got. She toyed with the idea of adding the woman who works in the drugstore, but being a little snotty with customers doesn't really count as a capital crime. Then there was that guy who was leering at her through her window when she was in her underwear. Okay, so maybe not leering. And yes, he did have an excuse to be there, seeing as how he was the window cleaner. And actually, he was kinda cute… Okay, so what about that coffee vendor who called her a bitch? Sure, except that he might have been saying that she must be *rich*, because she forgot to pick up her change. His pronunciation wasn't so good.

See? See my problem? Encountering people to hate isn't easy, even when you're on a mission to seek them out. All these people, and not one of them with a victim sign hanging above their heads.

All these people. Which is, of course, another problem. She needs to be around people to pick out the rotten apples, but she needs to be away from people so she can do what needs to be done. It's a Catch-22 situation. How the hell can she walk up to someone and bop them on the head with a hammer, and then expect to get away with it?

She's beginning to think she should have gotten it over with during the hours of darkness. A mad dash around the East Village, decimating its population of undesirables and ne'er-do-wells. There are some who would give out medals for such community spirit. She could be Gotham's next caped crusader.

Listen to me, trying to make light of this. What am I thinking? I have a hammer and a knife in my purse. I'm the grim reaper. Could that be any more serious? Someone – maybe you, or you, or you – is about to die at my hands. How can I be so cavalier?

Because I have to be. It's precisely because this is oh so fucking serious that I can't give it the serious consideration it deserves. If I did, I wouldn't be here. I wouldn't even be able to step out of my apartment building. I would stay in my bedroom and I would crumble and I would lose my baby.

And in that realization, it seems to her that the people around her take on a new dimension. They mutate from a milling collection of innocents into a seething mass of distrustful and cynical beings. They sense her anxiety and her predatory nature. They are a herd of wildebeest, alert to this lioness on their territory, waiting tensely for her to pounce. They know, and they are ready for her, and they will fight with every fiber they possess to protect themselves. And somewhere out here, somewhere in their midst, is…

'I'm getting bored, Erin.'

Yeah, him. He's out there. Maybe not far away. A mile? Yards? Feet?

You. Yeah, you. The guy with the headphones. Is that really music you're listening to? And that iPod or whatever it is you're holding, is that picking up the video feed from this ugly piece of crap fastened to my coat? And what have you done with Georgia? Where have you left her?

Aargh! This is crazy! I'm losing it. This torture is frying my brain, and soon I won't be able to function at all.

'Did you hear me? I said I'm getting bored.'

He checks in every few minutes. Just to let her know he hasn't gone away. Just a gentle reminder that he's with her at every step. Like a tooth-ache that keeps flaring up.

She puts a hand over her mouth as she speaks. Just in case anyone should think she's mentally unbalanced. They shouldn't think that. A serial murderer is all she is.

'What do you expect me to do about it? Why don't you go put the TV on or wash your socks or something? I can't rush into this.'

'Just saying, is all. I thought you were more decisive than this.'

'Yeah, well that just goes to show how you don't really know me at all.'

'Oh, I think I know you well enough, Erin. Better than you know your-self, in some ways.'

There he goes again. His claims to supernatural knowledge of my mental processes. Well how about this, Svengali? See that picture in my mind of a hand flipping you the finger? See that, asshole?

She walks some more. She's pretty tired of walking, and she's actually feeling hungry. She didn't think she'd be able to eat anything today, but now her stomach is rumbling. She spies a small coffee shop just up the street, and heads toward it.

As she draws level, she realizes that it's a tiny place. Three tables in the window, with two chairs apiece, and a counter along the far wall. But every chair is taken, there's a line for service, and the staff have big smiley faces. Good enough. She enters, and waits her turn.

'Erin, what are you doing?'

She can't answer, not in here. So she just beams him some more telepathic messages. Like: Go fuck yourself.

'Wasting time, Erin. Wasting valuable time.'

She rummages in her purse. Takes out the cellphone that she has hardly used since she came to New York. She types a text message on its screen, then holds it up in front of the brooch. It says: Hungry. Leave me alone.

She puts the phone away, then stares through the glass counter at the muffins and the cookies. She can hear the bubbling and the spouting of steam, and the smell of coffee on the air is potent. But then another noise catches her ear. Nobody else notices, but Erin does.

A gurgle. Not of a coffee making machine, but of a baby.

She cranes her head and looks up the line. Sees that the woman at the front is carrying a baby in a papoose. It's tiny, almost lost in all the layers of clothing it's wearing. Its face is all scrunched up and its eyes tightly closed.

The pang of loss stabs Erin in the heart. That should be me, she thinks. Doing stuff with my baby. Ordinary stuff like wandering into coffee shops, and then maybe later going shopping for baby clothes. Watching the faces of people as they coo over the baby and ask questions about her. Does she sleep well? What's her name? Where did you buy that adorable hat?

That should be me. That *was* me.

He ruined it. He took it all away. He cut us in two.

Then she sees the man. He's big and dark and grim-looking. Dressed in a leather jacket, jeans and black Doc Martens. He marches in off the street and straight up to the front of the line. No apologies or explanations. Just pushes right in there.

'Excuse me,' he says, but then doesn't even give the staff time to reply before he adds, 'Hey! You!'

Behind the counter, a young Hispanic girl turns to look at him. 'I'm sorry, sir, but you'll have to wait in line.'

'No,' he says, loudly so that everyone in the shop can hear. 'I did that already. What's wrong with your memory? It was only about a minute ago.'

Another Hispanic staff member bustles across. 'That was me, sir. I'm the one who served you. Is there a problem?'

He looks at her as if to say, *How dare you have a similar appearance to that other girl? You got a policy of trying to confuse your customers?*

'A problem? Yeah, there's a problem.' He holds aloft the paper cup he's carrying. 'This is a latte, and I ordered a cappuccino.'

'Actually,' says the girl. 'I'm pretty sure you ordered a latte.'

'Well, pretty sure ain't the same as absolutely sure, now is it? You got it wrong, sister. I know what I ordered. It was a cappuccino. But that's not what you gave me. Do you understand what I'm saying to you?'

He says his last sentence slowly, as if to imply that the girl is either stupid or lacking in her comprehension of English. He also keeps his volume up, because clearly he's a man who enjoys an audience.

'Yes, sir,' says the girl. 'I understand perfectly. Would you like me to exchange it for a cappuccino?'

'Yes, I would. I would like a cappuccino. Like I freaking well asked for in the first place. But now that you've admitted it was your mistake, I think you should give me my money back too.'

The woman shakes her head. 'I'm sorry, sir. I can't do that. I can give you a cappuccino or I could give you your money back, but I can't do both. I don't think that would be fair.'

Erin looks around. Everyone in the place has been stunned into an anxious silence. Waiting to see what happens. Hoping this will be settled amicably and the man will take his coffee and leave them in peace. Hoping that it doesn't get any nastier than it already is.

'Fair? What do you mean, fair? You messed up, sister. All I'm asking is that you make a little restitution for your mistake. A little compensation. That's what I think would be fair. Is that so much to ask?'

'Sir, would you like me to make you a cappuccino? Is that what you'd like me to do?'

The man sighs. A deeply exaggerated expression of his unhappiness. 'Why is this so hard for you to understand? Am I talking in Swahili here?' He turns on his heel, sweeping his hard gaze across the other customers, none of whom seem capable of meeting his eye. 'Anyone else here think this is so difficult to grasp?'

He turns back to the girl, who is trying to stand her ground but is looking more and more like she's about to run away in tears. 'One more time. I'll speak nice and slow, just for you. Give me my fucking money back, get me a cappuccino, stick this latte up your fat ass, and then everyone is happy. All right?'

'Sir, I'm sorry—'

'NO!'

The slam of his palm on the countertop is like the sound of a firecracker. The girl takes a whole step backward. Erin notices that the baby also jumps at the sound, and then it opens its mouth to scream.

'No,' the man repeats. 'No excuses. You're already in my bad books for fucking up my day, so don't make it any worse for yourself, okay?'

And that's when the mother decides to step in. It was an uncomfortable enough situation already, but now her baby has been alarmed, and that's a step too far. That's over the line.

'Hey,' she says, 'would you mind cooling it a little? You're upsetting my baby.'

The man rounds on her, eyes blazing. 'For one thing, I wasn't talking to you. For another, why the fuck do you bring a baby to a coffee shop if it's peace and quiet you want? Why don't you take it to a fucking church or a library or something?'

'Woo-hoo,' says Erin's commentator. '*Which charm school did this bozo go to?*'

As if responding to the verbal assault, the baby steps up its crying. The woman starts to stroke its back and bounce it gently while she sends hushing noises at it. Erin can feel her own anguish building. This baby is younger than Georgia, but still she can picture her own child making these screams. This is like an attack on herself and her baby, and she finds herself being inexorably drawn into this conflagration.

Says the woman, 'The girl told you what she can do. She made you a good offer. She didn't even have to do that. It's a cup of coffee, for crying out loud. What's the big deal?'

And now the man is squaring up to her. Straightening up and showing her how tall and broad and immovable he is. Demonstrating what a fine specimen of testosterone-fueled manhood he is.

'Oh, shut the fuck up, bitch. This ain't none of your business. You or your ugly little rug-rat. Keep your big nose out of it.'

The baby screams louder. The sound drills into Erin's skull and sets her brain on fire. Through the flames she sees images of Georgia. Sees her lying on her back, fists clenched and cheeks red-hot as she throws every ounce of her little might into pleading for her mother's help.

'Are you thinking what I'm thinking, Erin?'

Erin steps out of the line. An I-am-Spartacus moment.

'Hey! What is it with you? You got a complaint, fine. You don't have to make an asshole out of yourself to do it.'

The man turns his gaze on her now. He looks dumbfounded at first, then he finds his voice again.

'What the hell is this place? A dykes' convention or something? Am I upsetting one of the chief rug-munchers here?'

'Ha! This guy's a hoot. Is he on something?'

There was a time when Erin would have stayed silent. There was a time when, faced with aggression like this, she would have slinked into a corner and cowered. This time, though, something makes her refuse to back down.

'What is it with you? Why do you have to be like this? Why can't you just be nice?'

The man takes a few steps toward her. Erin brings her hand up and rests it on the mouth of the tan leather bag slung over her shoulder. Come on, she thinks. Try it with me, asshole. Let's see how those muscles of yours cope with a pound of steel coming at your ugly face.

'Nice?' he says. 'Nice? Jesus. And people wonder why the country's falling apart.' He points to the girl behind the counter. 'She fucked up. All I'm doing is letting her know about it, in words she might just understand. Nice don't get you nowhere.'

'First of all,' says Erin, 'we might all understand you better if you spoke proper English. Second of all, I believe the girl when she said it was your mistake. And thirdly… you're an asshole. And that means you deserve zip.'

'Great speech, Erin. Very succinct. Were you in the school debating team?'

She sees his face harden. It tells her he is no stranger to violence and intimidation. They are tools he will deploy as readily as most would attempt rational debate. When he steps even closer to her, she allows her fingers to dip into the bag.

'What did you say?' he asks.

The baby continues to cry. Everyone else hides behind its wail. Nobody voicing an opinion or coming to her aid.

But still she doesn't back off. From somewhere she finds the courage to play him at his own game.

'Now who doesn't understand? You want me to say it again, nice and slow and loud like you did with the girl?'

'Go, Erin. I think you're winning on ball size here.'

'You say one more fucking word, bitch, and I'll make sure you never speak again.'

'Them's fighting words. Does he know who he's talking to? Maybe you need to show him Mr Hammer.'

'Uh-huh?' she says. 'You get off on hitting women, is that it? Is this really about the coffee, or are you just fulfilling your pathetic need to demonstrate that you can be tougher than a woman? Is that it? Something to do with the size of your dick, maybe?'

He's on her then. Too fast for her to respond. He has his huge hand clamped around her throat and he's pushing her up against the glass fronted cabinet containing all those muffins and cookies, and his body is tight against hers, so tight that she cannot move her right arm, cannot push it into the bag and grab the hammer, cannot fight him off, and God what have I done, why did I think I could deal with this situation, why didn't I just keep my big stupid mouth shut?

He puts his face right up to hers. When he speaks she can feel the spittle flying from his mouth. He says, 'Don't you *ever* talk to me like that. Do you understand? Well, do ya, bitch?'

She tries to twist and turn, to get that arm free, to get those fingers to the wooden handle in her bag. Around her now there is consternation. The woman with the baby yelling at him to let Erin go. The serving girl announcing that she's calling the cops. The baby still screaming, screaming, screaming like Georgia.

And then suddenly he releases her and steps away. He looks around at everyone in that small, cramped space, utter disdain on his face.

'This is a fucking shithole,' he says. 'Keep your fucking coffee.'

He pulls back the hand still holding the coffee. Launches the cup at the girl behind the counter. She ducks, and the cup explodes against the wall, its contents bursting across the shop. Erin feels a few drops of the hot liquid hit her on the side of the neck. Her hand finally finds the hammer. She grips it tightly, thinking, Come back here. Try that again now I'm ready for you.

But he doesn't come back. He marches toward the door, flings it open so hard it slams against the back of a chair in which an old lady is seated, then leaves.

Erin takes a step forward, feeling dazed and confused, her eyes on the street outside. People are talking to her, babbling. She catches fragments of the chatter. They're asking her if she's okay. Saying what an asshole the guy was. The Hispanic girl is thanking her and offering her anything she wants, on the house. But rising above it all is one voice.

'What are you waiting for, Erin?'

And he's right. She was on the verge of taking that guy's head off. Would've done it too if she'd been able to get to her weapon. Isn't that what she's been looking for all morning? Well, isn't it, Erin?

She leaves. Ignoring the blizzard of concerns and the all-too-late outrage, she gets out of there.

She starts walking up the street, in the direction the man went, but she can't see him anywhere. She picks up her pace, her eyes scanning the street ahead for any sign of her quarry. Where is he, damn it?

She reaches the pizzeria at the end of the block. The pedestrian lights are against her. Did he beat them? Is he already on the next block, putting further space between them?

And then she sees him. Not ahead, but to her right. He'd turned the corner, and now he's heading downtown. She pulls away from the knot of people waiting to cross, and hastens after the man.

She follows him for another block. She checks the street signs. They're on Pitt Street. Ahead she can see the low, slanted beginnings of the Manhattan Bridge. There are fewer people on the sidewalks here, because there's nothing to see. No stores or restaurants; just tall brown apartment buildings. It suddenly occurs to her that if he should happen to turn, he will spot her instantly. As she walks, she reaches into her bag and takes out her woolen hat and scarf. They were knitted for her by Clark's grandmother. She puts on the hat. Pulls it low over her forehead, then wraps the scarf around her neck and across her face, so that only her eyes are now showing. It's not that cold right now, but it's the best makeshift disguise she can manage. Whatever that maniac remembers of her, it will not be that she was wearing bright red knitwear.

The man takes a left. Up a narrow path and into one of the buildings. Erin's pace becomes almost a jog. If he leaves the lobby before she gets there, she'll never find him in this huge monolith.

She pushes through the door, breathes a sigh of relief through the scarf as she sees he is still there, waiting for the elevator to arrive. Alongside him is a broad-shouldered black woman, resting her substantial bones on an aluminum walking-frame. The lobby is dimly lit and smells of industrial cleaning fluid. One of the fluorescent lighting tubes flickers as if sending out Morse code.

Erin focuses on the man. She notices he is now wearing earphones, the white leads trailing down to his side pocket. He taps the fingers of his right hand on his thigh, and she wonders what he's listening to. She bets it's nothing as the interesting as the transmissions she picks up on her own earpiece.

'Why not do 'em both?'

Right on cue again. I think of him, and he jumps in. Uncanny.

'Go on, Erin. Nobody will see you here. That'll take you up to four in one swoop. What's to think about?'

She turns her gaze on the woman. Tries to imagine herself caving in the back of her skull. No. It's not an image she's comfortable with. She couldn't do it.

But *this* guy... Well, that's a different matter.

She fingers the handle of the hammer again. She could do it right now. Just step up to him and bam! The old lady wouldn't be able to stop it. Wouldn't know what the hell was going on.

But not yet. Wait. Patience. Choose your moment carefully.

The elevator arrives and the door stutters open. The three of them shuffle inside. Erin watches the man's face as his eyes pass briefly over her and register no interest. Good. No need for a fight just yet.

Erin leans against the rail at the back and waits for the others to select their floors. There are twenty in all. The man hits 17, but doesn't bother to ask what anyone else might want. He just faces out into the lobby and puts his hands in his pockets. The woman makes a smacking sound with her lips as she slowly locates the button for the fifth floor. Then she looks over at Erin.

'You got a floor, or just here to enjoy the ride?'

She laughs after she says this. A breathless cackle that turns into a phlegm-filled cough.

Erin reaches across and stabs the top button, just as the door squeals shut.

'End of the line, huh?' says the woman. 'Nice view from up there.'

Erin just nods and smiles with her eyes, the rest of her face still hidden behind her scarf.

The elevator hauls itself painfully up through the building, rattling and shaking as it goes. Erin stands in silence, staring at the back of the man's head. She can hear the tinny beat of his music. Gangsta rap, she guesses. It would suit him. Stuff about killing cops and abusing women and taking drugs. Yeah, that's him, all right.

The elevator slows, if going any slower were possible, then grinds to a halt. Its door struggles with the effort of opening. The man makes little effort to move aside as the old lady squeezes her walker past him, and he snaps her a look of disgust when she brushes against his arm. She is hardly through the opening before he stabs angrily at the button to close the door again, and when she has gone he shakes his head in disbelief at the gall of the woman.

And then they're moving again. Alone. Just him and her. He's nodding his head and tapping his fingers and listening to crap about what it's okay to do to women because they're worthless anyhow, and she's slipping her fingers around that handle again, closing them tightly around that hammer, thinking about what he did to her, what he said to her, the sheer contempt he exhibited toward her, and when other thoughts try to push their way in – wishy-washy liberal thoughts about how maybe he just had a bad day, maybe he lost his job, or maybe somebody in his family died, and so his attitude isn't really his fault – she forces them back again, because yes, it is his fault, there can be no excuse for acting as he did, and anyway somebody needs to die, so it may as well be him.

Somebody needs to die? Did I hear you right? Did you really just think that, Erin? This guy *needs* to die?

Fuck off. Yes. He needs to die. There, I said it again. What are you going to do about it?

And now she glances at the floor indicators and sees that they have reached the twelfth, and despite the snail's pace crawl of this box, they'll get to his destination soon, and that could be too late. He will get out and she will have to follow him and he will become suspicious and maybe there will be other people on that floor and her opportunity will be gone, so it's now or never, Erin. Now? Or never?

'*What are you waiting for?*'

So she pictures it again. The scene back in the coffee shop. His hand around her neck as he spits into her face and calls her a bitch and tries to make her feel like the most unworthy pond life, and when she would gladly have brought the hammer out if she had been able to, would happily have smashed it into his ugly, hate-washed face. And it works because now the hammer is out of her bag, it's here in the open, and there in front of her is the back of this man's head, waiting there like a coconut on a shy, just waiting to be struck – two fairground games in one: test your strength and knock the coconut off. Go ahead, Erin, win that fucking coconut and take your prize home…

'I'm not a bitch,' she says.

But he doesn't hear her over his music. He's not interested in anything outside of his own pleasures.

'I said I'm not a bitch.' Louder now. Hear that, asshole? Show me you heard that.

And he does. Or at least she takes it that he does. A twitch of his head to the left and a slightly puzzled brow, as if he's trying to make sense of a phrase that doesn't quite fit in with the other lyrics about bitches and whores.

That'll do it. Say goodbye, creep.

It doesn't go as she expected. Despite the striving for independence symbolized by her move to this city she is not well versed in the use of a hammer, save for the fixing of one floorboard, and that didn't demand much effort. And her only recent thoughts about skull strength – a subject that tends not to dominate her thinking – were in relation to Georgia and the need to protect her soft, expanding dome. Both of these are factors in Erin's woeful lack of force in applying the head of her weapon to the head of her chosen victim.

Oh, it makes a nice enough noise. A kind of thwack that sounds as though it should do some serious damage, all right. But does he drop down dead on the floor? No, he does not. Doesn't even bother to go horizontal. He just yells and clutches his head and bends at the waist. Well, that's hardly good enough, is it? That's hardly what you'd call playing along.

'Again, Erin! Again! Hit that motherfucking sonofabitch!'

So she hits him again. Harder this time. And now the thwack is accompanied by a higher-pitched note that definitely suggests something is breaking. It's like the magnified sound of an egg-shall being cracked open. And this time he does go down. He grunts and he drops, but he's not dead because now he's making all kinds of curious noises that don't even sound human, and worse than that he's reaching a hand out toward Erin – sliding it along that filthy, dusty elevator floor toward her ankles, and she can't allow that, she can't allow him to put his disgusting, women-hating hands on her again, because that would be a violation, that would be all the things in the lyrics still beating into his thick cracked skull, it would be him making women into worthless objects and him making babies cry and him just being a hateful piece of shit that deserves to…

'DIE!'

Thwack!

Down goes the hammer. And *in* goes the hammer. Yes, actually in. She has swung it so hard this time that it has actually penetrated his cranium. It has smashed its way through his bony armor and found his spongy, hate-filled brain. And so now he's flapping about on the floor like a wounded bird, and she wants to vomit and get away from him, but the hammer is stuck, held fast in his head, as if his brain has taken hold of it and refuses to let go in case she strikes again, and while this tug of war goes on, what should happen but for the elevator door to start opening, because this is the seventeenth floor, where this guy lives, welcome home. And her worry now is that there might be other people on the other side of the door, standing there in the hallway, waiting to climb aboard this death capsule. When this door – which, hallelujah, is finding it a struggle to get its aging mechanism to cooperate – finally yawns open and offers up this gruesome spectacle, won't they suspect that all is not quite as it should be?

In her panic, she puts all of her might into freeing the hammer, and away it comes with a sickening crunch and an upheaval of skull fragments that erupt through the man's undulating scalp. Her momentum carries her back-pedaling into the wall of the elevator, and the shuddering of the box seems to act as the kick the door needs to spur itself into action. It opens. Erin pants and stares and waits and tries to decide what she should do next.

There is nobody there.

She is staring into an empty hallway. There is hardly a sound out there. A waft of warmer air carries to her the smell of over-cooked cabbage and stale food. Erin breathes out hard, both to release her tension and to blow away that nauseating smell, and the breath becomes a bark of laughter when she realizes she is holding the hammer out of sight behind her back. How ridiculous is that? What was I going to do – say he was like this when I got in? Say that he turned his music up so loud it blew his brains out? Oh, and this in my hand? Well, I always carry it with me in case there are things need fixing, you know?

Her light-heartedness is fleeting. At her feet, the man twitches, prompting her to raise the hammer in alarm. It has to be a death-throe.

Doesn't it? I mean, he can't still be alive. Not after what I did to him. And just look at what I did. Look at that hole in his head where there isn't meant to be one. Look at that red goo and icky stuff inside the hole. Why did I think this would be so clinical, so clean?

'*Way to go, Erin! That'll clear his head, dontcha think?*'

The voice laughs then. Like this is all just good fun. Like he's watching a TV show. And maybe that's how he sees it. It's just a show, put on for his personal entertainment.

The door starts to close, and panic pulses through her again. Does it always close after a while, or has somebody called the elevator? Are we about to scare the life out of some old lady on a lower floor?

She shoots a hand out and grabs the door's inner edge. It continues to push against her, and for an anxious moment she worries it will crush her fingers into the recess. But then it seems to recognize her resistance, and reluctantly it pulls back.

Okay. So far so good. Now what?

'*Drag him out, Erin. Dump in the hallway, then take the elevator down again.*'

She considers this. 'I was going to leave him here and take the stairs.'

'*Really? As soon as you step out of that elevator, somebody might call it. You think you can make it down seventeen stories before someone finds the body?*'

It's a good point. For once he's actually being helpful.

She wipes the head of the hammer on the man's pants, leaving an oozy red trail there, then puts the hammer back into her bag. She steps into the doorway and bends to grab hold of the man's ankles, then starts pulling. He's heavier than she imagined, or else she's weaker than she believed, and he doesn't move easily. As if with growing impatience, the door attempts to close several times, but each time decides it is not up to the task of cutting through the mass of flesh and bone in its path.

Erin starts to perspire as she heaves the body out. The rap music sounds even louder to her now, as if it's leaking out of the aperture in his skull. Eventually she gets him out of the elevator, and she makes a move to get back in.

'*Hold up, Erin. Aren't you forgetting something?*'

Shit. Not this again.

But she knows she has no choice.

She gets the hammer out again. Places it in the doorway to prevent the door closing. Then she takes out the kitchen knife. Swallowing back her distaste, she does what needs to be done.

Heading back down in the shaky elevator, she meets nobody. And it's not until she's well away from the building that she allows herself to picture some unfortunate person encountering the grisly corpse at the end of their hallway.

12.07 PM

Seventeen floors is a lot of stairs.

There are two elevators in this building, but one is out of action because it's always on the fritz, and the other is out of action because it's now a crime scene and has been halted on the seventeenth floor. That means anybody who wants to get anywhere in this building has to walk. And that includes ace detectives such as Doyle and LeBlanc, who get no special dispensation. As fit as they are, they are huffing and puffing by the time they get close to their destination.

'Aren't you younger than me?' Doyle asks, looking down the steps at his trailing partner. 'Why aren't you racing ahead?'

LeBlanc halts, his hands on his hips as he tries to fill his lungs. 'I'm holding back, old man,' he pants. 'Trying to let you feel good about yourself.'

'Uh-huh? Well, for your information, I feel pretty good already. Least I can climb a few stairs.'

'A few? There's at least a million. If I have a coronary, I'm gonna sue.'

'If you have a coronary, it's because you're outta shape. No wonder you never get the girls.'

'Oh, here we go again with that. I shoulda known you weren't done.'

'Just thinking of you, Tommy. Young, single guy like you should be crawling with babes looking to get hit by the Tommy Gun.'

LeBlanc laughs breathlessly. 'The Tommy...? Shut the fuck up, Cal. Just because you're old and married and have no future, it doesn't mean you can try to live your life through your younger, more handsome partner.'

Doyle turns and carries on up the stairs. With his face now hidden from LeBlanc, he allows his smile to break through.

'Just saying, is all, Tommy. You don't have to get so defensive.'

'Defensive? Who says I'm being defensive?'

'Well, sounds to me like you're protesting a little too much there, pal. It's okay, you know. This is the twenty-first century. You can be whatever you want to be.'

'What?' says LeBlanc, his tone rising in pitch. 'What the hell are you talking about?'

Doyle doesn't answer. His grin is wide now and threatening to break into a laugh, and he doesn't want to put an end to his sport just yet.

They eventually come through the doors on the seventeenth, and both of the detectives have to lean against the wall while they get their breath back.

It's pretty crowded in the narrow hallway. Crime Scene, precinct detectives, homicide detectives, photographers, uniforms and the Medical Examiner all vie for space here. Even though the uniforms are making sure that the area is kept clear of nosy residents, and that potential witnesses on this floor remain inside their apartments until the detectives need to talk to them, it's still a hive of activity. It doesn't help that word has already spread amongst the cops that this is possibly the latest in the string of 'number victims', meaning that everyone wants in on what is potentially a high-profile case.

Norman Chin breaks away from the swarm of people buzzing around the corpse and wanders over to join Doyle and LeBlanc. Unusually for him, he's wearing a smile.

'Join the party, guys,' he says in his solid Brooklyn accent. 'What, a few stairs too much for you? When I was your age, I coulda run up here without breaking a sweat.'

'Don't you start,' LeBlanc mutters.

Chin looks at Doyle and jerks a thumb toward LeBlanc. 'What got up his keister?'

'That's a very good question,' Doyle answers. Feeling the burn of his partner's glare on him, he changes the subject. 'What's that on your face, Norm?'

Chin brings a hand to his cheek. 'What?'

'Sorry. My mistake. I thought it looked a little like a smile.'

'Ha! You guys. Always with the joking around.'

Doyle narrows his eyes. 'Are you feeling okay, Norm? Sure you're not coming down with some kind of winter virus or something?'

'I'm fine. Never better. Which is more than I can say for you two.'

'Why?' LeBlanc asks. 'What's wrong with us? I know you're a medic, but that's the quickest diagnosis I ever heard of.'

'Ha!' Chin exclaims again. 'What I'm trying to say is I'm concerned for your mental wellbeing.'

LeBlanc seizes his chance to take some revenge on Doyle. 'Well, I already knew that about Cal here.'

Doyle glances at him, then shifts his puzzled gaze back onto Chin. 'Norm, what the hell are you talking about?'

'Brain fatigue. Maybe not now, but when you see this guy. I hope you like puzzles.'

'Puzzles? No, I hate puzzles. I like my cases straight. If there's a body, I like to see somebody standing over it with a smoking gun.' He looks over to the knot of people along the hallway. 'Is this our numbers killer or not?'

Chin laughs again. 'You tell me. You're the detectives. Why don't you come over and take a look for yourselves?'

He leads them across, still chuckling. Doyle and LeBlanc exchange mystified glances and pull on their latex gloves.

'Make room! Make room!' says Chin to the row of backs in his way. 'The Eighth Wonders have finally graced us with their presence. Let them see and pronounce judgment.'

Doyle notices how LeBlanc reddens a little at this further embarrassment. Chin always has been a master of making the cops around him feel about two inches tall.

Doyle looks down at the body. Male. Leather jacket and jeans. Music phones in his ears. Hole in his head.

'What is that? Gunshot wound?'

Chin shakes his head, still wearing his smile. 'Blunt force trauma. Somebody hit him with something heavy.'

'And that was the sole cause of death?'

'Far as I can tell here, yes.'

An uneasy feeling creeps into Doyle. If this is a lengthening of the string of victims, then the change of MO is unusual. Worrying, even.

'But this is the next in the sequence, right? This is number four?'

More chuckles. More shaking of the head. And now Doyle is starting to get irritated.

'Norm, I asked you back there if this was our guy. Why the hell didn't you just give it to me straight?'

Chin holds a finger up. Wait. And learn.

'That was a different question,' he says. 'Now you're asking if this is number four.'

Squatting, Chin takes hold of the body and turns it, just enough for the onlookers to see the number carved on its forehead:

'Like I said – I hope you like puzzles.'

12.27 PM

She wishes Clark were here. And hates herself for thinking that way.

She came here to start life afresh. To be a new, independent woman. Bringing up baby all by herself. Making new friends. Maybe starting a new job. She had thought about taking a course. Accountancy, maybe – she's good with figures. Or a computer course. Learn some new skills.

And now she decides she's so pathetic. Thinking about Clark. Wanting him to be here, telling her it'll be okay. And then he'll dash off on his white charger and vanquish the dragon and life will be back to normal. Just like the story books. Happy ever after.

But he's not here. She will have to sort this out herself. And that seems like a gargantuan task at the moment.

'Feeling proud of yourself, Erin?'

Proud? Not exactly the word I have in mind. Try frightened, or inadequate, or weak, or any one of a million descriptions that come nowhere near pride.

'You should be. Half way there, Erin. Half way there, and you still have half the day to go. You're easily on schedule.'

Schedule. Like she's a bus driver or something. Pick 'em up, drop 'em off, move on. So mechanical and effortless you don't even have to think about it.

Except she can think of nothing else. Her mind is filled with images of blood and gore and twitching, dying bodies. She suspects she has seen more of those in half a day than many soldiers see in their whole careers. The likelihood is that she will be permanently scarred by this experience – mentally traumatized and beset by nightmares for the rest of her life. What impact will that have on her relationship with Georgia? Will she get her child back, only to discover that she is no longer capable of looking after her properly? Is this all worth it?

'Could you do this?' she asks.

'Do what, Erin?'

'Kill people. Up close. Could you do that. Have you ever done it?'

A pause. *'Doesn't matter what I've done, or what I could do. What matters is what you're proving to yourself. Look at how you stood up to that guy in the coffee shop. Do you think you could have done that before today?'*

She knows she couldn't. A day ago she would never have had the guts to make even a squeak of complaint about someone acting like that, especially one so aggressive and seemingly capable of handling himself. But she showed him, didn't she? She proved to that sonofabitch what a—

NO!

What am I doing? It's not about that. Don't let him bend your mind like this.

'Is that how you see yourself? As some kind of self-improvement guru? What kind of warped view is that? Or is that just how you choose to defend your actions to yourself? You pretend you're doing some good, helping me out, when all you're really doing is getting your rocks off. You talk about me seeing the light, well how about you facing up to the truth for once? You're a pervert, that's all. You're the one who needs the help, not me. You're sick, but you've deluded yourself into believing you're some kind of savior. I'm right, aren't I? You know I'm right.'

He gives her the silent treatment again. When he does this she never knows whether he's sitting there trying to wash away the pain of her wounding words, or whether he's become bored and switched off while she gets it out of her system. Whichever it is, his calmness when he eventually comes back to her is infuriating.

'You haven't finished the task yet, Erin. Still three more to go. Judge me then, when it's all over.'

'No. I judge you now. There can be no excuse for what you're doing. None. Even if, by some miracle, I get through this and Georgia is in my arms again, even if I discover powers inside me I never knew I had before, you will not go up in my estimation. What you are doing is monstrous. I have never thought this about any human being before, but you deserve to burn in the fires of hell.'

'*Really, Erin? Really? Well, if you insist on getting all holier-than-thou about things, then consider this. Which is worse – someone who takes a baby, but then cares for it and gives it back, or someone who kills three innocent people in cold blood? Which of those two deserves to burn, hmm?*'

'No. Don't even go there. It's not as black-and-white as that, and you know it. You're just as guilty of those killings as I am. Yes, I've done a terrible thing, and I will pay for it one day. But you will pay too. You have a choice in this, but I don't.'

'*You have a choice too, Erin.*'

'What – to give up the life of my baby? You call that a choice? Do you even come close to understanding why that is no choice at all? Are you that detached from your own humanity?'

Another impenetrable silence. She wills him to yell at her. Come on, scream at me. Lose your temper. Show me that I'm getting to you. Show me that the sight of people being slaughtered isn't the only thing that can bring out some emotion in you.

But she fears that's the case. This man is dead inside. The only thing keeping him going is the torture and misery of others. The ability to play God. Isn't that always what the Devil wants most?

And when he finally breaks into her thoughts again, it's not to disabuse her of that view.

'*You never did get that coffee and muffin, did you, Erin? You should eat now. You've got a busy afternoon ahead.*'

1.38 PM

'**I**'m getting a headache.'

This from Lieutenant Cesario. And he's not the only one whose head is pounding with the facts of this case. He has a knot of detectives standing in front of him in his office, all of whom are struggling to wrap their brains around this one.

'Everyone wants to know what the hell we're doing about this. And by everyone, I'm talking about the Captain, the Chief of Detectives, the Commissioner, and even the mayor. And because I'm getting my ass kicked about it, I need to pass the ass-kicking on to you guys. These crimes took place on our turf, so that makes it our problem, and I want to put a stop to this before Homicide South or some other unit solves it and shows us up as fools. So tell me, in simple sentences my aching brain can understand, where we are with this.'

For a while, nobody speaks. There is some shuffling of feet, and a couple of nervous coughs, but nothing of substance. Simple is what the Lieutenant wants; but the simple and truthful answer to where they are right now is 'no place'. The detectives of the Eighth Precinct are nowhere near catching the perpetrator of this string of homicides.

Doyle decides that such negativity, accurate though it might be, is probably not what his boss wants to hear. So he tries to sound upbeat in his summation.

'Okay, we got three male DOAs, each with a different number on his head. What we can't figure out is why the numbers go in the order they do. A two, then a three, then a one. This morning we figured the perp was just counting up, and that we just hadn't seen number one yet. Now it doesn't look that way.'

Cesario sighs, and Doyle reckons he's seeing this for what it is: a whole heap of nothing.

'What does the ME say about the order?'

'Yeah, we thought about that. But Norm says the third guy isn't a dump job. He was definitely killed after the other two. The order is two, three, one – no doubt about it.'

'Two, three, one. What the hell does that mean? Why that particular order?'

Nobody answers. Then Jay Holden pipes up.

'Just a thought. What if it's not a one on this guy? What if the killer started to draw a four, but got disturbed and had to run?'

Silence in the room while everyone thinks about this. All the cops mentally drawing the number four. You might make the vertical stroke first, then add the diagonal and the horizontal to build a four. And if you only got as far as the vertical…

The cops all look at each other, waiting for someone to shoot the theory down.

'It's possible,' says Cesario. 'And to be perfectly frank, I prefer that explanation. Simple counting I can cope with, but some kind of coded message to us I could do without.'

'I don't buy it,' says Doyle, and he senses a slight hostility as he voices his demurral. Cops like simplicity; they hate complicated. Doyle himself wants this to be straightforward. But he has a bad feeling about it.

He says, 'The perp has gone to a lot of trouble to send these signals to us. I don't see it being allowed to go so badly wrong now. There's a big difference between a one and a four. I don't see the perp letting that kind of confusion creep in.'

'But Holden's point is that it wasn't in the plan,' says Cesario. 'Something spooked the killer, and he booked the scene before he could finish writing.'

'This killer doesn't spook easily,' Doyle says. 'From what we can put together, the guy's body wasn't discovered until at least twenty minutes after he was killed. Plenty of time to write a four if you wanted to. Three cuts, right? How long does that take? Not much longer than it takes to make one cut. If I started to draw a four, I'd finish drawing a four.'

Other voices start up in the room now. Everyone arguing over what might have happened and what the killer might have intended.

'Quiet!' yells Cesario, and the hubbub dies down. 'This is all guess-work. Either way, we have a problem. If it was meant to be a four, then we still haven't found number one. If it was meant to be a one, then I don't know what the hell we've got here.'

Cesario puts his index fingers to his throbbing temples. 'For the sake of argument, let's suppose it was meant to be a one on this guy's head. Is there anything about the three vics that would make that sequence of numbers meaningful? Anything at all?'

LeBlanc consults the notes in his hand. 'The latest DOA is William Fischer. Unemployed. Lived with his girlfriend until she moved out last week. Neighbors say he's an asshole. Plays his music too loud, gets into arguments – like that.'

'Okay, so putting them in numerical order gives us Fischer, then Vern the homeless guy, then Steppler the kitchen salesman. What does that tell us?'

Silence.

'Anyone see a pattern of any kind?'

More silence.

'Shit,' says Cesario. 'Me either. Can anybody give me some good news? Something positive in this mess?'

'Yeah,' says Doyle. 'Mrs Darby.'

'Who the hell is Mrs Darby?'

'Old lady lives on the fifth floor. She got into the elevator with Fischer on the first floor. Says another woman got in with them too.'

'Another woman? You manage to locate her?'

'Nope. Not much of a description either. She was wearing a red woolen hat and a scarf around her face. But when Mrs Darby got out at her floor, this other woman stayed in the elevator with Fischer.'

Cesario considers this. 'Steppler got his pecker out for someone in his car. Is that what this is? Is our serial killer a woman?'

Doyle shrugs. 'Could be. Norm says Fischer was killed in the elevator, before being dragged into the hallway. On the rough timings we've got, it could be the one Mrs Darby saw.'

Cesario addresses the gathered group. 'Find this woman. Check every apartment in that building. Put an alert out for any woman wearing a red woolen hat and scarf – I don't care if that means stopping ten thousand of 'em. And find out what Fischer was doing before he came into his building. She might have followed him there. If she did, I want to know exactly where she followed him from.' He pauses, becomes thoughtful again. 'Something else I don't get. The change in MO. Quick stabbing for the first guy, frenzied attack for the second, then a completely different weapon for the third. There's no consistency.'

Again he gets no answers – just the silent thought balloons of a million other questions hanging in the air. Why is this woman doing this? Is she just whacko, or is there some rational thought process taking place here? How does she select her victims? Randomly, or with precision?

And who's next?

1.57 PM

'*You're not eating.*'

'I had some toast.'

'*You had one small triangle of toast. That's not enough. You need energy.*'

'I'm not hungry.'

'*You should eat.*'

'If I eat, I'll throw it back up. I don't want it.'

She gets a feeling of déjà vu. Back to when she was a teenager and she'd fallen out with her boyfriend – some dickhead called Brian – and her mother was trying to persuade her to eat, even though she truly believed she would never be able to eat again, because her world had come to an end.

Oh, for such trivial problems now. A mere tiff with a boy. Peanuts compared to this. Try this on for size, teenage version of me. Try dealing with multiple murder and a kidnapped baby you might never see again. Not such a catastrophe now, huh?

She has made toast and scrambled egg. She thought it would be easy to swallow, but the smell of the egg has made her feel nauseous. Even her coffee tastes old and bitter and poisonous.

'*Try something sweet. You got any candy bars? Any chocolate?*'

Yeah, because everything can be cured with chocolate, right? That's all a woman needs when she's got somebody else's blood on her hands. A few cubes of chocolate will take away the misery and the guilt and the utter hopelessness.

'You know what I want?' she asks.

'*What's that, Erin?*'

'I want to hear my baby.'

'*What?*'

'I said I want to hear Georgia. Not crying. Not in pain. I want to hear her like she is most of the time, when she's with me. I want to hear her laughing.'

'*Why?*'

'What do you mean, why? It's such a strange request, me wanting to hear my baby being happy?'

He makes her wait, and she thinks he's going to deny her. But then:

'*All right, Erin. If it'll help. Wait a minute...*'

There's a scuffling noise, like that of a microphone brushing against something. And then...

Gurgling. Soft, tiny explosions of breath. And then – yes! – a word. Not a real word. Not anything intelligible. But something that sounds like it could be a word in some foreign language.

'Make her laugh,' says Erin.

'*How?*'

'Tickle her belly. Gently. Don't hurt her.'

More scuffling. Erin waits, and prays. She will know if this is not Georgia. She knows her laugh. She could pick it out in a whole roomful of babies.

And then it comes. A high, cheeky chuckle. Tentative at first, and then growing in intensity. Loud and clear over the earpiece, it plucks the strings of her brain and sets them singing. She closes her eyes and puts her arms out as if they are holding her baby, and she can imagine her, can see her Georgia in her arms, giggling at some secret knowledge into her mother's ear. And she doesn't want to let her go, not ever let her out of her arms, out of her sight, because Georgia is Erin, and Erin is Georgia. They should never be separated, because they are one and the same, and to take Georgia away is to cut Erin in two.

For a minute, a whole minute that is the most emotionally filled minute she has ever experienced, Erin listens to that most sublime of sounds and lets the tears fall.

2.10 PM

In the interview room Doyle drops his sheaf of reports and a brown bag on the table, then goes across to the cage. Still sitting on the bench, apparently in the exact same spot he was in when Doyle left him, Albert cocks his head and turns one roving eye on the approaching detective.

'Did you bring a rabbit?'

'Uhm, no,' says Doyle. 'I did bring you something, though.' He unbolts the door and swings it wide. 'Come on out, Albert. Stretch those legs.'

Albert doesn't move. 'I don't want to stretch my legs. They'll be too long for my body. I like to be in proportion.'

'Figure of speech, Albert. Come over here, see what I got.'

Albert stands, then shuffles to the doorway of the cage. He pauses at the threshold and looks around, a little like an animal that's not too sure about sacrificing its familiar surroundings to gain its freedom in the wild, dangerous outdoors. Doyle backs away to the table and waits there, so as not to add to the man's stress levels.

Eventually, Albert plucks up the courage to step out into the room. He meanders over to join Doyle, taking a roundabout route that makes sense only in his mind.

Says Doyle, 'Take a seat, Albert. I brought you some lunch. Thought you must be getting hungry by now.'

Albert sits. His gaze shifts to the bag on the table. He points. 'What's in the bag?'

'Uhm, that's your lunch. It's not in my pockets, Albert. It's there, in the bag.'

'Oh.'

He makes no move to touch the bag, and his eyes start to rove again.

'You wanna see what I got you?'

Albert stares at something in the corner of the room, and Doyle has to fight to prevent himself following suit.

'Sure,' says Albert, without enthusiasm.

Doyle opens up the bag. 'First of all...' He reaches in, pulls out a can of soda. 'Ta-da! Seven-Up! Didn't you say you liked Seven-Up the best? And guess what else? Go ahead, Albert, guess.'

But Albert is now too busy looking at the huge two-way mirror on the wall.

'Why do you have such a big mirror in here? Do you get dressed here? Is this where all the cops try their uniforms on?'

'Something like that.' He snaps his fingers a couple of times. 'Here, Albert, look. Guess what else about the soda?' He slaps his palm on the table in a show of glee, causing Albert almost to shoot out of his chair. 'It's only from the Seven-Eleven. Your favorite store, right? Whaddya think of that?'

But already Albert's eyes are elsewhere. A tough customer to please, thinks Doyle. Okay, I lied about going to the Seven-Eleven, but he doesn't know that, so could we show a bit of interest here, please?

'I got you a cup too. From the water cooler. I know you like those cups. And you know what else I got?' He reaches into the bag again. 'I met a guy when I was working a case not so long ago. Reminds me of you a little. He had a thing for corn chips, and especially these...'

Doyle pulls out a bag of Doritos. 'You like these, Albert? I bet you do.'

Albert scratches behind his ear. 'Yeah, they're okay. Although I prefer Cheetos.'

'Cheetos, huh? Okay, well, you can leave these if you want. But here's the *piece de resistance*. Are you ready?'

Doyle pulls out the final item in the bag. It's a sandwich. Ordinarily not something he would make such a fuss over, but hey, whatever works here.

'What is it?' asks Albert.

'It's a BLT. I took a wild guess at what you might like, but you seem like a BLT kinda guy to me. Am I right? Do you like BLT?'

'What's a BLT?'

'You don't know what—? It's bacon, lettuce and tomato.'

'So why isn't it called a bacon, lettuce and tomato sandwich?'

'Well, it is. Kinda. See, BLT. It's the initial letters. B for bacon, L for lettuce, T for tomato. Sound good to you? Was it a good choice?'

'Yeah.'

'Yeah? Cool. That's what I was—'

'Except for the lettuce.'

'The lettuce?'

'Yeah. I don't like lettuce. It's cold. And wet.'

'Okay, we can take out the lettuce. Here, let me do that for you…'

'And the tomato. It's also cold and wet. And technically it's a fruit. I don't do fruit sandwiches.'

'No,' says Doyle. 'When you put it like that, it does sound a little weird. Okay, so out with the tomato. Here – we've gone from a BLT to just a B. That okay now?'

'Yeah.'

'Okay, then, so eat. Go ahead.'

'Yeah.'

For a few seconds, Albert does nothing except scan the room. Then, abruptly, he pounces on the sandwich and takes a bite and starts chewing. And keeps chewing.

'Uhm, you enjoying that, Albert?'

Albert points to his mouth to indicate he can't speak right now. Doyle waits. And waits. Finally, Albert makes a huge swallowing noise and smacks his lips.

'My mom says I have to chew my food properly, or it'll stick in my throat. She also says I shouldn't talk with my mouth full.'

'Good advice, Albert. It sounds like your mother really wanted to keep you safe. She must have loved you. And I bet you loved her too, right?'

Albert's eyes flicker onto Doyle's, then drop back onto his sandwich. He grabs it again and takes another bite, as if using it as an excuse for avoiding the question.

Shit, thinks Doyle. Sonofabitch is smarter than he looks.

'Am I right, Albert? You loved your mother, didn't you? You would never want to hurt someone close to you like that.'

Chew, chew. More of the snap glances. Only not around the room anymore, but down. Down to the table.

'You ever argue with your mother? Ever get angry with her?'

He's not sure Albert is even listening. The table has become a lot more fascinating than Doyle's questions. So much for my interview technique, thinks Doyle.

What the hell's he looking at, anyhow?

The corn chips? The soda?

No, not those. Farther away from him. More toward my side of the table.

Doyle looks down. The only things here are the reports he's been carrying around. Why would Albert—?

He sees it then. Realizes what has grabbed Albert's attention.

When Doyle came into the room, he casually tossed his paperwork onto the table. The top report shifted out of line a little, exposing the one beneath. And on that second report down is an artist's reproduction of the numeric digits on the victims' foreheads. Currently only two of the symbols are visible, the third still being hidden beneath the uppermost document:

'What is it, Albert? The numbers? You find them interesting?'

Chew, chew.

Doyle waits for him to finish, then asks again: 'Is there something about these numbers?'

'Yeah,' says Albert. 'Two is prime. Three is prime. Two plus three is five, which is prime. Twenty-three is prime.'

Doyle nods. 'Prime numbers again, huh? You really like those, don't you?'

Albert chomps down again. Gives his jaw some more intense exercise.

Doyle stares at the drawings. Tries to see them as someone like Albert might see them. Is there something here? Some mathematical property that hasn't jumped out at them? Some religious or mystical significance, perhaps? Hard to tell with just two digits.

He waits for the audible swallowing signal, then holds up a finger. 'Wait up, Albert. I know you're hungry and all, but you mind taking a break for a second? I need to ask you something.'

Albert sits there with the sandwich half-raised to his lips, seemingly unsure as to what to do. Then he makes one of his sudden decisions and practically throws the sandwich back onto the table. His eyes flutter in a way that suggests he's a little perturbed by this interruption to his eating.

'It's okay,' says Doyle. 'You're not in trouble. I just want your help here.'

He picks up the sheaf of papers, then takes off the top report and puts it to the back. He slides the whole lot across to Albert, who is already staring with puzzlement at the mirror again.

Doyle taps the paperwork. 'Albert. Look, here. The numbers.'

Albert sneaks a sidelong glance down at the table. It's so quick that Doyle wonders whether he has taken in the row of three symbols that is now clearly visible:

'Albert. Did you see them? Did you see the numbers?'

'Yeah.'

'And?'

'And what?'

'Whaddya think?'

'About what?'

Jeez. This is like pulling teeth.

'Okay. One step at a time. Two is prime, right? And three – also prime. What about the one? Is one a prime number?'

A quick look of disdain. 'No.'

Doyle is starting to feel a little stupid. He feels he should know this stuff, but it went out of his head long before he became a policeman.

'Remind me,' he says. 'What's the definition of a prime number again?'

'A prime number is any number that is divisible only by one and itself. You know, this doesn't make a great changing room, even with the mirror. For one thing, there are no clothes hooks.'

'No. You're right. But about these primes. Doesn't the number one fit the description you just gave me?'

Another withering look. 'Doesn't count. If you counted one it would violate the fundamental theorem of arithmetic.'

'Of course,' says Doyle. 'Right.' He has no idea what the fundamental theorem of arithmetic is, but he doesn't want to be made to feel any more dense by requesting an explanation. The number one isn't prime, Doyle, you dumbass. Accept it and move on.

'So what if we put the three digits together? Two hundred and thirty-one. I'm thinking that could be a prime, right?'

It's a fifty-fifty shot. Doyle knows he should be able to work it out for himself, but he'd rather risk the humiliation.

'Ha!' says Albert. Which tells Doyle all he needs to know about his gamble.

'It's not prime?'

'Course not. It divides by three and seventy-seven. It divides by eleven and twenty-one. It divides by—'

'Okay, okay, Albert. I get the picture. It ain't prime.' Sheesh, rub it in, why don't you?

Doyle sighs. Wonders if this is a total waste of time. But he's not giving up just yet.

'All right. One more thing. Suppose we think of this as a sequence. Two, three, one. Would that mean anything to you?'

Albert says nothing. But there's something in the way he says nothing. A certain tell in the way he steadfastly chooses to remain silent.

'Albert? Two, three, one. That sequence of numbers. It means something, doesn't it?'

Another scratch behind the ear. The beginning of a slight rocking to and fro.

'Do you know what comes next? Is that it? You know what the next number is?'

The swaying increasing in intensity. The fingers coming together, tapping, tapping.

'Albert, this is important. It could save someone's life. Please help me if you can. What does this sequence mean? What's the next number?'

He's humming now. It's increasing in volume. On its way to drowning out all external noises.

'Albert, tell me about the sequence. Tell me!'

And then Albert moves. Doyle takes a step back, not sure what to expect. Violence? Screaming?

But it's neither of those. Albert grabs the rest of his sandwich. Stuffs the whole thing into his mouth. Starts to chew.

It's his way of shutting himself up, of preventing himself from telling Doyle what he wants to hear. Doyle knows this.

Which means there is something. There is something about these numbers. They have meaning, and comprehending that meaning might help to catch a killer.

But at the moment, the key to the code is locked away tightly.

Inside the head of another killer.

3.31 PM

She's spoilt for choice here, and she wonders why she didn't think of it before.

Tompkins Square Park, or TSP as it's known locally. A small square of green, with spreading elm trees, a basketball court, playgrounds, a dog run, and – meandering past them all – winding walkways lined with benches. Captured in the briefest of terms like that, it sounds an idyllic oasis. A haven from the hustle and bustle of Alphabet City here on the East Side.

Erin knows its recent history. She knows that during the twilight years of the twentieth century TSP symbolized all that was wrong with New York. Drugs, prostitution, violent crime, homelessness, the dregs of society generally – all were represented in overwhelming concentrations in this tiny quadrilateral.

It's clean now, though. Safe. That's what they told Erin when she moved to the city. Go see for yourself. Watch the children playing there. See a live performance or listen to one of the many bands that play for free. Enjoy the antics of the dogs. Have a picnic and strike up a conversation with your fellow citizens.

But…

And that's the problem. There's always a 'but'. The people who were so full of praise for their local park never, ever forgot to tag on that brief but oh-so-significant word. That's what should have given Erin the clue.

In a curious way it reminds her of the movie Gremlins. You're given this cute furry pet. It's just the sweetest thing on the planet. It smiles and chirrups and sings and rolls its big wet eyes and even repeats the occasional word. Totally adorable. You can keep it, you can look after it, it's yours. But…

Well, we all know what happened next.

The park is safe. But…

Yeah. Like the song says, I Like Big Buts. A huge, ugly, in-your-face but.

It's weird. There are normal people here. At least they appear fairly normal to Erin. Some of them even look pretty happy. But it's as if they can't see what's going on around them. They have somehow blinkered themselves to the degeneracy and the lunacy and the sheer bizarreness of the other denizens of this place.

Erin sees it, and she wonders how can she perceive what others cannot. Is it because she still thinks of herself as an outsider? Would she become like them over time, accepting of the unacceptable?

She sees the homeless guy with the huge white beard, unashamedly reaching into his pants and then pissing against a tree, while not forty yards away children play tag. She sees three youths laugh as they toss lighted matches at another vagrant lying on the damp grass. She sees the man with the traffic cone on his head, apparently talking to his shoes. She sees the fat middle-aged woman in a disgustingly undersized mini-skirt, singing to the dog held in a papoose strapped to her chest. And she sees the thin, sallow figures in the shadows, slipping things to each other in furtive handshakes.

None of this escapes her in her brief stroll around the park, and it astounds her. There was nothing like this back in Brookville. The occasional drunk sleeping it off on a park bench, yes. But he would soon be woken by the police and moved on. Where are the cops here? Why doesn't anybody call them? Do these people even care about their environment and its effects on their children? Why doesn't somebody do something, for Pete's sake?

I could do something, she thinks. I could quite happily start cleaning up this park. I mean, really clean, not pretend clean. Sanitized.

I could take a hammer to each and every one of these low-lifes and undesirables. I could flit from skull to worthless skull like a bee visiting flowers. Bop, bop, bop as I go. Leaving them fallen in my wake. And then maybe some of the decent law-abiding people here might actually cotton on to the fact that it doesn't have to be like this. Things can be changed. Maybe they will actually start to cheer and applaud. Maybe they will even join in and turn this park into the place of serenity and beauty and joy it's supposed to be.

But she doesn't do that. She doesn't take out the hammer. Not yet. Instead she sits on a bench and waits for them to come. Because they *will* come. She is an alien, not accepting of the ways of these feral creatures. They will sniff her out and they will eye her with suspicion and fear. She is not afraid to meet their collective gaze, and many will back down at that most primitive of challenges. But some – the hungriest – will be unable to resist. And as the light fades so early on this mid-winter day, they will grow bolder. And then they will come.

The first is a pervert.

He is bald and bespectacled and wears a heavy parka, but his beige pants are of thin baggy cotton. And when he pulls his coat aside in front of Erin, it is obvious through the flimsy material that he is sporting a full erection.

'Hey, Erin,' says the voice in her ear. '*Looks like you got a new boyfriend.*'

She doesn't run away. Doesn't scream. Doesn't even flinch. Doesn't give any of the reactions he is probably used to.

She just stares for a moment at the man's crotch, then lifts her impassive face.

'Okaaay. So now what do you expect me to do?'

He looks nervous. He has clearly never been in this situation before. Why isn't she scared? Where's the disgust, the loathing?

He passes a tongue over his lips.

'Y-you c-can touch it if you w-want.'

'*Best offer you've had all day, Erin. How could you possibly turn him down?*'

Still not showing any emotion, Erin reaches into her bag. 'Yes,' she says. 'I could do that, couldn't I? I could touch it with this...'

She shows him the knife. A glimpse is all it takes, and he's gone. Coat pulled tightly closed, he walks as fast as his cold bony legs will take him.

She could follow him. She could get up from this bench right now and follow that freak. Wait until he disappears into a stand of trees or the public toilets or wherever he hangs out between his public displays of affection. And then…

But no. Not yet. There's better to come. She's sure of it.

And she's right.

It comes in the shape of a man who looks to be in his mid-twenties. He makes as if to walk straight past Erin at first, but she catches the side-long glances. She sees that he finds her of interest. It's no surprise when he veers toward her.

He's wearing a green thigh-length jacket, zipped right up to the chin, and his hands are thrust deep into the pockets. His jeans are faded and stained, and look as though they haven't been washed for weeks. His collar-length hair is dark and shiny with grease, and a trail of mucus runs from his beak-like nose to his upper lip. His skin is peppered with zits, and when he affixes what is supposed to pass for a smile she sees that his teeth are nicotine-stained and crooked.

The man of my dreams, thinks Erin. Where have you been all my life?

'Hey,' he says. 'You looking for something?'

Yeah. I'm looking for an excuse to cave in your skull. Want to provide it for me?

'Maybe,' she says. 'What've you got?'

He gets straight to the point: 'Maybe some weed. You looking to chill tonight? I can get you the best weed ever.'

She turns her face to the side and stares into the distance, acting unin-terested. 'That the best you can do?'

He barks a laugh, then sniffs back some of his escaping slime.

'The best I can do? The best? What do you mean by that, the best?'

'A little weed? I can get that shit anywhere. Hell, I can get that in any bar in the Village.'

She doesn't know if that's true. Truth be told, she has no idea about how to get hold of marijuana or any other kind of drug. It's not something she has ever researched.

'So, what then? You telling me you're looking for something stronger?'

She brings her eyes back to his face. 'Maybe. You telling me you can help me out?'

He stares down at her for a while, then looks around him. He wipes the back of a hand across his nose, looks at the mess he's made on his hand, then puts it back in his pocket. Erin wants to barf.

He says, 'Are you a cop?'

She nods. 'Yeah. That toy poodle over there is my backup. You'd better watch out, because he's carrying a shotgun under that coat of his.'

'You don't look like no user,' he says.

'And you don't look like someone who's got the first clue about getting what I need, so why don't you just get lost?'

But he doesn't budge. He looks around some more, and then makes a decision.

'Aiight. Supposing I can get hold of some stuff for you. You got money?'

'I'm not offering sexual favors, if that's what you're asking. Yeah, I got money.'

'We'll have to go somewhere.'

'Where?'

'A place I know. Not far from here. I'll get you what you want.'

A sudden anxiety grips Erin's insides. She realizes then that her bravery thus far has come from being in such a public area. Despite the preponderance of low-lifes around her, the chances of something serious happening to her have been slim. She has been able to relax, to pass judgment, to feel and act superior. Now, though, with the possibility that she may have to swap her secure position for one of unknown threat, she begins to feel her confidence diminish.

'Come on, Erin. He's practically begging you to waste him. Go with him.'

'How do I know you're not trying to rip me off?' she asks, and then regrets it, because now she's showing weakness.

The guy shrugs his shoulders. 'Up to you, doll. You can go with me or you can stay here and watch the little doggies sniffing each others' asses.'

He's got the upper hand now, and he knows it. But, she reasons, that's probably a good thing. He should feel like he's in control. He should feel as though he can terminate this partnership at any time. Right up to the moment when he's the one being terminated.

'All right,' she says, getting up from the bench. 'Let's go.'

He looks surprised, and for a second she wonders if she's arousing his suspicion by making things too easy for him.

'I'm warning you, though,' she adds. 'One false move and I'm walking away.'

His smile tells her he seems happier now, and he turns and starts shambling out of the park. She follows him, at a discreet distance.

'I never had you pegged as a stalker, Erin. Was it his aftershave that got you hooked?'

'Shut up,' she says in a low voice.

Up ahead, the guy glances back over his shoulder, and Erin tries to act like she hasn't just been caught talking to herself. Wouldn't want him to think I'm crazy. Wouldn't want him to start thinking he's the one in danger here.

They walk for just a few minutes. On East Sixth Street the man stops and waits in front of a gate set into a chain-link fence bordering a vacant lot. When Erin draws level with him, he waits a while longer, watching the street until it seems nobody is looking. Then he flicks off a loop of rope holding the gate against the fence, and pulls the gate open.

Erin says, 'What, in here?'

'You want the stuff or not? Get in, before someone sees.'

She steps through, and the man follows. He leads her down to the back end of the lot, then bends to squeeze through a hole in the brick wall.

Erin hesitates. Out here on the lot she could still be seen from the street if someone walked by. She could scream for help and someone could see. She sacrifices that hope as soon as she disappears behind this wall.

On the other hand, she needs to make sure she's not visible when she snuffs out the life of this insect.

She bends, clambers through the hole.

She's in a backyard, behind an abandoned tenement. A building destined for greater things, no doubt, but right now in a hiatus that has probably allowed all kinds of lower life forms to infiltrate it.

The man picks his way through mounds of garbage, then ascends a short stoop. He grabs hold of the sheet of corrugated metal in front of the doorway and pulls it to one side, revealing a triangle of blackness within.

'In here,' says the guy.

She wavers again. In there? Inside that dark, decrepit building where he could attack me, rape me, murder me? Why would any sane woman go through that doorway with this scumbag?

'Why don't I wait here? Why don't you just go in there, get the stuff and bring it out to me?'

He shakes his head. 'Don't work like that, doll. I have to buy the shit from somebody else, and he'll want to check you out first.'

She glances up at the building. There are other people in there? Damn. That could make things difficult.

Get out of here, Erin. This is too dangerous. Say you've changed your mind, and walk away.

'He's bluffing, Erin. There's nobody else in there. He just wants to get you alone. Be ready for him. Go with him, and then do what you have to do.'

'You coming, or what?'

'I...'

'Think of Georgia, Erin. Time's running out. You're only halfway through. Don't let this opportunity pass you by. Who knows how long the next one will be?'

'Okay,' she says, answering both of her questioners.

But it's not okay. She doesn't feel okay at all. As she climbs the steps leading up to the building, the cautious part of her brain warns her this is one of the least okay things she has ever done in her life.

When she gets to the top step, she considers making her move. But the guy is watching her carefully. She is not sure she can take him by surprise just yet.

Okay, so let's get inside. Do it as soon as we get in there and his guard is down. Ready, Erin? Ready?

She stoops and enters the building.

It's darker in here than she imagined, and she realizes then that all the windows are boarded up. The only light is that finding its way in from the doorway, and that lasts only a second before the guy comes in behind her and lets the barrier fall back into place.

And now she cannot see a thing. Her other senses kick into overdrive and the stench in here overpowers her. Urine and feces and the unmistakable odor of marijuana.

She listens for the man's footsteps, but is unsure as to where he is. Her hand drops into her purse. Grabs the hammer tightly. Her heart is pounding now as she blinks furiously, trying to make her eyes adjust to the blackness. What's he doing? Where the fuck is he?

A whisper in her ear that startles her: 'Wait.'

She hears creaking floorboards, then a rustling sound. Jesus Christ, what is he going to do? What the hell was I—?

A rasping sound that makes her jump again. And then light as a match flares into life. The man is standing over a packing crate, on top of which are some candles. He lights two of them, then snuffs the match out with his fingers and tosses it to the floor.

'That's more like it,' he says, grinning. 'Some romantic lighting.'

Romantic isn't the word that jumps to Erin's mind. She's in a narrow hallway. There is no furniture here, no carpeting. The flickering candles pick out on the floor the occasional bundle of rags, garbage and other items she has no desire to identify. To her left, a staircase rises into the gloom above. Ahead is the lobby of the building. In the right wall, graffiti-adorned apartment doors lie open, but not exactly welcoming.

The man leads her further inside, to the foot of the staircase. He seems more nervous now, and she knows he has a plan. She knows this for certain by the way he is acting. He is going to do something, and it's going to be soon, and it's going to be unpleasant.

'You got money?' he says.

'Yes,' she answers. 'Yes, I've got money.'

'Show me.'

He licks his lips. His fingers are twitching. He's practically salivating. 'Why?'

'Because I need to tell the guys upstairs that I've seen your dough. Come on, show me the green.'

He puts out a hand. Flicks his fingers into his palm several times. Show me.

Erin glances up the staircase. She doubts there is anybody up there. This is just the guy finding out how much he can make here. This is him getting all excited about how better off he's about to be when he attacks her and robs her and does all manner of unspeakable things to her in this god-forsaken place that nobody will venture into in a million years if they have any sense. This is his idea of foreplay.

So she reaches into her purse. She doesn't need an excuse to do so, because he's asked her to. He has issued an invitation. Show me. Give it to me. Let me have it, doll.

So, here. Have it.

He moves more quickly than she hoped for. Pulls his head back as her arm whips toward him. The hammer catches him a glancing blow on the cheek and he yells and staggers back, falling onto the stairs, and she has to rush at him because she can't give him time to recover and fight back. He might look like shit, but he's young and wiry and possibly very strong, and so he has to get her blows in first, has to finish this thing quickly. So she leaps forward, but again her attack is thwarted when he raises an arm and wards off her blow – Jesus, why does he have to keep messing this up? Why doesn't he just accept what's coming to him, the thing he's been asking for ever since he came up to her in the park? Why can't he just put his head on the chopping block and wait for the fateful strike?

But she doesn't relent. She keeps up the pressure. Raining the blows down on him. Fighting through his meager defenses – die, you stubborn sonofabitch, die! – until all her blows are finding their target, smashing into his cheeks and his jaw and his eye sockets and his skull bones, crack, splinter, thud. Let me get rid of those zits for you, buster, like this and this and this. Let me take that huge shnozz down a size or two for you. Let me do something about those misaligned teeth of yours – pop, pop, pop, until his face is suddenly more malleable and less angular beneath the purple swollen flesh, and he stops yelling and fighting and thinking and breathing.

She halts eventually, unsure as to how long she has been hitting her prey. Unsure as to how many times that hammer has risen and fallen. It suddenly occurs to her that she has hardly breathed during her exertion, and now she sucks in huge lungfuls of air to compensate. She stares down at what she has done, and can almost make no sense of it. Did I do this? Has this really just happened?

But now all she wants to do is to get out of here. There is something profoundly disturbing about this deserted building, as though it is haunted by the ghosts of its ex-tenants, all standing here and watching her. She needs to escape.

'Attagirl, Erin. Great show. One of your best yet.'

'Shut the fuck up,' she says.

She swaps the hammer for the knife. Adds her touch of artwork to the victim. Time to go. Get out, Erin. Get out now. There's something not quite right about this place. You need to—

She hears the noise then. Slight, but definitely there. Behind her.

She whirls.

In the doorway of one of the apartments, a man. Young, like the guy now lying dead on the stairs. He wears a black biker's jacket and jeans. His hair is blond and weak-looking, and there is a vacant stare in his eyes. He props himself up against the door jamb, and looks as though he could slide to the floor any minute. He is obviously still coming down from a high.

'Wow,' he says. 'That was intense.'

'Nice timing. Introduce him to Mr Hammer, Erin.'

She knows he's right. This guy has seen. He has witnessed. He can't be allowed to tell others what she has done. And he's a junkie. That makes him no good. He ticks all the boxes.

So she starts moving toward him, the knife still in her hand. She's banking on him being too stoned to sense the danger he's in.

But she's wrong.

She realizes that when she sees him raise his arm and point the gun at her.

4.23 PM

Doyle stares at the numbers again.

Two, three, one.

What could they possibly mean? And how is it that Albert is able to attach meaning to them when Doyle, super-intelligent detective that he is, sees just a bunch of digits?

Okay, super-intelligent is stretching it a little. You didn't know what a prime number is, did you? You couldn't have worked out all those factors of 231 the way Albert did, without even having to pause for thought.

See – factors! I remember factors from school. I remember what they are.

Not gonna help you here, pal. Not gonna cut the mustard. Face it: math – even basic arithmetic – was never your strong point. At school the only equations you were interested in were of the form You + Attractive Girl = Fun.

But maybe I'm looking at this too deeply. Maybe what Albert sees in these numbers bears no relation to what I need to see. Why should there be a relationship between the two? For all I know, 231 could be the number of times Albert has tied his shoes today. That's the way his mind works. He doesn't think like I do. He doesn't need to catch a serial killer.

I do, though. And that means I still need to understand these numbers.

So let's start again. Ignore Albert. Take him out of the equation (see what I did there with the math speak?) and let's see what we have.

Our killer wastes three guys. She – because yes, unlikely though it might seem, all the signs point to this being the work of a female – carves numbers on their heads. Why is she doing this? Two possibilities. First is that she's just batshit crazy. She just lays down the first number that comes into her addled brain, or she throws dice or something. Whatever, if that's the reason then there's no point me looking at these figures any longer. It ain't gonna tell me shit about why she's killing or who she's gonna go after next.

But that seems unlikely. Killers who leave signatures are usually more consistent, and that's especially true when their minds are fried. If she had left, say, an upside-down cross on each victim, or even what we initially believed was the mark of Zorro, that would have made more sense. That would have been more in keeping with what's known about psychopathic serial killers.

So that brings us to the second possibility. She's trying to send us a message. Trying to tell us something.

It must be the order. Why else would you put the first three numbers on three victims, but not in the usual sequence? The order must mean something. Not something mathematical, like Albert is probably think-ing, but something more personal about the victims.

But what?

Two, three, one. Vern, then Edwin Steppler, then William Fischer.

Put them in numerical order and we have Fischer, then Vern, then Steppler.

Does that help? Does that tell us anything?

Shit, I hate puzzles.

'Detective Doyle?'

He looks up to see a woman at his desk. Attractive. Looks a little like Whitney Houston. She wears a suit and carries a briefcase. He hopes she has appeared in answer to his musings. She will wave a wand over the numbers in front of him and their secret will be revealed, and then she will vanish in a cloud of smoke.

'Uhm, yeah,' he says, standing and proffering his hand.

Her grip is firm, businesslike. 'Vanessa Maynard, from Psych Services.'

'Oh,' he says. 'Oh, yeah. Please, take a seat. Can I get you a coffee or something?'

'No, I'm good, thanks. I hear you have somebody you'd like me to talk to.'

'Yeah. Albert.'

She opens up her briefcase and takes out a notepad and pen. 'Tell me about him.'

So he tells her. And while he talks to her he is utterly self-conscious about how he is coming across. He has a thing about shrinks. He always gets the feeling that, no matter what he says or how he says it, he is being analyzed and judged. He could tell them something perfectly innocuous, such as his favorite color, and they will read all manner of things into it. From one simple piece of information they will dig deep into his psyche and discover all kinds of hidden tidbits that have lain there since his childhood. He doesn't like the idea of people knowing stuff about him that he doesn't know himself.

And so he remains guarded in his words. He does his best to stick to the facts and not to stray into opinion, not to venture anything that might offer an insight into his own thought processes or emotions. He particularly avoids mentioning how annoyed he is that it's taken this long for Psych Services to get someone out here, for fear it will give her the impetus to go to town on dissecting his mental health. It's probably the most uncomfortable conversation he's ever had at this desk since he arrived at the precinct.

She doesn't let him off lightly, either. 'What do you think?' she asks. 'Do you believe he killed his mother?'

Doyle's mouth opens but no words come out for a few seconds. Did he kill his mother? Could there be a question more psychologically loaded than that? Will she ask me about my relationship with my own mother next? Will whatever I say cause her to form an opinion about my sexual adequacy?

Get a grip, Doyle.

He bites the bullet: 'In all honesty, I don't know. I hope not. If you must know, I kinda like the guy.'

There. I said it. Read into that what you will. Open up that briefcase and take out the straitjacket if you think you need to.

But what she does is to smile at him. Playfully, she reaches out and flicks the bobble-headed leprechaun on his desk.

She says, 'Then let's go see if you're right, shall we?'

As Doyle looks down at the vibrating plaything, it seems to him that there's all kinds of things he could make of such a gesture.

He decides it's best not to go there.

4.37 PM

So now she's in his apartment.

Not the one in the derelict building – the one in which this guy had been sleeping after his drug fix. This is his real apartment, where he lives. She walked a whole two blocks with this man and made barely a squeak, despite passing several people on the street. But what was she going to do when he was pressing a gun into her ribs? Even if she hadn't believed he would shoot her, she wasn't exactly inclined to draw attention to herself after what she had just done.

So she came with him. All the way to this tiny little apartment.

And tiny it is. Just two rooms: a bathroom and a room containing everything else. A minuscule space like this needs to be kept tidy, and it isn't. The sofa bed is still in bed mode, its grim gray sheets only half covering the yellow-stained mattress beneath. The counter top along one side of the room is littered with unwashed plates, open food-cans and cups half-filled with cold coffee. The sink is crammed with pots and pans containing the remnants of meals going back several days. The stove is spattered and smeared with grease and baked-on food.

'What are you doing?' she asks. 'Why did you bring me here?'

'Shut up,' he says. 'Turn around.'

She follows his instruction, and when her back is to him he snatches her purse from her shoulder and flings it to the floor. Then he grabs her coat and yanks it off her. She sees it fly past her and hit the wall before landing on the floor, and she notices that the brooch is facing her, watching all that goes on here.

'Don't worry. I can still see and hear. I'll get you out of this.'

She hears the words over her earpiece, but they don't comfort her. She doesn't trust either of the men who have their eyes trained on her right now.

Something presses into the back of her neck.

'Don't move,' says the junkie, 'or I'll blow your fucking head off.'

The guy's other hand starts to slide over her waist, and she flinches.

'I said don't move. I'm gonna search you. Make sure you got nothing.'

His hand slips into the left pocket of her pants, then he brings it out and checks the one on the right.

She closes her eyes, waiting to swallow back her disgust when he checks out the rest of her body. But it doesn't happen. Instead, he brings his lips to her ear and says, 'Those tight pants and sweater of yours, I don't think I need to frisk you for a gun or nothing. Course, I might change my mind about that if you try anything. You understand me?'

She nods, and he pulls the gun away.

'You can turn around again.'

Slowly, she faces him. He's still got the gun out, holding it waist-high. She didn't need his warning. She has no intention of making any sudden moves when there's the barrel of a pistol being pointed at her.

He studies her, saying nothing.

'What?' she asks.

He moves his head from side to side, a smile growing on his boyish features. 'Shit. I can hardly believe it. What you did back at that building. Crazy shit, man. Why'd you do that?'

'Tell him you don't like lowlife junkie fuckwits.'

She ignores the suggestion. Shrugs. 'He deserved it. He tried to sell me drugs.'

The man's eyes widen. 'Ha! What are you, some kind of one-woman clean-up campaign? Nah, there's more to it than that. That was some seriously fucked-up shit back there, man.'

She doesn't like her actions being described in this way. It unsettles her. She did what she had to do, and that's it.

'I didn't like him,' she says.

He laughs at her. 'No kidding? And there's me thinking you had the hots for him. Come on, what's the story? He your ex or something?'

She gives him a look of disgust. 'I wouldn't touch him if he were the last man on earth.'

'Yeah, but you did touch him. You touched him with a fucking hammer, man. And then you sliced up his fucking head, man. I mean, you went to work on that guy. You musta had a reason.'

'He was going to do something to me. He didn't take me all the way there just to sell me drugs. He had a plan.'

'A plan? Woo-hoo! Well, now, that explains everything. Explains all that shit. A plan? Unforgivable. What was he thinking? Can't let a guy have a plan, no sir. Someone with a plan needs his fucking balls cutting off.'

Erin listens to the biting sarcasm and finds she cannot shrug it off. 'You're laughing at me.'

'Yeah, I am. But I ain't having half as much fun as you were in that building. You were soaking that shit up, man.'

Erin folds her arms across her chest. She suddenly feels cold and shivery. 'No. You're wrong. I… I didn't enjoy it. It was… necessary. I was just… protecting myself.'

She has trouble finding the words. It worries her that they don't seem to sit right.

'Well, you weren't exactly part of the audience, you know what I'm saying? I saw what I saw. You were in the zone, man. You were gone…'

No, she thinks. He's got it wrong. It wasn't like that.

'Protecting yourself? Fuck. You was hitting him long after he was dead…'

No, I… please, no.

'And then that knife thing? Taking a blade to the man's dome like that? I ain't never seen—'

'SHUT UP!'

Her yell bounces around the apartment, and her abductor responds by bringing up his gun arm, leveling the weapon at her frightened, confused face.

She stares down the barrel, her lower lip trembling. Is that how he saw me? Could I have really acted that way? As though it wasn't about Georgia? As though I was… having fun?

She wants to be sick, and she sees in the man's face the recognition that he's pursued this thread as far as he can.

He lowers the pistol again. 'What's your name?'

'Erin.'

'All right, Erin. You can call me Bruce, okay? It ain't my real name, but I like Bruce Willis. You dig the Die Hard movies?'

She gives a subtle shake of the head. 'I… I haven't really watched them.'

'Yeah, well you should give 'em a try. Best movies ever. Yippee Ki-Yay, and so forth.'

She doesn't know what he's talking about, so she just flashes him a weak smile. She's scared, but what helps her to keep it together is that, for whatever reason, he wants her alive. Otherwise he could easily have killed her back at the empty building.

'Why did you bring me here?' she asks.

'Good question, Erin. Wondered when you'd get around to it.'

The man who calls himself Bruce – even though he looks nothing like Bruce Willis or a Bruce of any kind for that matter – chews his lip and studies her, as if debating how much detail of his grand scheme he should reveal to his captive.

'I can sell you,' he says.

She wants to laugh, but is too afraid of angering this man, and is not so sure it's funny. What's he talking about? Human trafficking? Is he serious?

'Sell me to who?' she asks.

'The cops. You're worth something to them. Gotta be.'

She shakes her head. 'What? Why would I be worth anything to the cops? They don't even know about what just happened. What makes you think—?'

'How many?' he interrupts.

She stares, open-mouthed. 'How… How many what?'

'How many people have you killed?'

It's a shot in the dark. Has to be. He couldn't know what I've done.

'I don't understand. It was just him. Just that one guy. I—'

'LIAR!' he yells, and then he's advancing on her, gun raised again. 'I heard on the radio. About the homeless dude. Found dead with some kind of fucking Zorro mark on his head. That was you, wasn't it? *Wasn't it?*'

'Yes! Yes, it was me, okay?' She has her arms raised, and her hands tremble in the air. Her gaze flicks from the blackness of the gun barrel to the unfathomable eyes of the man who might be on the edge of sending a bullet exploding from it.

They stand frozen like that for some time. A dance with no movement but bursting with energy.

And then a smile tugs at the corner of his lips.

'Fuck,' he says. 'I knew it. I knew that had to be you. The chances of two different flakes running around cutting folks up like that...'

'I'm not crazy,' she says.

'No? He deserved it too, right? So that's two. How many others?'

'Don't tell him. Stick with two. He doesn't need to know more than that.'

But she wonders what the point is of withholding that information. Two victims or four – what's the difference to him? He heard about Vern on the radio. Maybe he's heard about the others too.

'It's four in total.'

His eyes widen and his jaw drops. 'Four? You're shitting me, right? Four? Jesus Christ, girl, what's gotten into you? What did these people do to you?'

She doesn't know how to answer that. They were available, that's all. They were in the right place at the right time. At least for Erin they were. But can she tell him that? Of course not. That would just sound crazy.

But the true story would sound even crazier.

Says Bruce, 'You know the cops will be chasing your ass, don't you? I mean seriously hunting you down, man. Four people on the slab because of you? Five-O will be crapping theirselves over that. That makes you Public Enemy Number One, girl. And that makes you worth something.'

She can almost see the dollar signs in his eyes. The plans being formulated in the brain cells that the drugs haven't destroyed yet. He's seeing big money. Enough to buy a ton of drugs and stay wasted forever.

'Fuck,' he says dreamily, his gaze drifting. 'I don't believe this.'

'You need to get ready to make a move, Erin.'

The warning unnerves her. A move? What kind of move am I supposed to make against a junkie armed with a gun? Is he serious?

Bruce snaps back into reality. He starts looking around him.

Erin narrows her eyes. What's he searching for?

'It's going to be soon, Erin. Before it's too late. Be ready on my signal.'

Signal? What kind of fucking signal? What's he going to do, fire a starting pistol in my ear?

'Turn around,' says Bruce.

'What? Why?'

Bruce glares at her. 'Because I said so, is why. Now turn the fuck around.'

She turns, so that she's now facing the disgusting bed. From behind comes the sound of drawers being opened and closed.

'I can see him, Erin. I'll be your eyes. Are you ready?'

She twists her head slightly to the left. She can just see her coat out of the corner of her eye, and she tries to throw it a question in her expression: Ready for what?

She doesn't know whether he understands her query, but he comes back with a response: *'When he's not looking, you need to attack, hard and fast. Do you hear me, Erin? Are you ready?'*

No. I'm not ready. I can't do this. What are you talking about?

But then there is no more time for debate, because the order arrives, loud and clear.

'NOW, ERIN! GO, GO, GO!'

It's as if she is not in control of her body. The words in her ear act like hypnotic suggestions. She cannot defy them. She doesn't know what form her attack will take, but suddenly she's spinning around, ready to pounce, ready to jump on this sonofabitch's back and rip his throat out, ready to—

But that's impossible. Because Bruce doesn't have his back to her. He is not rummaging in drawers. He has found what he wanted and is already facing her. And before she can take a single step forward he is lifting his gun hand again and a snarl is forming on his lips and his eyes are bursting with the heat of death, and he is about to shoot, about to kill...

'What the fuck?' he screams, his voice shrill and scared and angry. 'What the fuck are you doing? I told you. I fucking told you!'

He steps right up to her. Puts the cold steel muzzle to her temple. Presses it hard against her skull. If she were thinking logically now she would stand stock still and she would pray and she would plead and she would hope for mercy.

But she's not thinking logically. She is breaking inside. Snapping. Not because of Bruce. Bruce is secondary now. Bruce is an irrelevance.

She is not even aware of Bruce as she pulls away from him and turns toward her jacket on the floor and unleashes her fury.

'What the fuck was that? Are you trying to get me killed? Are you trying to keep me from my baby? Why did you do that?'

She expects an apology at least. An admission of error, maybe. What she gets is laughter.

He laughs uproariously in her ear. This is what he finds funny. Sick, insane situations like this are what floats his boat. He finds this hilarious.

'NOO!' she screams. 'STOP IT! STOP IT!'

And the laughter stops. In an instant. No tailing off or fading away. Just a dead stop, as though he has turned off his microphone.

She stares at the coat, at the brooch. She is panting heavily, like a lioness that has just chased down a gazelle. And like that lioness she could tear someone limb from limb right now.

And then she remembers she is not alone.

She turns to look at Bruce, and she sees in him what she would expect to see in anyone who has just witnessed a woman shrieking at an invisible companion – a woman who, not too long ago, was hammering the life out of a man before carving up his head. She sees in Bruce's eyes the uncertainty that anyone would feel in the presence of sheer insanity.

Bruce doesn't speak for a long time. It's as though he's not sure how to handle this. Not sure what he's gotten himself into here. This is beyond his wildest experience, beyond his understanding. She can tell he's afraid, the fear arising from the certainty he is not dealing with a rational being.

'You need to turn around now,' he tells her. His voice is not forceful, but quiet and tremulous. Despite that, she knows she must obey, because Bruce is even more likely to kill her now. He is scared of what he doesn't understand, and will gladly put a bullet in this untamable creature rather than risk falling victim to it.

So she does as she is told, and when he orders her to lie on the bed she does that without hesitation. And when he tells her to stretch out like a starfish so that he can tie her limbs to the corners of the bed using the cord he has just found in one of his drawers, she does that too. And when he pushes a cloth into her mouth and ties it in place with a second cloth, she doesn't try to fight it.

And when Bruce leaves the apartment, leaves her alone with her face buried in his grease-stained pillow, she tries to come to terms with the near certainty that she will never see her baby again.

5.22 PM

Doyle taps his fingers on his desk and stares at his bobble-headed leprechaun. It perturbs him that it was so recently and so intimately interfered with. It perturbs him even more that he's perturbed by such a minor thing. Better not tell Vanessa, he thinks. She'd have a field day with that confession. Tell me about your childhood, she would say. Tell me about what other little flexible possessions of yours were interfered with.

She's good, he thinks. Vanessa the shrink. She's good with the questions, good with her technique. She seems unflappable, with the patience of a saint. Every time Doyle has gone to watch her through the two-way mirror, he has been impressed by how professional she seems, how in control. He's glad he's not across the table from her, the subject of her scrutiny. He feels he would break down in seconds, tell her everything she wants to know, whether she asks directly about it or not.

But Albert is better.

Albert is a paragon of secrecy. He would make a great spy, able to withstand the most probing of interrogation techniques. He's giving nothing away except his love for numbers, Edifix construction sets and the water coolers. And the funny thing is, Doyle finds himself rooting for Albert. Perverse though it seems given that there's a possible corpse at the bottom of all this, Doyle will almost let out a cheer if Albert manages to withstand the psychological shenanigans of the mind-prober sitting opposite him.

Doyle doesn't think he'll tell Vanessa about those thoughts either.

Doyle's phone rings, and he picks it up.

'Cal? It's Marcus.'

Sergeant Marcus Wilson at the desk downstairs. Doyle suddenly realizes that he's well into the next four-to-eight shift already, and with that realization comes an immense feeling of tiredness. He has not been home for over twenty-four hours, and has been without sleep for even longer. He needs sleep, he needs his bed, he needs his family.

'Hey, Marcus, what's up?'

'Got a call here from a guy says he wants to talk to whoever's in charge of the murder investigation.'

Mentally, Doyle sighs. Whenever a homicide hits the news, the bedbugs come out in droves. They all know something. They've all got a story to tell. They've all got a theory.

'He say which murder investigation?'

'Nope. Says he's got some hot information, though. You wanna take the call?'

I have a choice? thinks Doyle. 'I guess so, Marcus. Patch him through, will ya?'

Doyle waits while the connection is made.

'Detective Doyle. Can I help you?'

'Y-yeah. I think so. They say you're in charge of the murder investigation. Is that right?'

'Depends. Which murder are we talking about here?'

Give them nothing – that's the rule. Don't volunteer any info, because this could be a newspaper reporter or some such. Let them show their hand first.

'Murders plural,' says the caller. 'Four of them, to be exact.'

And now Doyle suddenly forgets his tiredness. Now he is sitting bolt upright, pen in hand to take notes. This could be a shot in the dark, but something tells Doyle it's not.

'Four murders? Would you care to be a little more specific?'

'You know what I'm talking about. Actually no, maybe you don't. It's prob'ly too soon. Maybe you only know about three of them. Am I right, Detective? You know about three murders, all done by the same killer?'

Doyle knows he has to dance the dance. This could still be a fishing expedition. This could still be a reporter who suspects there's a serial killer on the loose, but isn't certain about the numbers involved. Try four to begin with. If that doesn't work, try another number. Keep going until you hit the jackpot.

'Excuse me, sir,' he says, 'but do you mind telling me the purpose of your call? You got some information you'd like to pass on to me?'

A snort of laughter. Then: 'Oh, yeah. I got information. Man, I got the best information money can buy.'

So that's it, thinks Doyle. This guy's looking to make a few bucks. Okay, well let's see what he's got.

'Sir, if you know something about a case we're working on—'

'Let's cut the crap, shall we, Detective? We both know what we're talking about here. A bunch of dead bodies, all killed by the same nutso woman, all with weird shit cut into their heads. Ring any bells with you, Detective Doyle?'

Ding-ding-ding. Yessir, those bells are ringing loud and clear. And now Doyle is spinning in his chair and waving his arms frantically at Tommy LeBlanc, who is too engrossed in his reports to notice – that is, until Doyle picks up his bobble-headed leprechaun and throws it at him.

Doyle gestures to LeBlanc to pick up his own phone and connect to the same line. 'Maybe,' says Doyle into the receiver. 'You mind telling me where you heard about this?'

'Straight from the horse's mouth. The woman herself.'

Doyle hears the pride in the man's voice. The smugness that comes from believing he's way ahead of the cops on the biggest case in the city. Which Doyle is starting to think might be the truth.

'Wait a minute. This woman, whoever she is, *told* you she committed some murders? Why would she do that?'

'Don't matter why. You interested in doing business with me or not?'

'I like to know who I'm doing business with. Who are you?'

'Far as this goes, you can call me Bruce. Just so you don't go wasting any precious police time tracking me down, it ain't my real name.'

Doyle looks across at LeBlanc, who just raises his eyebrows. He has heard only a fraction of the conversation, and doesn't know what the hell is going on.

'Okay, Bruce. But what you have to realize is that we get a lot of calls like this. People claiming to know a lot more than they do, and hitting us for handouts.'

'I don't care what you get. This is the real deal. I know who's doing these murders.'

'I'd like to believe you, Bruce, but I gotta be sure. You're gonna have to give me something more. All you've said so far is that it's a woman, which already is starting to sound a little far-fetched, if you know what I mean.'

'Yeah, well, you haven't met this crazy bitch. You haven't seen what she can do.'

The line goes quiet for a second. Doyle exchanges glances with LeBlanc again. They both sense this could be the break they've been waiting for.

Bruce comes back: 'All right, you want proof? There's a vacant lot on East Sixth, opposite a place selling automobile spares. Right next to the lot is an empty tenement, only it ain't so empty now, if you catch my drift. Check it out. See what this nice lady did. Nobody else knows about this, not even you, right? So go see, then maybe we can talk. Catch you later, Detective.'

'Wait,' says Doyle, but he's too late: the line has gone dead. Doyle puts the receiver down and stares at LeBlanc. LeBlanc puts his own receiver down and stares right back.

And then they spring into action.

5.45 PM

'*One hand, Erin. That's all it takes. One hand.*'

She tries to yell back, but all she can manage through the cloth stuffed into her mouth is a muffled, unintelligible sound. But still she tries to inject all the venom she can into that sound.

Ever since Bruce left the apartment, she has been desperately attempting to pull her hands free from the cords that bind them to the bed rails. She is fully aware – Lord knows, she has heard it enough times over her earpiece – that all she needs to do is get one hand free, and then she can untie the knots holding her other limbs. But it's not working. Her wrists are sore and swollen, which is only making things worse.

'*Come on, Erin. He'll be back soon. He'll—*'

Another stifled yell. 'Shut up! Shut the fuck up!' is what she's trying to tell him. She wants to know why the hell she should listen to his advice any longer, especially after the stunt he pulled earlier. She still finds it hard to believe he did that. Bruce could have blown her head off. He was standing right there, with his gun pointed at her, and he could have shot her dead. Why the hell was she put in that situation?

And the worst thing of all? The way he laughed. The way he thought it was the funniest thing ever that he almost got her killed. As if her life means nothing to him, just as he said Georgia's life means nothing to him either. She is starting to believe that now. He has no feeling for others, no empathy. He is a true psychopath, with no comprehension of the pain of his playthings. Like a kid tearing the wings of flies. He is interested, fascinated, but cares nothing for any agony or distress they might feel.

And what that tells her is that she is on her own. She cannot rely on anything this man might tell her. All that stuff about protecting her, getting her through this, making her stronger – it was all horseshit. So far he has done nothing to help her – quite the reverse, in fact. He will bring about her death if it suits him, if it amuses him, and he will do the same to Georgia.

It is a profoundly sobering and frightening realization. Much as she has never fully trusted this man anyway, she has always believed he would at least do his utmost to keep her alive until the end of his sick game.

But that also puzzles her.

Isn't the game the whole point of this? Whether or not he has an ounce of compassion in his body for Erin and Georgia, doesn't he at least want to see this play out to the end? Six bodies, he said. He was very specific about that. And so far he has only four.

So why endanger his plan? Why put his only means of executing that plan in the path of such immediate danger?

It doesn't make sense.

But none of this makes any sense. And now it doesn't matter, because the game is over anyway. Bruce is going to sell her to the cops for whatever drug money he can get. And that means she can never complete her mission. She cannot save Georgia.

'NOOO!' she tries to yell, and cannot even do that. In her frustration, she yanks furiously at the ropes again. Twists and turns her hand this way and that, feeling the cord bite into her flesh, feeling the burning as it sloughs off the top layer of her skin. She bites down on the cloth, tears running down her cheeks and onto the grimy pillow that smells of sweat and grease and cigarette smoke.

'You can do it, Erin. Come on. You can do this.'

But she has already given up. She is exhausted and racked with pain and guilt and the sordidness of it all. This is the end. This is the end.

When she hears Bruce come through the door, she almost finds it too much just to turn her head and look at him. There is a stupid smile on his face.

'Won't be long now,' he says. 'I gave the cops a heads-up. Sent them to check out what you did. Soon as they see that, they'll take me a little more serious. Won't be long now, girl.'

No, she thinks. It won't be long. Not long until you bring about the death of my little girl. You have no idea what you're doing.

No idea at all.

6.08 PM

They exercise caution going in.

A call like that, it could be a trap. Something designed to lure cops into a situation where there is a gun or several pointed right at them.

Some people are weird like that.

But Doyle senses it's the genuine article. Trailing behind all the ESU cops with their body armor and high-powered weapons as they crash into the building, he has the feeling that they will find one thing and one thing only in here.

A body.

And there it is.

Collapsed on the stairs. Hunched over there as if he has just fallen asleep. Flashlights play over him as the cops fan out to search the rest of the building.

But this is all, thinks Doyle. This is all we will find. All we are meant to find. This killer is careful, and works with precision. A dead body, a number cut into the forehead – there, over to you, detectives. Go figure it out.

Except…

This time she (she? Doyle still has difficulty getting to grips with that) wasn't so careful. Somebody saw her. Bruce. He knows who she is. He can lead us right to her door.

Doyle feels his pulse race. The excitement of a chase that could be nearing its climax.

Play it cool. By the book. Don't fuck this up now.

He moves toward the body. Something on the floor, at the foot of the stairs, glints at him. He bends over to take a closer look. A knife. Its tip is covered in blood.

So again this is something different. She has never left a weapon before. What was different this time? What caused her to drop the knife? Did she see Bruce watching her? Did she panic and run?

Doyle shifts the beam from his flashlight up onto the corpse's face. It's a bloody pulp of a face, but the numeral that was slashed into the thin flesh above the eyes is clear enough.

LeBlanc shuffles over. 'Number four?'

'Yup,' says Doyle. 'Number four.'

6.52 PM

'How much longer?' she asks.

She looks at Bruce, who is sitting the wrong way round on a wooden chair, his chin resting on his arms which are on the back of the chair. He has taken the cloth from her mouth, allowing her to speak.

'I'll give 'em a few more minutes. Cops are slow. They're not as smart as they are on the TV.'

'Okay, so you give them a few more minutes. Then what?'

She notices how he creases his brow in puzzlement. He's not such a smart cookie, and right now that's the only thing Erin has on her side.

'What do you mean, then what? I call them up. We negotiate a little. We make the transaction. That's it.'

She lets out a mocking laugh. 'Yeah, right.' Then she turns her head away from him.

Wait, she thinks. Wait for him to take the bait. Give it time for the doubt in my voice to percolate down through his barely functioning brain and kick-start a few of those long dormant neurons back into life.

'What, you think this is complicated? It's not complicated. It's a simple business deal. They pay me, I hand you over. Easy as.'

She turns to face him again. 'Sure. You're right. It'll be easy.'

He's chewing his lip now. Worried.

'Why shouldn't it be easy? The cops want you. They want you bad. Why wouldn't they pay?'

'Think about it, Bruce. Did you ever meet a cop you could trust to stick to their end of the bargain?'

She knows what his answer will be. This man is a slime-ball whose past history with cops will not be the fondest of memories.

'Cops pay out for information all the time.' His voice is almost a whine now. Like a kid trying to justify why he should be allowed to stay up as late as his older brothers.

'Information, sure. A few bucks for a little piece of gossip someone has overheard in a bar or someplace. But we're in a different league here, don't you think, Bruce? A whole new ball-game, in fact. You're withholding information on the whereabouts of a multiple murderer. That's a crime, Bruce. You could go to jail for that. And then there's the kidnapping…'

'Kidnapping?'

'What do you think this is? You brought me here at gunpoint, threatened me, tied me to the bed. That's kidnapping and imprisonment. Now we're talking about a federal rap. And the gun, Bruce? Do you have a license for that? I thought not. What about other offenses? Any outstanding warrants you haven't mentioned? Drugs, maybe? Oh, yeah, and what about the way you just stood and watched while I killed that other guy in the apartment building? You had a gun. You could've stopped it. But you didn't. You just let it happen. What do they call that – accessory to murder?'

Bruce is off the chair now. Starting to pace as he considers the barrage of thoughts she is firing at him.

She presses home her advantage: 'Why should they pay you? When they've got all that on you, why should they pay when they could just threaten to throw your ass in the slammer? You know what the best you can hope for is? That they overlook one or two of your more minor crimes. They give you a pass on a drugs beef or something. Maybe that way you'll serve a little less time in jail.'

There is anger and fear on Bruce's face. He waves his hand at her. 'Nah, you got it wrong. It ain't gonna work like that. You're too valuable.'

'But that's just the problem, Bruce. I'm big news. And when this story breaks properly, you'll be big news too. All kinds of people will be asking about you. The cops know that. They know they've got to do this by the book. They can't just hand over money to a criminal like you and let you walk away.'

Pace, pace, pace.

'So what are you saying? You got a suggestion to make?'

Here we go, Erin.

'Yeah. Let me go.'

He scoffs. 'What?'

'Let me go, Bruce. Untie me, let me walk out of here. Nobody will know. I'm not exactly in a position to go running to the cops, am I? If you don't, if you try to see this thing through, it will go wrong. You can't do this, Bruce. Yes, the cops are dumb, but they're sneaky too. They'll promise you everything and give you nothing. In fact they'll take everything away from you. We could end up sharing a prison cell. Just you, me, and some broken promises. You don't want that. You don't need to take this risk. Let me walk away, and you'll be safe.'

So that's it, she thinks. End of speech. The best I can do. What do you think, Bruce? Gonna give this girl a break? Show this psycho-killer bitch a little felon fellowship?

He stares at her for a while. He pushes his fingers through his hair, scratches his neck, rubs his hand across his dry, flaking lips.

And then he comes toward her. Bears down on her, looking as though he wishes he had never met this crazy woman and just wants to throw her out of her apartment and pretend none of this ever happened.

His gaze shifts to her chafed wrist. He reaches for it.

He's doing it, she thinks. He's going to release me. It worked!

He grabs hold of the cord...

Yes!

... and tightens it. Pulls it hard into her sore, swollen flesh.

'Nice try,' he says. 'For someone so insane, you got a way with words. No wonder you're so dangerous.'

And when he pushes the cloth back into her mouth and fastens it in place, she knows she has lost everything.

7.16 PM

There are just three of them in the squadroom: Doyle, LeBlanc and Cesario. Everybody else is hitting the bricks. Everybody else is running around like headless chickens, chasing a killer who as yet has no name, no face, no predictable pattern of behavior. How do you stop somebody like that? When you don't know where they are going to strike next or when, what can you do except saturate the streets with cops and hope to get lucky?

Well, maybe this is what you can do. Maybe you can sit and stare at a phone and pray for it to ring and for the caller to be a man called Bruce who says, 'This killer you want? Here she is, boys.'

That would be nice. That would be perfect. That would bring the working day to a satisfying close.

Working day? How long is one of those? Time doesn't make a lot of sense to Doyle anymore. He has been at work for a year, it seems. His mind is starting to turn to mush. LeBlanc, too, looks as though he could close his eyes and fall asleep in a heartbeat.

The squadroom is deathly quiet. No two-fingered hammering of keyboards. No swearing, laughing, joking. No sound at all.

And then the phone on Doyle's desk rings.

Cesario points at LeBlanc – the signal for him to pick up his own phone and instruct the guy from the Technical Assistance and Response Unit to trace the incoming call. Then Doyle and Cesario simultaneously pick up their own receivers, and Doyle hits the line answer button.

'Detective Doyle,' he says.

'Hello, Detective. Busy day?'

Doyle is confused. This is a woman's voice. The killer? Could it be her?

He sees the questioning look from Cesario, and he shakes his head.

'Uhm… I'm sorry, but you are…?'

'Forgotten me already, Detective? It's Vanessa Maynard. Psych Services?'

Doyle feels the tension flood out of his system again. His answer is yes, he had forgotten all about her. Forgotten too about Albert, still cooped up in an interview room.

'Oh. Oh, yeah. Listen, do you mind if I call you back? I'm right in the middle of—'

'Yes, you can call me back. That's the good news. The bad news is I can't tell you anything about your boy Albert. Nothing pertinent to the murder he confessed to, anyway. On that he's keeping quiet. I spent hours with him, but got nowhere. He's put up some strong barriers there, Detective. It's going to take more than one session with me to break them down again.'

Doyle realizes that Cesario is using his finger to make throat-cutting motions, urging him to free up the line.

'Okay, thanks. But you still think it would be worth my while calling you back?'

He intends it purely as a work-based enquiry relating to Albert, so it surprises him when what he gets back is a soft purr of a voice.

'Yes, I do, Detective. We can talk about the psychological effects of me fingering your bobble-head.'

Doyle almost gulps audibly. He wasn't expecting a come-on like this. He certainly wasn't expecting to get it when two other guys were listening in to his conversation.

'Yeah, okay, listen, I gotta go. I'll call you.'

He hangs up quickly, instantly putting out of his mind his promise to call her again. Less easy to dismiss is the embarrassment he feels when he sees the expressions on the other men in the room. LeBlanc in particular seems to be enjoying himself.

'Fingering your bobble-head?'

'Uhm, yeah. I… She's referring to… Oh, never mind.'

Cesario doesn't let it go, but for different reasons. 'Don't tell me we've still got that water-cooler guy here – what's his name?'

'Albert.'

'Albert, yeah. What have you done with him?'

'He's, uhm, he's in the cage.'

'And?'

'And what?'

'Well, has he committed a crime or hasn't he?'

Doyle feels like squirming in his chair. 'I don't know yet. That woman on the phone – Vanessa? – she spent a coupla hours with him, and she doesn't know either.'

'That much I gathered. So what's your next move?'

Doyle shrugs. 'We're trying to find out where he lives. I sent his picture out. Problem is, everyone's so tied up with the DOAs, nobody's got time to go knocking on doors looking for people who recognize him.'

'You can't keep him here forever, Doyle. He's got rights, whether he knows it or not.'

'I didn't drag him in here. He came to us.'

'Then make a little more use of that cooperative nature of his. Find out what the hell he knows. If you can't, then you'll have to turn him loose. Either way, I don't want him tying up my interview room for much longer. He should be downstairs.'

Doyle lapses into silence, considering himself rebuked. Albert shouldn't be downstairs, he thinks. Albert is different – in more ways than one. There's more to his story than he's saying – which, admittedly, is not very much. The problem is getting at it. What did you do, Albert? What's going on in that head of yours?

Oh, and yeah, what do you know about these numbers?

Two. Three. One. Four.

As if responding to an eccentric countdown, the phone on Doyle's desk bursts into life.

7.23 PM

I need to be more like Bruce, he thinks.

It's a nerdy name, Bruce. But there is no doubting that Bruce Willis is the coolest guy on the planet. Bruce Lee was also pretty cool. And Bruce Wayne.

Come to think of it, why does the name Bruce have such a bad rep?

I should think and act like Bruce. Yippee Ki-Yay, motherfucker. Bruce would know exactly what to do here. He would make all the right moves, say all the right things. He would always be the one in control.

Right now, Lemmy Bilinski doesn't feel in control. He feels like a rabbit facing up to a pack of wolves. One false move and they'll rip him to shreds. The vast might of the New York Police Department is on the other end of this phone line, and all he's got is his wits.

Gotta be careful here, Lemmy.

He wishes he hadn't listened to that crazy murdering bitch. She put doubts in his head. Before that, he knew what he was doing. He had it all planned out.

Well, actually, that's not strictly true. He had *some* of it planned out. Like many a story writer, he had a beginning and an end in mind, and was hoping that one could be made to lead seamlessly into the other. He hoped to wing it in between.

But now the bitch has made him hold up a magnifying glass and scrutinize the detail, and he's no longer certain he can overlook the plot holes in this story. He's not sure he can pull it off.

Shit!

'Eighth Precinct. Detective Doyle.'

Too late now, Lemmy. You're committed, guy. The light's on green and you gotta go.

'Yo, Detective. It's me again. Bruce. You remember me?'

He thinks that sounds good. Confident. He's the man.

'I remember you, Bruce.'

Course you do, Doyle. You need me, man. I'm gonna make you famous. Gonna hand over a serial killer and make this city safe. Because you dumb cops can't do it without me. That's why this will work, because you *need* me.

He says, 'You checked out my info, right? You know I'm the real deal here, right?'

'We know it. Where did you hear about it?'

Lemmy has prepared himself for this. He knows how the cops play. This isn't one guy on his phone, all by himself. This is a whole team of cops listening in. A couple of tech-heads pressing buttons and shit to track him on the phone network. Lemmy has seen enough movies to know that this cop will try to stall for time until they can pounce on his ass.

'Don't try to get me into no long conversations, Detective. I know how you guys work, so I ain't hanging around. Now are you gonna pay for this bitch, or what?'

The answer isn't immediate. Lemmy makes use of those few seconds to take a good long look around him. He's at a payphone on the corner of a block, just outside a bodega, with a good view of approaching pedestrians and traffic. A different payphone from the one he used last time, which probably has cops swarming all over it. That's something else he learned from the movies. Keep moving, keep changing your routine. Don't, whatever you do, make use of a cellphone. Those satellites can home in on your ass from a thousand miles up, wherever you are.

'You there, cop? Don't fuck with me, man, or I'm gone.'

'I'm here, Bruce. Don't hang up. We'll pay, okay? If your information leads to an arrest, we'll pay.'

The magic words. *We'll pay.* Well, fuck me sideways. How easy was that?

Lemmy starts to think numbers. How far can he push this? Five thousand bucks? Ten thousand? Nah, gotta be more than that. This woman is a menace to the city. She's running rings around the cops. Start at twenty? Better to aim high and come down rather than go home regretting he didn't ask for more. Better to—

Wait a minute. Hold the bus.

What did the cop say?

'What do you mean, if it leads to an arrest?'

'Just what it says, Bruce. If what you give me is solid, and we can make an arrest on the strength of it, then you get your money.'

Lemmy doesn't like the sound of this. This doesn't sit right with his plans at all. What he's got is solid, all right. It's cast iron. He can fulfill his side of the contract, in spades. But what's shaking his tree right now is the small print. The terms and conditions. These are worrying.

'Uh-uh. I don't like that *if* business. You gotta pay in advance, dude. You get me the money, then I deliver you a killer.'

'Sorry, Bruce. It don't work like that. It's obvious you know more than most about this case, but that's as far as it goes. Shouldn't be a problem, though, right? We're the law, Bruce. We ain't gonna scam you.'

In Lemmy's experience, anyone who says they ain't gonna scam you are going to do exactly that. Cops in particular rank especially low on his list of people who are trustworthy.

'I don't care how you usually do things. This one is different. This time I tell you how to get me the money, and when it's in my hands and I know I'm safe, I'll tell you where Suzie Psycho is.'

The response is immediate. Not even a second to mull it over. 'Forget it, Bruce. We can't do it that way. What are you worried about? Your intel is good, right?'

'My intel is fireproof,' he snaps back.

Which makes it all the more difficult. Lemmy knows what a prize he has in his hands. He knows she is worth more money to him than he has ever had in his life. His plan was to get the money, tell the cops where she is, then leave the city. Just take that money and hop on a Greyhound and get the fuck out of here.

But what if the cops know who he is and where he lives even before he has the money? What if they become aware of the kind of person they're dealing with? Will they still be willing to play ball then?

Kidnapping and imprisonment, the bitch said. Illegal possession of a firearm, she said. Drugs offenses, she said. And then there's what she doesn't know about. The fact that he's on parole. One minor infringement and he's back in jail.

With that kind of leverage, why would the cops even consider bargaining with him?

This is starting to look doubtful. All that money, just out of reach. So close and yet so far.

'What if,' he says, 'what if this intel I got, it was obtained by some slightly dubious means?'

A pause. Lemmy can imagine the cop grinning to himself, thinking the scales are quickly tipping his way.

'How dubious, Bruce?'

'Felony dubious, maybe.'

'We can talk about that. See what wriggle room there is. Nothing is impossible. The important thing is to get this deal sorted out.'

Lemmy can see the money slipping away, and it's killing him. The cop is being evasive, trying to make light of what is a serious issue here, namely Lemmy's freedom. The cops don't want him thinking about that. They want him to remain focused on the money, to picture himself surrounded by piles of lovely green dough. And he wishes he could do that, but it's all blowing away. It's all disappearing.

The bitch was right.

He knows that even more when he hears the siren.

This city, sirens are not a surprising sound. But this one, this particular one, Lemmy knows is not good. It's one of those whoop-whoop *get the fuck out of my way* type sirens, coming from around a corner of the next block. And when the police cruiser finally rounds the corner, it makes no more noise. It does this because its occupants are hoping to sneak up on Lemmy. He knows this. He sees how the stupid cops try to hop their car around the traffic without attracting his attention, and he knows it's intended for him.

'You cocksucker!' he yells into the receiver. 'Fuck your deal!'

'Bruce...'

But Lemmy has stopped listening. He is already sprinting down the street, heading for home, running hell-for-leather away from those dirty bastard cops, and wishing he were more like Bruce Willis. He dodges traffic, he dodges people, and he is almost crying over the money he never had but which he feels has just been taken away from him. The money he was allowed to sniff but not touch. It was cruel, so cruel.

He stops running only when he gets to his apartment building, and as he pauses to catch his breath in the lobby he tries to decide what he should do next. He tries convincing himself that all is not lost. He still has the bitch, and the cops still want her. There has to be a way of making a sale here.

But his doubts increase with each step he takes up the staircase. He didn't trust the cops before, and he trusts them even less now. They kept him on the phone. Kept him talking while they tracked him down with their fancy-dancy equipment. And then they sent the dogs after him. They had no intention of making any deals. The bitch was right. The cops want her *and* him.

So what to do? Jesus Christ, I got a crazy-ass killer tied to my bed. Can you believe that? Not an everyday turn of events. Hey guys, I got a hot chick in my bedroom. Want a piece of her? Yeah, well, you'll need to bring protection. No, not that – I'm talking about something that will stop your head being caved in.

He can't release her.

He's already decided that. If the cops get her, which they will eventually, then she'll blab about him. Why wouldn't she? And if she kills more people before they catch her, won't that make him some kind of accessory to murder? Even if she doesn't kill anyone else – even if he dumps her someplace and calls the cops – she will still blab and the cops will still throw him back into prison.

He's not going back there. Uh-uh.

So what does that leave?

Not a lot. Not a lot of options, my friend.

Christ, what a mess. What a fucking weird mess.

I'll have to waste her.

I got no choice. She's a liability now. A fucking seagull around my neck. No, not a seagull. That other big fucking sea bird. Whatever. She needs to go. She needs to be out of my life before she fucks it up even more than it is already.

Shit.

So in he goes. Into his apartment. His mind occupied with the logistics of how he's going to do this. How he's going to kill her and dump her and restore order to a situation that he never should have gotten into in the first place. In he goes and turns his eyes directly on the bed where Erin the psycho-killer mad crazy fucked-up bitch is lying and waiting and hoping that he hasn't brought bad news.

Except she isn't.

On the bed.

Where she is, God help me, is to one side of the door. Holding a hammer. Swinging a hammer. Bringing that hammer in a wide arc so that she can drive it into the side of my skull. That's where she is.

Oh, crap.

This never woulda happened to Bruce Willis.

8.28 PM

The break the cops get comes far too late for Lemmy.

It comes in the form of fingerprints found in one of the first floor apartments of the abandoned tenement building. The prints are on a beer bottle next to some recently used drug paraphernalia on the dusty floor. The Latent Print Development Unit identifies them as belonging to one Lemmy Bilinski, currently out on parole having served time in Rikers for burglary, and now residing on East Sixth Street, practically a stone's throw from the derelict tenement.

So the cops hurry on over there en masse, and they enter Lemmy's apartment without even the courtesy of a knock, the manners of some people, and what do they find there? The lifeless corpse of Lemmy Bilinski himself, one side of his head caved in and a nice big numeral sliced into his forehead:

'Shit!' cries Doyle as he slams his hand against a wall. 'Too fucking late again. Why are we always one fucking step behind?'

He's tired. Really, really tired. Each killing has drained a little more out of him, and he can see no end to this carnage. He has nothing to go on. There is no logic here, no apparent pattern. Well, except for the numbers.

Those damned numbers!

Five victims, numbered one to five, but not in precise sequence. Why not in sequence? What the hell does it mean?

It's counting. It has to be counting. But who the hell counts like that? Everybody else on the planet counts one, two, three, four, five. Nobody takes the one and puts it after the three, keeping everything else the same. Why would you do that?

He looks to LeBlanc for help. 'Do you get this? Do you understand what the hell is going on here?'

But LeBlanc shakes his head. 'I'm just a simple country boy. This is far too complicated for me.'

Doyle stares down at the body. Is it complicated? Or are we just making it complicated? Could it be a lot simpler than it appears?

If only they had managed to grab Lemmy at the payphone. Or at least get close enough to make a positive ID. Shit!

Doyle worries that he mishandled the phone conversation. Maybe he should have given in to Lemmy a bit more, in which case Lemmy might have given them something more in return. Maybe then Lemmy would still be alive and the killer would be in their custody.

Jeez, I am so tired.

8.45 PM

'**N**o more,' she says. 'I'm done.'

'*Come on, Erin. You can't give up now. Look at how close you are. Five down, and only one more to go. One more. You can do this.*'

'No, I can't.'

'*You can. You've proved how resourceful you are. Think about what you just did. You were tied up, with no hope of escape, and yet you did it. You did escape. That's the kind of person you are, Erin. You're stronger than any other woman I've ever met.*'

She doesn't feel strong. She feels wasted. She feels like a crumpled-up dishrag, all limp and worthless. What happened back there wasn't down to her strength; it was luck, that's all. Sheer good fortune.

She remembers the desperate, furious way in which she fought against those bindings. Pulling and twisting and bucking, without any real thought for what she was doing. Just hoping that something would give way, something would break and release her. She recalls the burning of her skin against the cord, the squeaking complaints of the lumpy mattress, the rattling of the cheap metal bedrails.

Ah yes, the rattling.

Even now she's not sure what led her to focus on the rattling. She remembers raising her eyes, bending her neck back as much as she could so she could watch the bedstead as she pulled on it. Rattle, rattle, rattle. And, running along the top of the vertical posts, a single black horizontal rail, fixed to the others by a brass knob.

And the brass knob was jiggling.

It was loose.

All that time fighting with the cords, and it was the bed that was the weakest link.

It was quite a stretch getting her hand to the top of the rail. She didn't think she was going to make it. It felt as though her arm was coming out of its socket as she slid it as far as she could up the post. And then more stretching – her fingers crawling slowly over the metal as she sought the brass knob. Then an agonizingly long period of time as she unscrewed the seemingly endless thread, her body crying out for mercy until, eventually, the knob came away with a jolt and the whole bedstead practically fell apart, freeing her hand and allowing her to undo the other knots holding her there. She managed it just in time, barely seconds before Bruce put his key in the door. Just time to grab the hammer from her purse and make it across the room so that she could stove that creep's head in. And after that? Business as usual, only this time with Bruce's own knife, from his own vomit-inducing kitchen.

She did nothing clever there, nothing courageous or strong. She got lucky. Throughout all of this she has come several times within a whisker of being caught or hurt or killed, and all that has saved her has been luck. But luck doesn't last forever.

'You were supposed to help me,' she says. 'You told me you would look after me.'

'*You're here, aren't you? Back in your own apartment. Safe and sound.*'

'No thanks to you. Why did you do that, in Bruce's apartment? Why did you make me attack him at that moment, when he was ready for me?'

'It was a test.'

'A test? What kind of test?'

'*A test of him, to see what he was capable of, and a test of you, to see how much you trusted me.*'

'Right. I see. Never mind that he could have killed me. Well, you know what? It's backfired, mister. Because now I don't trust you an inch. I don't trust you to keep me safe, I don't trust you to look after my baby, and I don't trust you to give Georgia back to me when this is all over. How about that? Is that what you wanted?'

'*You're making something out of nothing, Erin. You're alive, aren't you? You're free from that crazy junkie.*'

'I was nearly killed. And you found it hilarious. You thought it was the funniest thing ever.'

'Well, you should have seen it from here. It was pretty funny. You running at Bruce. Bruce not knowing whether to empty his gun or fill his pants. It was like something from a comedy show.'

'Yeah? I'm glad it amused you. I'm so happy you've had your fun. Make the most of it, because there's no more. Show's over, asshole.'

'Don't be such a killjoy, Erin. It wasn't so terrible.'

She doesn't answer him. She wants to let him know how badly he's misjudged things. Not that he will necessarily make that inference. He doesn't think like other people do. His mind runs on different tracks.

And that's why she has given up trying to second-guess him. He is too erratic, too unpredictable. His responses are just downright weird.

It was dangerous out there tonight. Life-threateningly dangerous. She has never looked down the barrel of a gun before, and hopes she never has to again. But that fear pales into insignificance in comparison to what she now knows to be true.

She is not getting Georgia back.

This man's promises mean jack. His assurances mean jack. He is using her, and using her child, to get his kicks. After that… well, after that, it's the end.

Earlier, in Bruce's apartment, she had puzzled over why her tormentor should jeopardize his plan by getting her killed before she had accomplished her mission. Now she understands.

There is no mission.

At least not in the precise sense of killing six people before midnight. That was a crock of shit. Six was just a number. He could have chosen five or seven, or fifty. Similarly, midnight was just a time. He chose those parameters because he thought they were the most he could get away with. He viewed those as the upper limit of his victim's acceptability threshold. Too many bodies stretched over too long a period would just be seen as impossible, and his plan would come to naught.

All he wants is to be entertained.

Sex doesn't do it for this guy. He's not interested in her body. What he wants is to live vicariously through a killer – seeing, hearing and experiencing what it's like to murder without actually having to do it himself.

And he wants to do that for as long as he can.

The only reason he told her to attack Bruce was that he got bored. It wasn't a test, as he claims. Because she had been caught, the pace of the game was flagging, and so he needed to spice it up a touch.

And that's why she knows that when this is over, when she has killed her sixth victim, he will lose interest. The game will be at an end. He will dispose of Georgia because she is no longer useful to him, he will abandon Erin to whatever fate awaits her, and he will move on – probably to another unsuspecting victim in another perverted game.

But what if she doesn't go after her sixth victim? Well, then the outcome remains the same, doesn't it?

You're damned if you do, Erin, and damned if you don't.

So you might as well go down fighting. You might as well cheat this man of his prize. And there's only one way you can do that.

The movement is quick, before he can say anything that might stop her. In one swift motion she snatches out her earpiece.

She holds it up in front of the camera still attached to her jacket.

'I know you can see this,' she says. 'I know that you're probably making all kinds of threats now. But I can't hear you. More to the point, I can't hear Georgia either. I know you're going to hurt her, but I believe you've always been planning to do that anyway. It's just a question of when. So you might as well do it now. Go ahead, kill her. I can't stop you. I never could stop you. But what you need to know is this. I win. I win the game. You asked for six victims, but you're not getting them. I refuse. And that means I win. You're a loser. You will always be a loser.

'You might be wondering how I can possibly do such a thing, how I could willingly give you the excuse to hurt or kill my baby. The answer is, you did that for me. While you were enjoying living through me, I was changing. I was becoming what you don't have the balls to be: a cold-hearted serial killer. Bruce saw that in me before I realized it myself. He saw how wrapped up I was in the killing of that junkie friend of his. I was shocked when he told me. I didn't believe it. But now I know he was right. Nobody can do what I've done without being changed in some way, without becoming desensitized to the act of murder.

'You kept going on about the lesson I would learn from all this. I think you were talking through your ass. You had no idea what would happen to me, and you didn't care. But the ironic thing is that I have become stronger. Nothing matters to me anymore. You can't hurt me. So I have only one thing left to say to you.

'Goodbye.'

9.38 PM

'What do you mean, it's not my case anymore?'

Doyle does his best to sound affronted, but he was expecting this. This thing has grown too big, become too high-profile. Somebody has murdered five people in a single day, and there's no sign of the rampage coming to an end. Unable to contain the pressure any longer, the police top brass have finally gone public and confirmed what news reporters were already suggesting, namely that a spate of unexplained homicides on the East Side are linked – are in fact suspected to be the work of a single killer. Members of the public have been advised to exercise extreme caution and to be vigilant until such time as the perpetrator has been apprehended. Other than that, have a nice day.

Doyle would not normally be back in the squadroom so soon after attending a homicide scene. He would be canvassing. He would be talking to witnesses. He would be chasing up friends and relatives. But he has been dragged back here, along with LeBlanc. Ordered to return to base, leaving others to work the case. He knows what's coming.

'It's the Task Force's baby now,' says Cesario. 'No offense, Cal, but there's no way they could leave a precinct detective running the show. Doesn't matter how good that individual cop is, the people will expect to see a proportionate response. Besides, you're ready to drop to the floor. Both of you.'

Doyle looks across at LeBlanc. He sees that there is no resistance there, no inclination to fight the good fight any longer.

He turns back to Cesario. 'So what are you saying?' An unnecessary question, he knows, but his brain can deal only with plain speaking right now.

Cesario sighs. He sounds tired too, and he's been awake for only half the time that Doyle has.

'I'm saying go home. Get some rest. You're no good to me as you are. With any luck we'll catch this lunatic before the night's out. If not, come back in the morning and help out. It might not be your case, but you can still work it.'

Doyle nods. He feels he should be arguing against this, but his mind and body won't let him. They're saying, *We want sleep, damn it!*

Besides, a small part of him is glad to be shut of this case. Let somebody else feel the frustration of not catching this perp. This one's impossible. There's no logic, no sense, no—

Yeah, haven't we done this already? Don't I keep telling myself how there's no pattern here, that there's nothing concrete to hang my hat on? Not that I would hang my hat on something made out of concrete. And not that I ever wear a hat either, but anyway…

See, that's what I mean. That's how fucking tired I am. I'm rambling. I'm delirious. I need to get away from the job for a few hours. Away from the fruitcakes and craziness and the horror.

So, okay, Lou. You win. I'm going home. Call me when it's over and the world is back to normal.

Doyle forces himself to stand, even though he could quite happily go to sleep in this hard, uncomfortable chair. He beckons to LeBlanc, who follows him to the door.

'Oh, and before you go home,' says Cesario, 'you got some tidying up to do.'

Doyle pushes up his eyelids to get another look at his boss.

'Tidying up?'

'Alfred. Albert. Whatever the hell his name is. I want him off this floor.'

Crap, thinks Doyle. He'd almost forgotten about Albert again.

'What am I supposed to do with him?'

'I don't care,' says Cesario. 'Take him home. Leave him on somebody's stoop with a note to look after him. Whatever, put him someplace that isn't here.'

An impulse to resist starts to rise up Doyle's chest, but fails miserably to reach his mouth. Cesario is right. They've got nothing on Albert. He says he killed his mother, but lots of people say lots of things to police officers, an extremely high proportion of those things being untrue. People have passed through this station house asserting perpetration of every crime in the book, from attempted assassination of Donald Duck to sex with an underage muskrat. Doyle would like to believe that Albert wouldn't lie so baldly to him, but at the same time he wants Albert's claim to be a figment of his unfathomable imagination. Whatever the truth of the matter, Doyle accepts he has failed to investigate Albert's story as fully as he might. But hey, things have been kinda hectic around here.

So is Albert a killer or not? Doyle doesn't know. What he does know is what Cesario has said to him before. The man has rights. He can't be kept here indefinitely. If he had a lawyer fighting his cause, he'd have been out of here hours ago.

Doyle nods wearily. He has failed to stop a serial killer and he has failed to give Albert the commitment he deserves. This whole day has been one of failure.

Ho-hum.

9.42 PM

She's dead. Georgia. She's dead.

Erin can feel it in her bones. It has been almost an hour since she took out her earpiece. She has sat and stared at it lying there on her nightstand, constantly tempted to succumb and put it back in and issue a groveling apology for her outrageous defiance, sorry, sorry, sorry, I didn't mean anything by it, please don't hurt my baby, please don't.

But she hasn't surrendered. She has stuck to her guns, even though they have been aimed at her own child. In a sense she has also been the one to pull the trigger.

Do you hear that, Erin? Do you understand what you've done? You have condemned your own child to death.

Yes, yes. I know it. I understand fully. It's over. It's done.

She wonders whether she will kill herself, and thinks that she probably will. Why not? What is left to live for?

It was the right thing to do. The *righteous* thing to do. He was always going to kill Georgia, and he was going to find it all the more enjoyable in the knowledge that he had won his mind game with the baby's mother.

Well, that's all been shot to pieces hasn't it, mister?

You lose.

I win.

And I think now it's time to go. Time to leave the world.

Erin stands. Her eyes still on the earpiece, she mouths words at it: *Goodbye, Georgia. Forgive me.*

Then she tears her gaze away and starts to think about other matters. How to do this. How to end things. How to take away the pain.

The noise of the door buzzer seems unreal. A distant drone, unconnected with her location in either time or space. And so she ignores it. It has no meaning.

But it doesn't go away. It returns, again and again, each call for attention stronger than the last. And finally it penetrates her bubble. It makes itself perceived by the emaciated part of her consciousness that clings to the real, horror-filled world. It demands to be dealt with before she is allowed to slip completely into comfortable numbness.

She decides it will be quick. Hello and goodbye, with as little as possible in between. I have to go now, if you don't mind; I have wrists that need slitting.

At the door is Mr Wiseman. She might have guessed. Nobody else comes calling here, which says everything about the success of her new start in this city.

He holds up a Tupperware box. Sloshing around inside it is some viscous pale liquid.

'Chicken soup,' he says. 'I made extra. I thought you might like some.'

How surreal, she thinks. The end of my life marked by a serving of chicken soup.

She goes to take the container, then thinks better of it. He might never get it back. When the authorities come to clean up after her, it won't occur to them to go looking for the rightful owner of the box.

Such a trivial matter, and yet it seems so important.

'It's very kind of you,' she says. 'But actually I'm not very hungry.'

'When did you last eat?' he asks, as though her lack of nutritional intake today is patently obvious. But his voice is not inquisitorial; it is overflowing with concern. And because of that she finds it difficult to respond. Finds it hard to hurt him with a harsh rejection.

He presses on: 'You should eat. You should look after yourself. You don't... you don't seem happy.'

Again, what to answer? I'm ecstatic? I'm delirious? He knows that's not true. But what the hell does it matter what he knows? It's over. Take the soup and close the door. Leave the Tupperware to him in your will, if that's what's worrying you.

'I'm okay,' she says. 'It's not been a great day, but I'm surviving. Tomorrow will be a better one.'

Except that there is no tomorrow. There are no more days after this. This is my last conversation, and it's about chicken soup. That's funny. That's hilarious.

Wiseman looks over her shoulder, as he did the last time he was here. 'Is... Is your baby home again now?'

He had to ask, didn't he? He had to go and ask about Georgia. But when she searches his face she understands why he's asking. He knows something's wrong. Shit, it doesn't take a genius to work out that something is very badly amiss here.

'Yes,' she lies. 'She's sleeping.' A deep sleep. The deepest sleep of all.

She can see in his eyes that he doesn't believe her. But what the hell? It doesn't matter anymore. Believe me or don't believe me. I don't care.

'Erin,' he says. 'Forgive me if I'm being intrusive in any way, but... I think you need help. I think you need to talk to someone.'

Help? I'm beyond help now, but thank you for asking.

'Yes,' she says. 'Maybe I'll do that.'

She doesn't tell him that she has been talking – or at least listening – to someone almost incessantly for the past twenty-four hours. Her constant companion, always there but never seen. And what a help he's been. Sure, look what he's done for me.

Says Wiseman, 'Is it about your... your baby?'

Her eyes widen at the mention of Georgia. She finds herself suddenly on the defensive in response to this sign of someone showing an interest in her offspring. Like a feral animal protecting its young, she wants to bare her teeth and hiss.

But why? She has already surrendered her child. Georgia is beyond hurting, beyond the need for her mother's shielding presence.

'What makes you say that?' she asks.

'Some mothers,' he begins, 'they don't cope too well. Especially with young ones. Please don't think I'm being disrespectful when I say that. My wife was the same. With Leonard, I mean. She could never understand why this had to happen to us. What did we do wrong? What sins had we committed that made God feel he had to punish us in this way? I don't think she ever really came to terms with it. I don't think she would have died as young as she did if she had learned to accept that sometimes life is just like that. You have to take the rough with the smooth.'

'What happened to her? Your wife?'

'A stroke. When she was only fifty-two. She was too stressed, too anxious. Her blood pressure was through the roof. She smoked like a chimney. All the danger signs were there, but she refused to see them. It was like she was driving through every stop light at eighty miles an hour. There are only so many times you can do that without crashing into something.'

This is news to Erin. All the times she has spoken to Wiseman, and this is the first time she has heard about his wife. Or perhaps not. Perhaps he has related all this to her before, many times, and she has been too strangled by her own affairs to listen.

'So, basically you've been looking after Leonard by yourself for all these years?'

'Yeah, I guess so. Did the best I could, anyhow. But that's what we do, isn't it? As parents, I mean? We do the best we can. We don't always get it right, but we try. We give our children everything, because they are the most important things in our lives. They are why we exist, to give life to others so that they can carry forward what we have started. Sometimes, like with Leonard, things don't turn out as we hoped. But that doesn't make him any less valuable in my eyes. He is in me, and I am in him, even with his problems. But it's not always easy. There are many days I've cried over what happened to Leonard, and what will become of him once I've gone. But I carry on. I do what I can for him. And I hope others will help him once I've gone.'

His old eyes are suddenly a lot more moist, his face sagging with the weight of years of hardship.

'I think what I'm trying to say here, Erin, is that it's okay to ask for help. It's okay to admit we can't do it alone. Being a parent is the hardest job in the world, and sometimes it gets too much. But don't give up. Don't lose sight of what's important.'

She suspects that he's talking partly to himself, but it doesn't dilute his message. He's right, of course. So fucking right it hurts. The painful truth of it stabs deep into her heart. We live for our children. They come first. Georgia comes first, always. And if there is a chance, no matter how remote that her life can be spared, then that chance should be taken.

It doesn't matter if I die, she thinks. It doesn't matter if I have to spend the rest of my life in prison. And, most of all, it doesn't matter if Georgia's abductor wins his stupid game with me. A *game*, for Christ's sake! What was I thinking? Why did I feel it important to deny him his prize? Yes, he will probably murder Georgia when this is over, but the key word there is *probably*. It's not a certainty. It's not set in stone. I still have a chance of keeping her alive.

Or do I?

She is suddenly in Wiseman's face. Kissing him on the cheek, much to his surprise. 'Thank you, Samuel,' she says. 'That could be the most meaningful thing anyone's ever said to me. Thank you.' And then she's closing the door on him, giving him smiles that say everything's all right now, it'll all work out. And he looks bemused but happy to be of service. And when the door clicks shut she runs into the bedroom. She snatches up the earpiece, makes a point of flashing it in front of the brooch, plugs it back into her ear.

'I'm back,' she says, her words tumbling out in a rush. 'I made a mistake, okay? But now I'm back. Forget what I said before. I was stressed out. I lost it. But it's okay now. I'm on it again.'

Nothing. Silence. She puts a finger to the earpiece and pushes it in as far as it will go. She strains to hear the slightest sound. But still there is only empty, heartbreaking silence.

'Okay?' she says. 'Did you hear what I said?'

No response. And now her panic is mounting. Has he abandoned his game? Has he decided to find his amusement elsewhere, with Georgia?

No, no. Don't let it be like that.

'I was wrong, okay? Is that what you what you want me to say? Tell me what I have to say to you. Tell me what I have to do.'

Not a breath. Not a murmur. Not a whisper. Just her own pulse pounding furiously in her head.

'TALK TO ME, YOU SONOFABITCH!'

But it is starting to sink in that her mistake was a fatal one. She offered up her daughter, and her daughter was taken. What could be simpler?

Why should she even suppose he would shrink from carrying out his threat?

'PLEEEAAASE!'

And then:

'*Welcome back, Erin.*'

His voice. As welcome now as it was detested before. She has to fight to prevent herself from descending into a wailing state of gratitude and obsequiousness.

'I made a mistake,' she repeats. Tries to make it sound matter-of-fact. A glitch in the system. Nothing irrecoverable, so let's pick up where we left off.

'*A mistake? Surely not, Erin? Not where your daughter's life is concerned? Nobody makes a mistake of that magnitude, with that much at stake.*'

'I… I'm tired. I'm out of my mind with stress and worry. I didn't know what I was doing. But it's all good now. I just want to do what's best for Georgia.'

'*I see. Her welfare is at the heart of this. So when you said I could go ahead and kill her…*'

'I didn't mean it. I thought you were planning to kill her anyway, so I just thought… I misjudged you, okay? I thought you wouldn't honor your side of the bargain, that you wouldn't give Georgia back to me even if I did what you asked.'

'*But now you suddenly understand how serious I am? Tell me, Erin, what led to this miraculous epiphany?*'

'You saw me talking with Mr Wiseman. You heard what was said. He made me realize something. About what's really important. About why we even bother to go on living.'

'*Hurrah for Mr Wiseman. What a saint that man is. Okay, Erin, so now you know I'm a man of integrity, right?*'

Not exactly how I'd put it, she thinks. But…

'Yes.'

'*So you understand that if I say I'm going to do something, then I will do it?*'

Just like how you protected me the way you promised, she thinks. But…

'Yes.'

'And what did I say I would do if you defied me again, Erin?'

No. Please. Not that.

'You… you haven't…'

'What did I say, Erin?'

'I… I don't know. You're—'

'Yes, you do know. You remember precisely what I said.'

She feels his pressure. She is a spineless lowly life-form and he is standing on her, squishing her into a wet mess of protoplasm.

'Is she still alive? Is Georgia alive?'

'You said I was a loser, Erin. You said I would always be a loser.'

'I was angry. I was confused. I didn't mean it. Please. Tell me. Is Georgia okay?'

'I made it very clear to you how I would punish you, didn't I?'

'Yes, but—'

'Didn't I?'

'Yes. Yes, you did. What have you done? Is she dead? Please tell me you haven't killed my baby.'

The pause. The lengthy silence he always knows when to interject for maximum impact. Several seconds of excruciating agony.

'No, I haven't killed her.'

Something in the way he says that.

'Then… what? What have you done to her? She's just a baby.'

'I told you I would punish you, Erin.'

'What have you done?'

'Let's just say that there is a lot less of Georgia than there was before.'

Oh. Oh, Jesus. Oh, God, no.

Images flashing before Erin's eyes. Gruesome imaginings of sawn-off body parts and a child who cannot comprehend why this world is so painful and cruel.

Erin opens her mouth, but the words won't come. They are replaced by primitive spasmodic sounds of extreme loss and horror and disbelief.

'I tell ya,' says the voice, *'that kid really knows how to fill a diaper.'*

At first the comment seems such a non-sequitur that it just sits on the fringes of Erin's consciousness, unable to push through the barrier she has put up against further demolition of her fragile mind. But gradually she becomes more aware of it, senses the importance of it.

'What?'

'There must be a gallon in there at least. That's what I was saying. About there being less of her now.'

She rolls this around in her mind, examining it in minute detail for a catch. What is he saying? That it was just a joke? That Georgia is still whole and perfect and unharmed?

'You haven't... you haven't hurt her? She's okay?'

'She's fine, Erin. I haven't hurt her.'

'Why? I mean, thank you. But why?'

'Because I knew you'd be back. You don't need threats from me anymore. You know what you need to do, and you're too close to give up now. One more killing, that's all. And then you and Georgia can be back together again.'

So it was a joke. A twisted prank, about which she should be spitting fire. She should be ranting and raving and filling the air with curses that would make a trooper blush. But she isn't. She's grateful, so grateful. He could have hurt Georgia so badly. He had the perfect excuse and he chose not to exploit it. Bizarrely, she feels she owes him something. Even after all he has done to her, she feels somehow owned by him now.

He says, *'Would you like to hear your baby? She's making some cute noises right now.'*

It's the first time he has offered anything like this. The first time he has been... well, *nice*. The contrast with his previous manner strikes her so hard it causes tears to form. She should tell herself to stop it. She shouldn't fall into this emotional trap he has created. But she can't even think about resisting. She has no willpower left. She will do whatever he asks.

'Yes, please,' she says.

And as she listens to her baby one more precious time, she tells herself that this will not be the last of it. It cannot be the last. They will be reunited soon.

Just one more death.

That's all it will take.

9.55 PM

He plays it safe with a burger and fries. A plain burger. No mayo, no dill pickle, no tomato, no lettuce, no cheese, no nothing. Just a burger. With fries.

To Doyle's relief, Albert seems happy with the choice. He takes a huge bite out of the burger, then puts his finger in the box of fries and swirls them around.

'What are you looking for?' says Doyle.

'Ketchup.'

Doyle reaches into the paper bag for some sachets. 'You want ketchup? I got ketchup.'

'No. I'm checking there's no ketchup. I don't like ketchup on my food. Ketchup is made from tomatoes, which are technically a fruit. Why would I put fruit on potatoes?'

Yeah, thinks Doyle. How stupid am I? Ketchup is for fruit salads, right?

He allows Albert to eat for a while, then says, 'What's your favorite meal, Albert?'

'Lasagna. I like lasagna.'

'Yeah? Do you buy it in, from the supermarket, or does your mom make it?'

'My mom makes it. Nobody else can do it like my mom.'

'I'll bet. She's a real good cook, huh?'

'The best. She can do cakes and pies too. And ice cream. And toast.'

'Toast, huh? That's pretty good. What else does she do for you?'

'She washes my clothes. She helps me to read books. Lots of things.'

'Sounds like a wonderful woman. Sounds like the perfect mother.'

'She is. And her birthday is on the seventeenth day of the eleventh month. Those numbers are both prime.'

'Even better. I don't believe there are many mothers who could be all those things.'

'No. She's special.'

Doyle smiles and nods along. Sorry, Albert, he thinks, but I have to do this...

'So why would you kill her?'

Albert halts in mid-chew. He sets down the remains of his burger on its greaseproof paper. Then he reaches into his mouth and takes out the partly masticated sphere of food and puts that on the paper too. It's as though he has suddenly lost all appetite, as if the very thought of food is enough to make him balk.

Doyle knew what he was doing. A standard interrogation technique. Take the suspect along a comfortable path, something about which they are happy to wax lyrical. Get them into a steady flow. Then suddenly throw in a curve ball – something that comes so hard and fast they are unable to make the mental adjustments required to deal with it. That's when they slip up.

He had taken Albert into the zone. The poor guy couldn't even see beyond the present tense that Doyle insisted on using. Far as he was concerned, his mother was still on this earth, still tending to his needs, still loving him.

And then the whammy. The big fat reminder that she has gone. That, in fact, her absence is down to him. This is all his fault, and what has he got to say about that?

Doyle sees how the shock has registered with Albert, and he hates himself for taking such an advantage of the guy. But this is a last-ditch attempt. These are emergency measures. Sometimes you gotta be cruel to be kind.

And so he presses on: 'Tell me, Albert. Please, explain it to me. You've told me nothing bad about your mother. Everything you've said about her makes her sound like a saint. She did everything for you. She cooked for you, cleaned for you, helped you to learn stuff. Why would you hurt someone like that? What possible reason could you have?'

It starts then. The flitting gaze, the tapping fingers, the scratching behind the ears. Doyle finds himself growing irritated. He knows he shouldn't allow that to happen. Albert can't help it. And yet the actions are starting to feel like those of an annoying brat who sticks his fingers in his ears and sings loudly to avoid having to communicate.

'Did you really kill your mother, Albert? Really? I don't think so. I don't think you did it. I don't think you're giving me the full story, are you?'

Albert is humming now. Muttering. Legs trembling.

'Why don't you just end this now? Tell me your real name. Tell me where you live. Tell me what really happened to your mom.'

'I… I told you what happened.'

'No. No, you didn't. Not in any detail. Maybe it's not as bad as you think. But if your mom is hurt, don't you think we should go to her? Don't you think you should tell us where she is, so that we can help her?'

Albert starts slapping his head. 'It's bad, it's bad. She's dead. You can't help her. Nobody can help her. I killed her.'

'How, Albert? How did you kill her? What did you do?'

'I-I-I-I…' he says, as if stuck in a loop. And then the 'I' sounds become longer, more drawn out. They turn into whines, and then cries of pain. Something is boiling up inside him that threatens to explode.

Enough. Doyle resigns himself to the fact that this isn't going to work. It was his final attempt, and it hasn't worked. Today ends with another failure in a long of string of them.

What a shit day.

'All right, Albert. No more. I'm not going to ask you about it again. I can't make you tell me what you refuse to talk about. We're done here. Okay?'

Gradually, Albert calms down. His tics recede. He finds some peace in his tortured mind. Doyle observes the settling of these troubled waters and finds it strangely soothing himself. He is drained, and watching the extreme agitation leave Albert makes him crave the relief that sleep offers him.

Doyle stands. Grabs up his paperwork. He still has a DD5 to finish typing up. LeBlanc had offered to do it, but Doyle told him to go home. Still, it won't take long. And then to bed. Oh, yes.

And then something occurs to him.

What the hell, it's worth a try. What harm can it do?

He opens up his manila folder. Slides out a sheet of paper.

'One thing, Albert. Before I go. You mind if I ask you something?'

He gets a grunt from Albert that could mean anything. Yes, no, go fuck yourself – anything. But Doyle has no inclination to clarify the meaning. He's going to ask it anyway. He's got nothing to lose. It's not like there's a risk of destroying any kind of trust-based relationship here.

He places the sheet in front of Albert.

'Do you know what these numbers mean, Albert?'

He doesn't expect much of a response. He got little last time, and will probably get the same now. A simple no, perhaps, or a shake of the head. Maybe a quick glance at the sheet and then a comment on a totally unrelated topic. Nothing useful.

So it surprises him when Albert starts rocking. Starts scratching and humming again.

'Albert? What's the matter? These numbers mean something to you?'

The anxiety building. Albert folding and unfolding his arms.

'They mean something, don't they? What do they mean, Albert? Please. I could really do with your help here.'

No answer. Not in words, anyway. But the body language says everything. Albert sees something in this pattern of numbers. Something nobody else has seen.

'Albert. What is it? What's in the—'

'You lied!'

The accusation is flung in Doyle's face, before Albert turns his face away again. Doyle tries to make sense of it. What has he done to upset the guy?

'Lied about what, Albert? What did I say?'

'You said… You said you wouldn't ask me any more questions about what happened. But now you're trying to trick me. You're trying to catch me out. So you're a liar, that's all. Pants on fire.'

Doyle replays their conversation in his mind. What am I missing? These are two separate things. Albert and the serial killer aren't connected. They can't be. So how do these numbers relate to my questions about what happened to Albert's mother? What possible link can there be?

Gotta play this carefully.

'I'm sorry, Albert. I just had to ask, ya know? The numbers were on my mind. I got talking to you, and that just made me think of them again, so I had to ask. Numbers like these, they're everywhere, right? We can't get away from them.'

He sees that Albert is starting to relax again, but he leaves the sheet of paper on the desk in full sight.

Come on, Albert. Reach out a little. Pull me out of this quicksand I'm flailing about in.

'I had no idea it would upset you so much. The numbers, I mean. I shoulda thought about it more. I shoulda been more considerate. Of course it would upset you. These numbers… your mother…

Pick up, Albert. Take up the thread. Show me where it leads.

'I should've realized the connection. You saw it straight away, didn't you? Of course you did. Even when I only had three of the numbers, you saw it for what it was. You'll have to forgive me. I'm just a dumb cop. It wasn't obvious to me.'

Laugh at me, Albert. You have my permission. Agree that I'm stupid, but then tell me where I went wrong. Ask me how I could possibly fail to see the message in these stupid fucking numbers. *But at least tell me what the fucking message is!*

'Where's the other one?' says Albert.

Doyle stares at him. 'What? What other one?'

'The other one. There are only five here. There should be six.'

It's one of those moments. The hairs on your arms and your neck standing on end. Your whole scalp prickling.

'Six, Albert? Six numbers? Why? Why should there be six?'

But Albert is done talking. He gives Doyle a look that seems almost pitying. As though he feels sorry for the poor idiot of a cop who can't even figure out why there should be six symbols here, let alone work out what they mean.

And then Albert is on his feet and shambling back to the cage, leaving the cop staring speechlessly and wondering not only who the sixth victim will be, but what happens after that.

10.20 PM

She has picked a bar close to home. Just a couple of minutes away, in fact. There are too many cops on the streets for her to venture any farther. They are like hornets from a disturbed nest, buzzing angrily as they search for the cause of their unrest. She doesn't know how much information they have, but she guesses they have at least worked out that their prey is a lone female, wandering the streets with a deadly weapon in her purse.

And so here she is. The Wunder Bar, it's called. A well known haunt for guys looking for girls and vice versa. Which makes it perfect. She can't afford to piss away the little time she has left. She has just over an hour and a half to get this done. That's not a lot of time. It would certainly be difficult in that short period to find someone of the level of despicability of her last few victims.

Fortunately, she's not going to do that.

She has shifted the goal posts. No choice in the matter. She has decided to sit here, on a barstool, looking alone and in desperate need of a screw, until he comes along. Whoever he might be. She doesn't care. She has killed five people now. Count 'em – five people! She wasn't lying when she told Georgia's captor that he has turned her into a hardened killer. This is easy now. She could kill a priest or even a disabled guy – that's how detached she has become.

Better if they have at least something she can disapprove of, though.

Treating her like a piece of meat is good enough. Thinking they can come in here and simply assume – yes, assume – that she is here for the taking, here to serve them and satisfy their disgusting carnal desires, here just as an outlet for their sexual energy. Like some kind of socket – just plug yourself in and let it all out, why don't you? Because that's all I am to you, aren't I? Just a plaything, a device, an object.

'Quiet in here tonight.'

And here he is. That didn't take long. In different surroundings I would probably be pleased at being able to attract male attention so quickly. But not here. This makes me feel cheap. This makes me feel like a hooker. You hear that, fella? You know what you're doing to me?

He's not bad looking, actually. She saw him watching her as she slid onto the barstool, and she wondered whether he would be the one. She would have preferred someone a bit less clean cut, a bit more swarthy and villainous. But he will have to do. Beggars can't be choosers.

'People still recovering from the holidays,' she says.

'What about you? You don't need to recover?'

'I'm there already. I have a sturdy constitution.'

He smiles, and it's an attractive smile. Don't let it fool you. He's a bastard underneath. Must be to be hitting on me like this.

He gestures toward the barstool next to her. 'You mind?'

She smiles back. She thinks her own smile will look pleasant to him too. He won't know that she's smiling because she sees right through him. Sees exactly what he wants, what his plan is.

'My mother warned me never to talk to strangers. Especially those who are hairier and have more testosterone than me.'

'You should stay away from *my* mother, then,' he says, and laughs.

She joins in with the laughter, and has to tell herself not to let her guard down. Don't start to enjoy this. Don't let him disarm you with his witty, easy-going nature, this sonofabitch with a hard-on. He is the enemy. And he is also Georgia's savior. Don't allow yourself to like him.

'How about this?' he says. 'We exchange names, and then we're not strangers. Would that work for you?'

She swirls the ice cubes in her glass, loving the tinkling noise they make.

'It's a novel idea. Some might even say a bold one. I guess we could give it a try. My name's Erin.'

'Erin? As in Erin Brockovich?'

'As in Erin Vogel.'

Her real name, but what does it matter? He's not going to be able to reveal it to anyone.

The man puts out his hand. He is young and he is handsome and he is about to make the first intimate contact that will lead to that most intimate of moments. His death.

'Tommy,' he says. 'Tommy LeBlanc.'

10.44 PM

So this is goodbye.

It's not the most satisfactory of endings. A guy comes into the station house and confesses to a murder. We ask him some questions, get nowhere, and send him home again.

Not that it's so unusual. People come in here all the time saying they did things they plainly didn't. Some have assassinated the president. Others have the dead body of Elvis in their basement.

But this is different. Albert's story is amorphous: it has no precise shape that Doyle can perceive, and yet he feels that it overlaps regions of truth in a number of places. There is something to it that feels right. And yet so much about it that seems wrong.

He escorts Albert down the stairs. Albert says nothing, and Doyle cannot read his mind. In the twenty-four hours he has known Albert, Doyle feels he has not gone an inch further in understanding what happens in this man's head.

They get to the first floor. Step past the desk in the lobby. When he notices the huge frame of Marcus Wilson behind the desk, Albert brightens a little.

'One-three-seven-one,' he says.

Wilson smiles. 'Yeah. That's me. You might want to know I topped up the candy too. Got back to those prime numbers you like. Gonna keep it that way from now on. Looks right, somehow.'

Anyone else might smile back, give a nod of appreciation – something. Albert just stands there and scans the area. His eyes alight on the steps leading down to the cells, and he shifts his gaze away hastily.

'Come on, Albert,' says Doyle.

Albert doesn't move.

'Albert. Let's go, man.'

'I don't want… I don't like it down there. I—'

'Albert, I'm not taking you down to the cells, okay? Is that what's worrying you? You're not going back down there.'

'Yeah. Okay. Good.'

Albert turns and starts heading back to the staircase he just descended.

'Wait, Albert. Hold up. Not back that way either.'

Albert halts, looking confused. Doyle steps up to him.

'You're going home, Albert. I'm sending you home.'

Albert shakes his head. 'Can't go home.'

'Why not?'

'I told you. I did a bad thing. I killed my mom. That's bad. I have to tell the police when something bad happens.'

'Well, now you've told us. It's all going in my report, okay? You did your duty, and now you can go home.'

Albert's eyes dart. Doyle can sense the anxiety building again. Shit, why is nothing straightforward with this guy?

'I… I can't go home. My mom's there. She's dead. I can't go back there.'

Doyle is surprised to see that, for the first time since Albert arrived here, there are signs of tears forming in his eyes.

Don't do this to me, Albert. Don't turn on the waterworks. I hate it when people start crying.

'You're not giving me a choice, Albert. You've tied my hands. You won't tell me where your mom is. If you did, I could check it out. I could figure out what really happened. But you won't, and I can't keep you here.'

'I want to stay here. With you and one-three-seven-one. I like it here. You didn't shoot me or put me in the electric chair. You gave me Seven-Up and you gave me food, even though it had tomatoes. You didn't let them put me downstairs. You looked after me.'

Doyle sighs. This is hard. This is like the scene in that movie where the dolphin is sent away, or when ET finally goes home. Shit, kid. Don't do this.

'We look after everyone who comes in here, Albert. We're not the bad guys. We just want to help people. I want to help you, but you won't let me.

And when people won't let us help, there's nothing we can do about it. If you don't want us, Albert, then you have to go.'

Albert reaches up with both hands and grabs fistfuls of his hair. 'But… but… but…'

Doyle beckons to him. 'Come on. Let's get you out of here.'

Albert stays where he is. He's like a child who really doesn't know what to do, and can't handle the emotions that are bundled with not knowing.

'But… but… that's not helping me. You said you'd help me. Pants on fire. You didn't help.'

'You won't let us help, Albert. You won't tell us where you live, you won't tell us what your real name is, you won't tell us what happened to your mom…'

And then Albert says something that possibly opens up a door.

'The numbers.'

Doyle is suddenly wide awake again. 'What about the numbers, Albert? What's that got to do with this?'

'You said you understood. You told me you knew what the numbers meant.'

Doyle reaches into his jacket pocket and takes out the folded piece of paper he showed to Albert earlier. He unfolds it and thrusts it in front of Albert's face.

'I thought I did, Albert,' he lies. 'I really thought I did. But you see more than I do, don't you? You're smart, Albert. Smarter than I'll ever be. I wanna help you. Truly I do. But you need to help me first. You need to tell me what you know about these numbers.'

It's now or never. Doyle can see it in Albert's face. He's either going to spill what he knows or he's going to tip over the brink again, just like he has done every other time he's been quizzed.

Doyle holds his breath and waits. Keeps the piece of paper as still as he can in front of Albert's face. Thinks to himself, Do it Albert. Do it for you. Do it for me. Help us both.

And then the phone on Wilson's desk bursts into life and the spell is broken. Albert lets out a cry of frustration and starts slapping himself about the head. Doyle snatches the paper away. He wonders what the hell it takes to break through to this guy, and feels his own frustration at not being able to establish some form of meaningful communication. It's making him angry, not at Albert, but at himself, and he finds himself unable to contain it when he next speaks.

'Okay, Albert. Enough. I'm tired and I'm sick of this. Go home. If you change your mind about opening up to me, then you can come back. But not until you're ready to tell me everything.'

Albert is crying, and continuing to slap himself. Doyle looks over to Wilson for assistance, but the sergeant is busy on the phone. Doyle reaches out to grab Albert's arm, thinking he may have to manhandle the poor bastard out of here, but Albert dances out of his grasp. He takes off, wandering aimlessly around the lobby area and muttering to himself through his tears.

'What?' says Doyle, irritation evident in his tone. 'What the hell are you saying, Albert?'

Albert raises his voice. And that's when it happens.

'Two-three-one-A-five-something,' says Albert. 'Two-three-one-A-five-something.'

Doyle goes suddenly cold. He can feel his guts tighten up.

'What?'

'Two-three-one-A-five-something.'

Slowly, Doyle raises the paper again and stares at the symbols it holds.

'Two-three-one-A-five-something,' Albert repeats.

An 'A'? That's an 'A'? Well, it could be, sure. But why a letter? Why not a digit like the others?

'Albert, why do you—'

But Albert has moved on to another level. He is making loud keening noises, and he rocks his head back and forth as he stomps around the lobby. Other cops appear from the adjoining rooms to see what the hell is going on.

'Cal,' says Wilson. But Doyle holds a hand up to silence him. Something is happening here, and whatever it is, he needs to let it unfold.

And then: 'Three-zero-four-D-two-C. Three-zero-four-D-two-C...'

He says it again and again and again, and Doyle is still mystified. Still can't get a handle on this.

'Cal!'

He looks around at Wilson, who is holding out the phone toward him. 'It's one of my men,' says Wilson. 'He's off duty right now, but he got talking to a friend of his who thinks he's seen Albert in the area.'

Doyle takes the phone. He continues to watch Albert going through his weird act while he speaks into the receiver.

'This is Doyle. You got a line on Albert?'

He listens. Lets the off-duty cop speak. And what he hears he doesn't believe.

'What? Say that again.'

The words come once more, and still they carry the same jaw-dropping impact.

Doyle hands the receiver back to Wilson, his eyes wide. And then he looks again at Albert, still parading around the room and issuing his strange mystical chant.

'Oh my God,' says Doyle. 'Oh, Christ.'

11.10 PM

J ust wait till Cal hears about this, he thinks.

Tommy LeBlanc, lady killer extraordinaire.

To be honest, he expected this to be a washout. He thought coming here was a mistake. He should have gone home and crashed out. But all the stuff Doyle was saying has been preying on his mind all day. Every time another cop looked at him, LeBlanc wondered what opinions were being formed or confirmed.

It shouldn't bother him – he knows that. These are modern times. A person's sexual proclivities, or lack thereof, should have no bearing on whether that person is deemed fit to do their job. But at the same time he knows it's not as simple as that in an organization like the police force.

He'd be less bothered if he were indeed gay. But the situation now, if Doyle is to be believed, is that people have an inaccurate view of him. He's as straight as they come. He likes girls and they like him. It's just that he's put all his energy into his work lately. He's ambitious. Nothing wrong with that.

So, anyway. This is to prove Doyle wrong. Him and all the other gossip-mongers who think they have a right to put people into fictitious pigeon-holes.

And yourself, Tommy?

What?

I mean, isn't this a little bit about proving something to yourself too? Confirming what you already know – because this is not news, of course – that you're definitely one of the guys? That you're interested in sports and cars and women and that you're definitely not interested in musicals, even though that performance of Fiddler on the Roof the other night was pretty damn good?

No, it's not. I don't need to prove anything to myself. I'm comfortable in my own skin, thank you very much. This is for all the shallow dickheads who will only accept they're wrong when they see me with a woman on my arm.

Not that she'll end up on my arm. Or any other part of my anatomy, for that matter (see, guys, what I did there with the smutty testosterone-fueled jokiness? How about that Knicks game, huh?) At the most I'll get a phone number. Maybe her photo on my cell phone. But that could always lead to other things on another night. And at least I'll know – I mean, the guys will know. The rumors can be put to bed, even if I don't get this girl into bed (see, again with the bawdy male wordplay).

She's nice, this Erin. Not the kind of girl he expected to meet in a place like this. In a way, that made it easier to approach her. A girl sitting alone on a barstool at the end of the night in a seedy bar, you expect her to be a hooker. Or at least a girl of questionable morals. You expect her to have as much flesh on display as is possible without contravening public decency laws, and to start talking dirty every time she opens her mouth.

LeBlanc doesn't like that type of girl. I mean, don't get me wrong and all, they can be great to look at, right? What kind of guy doesn't like to get his pulse all revved up by the sight of a half-naked woman, huh? Sure. That's a given, right, fellas?

Maybe it's the way he was raised, by strictly religious parents. It was drummed into him that modesty is a virtue, and that girls who abandon it are destined for hell – even if they do seem to have an immense amount of fun en route. He has never quite managed to shake off that indoctrination. Girls who make the first moves have always worried him.

Erin, though, is different. She is pretty. Desirable without the need to be half undressed. In fact, it is surprising how little attempt she has made to appeal to the drifting male clientele. I mean, that's a big coat she's wearing. No danger of over-exposure there.

He could go for a girl like this.

But, as the old saying goes, what's a nice girl like her doing in a place like this?

Well, that's okay too. No need to doubt her intentions. He has already asked those questions. In a subtle way, of course. She came here to meet a guy. No, don't get me wrong: not just any guy, but a particular guy. And he stood her up, the bastard. She came all this way to have a drink with a guy who said he might be able to offer her a job, and he stood her up. How do you like that? Some people.

Oh, and she had no idea what this bar was like before she arrived. New in town, you see. Had no idea it was renowned as a pick-up joint. Still, might as well have a drink or two before heading home again, alone and forlorn. Nothing wrong in that. Anyone would do the same.

Yeah, she's nice.

So maybe he shouldn't have lied to her.

See, people can be funny when it comes to cops. Sometimes they hate them. Other times, even when they've got nothing to hide, they can feel uncomfortable around an officer of the law. He doesn't want Erin to feel uncomfortable. So, for tonight at least, he's a hotel clerk.

He picked that particular job because he thought it unlikely she would be find it interesting. The last thing he wanted was a shitload of questions regarding a form of employment about which he knows very little. But in fact the very next thing out of her mouth was a query about which hotel he worked for. So he said the Waldorf. And then she wanted to know if he had met anyone famous there, and so he had to pretend that he had signed a non-disclosure agreement, which sounded so unconvincing it provoked him to change the subject immediately, while bitterly regretting the fact that he had lied in the first place.

But what the hell? This isn't going anywhere. And even if it does, he'll fess up. He'll explain to her that he was so enamored with her that he didn't want to jeopardize the possibility of a relationship. That's what he'll say, and she'll love that. She'll appreciate his honesty and the strength of his desire for her, and she'll tell him how cute she finds it. He's got it all figured out.

'So...' he says as he watches her take a delicate sip of her drink, 'What are your plans now?'

Good question, he thinks. Puts the ball firmly in her court. Gives her an opportunity to say something like, 'That's up to you, lover boy.' Okay, maybe not that. Maybe something not quite so cheesy. But something that at least hints at a continuation of this togetherness into the small hours.

She takes a look at her watch. He's noticed she does that a lot. Why does she keep doing that? How is my animal magnetism not enough to stop her obsessing about time?

'I should be going home soon,' she says. 'Long day. And another long one tomorrow. A girl needs her beauty sleep.'

'Looks like you've had plenty of that to me,' he says, a little too quickly. Shit! Talk about cheesy. What kind of line is that, you freaking idiot?

She turns her gaze away, looking faintly embarrassed. As well she might after receiving such a moronic comment. Okay, Tommy, what are you gonna do now to rescue this situation, you putz?

'You want, I could give you a ride home,' he says. 'My car's outside.'

A step too far? She hardly knows me. Why would she agree to get in a car with a complete stranger at this time of night, especially since she seems so respectable?

'I… Well, we've only just met, and, well…'

See? Told you. A ridiculous suggestion.

'That's okay. No problem. Just thought I'd do the gentlemanly thing.'

She looks him up and down, a hint of a smile on her lips. 'You know what, I actually think you are a gentleman. You're a refreshing change. Most guys, coming up to a girl all alone in a bar, well…'

'I know what you mean,' he says. 'Conversely,' he adds, because 'conversely' is a good word, he feels, an intelligent word, 'most women who sit alone in bars…'

She laughs then, in a way that suggests she has entered into a secret pact of understanding with him. They are now both inside the circle looking out, and that makes all the difference.

She stares at him a bit longer. 'It's okay. I can get a cab. It's probably way off your route, anyhow.'

I would drive to the ends of the earth for you, is the next answer that jumps to mind, but this time he catches the ludicrous statement before it escapes. He decides he needs to stop watching so many old B-movies.

'Why, where do you live?' There. Sensible, down-to-earth question. No need for the melodrama.

'I'm not sure I should tell you. You might have ideas.' She says this playfully, as though toying with him, and he feels a tugging sensation in his pants. Okay, he thinks. Don't fuck this up now. Don't tell her that, actually, you *do* have ideas. Lots of dirty, disgusting, depraved ideas. See, guys? See how I'm just one of the boys?

But before he can think up a better response, she tacks on a question of her own: 'Where do *you* live?'

'Greenwich Village,' he says without hesitation, because he doesn't want her to think he has anything to hide. 'West Thirteenth and Seventh Avenue.'

She blinks. 'You're kidding.'

'No. Why would I be kidding about my address?'

'I live there! Well, not there exactly, but the next block. On West Fourteenth.'

Now it's his turn to blink. This is destiny. Has to be. Somebody is trying to tell him something and he needs to listen. The stars are all lining up.

'Seriously? That is so weird. We're practically neighbors.'

'Yeah,' she says. 'I guess we are. Howdy, neighbor.'

'Howdy. So… you still want to turn down my offer of a ride?'

'Well, now, I think that would just be downright rude, don't you? I accept your kind gesture, neighbor.'

He smiles. Tonight is working out just fine. Better than fine.

He forgets about what came before. The homicides he has been investigating. If he weren't so tired and his mind so preoccupied with this woman next to him, he might allow his thoughts to flit back to the events of the day and the realization that there is a murderer still out there somewhere. A female murderer.

But he doesn't. And even if he did, his mental picture of the killer would be of someone utterly unlike Erin.

Erin is just too darned nice.

11.17 PM

When he first steps into the apartment, it all seems so normal. A home like any other. No signs of anything untoward.

But then Doyle starts to search. He looks in the bedrooms. He looks in the bathroom. And gradually it starts to become apparent to him that something is very wrong here. This is not normal at all. This is a place of disturbance, of derangement, of extreme unhappiness. This is a place where bad things have happened. A place to send chills up the spine.

Doyle takes his time. Searching and searching. Putting the pieces together. Trying to understand.

Some of it he gets. But not all. Not the whole picture. There are things that still need to be explained, and there is only one person who can do that.

When he believes he has done all he can here, he starts to head toward the apartment door. He needs to radio in, make some calls. He opens the door, but turns to take one last look at the apartment that has so much of a story to tell.

That's when he sees it.

The tiny keyhole. Set into the wood-paneled wall on his left.

He walks back to it. Taps on the wall. Hears the hollowness that betrays the closet space behind.

It takes him a few minutes to find the key, placed on a shelf in the kitchen area.

He inserts the key into the hole and turns it. Swings the door open, wincing as it creaks eerily.

It is a simple utility cupboard.

It contains a vacuum cleaner, cleaning products, cans of paint, a rolled-up rug, some framed paintings, spare light-bulbs, an ironing board…

Oh, and a body.

A dead body.

Freed from its confines, it rolls and flops into the room, staring up at Doyle as if demanding to know who would dare disturb its peace. Doyle recognizes the face. He knows exactly who this is. Another piece of the puzzle slots into place, but still leaves many questions unanswered.

'Oh my God.'

The words are not Doyle's. He spins to confront their source, standing there in the open doorway.

'Who are you?' Doyle asks.

The old man cannot take his eyes from the corpse as he speaks. 'My name,' he says, 'is Samuel Wiseman.'

11.34 PM

'*You can't back out now, Erin.*'

She knows this. She doesn't need reminding. It's getting close to midnight. There isn't enough time to get rid of this guy and find somebody else. Not without rushing it and making mistakes that will get her caught.

But…

A cop, goddamnit!

Why did he have to be a cop?

She didn't know this before. He told her he was a hotel clerk, and she didn't question it. Why would she? Who goes around saying they're hotel clerks when they're not?

Cops, that's who. Dirty sneaky cops who are out to prevent me from keeping my baby alive.

A few minutes ago she had told him to pull over at a random building on West Fourteenth, saying it was her apartment. She told him she'd love to invite him for a coffee – a coffee, you understand; nothing more – but her mother was staying over. And then, surprise, surprise, he suggested going back to his place instead, only a block away. Again, you understand, just for coffee, nothing more, just coffee.

Well, she had said, I guess I could risk a coffee, and off they had driven. Here, to this apartment building, outside of which this man called Tommy had hesitated before getting out of the car because he had something to tell her. A confession, if you will.

So she asked what it was, and he told her what it was. Which was that, erm, actually he had lied about being a hotel clerk, and that he was in fact a detective in the NYPD.

A detective. In the NY-fucking-PD.

Aaaargh! How more unwelcome could that revelation be?

She did her best not to panic. Oh, she said in her best unruffled voice, you're a cop, so why didn't you tell me that? And he said he hadn't wanted to frighten her off. To which she could easily have responded, *Frighten me off? You've just made me crap my pants, you prick! Is that any way to deal with a murderer?* But she didn't. She said all the things she was expected to say, about what a silly fool he was, and about how sweet his attitude toward her was, and all the while laughing coquettishly like a character in a Jane Austen novel.

She thought about calling it off. Cops are a no-no. You can kill vagrants and hookers and drug dealers and street scum – they're all fair game. But not cops. That's when you turn the full machinery of the state against you. They will not rest until they find you, and when they find you they will throw the book at you. You will be history. Georgia will be history.

But the time…

She had glanced at the clock on the car's dashboard. Saw how late it was. She was Cinderella, and after midnight the gig was over. No opportunity to find another Prince Charmless in the time available.

So here she is. In his apartment. A cop's apartment. Which, actually, is not the scummy den of iniquity she expected it to be. It's tidy and it's clean and it has modern, expensive furniture – not like a typical bachelor's crib at all. She also sees now why he owned up to his true employment: if he hadn't, the various photographs of him in uniform would have given it away.

See, Erin, he's not a nice guy at all. He lied to you, and he abandoned his deception only when he was left with no alternative. He is after one thing, and will do whatever it takes to get it. That's why he was in that sleazy bar. Did he have the excuse that he was using it merely as a rendezvous point? No, he did not. Was he ignorant of the nature of that bar? No, he was not. He knew exactly what he was doing, and what he was seeking. He's a predator, and he deserves all that's coming to him.

As these thoughts pass through her mind, she is also dimly aware that she is repeating a process she has executed many times today. Seeking justification – that's what she is doing. Arguing herself into a state of mind that will make it easier to do what is necessary.

It's coming. It will happen soon. Georgia, are you listening? You're coming back to me real soon. There are only minutes separating us now. Minutes, that's all. We can last that long.

And so she chats to this cop, and she accepts his offer of a gin and tonic, even though she has no intention of drinking it – because wasn't this supposed to be about coffee and not something that could get her drunk and defenseless? – and she rests her arm on her lap with her sleeve pushed up slightly so that she can see her watch, and she counts away those minutes that are the only thing separating her from her baby, and she waits for her moment to end this ordeal, waits for that sweet, sweet time when she can declare this day, this nightmare, officially over.

He talks to her as usual. The man in her ear, not the cop, although he is speaking too. He goes through his same tired routine: *Kill him... What are you waiting for? ... This is the last one, Erin. Number six... You'll soon have your baby back in your arms again... yadda yadda.* But she's not really listening, to him or the cop. They are both just noise. Her entire focus is on finding an opportunity, an opening. Her purse is on the floor, next to her foot. Within easy reaching distance. She could reach in and grab a weapon in one swift motion. Lunge at this guy before he knew what was happening. But the timing has to be right. Yes, he is unsuspecting, and yes, his reactions must have been dulled by the alcohol he has consumed. But still, he's a cop. He must have been in physical confrontations lots of times. He has been trained to deal with such situations. Get it wrong, and he will break her arm, take the weapon off her and shove it up her ass.

She decides that it has to be the knife this time. It will do the most damage. Even if she can't kill him with the first stab, he will see the blood gushing out of him and he will panic and she will have the advantage. She can always get cleaned up in his bathroom before she leaves. Yes, it has to be the knife. Bruce's knife, in fact – the one she took from his apartment because he made her drop her own in that derelict tenement.

So clinical. Selecting the most appropriate murder weapon. Like she's some kind of professional assassin. It should sicken her, but it doesn't. Not anymore. Five victims or six – it really doesn't make a huge difference. In such a compressed time period they kind of all blend into one, anyway. They become an amalgam: one huge mass of blood-soaked flesh. She has lost the ability to see them as individuals with feelings and thoughts. She won't refrain from killing this handsome blond cop. All she needs is the opportunity.

She thinks she gets one when he stands up and turns away from her, still blathering on about something or other. She starts to reach into her purse, her eyes fixed on his back. Jump up quickly, she thinks. Push the knife into his ribcage, where his vital organs are. Now. Do it now.

But then he shuffles off his jacket and she sees it. The gun, on his hip. A big dark cannon of a thing. It puts her own armament to shame. Her puny hammer and tiny knife wilt in comparison. She cannot take her eyes off that weapon.

He glances at her, and seems to detect her unease. 'Tool of the trade,' he says by way of apology. And then he unhooks it from his belt and places it on top of a bookcase. Which, she notices, houses some surprising reading. Classics rather than cheap trash.

So he's cultured. What of it? Doesn't make him a good guy. Hitler liked opera music, didn't he?

She breathes a sigh of relief when he moves toward her again. Denuded of his gun, he is hers now. His big ugly friend on the bookcase is out of reach. It's just her and him and what's left of the night. Tick-tock.

He stops in mid-stride when his cellphone rings. Erin's heart jumps, first in alarm, but then in realization that this could be it. This could be the perfect opportunity.

He smiles at her and shrugs – another gesture of apology – then goes back to where he left his jacket folded over a chair. He reaches into the pocket, takes out his cell and answers the call.

Erin watches.

And waits.

11.47 PM

When he sees who's calling him, Tommy LeBlanc's face lights up. It's Doyle. Perfect timing, Cal. Just wait till you hear my news. I might even toss a casual question her way while I'm on the phone. Just so you can hear her voice. Got all the proof you need then, Cal. Ha!

'Hey, Cal!' he says.

He flashes her a smile as he says this, and she smiles back. She looks a little nervous, but that's understandable. This is a guy's apartment. A cop's apartment. She probably never got this close to a cop before. He hopes the sight of his gun didn't scare her too much.

'Hey, Tommy,' says Doyle. 'You weren't in bed yet, were you?'

Not yet, he thinks. Could be soon, though. And maybe not alone either.

'No. How come you're still up?'

'Had a stroke of good luck. Wanted to tell you about it.'

'Yeah? Well, things aren't going so bad for me either.'

Another smile at Erin. Let her know how grateful he feels to have met her. Show her what a lucky guy he is. Not that he's going to get any luckier tonight. That would be too much to ask. They barely know each other, and Erin just isn't that kind of girl. They will have a drink or two and then he will walk her back to her apartment. He will ask if he can see her again, and maybe she'll agree. He hopes so. He just needs to make sure he doesn't make a complete idiot of himself between now and then.

'Glad to hear it, Tommy. Anyways, I just wanted to tell you about a break I got on the case.'

LeBlanc chews his lip. It irritates him that Doyle didn't pick up on his subtle hint. Doyle should have asked him why things weren't so bad. He should have read between the lines. Should have pictured the nod and wink hiding behind his buddy's words.

And because he is irritated, he makes the decision that he doesn't want to hear about work right now. He doesn't want to hear about whatever it is that Doyle managed to discover about Albert. There are other things in life, Cal. Like, for instance, relationships. Would you like to hear about my relationship, hmm?

'Uhm, I can't really talk about the job right now,' he says. There you go, Cal. That one's loaded with implication. Get your mind off the job and focus, why don't you?

'You can't? I thought you—'

And then it seems to hit home. The pause suggests that Doyle has finally cottoned on.

Says Doyle, 'Wait. You got company?'

LeBlanc can see the big smile on his partner's face, and he cannot stop one creeping onto his own.

'Uhm, yeah,' he says.

'Female company?'

'Yes,' says LeBlanc, a little crossly.

A laugh from Doyle. Then: 'Are you sure? Have you checked yet?'

LeBlanc shakes his head. He should have expected nothing less from this idiot.

'I gotta go now, Cal. I'll talk to you tomorrow, okay?'

'No, wait. I'm fooling with you, okay? Have a great time tonight. If you can stay awake, that is.'

It occurs to LeBlanc that staying awake could be a big problem. In spite of his visitor's charms, sleep has become a distant memory. Add to that the sedative effect of alcohol and...

'I'll cope,' he says. 'What about you?'

'Dead on my feet,' says Doyle. 'Heading home soon, though. I've done the hard work. Let somebody else do the mopping up.'

'So you figured out Albert's story, then?'

'What? Oh, yeah, yeah. But I was referring to our numbers killer.'

And now Doyle has got him. This is the big story. The one LeBlanc thought would run for a while yet. Maybe the killings would stop, and maybe not. Either way, LeBlanc believed the perp would remain at large for some time. And now Doyle is telling him that he has solved the case? What the fuck? LeBlanc can't put the phone down just yet – not after a bombshell like this.

And so what he does is turn his back. On Erin. The woman who is sitting on his sofa, looking so nervous and yet so alluring. He turns his back on her because he needs to hear this. Needs to get the skinny on just what has happened since he left the squadroom. Needs to ask some questions. Needs to know.

He turns his back.

'You got her?' he says. In a whisper, of course, because he doesn't want to frighten Erin away. The gun was bad enough. She didn't like the look of that. She certainly won't want to hear him talking about a series of gruesome murders he's been investigating. Won't want to know that he's been spending all day dealing with mutilated corpses. What kind of picture would that paint of him? A delicate flower like Erin, she couldn't cope with knowing that kind of information about him. It would be like telling her he was a mortician or something. Nobody wants to start a relationship with someone who spends so much time steeped in death. Certainly not someone of Erin's sensibility.

'Well,' says Doyle. 'Not quite. But I got an ID. I got a name.'

'Yeah? How come? How'd you do that, supercop?'

'Long story,' says Doyle, a little teasingly. 'I'll tell you tomorrow. Get back to your conquest, stud.'

But LeBlanc can't let this go. Not now.

'Come on, Cal. How'd you do it? Who is it?'

A heavy sigh from Doyle. Teasing again. Saying, *If you really must drag this out of me...*

'You sure your girl there can wait?'

'I'm sure. Now who is it, damn it?'

'All right, Tommy. Chill. Before your friend starts worrying about you. Her name's Erin Vogel.'

A laugh explodes from LeBlanc's lips, but it's propelled by surprise rather than humor. And then the confusion washes in. His alcohol-fogged brain tries to make new connections to deal with this unexpected information. Is this a prank? Is that what this is? The guys have set him up with this date as a joke? How else would—

'How do you know that?' he asks.

'That's what I was about to tell you.'

'No. I mean about my... who I'm with?'

A pause. Confusion abounds now.

'What? Tommy, what are you talking about? Are you drunk? I'm trying to tell you about the perp. Erin Vogel.'

This still doesn't make any sense. There are two different people being talked about in the same conversation here. Two totally unconnected people.

Unless...

His mind is working slowly tonight. If he had time, he would blame his tiredness or the alcohol or both. Or maybe simply the fact that he's allowing his lust to override his normally pin-sharp judgment. But his mind doesn't get that far. It gets only as far as telling him that he should turn around now. He should stop listening to Doyle and start checking out things closer to home. Turn around now, Tommy. NOW!

It's a good thought. Wise advice.

But a fraction of a second too late.

He sees her. But she's not sitting on the sofa, looking demure and desirable and innocent. She's here, right on top of him, rushing at him. And there's an expression of jaw-clenched, wild-eyed determination on her face that is not at all attractive. It is frightening in its intensity, and what makes it worse is that she is causing him pain.

Pain?

Yes. Here, in my ribs, where she is hitting me. Why is she hitting me? What have I done to deserve this change in her? And why all the redness? All the...

Blood.

He tries to fight then. He drops the phone and he lashes out at this whirlwind of a woman who is giving him pain and taking away his blood. Not a fair exchange at all, he would decide if he had time, which again he doesn't because there is no time anymore. There is just flailing of arms and gnashing of teeth and pain and blood and yelling and terror and adrenalin, all mixed together, all blurring into a measureless event that defies human comprehension.

Time has no meaning here.

11.51 PM

Doyle knew he was doing wrong when he made the phone call.

He was driving when he called Tommy. On his cellphone, while driving. That's against the law. As a police officer he should have known better.

But he had to call. He was so proud of himself for cracking the case. Okay, maybe it wasn't such a stroke of genius. Anyone else would have made the same leap of logic. Even a kid would have seen it. But…

Well, hell, Doyle. Allow yourself some credit. Others didn't do it, did they? It was you. Crow about while you can. Tell someone, before everybody starts talking about how obvious it was and your ability to capitalize on this moment sinks without trace.

And who better than your partner?

Who, he thought at the time, is probably in bed, fast asleep.

But still. Worth a try.

That's what he thought when he made the call.

And now? How do you feel now, Doyle? Now that your conversation with LeBlanc has been brought to this unexpected conclusion? Now that all you can hear over the phone is what sounds like your young partner being attacked without mercy? Now that LeBlanc's earlier friendly banter has been replaced by his screams of terror and his pleadings for his attacker to stop? Now that there is only one name coming out of his lips, that name being Erin?

How does that make you feel?

Well, what it makes Doyle feel is sick to the core. Sick and scared and filled with just one thought: to save his partner.

He had been on his way home. He felt he had done his part. Cracked the case like the maestro of detection he is, then handed over the remains for others to pick at. He had felt good, and he had felt wasted, and he had decided he had earned his sleep.

But now he has only one destination in mind, and a determination to get there in the fastest possible time. He can be at LeBlanc's place in just a couple of minutes. Knowing this, he crushes the gas pedal into the foot well, ignoring the screams of complaint of his car's engine as he urges the vehicle onward like it's a racehorse. He yells and curses at it, pleads with it, begs of it.

When he gets to LeBlanc's apartment building, he practically falls out of his car and takes the stoop in almost a single bound. He leans on the intercom buzzers, pressing all of them except LeBlanc's. Keeps pressing until some gracious soul permits him entry. And then he is leaping up steps again, sailing over them two at a time until he gets to LeBlanc's floor. He doesn't wait, doesn't assess the risks to himself. He just pulls his gun and launches himself off the opposite wall, smashing his foot into the door – once, twice, three times before he manages to get it to fly open. And then he's in the apartment, gun outstretched in front of him. He sees LeBlanc slumped on the floor, his head against a gray radiator, and he's covered in blood, so much blood. His shirt is soaked in the stuff, and it still pours from the wound carved into his forehead, and he looks dead. And all Doyle can think is please, please don't let him be dead. He's thinking this even though there are other things that are demanding his attention, other matters that need to be taken care of before he can go to his young partner's aid.

Like the woman. Erin. Standing there pointing LeBlanc's gun at him.

11.58 PM

'*S*hoot the fucker. NOW! Shoot him! Before he shoots you.*'

She wants to obey. She thinks she should obey. She has done everything that has been asked of her. Her mission is over. Accomplished before the midnight deadline. She just needs to get out of here. Needs to get rid of this last obstacle blocking her escape route.

And so she raises that heavy, heavy gun, and her finger tightens on the trigger, and...

'Don't do it, Erin. Drop the gun.'

My name. He knows my name. Who is he? How does he know my name? Who else has he told?

'It's over, Erin. You don't have to do this anymore. No more killing.'

'*Don't listen to him. He's trying to trick you. Get you to lower your guard. You need to get rid of him.*'

And then the other voice again: 'I know everything, Erin. I've been to your apartment. I've spoken with Mr Wiseman.'

What? My apartment? Samuel Wiseman? This man here has done all this? He knows things about me?

'*Erin. Fire the fucking gun. Don't let him ruin it now. Your baby is here. I can give her to you. Just come and get her.*'

'Shut up!' she says. And then to the man in the doorway: 'Who are you?'

'I'm a cop, Erin. Detective Callum Doyle. You can call me Cal, if you want.'

'*He's fucking with your mind, Erin. They do this. Don't trust him.*'

'Shut up, I said.'

She sees the puzzled look on the detective's face. She says, 'You don't understand. I had to do this. I… I had no choice.'

'Okay, Erin. Then tell me about it. Let's talk. Let's both lower our guns, and then we can talk.'

She's not sure. Trust this man, or not? Shoot him, or not? But if I shoot him, he'll shoot me back.

And if I trust him?

'All right,' she says. 'All right.'

She starts to lower her gun. Sees that Doyle is doing the same.

And then: *'Damn it, Erin. You are not to do this, do you hear me? I swear I will kill this baby. Is that what you want? You want me to hurt Georgia again? You want to hear her scream like she's never screamed before?'*

'No, please. Please don't hurt my baby. I… I don't know what to do.'

'Erin,' says Doyle. 'What is it? What's wrong?'

'I… I can't say. He won't let me…'

'Who? Who won't let you? Is this about your daughter? Is this about Georgia?'

She locks her gaze onto him. He knows. He knows about Georgia. My God.

'I can't explain,' she says. 'He won't let me.'

'Who? Who won't let you?'

'Shut up, Erin.'

'I… I can't say. He'll kill her. He'll kill Georgia.'

'Enough, Erin! Shut the fuck up!'

The cop stares at her, and there is some sadness in those eyes.

'Erin,' he says. 'Your baby is already gone.'

His words hit her like a gunshot. What does he know?

'Gone? What do you mean, gone? You mean… dead?'

The cop nods. 'Yes. I mean dead. I'm sorry, Erin.'

She shakes her head. This is too much. He's hurting her too much. Why would he do this?

'No. He promised me. He said if I killed those people, he'd give her back to me. That's why I did it.'

She grabs hold of her jacket and twists the brooch to her face. 'I'm right, aren't I? Georgia's alive, isn't she? You promised. YOU PROMISED!'

But there is no answer, and the silence seems to her an admission of guilt.

'No,' she says. 'No. Talk to me. Tell me she's alive.'

'Erin,' says the cop. 'Georgia's gone. You need to accept that. She's been gone a long time.'

The tears are streaming down her face now. 'You're wrong. I've heard her. Today. Lots of times. I've heard her laugh, I've heard her cry. It was Georgia. I know it. You're wrong.'

'Erin,' says Doyle, 'your baby has been dead almost a year now.'

THURSDAY, JANUARY 6
12.01 AM

He's no psychologist. He's not sure how he should be playing this. Probably getting it all wrong. But he's got to act like he knows what he's doing. Got to be the one in control here. Say the wrong thing, and she'll bring up the gun and it'll be game over.

It's hard, though. Difficult to act rationally when your partner is lying over there in a pool of his own blood, his forehead cut to ribbons. Doyle could so easily start blasting away at this woman. A part of him would feel that was righteous, after what she's done.

But a bigger part of him knows that he would regret it for ever more. There is another way to end this. He just needs to get through to her.

He sees the shock on her face. His words have registered somewhere in her brain. But he has no way of knowing how they are being processed, in the same way he could never cross that divide with Albert.

The intricate workings of the human mind. How easily they are made to go out of sync. How difficult to put them back in order. Like crushing a sugar cube and then trying to reassemble it, each grain precisely in its original position.

He wonders if reality is starting to seep through to her. That feels to Doyle to be the right way forward. Hammer home what is real, no matter how hurtful it might seem.

'No,' she says simply. 'No.'

'I've seen the death certificate, Erin. I found it in the drawer in your apartment. She died of meningitis when she was six months old.'

Images of her apartment come back to him as he says this. Most of the rooms were fairly normal and unsurprising. But then there was the baby room. Every inch of wall space papered with photographs of the child. Every inch of floor space piled high with baby clothes and diapers and formula. Like all Erin ever shopped for was baby stuff. It wasn't a normal baby room; it was a shrine. He knew that as soon as he saw it. Knew also that the person who had made it that way was severely disturbed. Finding the paper records just helped to flesh out the picture of tragedy and mental decline.

He watches her reactions now. She looks away from him. Up at the ceiling and then down at the floor as she considers his words. There is pain written on her face, as though she is struggling to dredge up razor-sharp memories that are cutting her inside.

'No,' she repeats. 'I heard her. She was crying. She's alive.'

'I know that's what you want. You were her mother. You loved her. You must want her back more than anything else in the world. But she's gone, Erin. All this killing isn't going to bring her back.'

'He said... He told me...'

'Erin, you know it's not true. Deep down you know it. That's why you asked for help. A part of you wanted us to stop you.'

Her brow creases in puzzlement. 'What do you mean?'

'Your message to us, Erin. Took us a while to figure it out. Too long, really, for such a simple message.'

'I... I don't understand.'

'Two-three-one-A-five,' says Doyle. He looks across at his mutilated partner, at the symbol carved into his forehead, and can't prevent a groan escaping his lips. 'And now a B. Two-three-one-A-five-B. Your address, Erin. 231 Avenue A, apartment 5B. You've been telling us all along where we could find you. That shows me a part of you understands that what you've been doing is so wrong. That's why I think there's still hope for you.'

She opens and closes her mouth. Looks around the room in confusion. The gun is still in her hand, and there's no sign of her letting go of it yet. LeBlanc still hasn't moved. He's dead, thinks Doyle. There's nothing you can do. Grieve later, but first get through to this woman.

He says, 'You need help. Put the gun down. Let me help you.'

'That's what he said. He was going to help me. He would protect me.'

'Who, Erin? Who told you that?'

'He... he talks to me. He watches where I go.'

'No, Erin. He can't. Nobody is watching.'

She reaches up a hand and pushes back her hair, exposing a hearing aid in her ear. 'Look. He put this here. He talks to me through it, telling me what to do. And this...' She points to the large brooch pinned to her jacket. 'It's a camera and a microphone. He sees and hears everything. He can hear you right now.'

Christ, thinks Doyle. She's a mess.

'I saw your records, Erin. Your medical file. You started hearing voices a long time ago. Don't you remember? You should be taking medication. Did you stop, Erin? Did you stop taking your meds?'

Her stare becomes that of a wild, frightened creature. She doesn't comprehend. She has lost touch with reality. And still she waves the loaded Glock.

'I... I don't need pills. I'm fine. My baby is fine. I've saved her. I'm going to get her back now.'

Shit, thinks Doyle. This isn't working. And while it isn't working, LeBlanc's bodily fluids continue to spread across his floor.

'Erin, I'm going over to my partner now. I need to see how he is.'

Her weapon hand jumps up, and for a moment Doyle believes a gun-fight is about to break out.

'NO! He's dead. He had to die so I could get my baby back. Leave him.'

Doyle backs off. He thinks she's right – that LeBlanc is dead. But he also thinks that if he were to prove her wrong she would freak out. She needs to believe that she has successfully completed her mission. The only way around this is to convince her that there is no mission – that it is all a figment of her disturbed mind.

'Please, Erin. Think about this. When's the last time you saw your baby?'

'I heard her today. Several times.'

'But when did you *see* her? When did you last look at her face? When did you last hold her in your arms?'

'Y-Yesterday. Before all this started. Before she was taken from me.'

'Really? Think about that. Think about what she ate. Did you go out with her? Where did you go?'

'I... We went...'

'And her age. How old did she look, Erin? I saw her birth certificate. She should be eighteen months old now. Did she look that old to you? Think about all the photographs on the walls at home. She's never older than six months in those photos, is she?'

Erin shakes her head, not in answer to Doyle's question, but as if trying to cast out the doubts infiltrating their way into her mind.

'We went out. I took her out in the stroller.'

'You never take her out, Erin. Your neighbor, Mr Wiseman, told me all about you.'

Alarm flashes across her face. 'What? What did he say about me?'

'He said you've got problems. He's no doctor, but he knows you're not well. He says he's never seen a baby since you moved in. Never heard one either. Every time he asks you about Georgia, you make something up or change the subject. And he says... he says you sometimes wander the building at night, yelling and banging on doors.'

'No. He's got it wrong. That's Miss Frodely. She's the one who does all that crazy stuff.'

'There is no Miss Frodely in the building. Frodely was your maiden name. The name you had before you married Clark.'

The name seems to strike a chord somewhere in the depths of her consciousness.

'Clark,' she says. 'Clark.'

'Yes. Clark. Your husband. You left him, didn't you, Erin?'

'We... we had to get away. He wasn't good for Georgia.'

'So you escaped. You came here to New York. Only he found you, didn't he? He tracked you down and came to your apartment.'

Tears run down her face. She's remembering, thinks Doyle. She's coming back.

'He said things. Bad things. He told me Georgia was dead. He said I was sick. He said I needed to see a psychiatrist. But he didn't realize. I knew what he was really doing. He was trying to get Georgia away from me. Trying to take her back for himself. I could see right through him.'

'Is that why you killed him, Erin?'

There. There you go, Erin. Remember all that? Remember the visit from your ex-husband that tipped you over the edge? Remember killing him to take away the agony he was bringing to your door? Remember how good you felt then, and how it seemed that killing might be the pain relief you'd been searching for all that time? Remember how your unraveling mind invented the whole abduction scenario so that it could give you a plausible explanation for the absence of your baby and some hope that you could get her back? Remember how each and every killing resulted in you believing that it took you another step closer to the baby that had been so cruelly snatched from you?

And yet, while all this was going on, do you also remember how you fought against it? Remember those tiny chinks of remorse and guilt that led you to leave the message that told others how to find you, if only they knew how to read it?

Do you remember all that, Erin?

She does. He can tell she does. He can see it in her eyes. Recollections drifting back, squirming through the chaotic murk of her thoughts and straining to make themselves heard through all the white noise.

But then something else clutches at her mind and turns it away. She cocks her head, listening. Her face contorts in fear and panic.

'No,' she says, but not to Doyle. 'Please don't do that. Don't hurt her again. I did everything you asked. We had an agreement.'

Doyle calls her, desperate to keep her here in this world. 'Erin! There's nobody there. The voice isn't real. You know that, don't you?'

'No. I can hear him. Plain as day. He's talking—'

'No, Erin. It's just a hearing aid. An ordinary hearing aid. It belonged to Clark. I saw it on him in your photographs. You must remember that.'

She stares at Doyle. Raises a hand to touch the hearing aid. Then she looks at the brooch. Slowly, she reaches under her jacket. Doyle tenses, ready to take her out. But what she produces is a small black box, from which a wire snakes up to her brooch.

'It's a transmitter,' she says. 'It's how he sees and hears things. It sends him everything. And he tells me what to do.'

'Open the box, Erin. Go ahead, open it.'

She looks at him for a few seconds, then back at the box. Holding on to the gun, she manages to turn a plastic latch on the box and raise the lid.

It's empty. Just an empty plastic container.

Her mouth drops open. This must be the final piece of evidence, thinks Doyle. Surely this must provide the slap that wakens her from her long nightmare.

'Put the gun down, Erin. Let's get you some help.'

She turns her gaze on the gun in her hand, as if only just realizing it's there.

Come on, thinks Doyle. Drop the gun. It's over, Erin.

But it's not over.

It's not over because somebody breaks the tension. There is a taut balloon in this room, expanded to its limit, and instead of allowing it to deflate softly, somebody sticks a pin in it.

It's LeBlanc.

A cough is all it takes. A single tiny expulsion of blood-stained froth. In that moment everything changes, and Doyle loses his handhold on the woman he was rescuing, as the demons of her dream-world drag her back to them. He hears her cry, hears her deny the truth of LeBlanc's feeble clinging to life, hears her yell that this cannot be so because of what it means for her baby. LeBlanc should be dead, she pronounces. He should have died so that her baby might live.

And Doyle hears his own cries. His calling to Erin not to do what she is about to do, not to continue with the inevitable. He calls knowing that it is in vain. He calls as she raises her gun to aim it at LeBlanc. He calls as he levels his own gun and snaps off two shots in rapid succession.

And then he watches her spin and fall and hit the ground, and he hates that it had to end so wastefully like this.

He goes to her first, but only so that he can move LeBlanc's gun from her reach. And then he is at LeBlanc's side and he is weeping and telling his young partner that everything will be all right, even though everything has gone horribly wrong, and he is barking into his cellphone for assistance, telling them that there is an officer down, a police officer, and they tell him they will be there as soon as they can, and already Doyle senses it will be too late, and all he can do is hold his partner close as he waits for the others to come.

It is barely a new day, and already the scent of blood hangs heavy on the air.

1.32 AM

How much punishment can the human body take?

Doyle ponders this as he paces the hallway of the hospital. He knows the doctors are working as hard as they can, and he keeps willing them to succeed, but a nagging voice at the back of his head keeps goading him with its suggestions that it's a lost cause. He lost too much blood, it says. He has too many knife wounds, it says. You took too long to get to him, it chides.

Fuck off, Doyle answers in his head.

And then he thinks, Shit, I'm getting as bad as Erin. Arguing with myself like this.

But there is another dark feeling that keeps haunting him.

He tries distracting himself. He makes some phone calls. Asks about Albert.

His real name is Philip Dorling, but Doyle continues to think of him as Albert. Detectives and the Crime Scene guys went to his home at 304 Avenue D, apartment 2C – the address that Albert gave Doyle in his cryptic way, thereby solving two cases in one fell swoop. What they found there was a story of profound sadness.

Edifix.

The construction kits that Albert loved to build. That's what did it.

He'd built a fire truck out of the blocks. He was probably immensely proud of it. Probably spent many hours rolling it to and fro on the floor.

Seems he left it there. On the floor. Where his mother stepped on it while she was carrying a knife she had just been using to slice cucumber. When she landed, the blade pierced her heart.

That's how it looks to the cops and techs, and Doyle is happy to accept that story. He understands now why Albert feels such guilt. It was his toy. He left it where he shouldn't have, and because of that his mom is dead. But still, it's better than an alternative universe in which an evil, violent Albert plunges the knife into the chest of his own mother. Doyle is glad he is spared that version.

He wonders now what will become of Albert, and vows that he will speak to him in person. He will do his utmost to convince Albert of his innocence. It wasn't his fault. He wasn't to blame.

I'm to blame, though, he thinks.

For Tommy, I mean. I'm to blame for that.

The only reason Tommy is lying on an operating table now is because he hooked up with Erin, and the only reason he hooked up with her is because I ribbed him about not having a girlfriend. That's why he's looking death in the face right now. That's on me.

Doyle's legs suddenly go weak on him, and he has to sit down. It's the exhaustion, he decides. When did I last sleep?

He would love to sleep, but he thinks it's a distant promise. His mind is too full of sorrow and remorse and fear for the life of a young man being operated on just yards away. Through those doors there. The doors through which a middle-aged surgeon is now exiting, heading toward me, his face grim, his scrubs splashed with blood. LeBlanc's blood.

He has news.

Please, please, please let it be good.

5.40 AM

She awakens.

She's not sure how long she has been out. What time is it, anyway? She sees the whiteness of the room and the glow of the monitors and the tubes sticking out of her. She feels the pain in her torso.

She remembers.

Remembers what she did. Remembers what the cop did to her. The cop called Doyle.

She recalls the loudness of the gunfire, the force of the bullets punching into her, the acknowledgement that she might die at that moment.

She wishes she had died. It would have been a merciful release.

The torment continues. It should have ended at midnight, but it did not.

Doyle said things to her. Lots of things. Crazy things. She almost believed him. It was plausible enough. It would have been a pretty good explanation, for example, as to why it all went so wrong in that junkie's apartment when she tried to jump him. She didn't know exactly what Bruce was doing because, in fact, there was nobody who could see him, nobody who could tell her.

Yeah, nice try, Doyle. You almost had me there.

He was good. Hypnotic. She doesn't understand how he managed it, but he actually had her believing she couldn't see the workings inside that radio transmitter box. That's how fucked up her mind was at that point. Doyle took advantage of her. He ruined everything. If he hadn't arrived when he did, she would have made sure that the other cop was dead. And then it would have been all okay. She would have got Georgia back.

'Oh, but you can have her back.'

She jumps at the voice, sending an agonizing spear through her ribs. Fighting the pain, she twists her body to locate the source. Above a red button on the wall is a small intercom grill.

Clever. Very clever. How does he do these things?

But then the meaning of his message penetrates her drug-fogged brain.

'What?'

'*Yes. I know how close you came to completing your task. You did your very best, Erin. And for that, I decided to give you a reward. I kept her alive.*'

'No. You're teasing me. You're being cruel again.'

'*No joke, Erin. I'm proud of you. Would you like to hear her?*'

Is this for real? Is he really offering this?

'Can I?'

'*Of course. Listen.*'

A faint chuckling and gurgling. Happy sounds. The happiest, most beautiful sounds she has ever heard. Erin listens and sobs and rocks to her baby's tiny sing-song voice.

'*She's yours, Erin. Just do one more thing for me.*'

'Anything. Anything.'

'*The cop who screwed things up for you. Doyle. Promise me you'll kill him, first chance you get.*'

'I promise. He deserves it. I wouldn't even hesitate.'

'*Good girl. Now rest. We'll talk again when you feel stronger.*'

She closes her eyes, content now, and then she sleeps.

Because the voice in her head has commanded it.

ACKNOWLEDGMENTS

It is often said that writing is a solitary business, but behind the scenes there is usually a whole team of people who go into making a novel what it is. First and foremost among those I'd like to thank is my wife, Lisa, without whose support and encouragement I couldn't do this job. I owe her doubly this time because of her creative work on the design of the book jacket for Cry Baby. I would also like to record my gratitude to family and friends, and to all those on Twitter who urged me on and helped to spread the word. Last, but certainly not least, I'd like to thank my agent, Oli Munson of AM Heath Ltd., whose presence and enthusiasm for this project has made all the difference.

Printed in Great Britain
by Amazon

61470945R00169